SOME
DIE
YOUNG

SOME DIE YOUNG

THE MAN FROM WACO

WILLIAM W. JOHNSTONE
AND J.A. JOHNSTONE

PINNACLE BOOKS
Kensington Publishing Corp.
www.kensingtonbooks.com

PINNACLE BOOKS are published by

Kensington Publishing Corp.
900 Third Avenue
New York, NY 10022

All Kensington titles, imprints, and distributed lines are available at special quantity discounts for bulk purchases for sales promotion, premiums, fund-raising, and educational or institutional use.

Special book excerpts or customized printings can also be created to fit specific needs. For details, write or phone the office of the Kensington Sales Manager: Kensington Publishing Corp., 900 Third Avenue, New York, NY 10022. Attn. Sales Department. Phone: 1-800-221-2647.

PINNACLE BOOKS, the Pinnacle logo, and the WWJ steer head logo Reg. U.S. Pat. & TM Off.

First Printing: September 2024
ISBN-13: 978-0-7860-5091-8
ISBN-13: 978-0-7860-5092-5 (eBook)

10 9 8 7 6 5 4 3 2 1

Printed in the United States of America

CHAPTER 1

"Pa," thirteen-year-old Tommy called out to his father, who was up in the hayloft throwing down some hay for the milk cow, "somebody's comin' up the path to the house, leadin' a packhorse."

Warren Bannack straightened up and leaned on his pitchfork while he looked in the direction Tommy was pointing. "Yeah, I see him," he answered. "And right at dinnertime as usual," he muttered to himself. It was the time of year when the occasional drifter happened upon the path up to his house. Usually it was a cowhand riding the grub line after the herds had been driven to the railroad and he was no longer needed. And Warren would have to explain that he was a one-man farm and not another cattle ranch. It usually ended up with the drifter getting a meal before moving on. *This one looks like a big fellow,* he thought. *I hope Kitty can scare up enough to feed him.* He sighed and went back down the ladder and walked out of the barn to meet the rider. *Maybe he's not a cowhand,* he thought as he got a little closer. He was leading a packhorse that looked to be loaded heavily and that was not typical for a cowhand seeking work. As the rider approached the barn, he appeared to be looking all around him as if trying to picture the entire homestead. Warren watched him carefully, thinking how he might have felt better if he was wearing his gun. The rider pulled the buckskin to a stop only a few yards short of him when Warren was suddenly struck with the realization. "John?"

"Howdy, Warren." He stepped down from his horse and nodded to the young boy standing next to his father. "Tommy?" Tommy nodded vigorously, still in awe of the big stranger.

"John?" Still amazed by the transformation of his younger brother into the imposing stranger facing him, Warren was rendered speechless for a few moments more before he decided it was really happening. "John?" He asked again to be sure when his brother stepped forward to shake his hand. "Tommy, run to the house and tell your mama that John has come home." Without a sound and eyes as big as saucers, the boy turned and ran to the house, only to reappear within seconds, followed by his brother and mother.

"John?" Kitty Bannack questioned as she ran from the house, still wiping her hands on her apron, also amazed by the rugged individual watching her approach. "What. . . ? How did you get. . . ?" She didn't know what to ask.

"Howdy, Kitty," John said. "You mean, what am I

doin' out of prison? It's a long story, but I can honestly tell you that I did not escape from prison. I was pardoned by the governor himself. And before I move on, I thought I'd see how you folks are doin'. And you might hear some wild stories about me, so I want to make sure you know the truth. I apologize for poppin' in on you so sudden this close to dinnertime, but I brought some fresh meat with me to cook. I shot a deer this mornin', so I butchered it right away. Otherwise, I would have gotten here earlier to give you a little more notice." He was aware that he must have changed drastically since they last saw him, judging by the four faces staring at him.

"It's a good thing you brought a deer with you," Kitty finally spoke. "Because I don't think I cooked enough to feed you." She thought about giving him a welcome home hug but decided to offer her hand instead.

"Let me unload my horses and take care of them and we'll get some of this venison on the stove," John said. "Or maybe we could build a fire outside and roast it? We're gonna want to smoke most of it to eat later 'cause it ain't gonna be fresh after tonight. As big as these two boys are, they're gonna need plenty of meat," he nodded toward Billy and Tommy.

It didn't take long for his brother and his family to realize that it was indeed still John inside the prison-hardened body that returned home more than five years after leaving. He told them how he came to be pardoned after saving the life of a judge. He also told them of the possibility that it might be overturned, if another judge had his way. So they understood why he hadn't come to stay. He was happy to see that the farm was doing well and the boys were old enough to help maintain it. He felt he could leave again with a satisfied feeling that his brother's family was doing well and he was not needed. In fact, if he stayed, he might make his brother's situation difficult again, just like it was when he originally left to go to prison. "I hope you'll forgive the surprise visit, even if it is right at dinnertime. You reckon we could get Tommy and Billy to gather some wood for a fire?"

"Yes, sir," Tommy responded. "Come on, Billy!" They ran to the woodpile behind the house to bust up some logs.

"You still got that spit in the barn?" John asked his brother.

"Yeah, we still have it," Warren said. "We might have to burn some rust off of it, though. We ain't used it in a long time."

Kitty watched Warren's reaction closely. She was well aware of the flood of guilt released into her husband's mind upon the return of his younger brother. It had taken Warren over a year to finally remove those feelings of guilt from his everyday thoughts. She gazed at the powerfully built man now as he untied the fresh meat wrapped in the deer hide and removed it from his packhorse. Then he and Warren took John's horses to the barn. They came back with the crude spit they had fashioned, using the metal axles and wheel rims from an old handcart. Warren was right when he said they had not used it recently. In fact, they had not used it since John went to prison. She found it hard now to envision the eighteen-year-old young man who had gone to prison for a crime he did not commit. She switched her gaze to her two sons eagerly awaiting the feast of deer meat roasted over an open flame, obviously impressed by their mysterious Uncle John. She decided then that she was glad John was not home to stay. She wanted that admiring look on her sons' faces to be cast in their father's direction. She immediately felt guilty for thinking it when she then thought of the terrible sacrifice John had made to keep her family intact. How could she not be eternally grateful?

Kitty was not the only one reading the faces of her family as they tended the roasting meat. Like his sister-in-law, John Bannack was studying her family's reactions to his sudden visit. He was especially observing Kitty's expressions and he thought he could read the deep concern in her face when she looked at her husband. He decided that it might have been better not to have come back. But it was too late for that decision. At least he had told them he would be leaving in the morning, in spite of Warren's urging him to stay a while longer.

When the meat was roasted to their satisfaction, they took it off the spit and carried it into the house. Warren sliced it into portions while Kitty brought the side dishes she had already prepared for dinner and placed them on the table. They decided the meat was fresh enough to cook some more for supper and smoke what was left for jerky.

"You know, John," Warren commented, "you could just stay on here with us. I hope you know you've always got a home here. I know the boys would be glad to give you your old room back."

John glanced at once toward Kitty to see the immediate frown that appeared on her brow. "Well, now, that's mighty nice of you, Warren," he said. "But there's some parts of Texas I've got a hankerin' to see. I reckon that's something prison does to a man. After being locked up in a tiny space for a long time, you get a need to wander." He looked at his sister-in-law. "You can understand that, can't you, Kitty?"

"Oh, indeed I can," she replied. "I don't blame you one bit."

"Besides," John continued, "I wouldn't wanna run the boys outta their room. I won't even do that for one night. I plan to bed down in the hayloft tonight." When Kitty started to protest, John went on. "It's what I'm used to, anyway. The whole time I was working for Judge Justice, I was sleepin' in his hayloft. I got to where I preferred it to sleepin' in the house."

She met his gaze with a smile. "You're serious, aren't you? The judge made you sleep in the barn with the horses and cow?"

"He didn't make me sleep in the barn," John insisted.

"He was gonna make room for me in the house. He was one of the most considerate men I ever met. But I preferred to sleep up in the hayloft. I got more room there."

"He is almost as big as a horse," Tommy remarked.

"Watch your mouth," Kitty scolded. "You better show a little more respect for your uncle." John and Warren both laughed.

"He's right, Hon," Warren said. "Uncle John sorta grew up when he went to prison, didn't he, boys?"

"I don't know how it happened when I think of the food I got in prison, though," John japed. "That's one reason why I can't come back here. I'm afraid I'd get so big eatin' your mama's cookin' that pretty soon you'd have to haul me around in the wagon."

"Or hitch you up to it," Billy commented, "and you haul us around in it."

"I declare," John said, pretending to be insulted, "you gonna let those boys talk to me like that?" The horseplay went on for a little while, causing Kitty to remember good times the family had before the tragedy that sent John off to the Huntsville Unit of the Texas State Prison. Even Warren was chuckling, showing her glimpses of his old persona instead of the almost constant remorse. She wished it would always be like this, while at the same time knowing that it was really not possible. John had told them of the very real possibility that he would become a wanted man, if Judge Raymond Grant had his way, and he had no intention of returning to prison. In view of that, she was determined to enjoy her brother-in-law's brief visit.

After the long dinner hour finally ended, Warren and John cut the rest of the deer up in strips to smoke cure over a smoldering fire of some green limbs and leaves. They left Billy and Tommy to keep the fire going while Kitty cleaned up the dinner dishes and decided what to prepare for supper to go with the remainder of the fresh meat. Then Warren took John for a little tour of the farm to show him the progress made while he was away. John was impressed. "You've done a helluva job, Warren, you and the boys."

Warren took him down near the river and showed him an acre-size piece of land adjoining his farm that he was in the process of negotiating with the owner of the property to buy. "Those two boys remind me of you, little brother," Warren said. "They're growin' into men pretty damn fast. I'm hopin' we can keep expandin' the farm, so it'll support both of them, if they have their own families one day."

"Big brother," John said. "That is sure enough what I hoped you would tell me when I came here today. I'm satisfied that everything has turned out fine for the both of us. The only thing I want now is for you to make peace with the past and rejoice in the fact that it all happened for the best."

They took a walk around the piece of land that Warren was planning to buy and he told John of his intention to turn it into a cotton field. John responded with enthusiasm for Warren's plans, although farming no longer held any interest for him. He decided then that he had made a good decision when he came back to the farm to visit Warren and Kitty. He now knew for sure that this was not the place he wanted to spend the rest of his life.

When they returned to the house after a walk of the entire farm, they found the boys still tending the fire smoking the venison. "I expect you'd best take the biggest portion of that jerky with you, if you're gonna be travelin' like you said," Warren suggested.

"I'll just take a little of it for when I can't find something to hunt," John said.

"Where are you goin'?" Warren asked. "You never said."

John shrugged. "West," he answered, then added, "toward Stephenville, I reckon, toward cow country."

"You wanna work with cattle?" Warren was surprised. Neither he nor his brother had shown any interest in raising cattle before.

"I guess so," John replied. He was not sure of it, himself. It was just something he thought he could do, if nothing better turned up. "I know I just feel at home on a horse."

"Well, when you get your fill of chasin' a bunch of ornery old cows around, you can come on back to this little farm and we'll raise cotton and corn and beans."

"Looks to me like you've got all the help you need to run this place," John said, nodding toward Tommy and Billy at the woodpile, chopping more wood for the meat still smoking.

"It's about time to roast the rest of that meat for supper," John remarked. "I'd like to clean up a little before we eat, scrape some of these whiskers off my face, too. You and the boys still go to the river to take a bath?"

"Sure do," Warren replied. "Kitty would probably appreciate it if I was to take one, myself."

When Warren announced to Kitty that he and John were going to the river to take a bath, she responded as if it was the best idea they'd ever had. "Why don't you take the boys with you?" she suggested.

"I swear," Warren replied, "you'd think we ain't ever took a bath before."

"I didn't say you haven't ever taken a bath before," Kitty came back. "It's just the first time it was your idea."

"She's got you there, Pa," Tommy said. "But me and Billy go swimmin' in the river almost every day this time of year."

So the Bannack men walked down to the river to take a bath. John took his saddlebags with him with his extra shirt and his razor. After he shucked his dirty shirt, he soaped it up and washed it, then hung it on a bush while he cleaned himself up. He was shaving with a razor and hand mirror when he became aware of young Billy staring at him, so he playfully flicked some water at him. "What are those holes on you?" Billy asked and pointed at the old bullet wounds in his chest and side.

Hearing Billy's question, Warren looked at John as well, just then noticing what had attracted Billy's attention. If he had to guess, he would figure they were bullet holes, so he waited to hear John's answer. "Just a couple of places I got poked with tree branches, ridin' through some thick timber," John answered Billy.

Warren realized that there was much about the time John was away that he had not shared with them. He couldn't help commenting, "They look like bullet holes."

"Yeah, I guess they do, at that," John replied, leaving the comment hanging there.

"That's because that's what they are. Right?" Warren insisted. "Damn it, John, I'm your brother. Tell me what happened."

John turned and looked him in the eye while deciding whether or not to explain. Finally, he said, "The one in my side was meant for somebody else. I just happened to get in the way. The one in my chest was meant for me, and the shooter's dead now. End of story." Warren nodded in response, knowing that was all the explanation he was going to get. When he saw Billy about to ask John another question, he shook his head at him. He knew then that there was a lot more about his brother that John was not anxious to share, so Warren refrained from pursuing it.

They finished their swim in the river and returned to the house to find Kitty roasting the last of the venison on the spit. "Good," she said when they arrived, "you can take over the roasting. I've got things in the kitchen to finish."

Supper that night was a repeat of the cheerful affair that dinner had been with both Warren and John recalling humorous incidents involving each other back before John left the farm. After supper, the grown-ups talked late that night with much of the conversation concerning where John was going when he left them. He tried to explain that there was little he could tell them because he wasn't sure himself. "Just west," he said. "I'll know when I get there."

CHAPTER 2

He was awakened the next morning by the sound of Billy in the barn below him, scolding the chickens for their lack of production. Having forgotten that his Uncle John was sleeping in the hayloft above him, Billy was informing the lazy hens of their disappointing lack of effort. And he was using some rather colorful adjectives in describing their performance on an occasion when there was a special guest for breakfast. John pulled his boots on and rolled up his bedroll. He strapped on his gun belt, then went to the ladder and dropped his saddlebags down to the barn below. They landed with a solid thump. "Mornin'," John said as he slid down the ladder to land behind a startled Billy in time to grab the egg basket he almost dropped when he jumped.

"Son of a buck!" Billy blurted before he could catch himself. "I forgot you was gonna sleep in the hayloft!"

"Sorry I startled you," John said. "Is your pa up?"

"He's gettin' up," Billy answered. "Ma's cookin' breakfast and she needs these eggs."

"Then we'd best take 'em in the house," John said and led him out the front door of the barn. When they walked into the kitchen, Warren was sitting at the table drinking coffee.

"Good morning," Kitty said, working at the stove. "Pour yourself a cup of coffee and I'll have you some breakfast in a few minutes." She slid a tray of corn-bread into the oven. "You still plannin' to leave us this morning?"

"Yep, I figured I'd give you the pleasure of my company for breakfast, and then I'll hit the road."

"Still aimin' to head up toward Stephenville?" Warren asked.

"Yep," John answered. He didn't confess that he was going that way only because he knew where the road to Stephenville was and it seemed to be heading in the right general direction. Maybe things might have changed since he was in prison, but there used to be some small cattle ranches in that area. At the present time, catching on at a cattle ranch was his only prospect. He had a little money to carry him for a while, since he had saved every cent he could of the salary Judge Wick paid him, but he hoped he could pick up some wages somewhere.

"I don't understand," Kitty said. "Why are you going to Stephenville?"

"I ain't goin' to Stephenville," John tried to explain again. "It's just a town on the way I'm headin'. Like I said last night, I'll know where I'm goin' when I get there."

"I don't see why you don't just stay here until you do know where you want to go," Kitty insisted. She was satisfied that he didn't plan to stay with them permanently, but she didn't understand why he was in such a hurry to leave.

He found himself running out of patience and when he glanced at the grinning face of his brother, it only added to his discomfort. "Because," he told her, "there's a very good chance that Judge Raymond Grant will have his way and I'll be a wanted outlaw overnight. And this is the first place they'll come lookin' for me, so I damn sure don't wanna be here when they do."

She shrugged and made a face. "I see your point," she said as she placed his breakfast on the table. "You're gonna have to settle for bacon this morning, unless you want deer jerky with your eggs."

He lingered over breakfast longer than he had originally intended, but he wasn't sure how long it would be when he might see his family again, if ever. It was close to midmorning when he finally struck the road to Stephenville, a small settlement almost one hundred miles away. There was a sense of sadness about leaving Warren, Kitty, and the boys again, but there was also a feeling of freedom as he struck out to the west. After three and a half days of uneventful travel, he rode into the little town of Stephenville at noontime on the fourth day. Ready to spend a little of his money for a decent dinner, he rode the length of the short main street, hoping to find a hotel or a café, but there was none. There were two saloons, however, and he wondered if one of them might serve meals. He saw that there was a sheriff's office, so he figured that would be a good place to ask. It struck him as ironic that he would ask the sheriff, but he felt very little risk that he was a wanted man yet.

Deputy Jerry Stubs looked up from his desk when the door of the sheriff's office was suddenly filled with the intimidating figure of John Bannack. A slight young man, Stubs was not sure if he was in trouble or not. He pushed his chair back, almost tipping it over, in his haste to get to his feet, only to find himself still straining to look the somber stranger in the eye. "You lookin' for the sheriff?" Stubs squeaked.

"Not particularly," Bannack replied, "I'm just passin' through town. Never been to Stephenville before and I thought this would be a good place to ask if there's a decent place to get a good meal." When Stubs didn't respond at first, other than a not-so-subtle sigh of relief, Bannack asked, "Are you the sheriff?"

"No, sir, I'm not. I'm Deputy Sheriff Jerry Stubs. There ain't no sheriff, and I'm tryin' to kinda watch over things since Sheriff Boswell left. As far as a place to get some dinner, the place to go is the Oasis saloon. They've got a good cook there, and that's where most folks eat."

"Much obliged," Bannack said. "I'll go see what they're cookin' today."

"Chicken and dumplings," Stubs said, "I just came from there not five minutes ago. That's what Pearl cooked up today and they were mighty good." *I'd still have been there if Ace Parker and two more of that crew from the Bar-W hadn't come in the saloon,* he thought. *They like to aggravate a man wearing a badge, so there weren't no use in me giving them the chance.*

Bannack walked out of the sheriff's office and looked down the street to spot the Oasis, only a little way down on the other side. He led his horses over and tied them at the rail with three other horses. As a precaution, he pulled his rifle out of the saddle scabbard, not willing to risk leaving the rifle while he was inside eating. Moe Price, the bartender, glanced up to see the solemn-looking stranger push through the batwing doors, and his first thought was, *Here comes trouble.* Unfortunately, this was often the first impression for most people upon meeting the peaceful man from Waco, so Moe studied him carefully as he approached the bar. "Whaddle it be, stranger?" Moe asked.

"Howdy," Bannack offered. "Deputy over at the jail said I could buy some dinner here."

"You sure can," Moe declared in relief. "We've got a fine cook and a special section for folks who just want to eat. We do a good business with the local folks who want to get a good meal while they're in town." He pointed toward the back of the saloon. "See those four tables in the back corner? They're reserved for our food business. There's even a back door to the outside for folks that don't wanna walk through the saloon. There's a customer who came in the back door eatin' dinner right now. See that young woman and her little boy? That's Emily Green. Her daddy owns the Rocking-G Ranch."

"I don't like to leave my rifle on my saddle when I can't keep an eye on it," Bannack said, "so I brought it in with me. Some saloons don't like you to bring a rifle in. You want me to let you keep it behind the bar till I leave?"

"No, we don't have no rule against totin' guns in here," Moe said. "Them three fellers right over there are wearin' guns." Bannack turned and saw three men who looked like cowhands get up from a table in the saloon and walk back to one of the four tables Moe had pointed out. They stared brazenly at the young woman.

"It's been a long time since I've had a drink of whiskey," Bannack decided. "I think I'll have one drink before I eat."

"What's your pleasure?" Moe asked.

"Just whatever you're pourin' will be all right," Bannack answered. "I ain't much of a drinker." He watched Moe pour it, then he sipped a taste before he tossed it back. "You know those three fellows?"

"Yeah, I know 'em," Moe replied. As they watched, one of the men went over and sat down at the table where the young woman and her son were eating. "That big one that sat down with Emily is Ace Parker. I ain't surprised he'd make trouble. Doggone it, Jerry Stubs was just in here a few minutes ago, too."

"So you're pretty sure Emily didn't invite him to join her?"

"I'm pretty sure of that," Moe said, and I'm gonna go see if I can do something about it."

"Looks to me like you're outnumbered," Bannack said. "Why don't you let me take care of Mr. Parker and you keep his two friends from shootin' me in the back?"

"Mister, you've got a deal, because I wasn't too confident of how I was gonna do any good."

"All right," Bannack said, "I'm goin' to eat dinner." He left a coin on the bar and walked to the four tables in the back. As he approached the young lady's table, he heard her asking her uninvited guest to leave her and her son alone.

Ace favored her with a devilish grin and declared, "I like a woman with a little bite in her. It's like breakin' a buckin' horse." He was surprised to see her looking up past him in alarm. He turned to see Bannack behind him, like a mighty oak tree that wasn't there a few seconds before.

"I'm sorry I'm a little late, Mrs. Green," Bannack said. "I stopped at the bar for a drink before we ate. Did you invite this fellow to join us for dinner?"

He waited to see if she realized he was trying to help, but she was still confused. "I didn't invite anyone to join Peter and me, and I've just asked this man to leave us alone."

"That's what I figured," Bannack said before she

had a chance to include him. "I told your daddy I wouldn't let you out of my sight till I brought you home. I hope you ain't gonna tell him I stopped to have a drink." He looked directly at Ace, who was speechless in his confusion. "Glad I could stop you from makin' a big mistake, cowboy. You can go on back and join your friends now. No harm done."

"No harm done?" Ace's brain suddenly started working again and he flared up. "Who the hell are you?"

"Now, don't let your mouth get you in trouble," Bannack scolded calmly. "I'm the fellow who was sent to look after Mrs. Green and her boy. My mistake for runnin' a little late, Mrs. Green." He glanced toward the kitchen door then to see a woman standing in the doorway, stopped on her way out. Remembering the name mentioned by Moe, Bannack said, "I'll be eating dinner, too, Pearl, and I'd like coffee with it." Back to Ace then, he asked, "Are you a little hard of hearing? If you are, I apologize. You can go back to your table now and Pearl can fix you up with something to eat. Like I said, no harm done."

Like Ace Parker, Emily Green was too confused to make sense of what was happening, but she gradually began to see that the stranger was acting on her behalf. Consequently, she remained silent while Ace got up from the chair. Standing tall, he found he still had to look up to cast his stare of defiance at the stranger. "She shoulda said she was meetin' somebody" was all Ace could think of to say before he went back to join his friends, who were waiting to hassle him about his attempted conquest. When he left, Bannack sat down at the table with Emily.

"I hope you don't mind if I sit down with you, ma'am, but if I don't, I'm afraid he's gonna know I was lyin' and he might be back to bother you."

"No, mister, please join Peter and me for dinner," she said. "How did you know my name?"

"The bartender told me," Bannack answered. He could see that she was still shaking from the encounter.

She waited until Pearl placed his plate and coffee on the table before asking, "Do you work for one of the ranches around here?"

"No, ma'am, I'm just passing through town on my way west."

"You're just passing through town and saw that I was having some trouble, so you decided to rescue Peter and me," she stated. He shrugged as if anyone else would have done the same and took a sip of his coffee. "What is your name?" she asked then.

"John," he said, thinking it best not to tell her his last name, since he wasn't sure if anyone might come looking for him.

"John what?" she asked. "What is your last name?"

"John Cochran," he replied at once, that being the only name that came to mind right away. It was his late mother's maiden name.

"Well, John Cochran, I want to remember that name. I want to tell you how much I appreciate your stepping in to save Peter and me from what might have been something I would rather his four-year-old eyes didn't see. Something like this has never happened to me before, and I've been in to eat here a couple of times since Mr. Rainey made this little section into a café. Of course, my husband was with me before. He couldn't come today. He's the foreman at the Rocking-G Ranch and they're moving a big part of the herd to some new grazing." She reached over and playfully ruffled up her son's hair. "But today's Peter's birthday and we promised him he could come into town and spend his birthday money." She smiled at her son. "So that's what we did, isn't it, Peter? And we met a nice man in the process." Then she stole a glance in the direction of the table where the three cowhands were sitting. "I'm afraid those three are going to cause you trouble, though. Did you know he had two friends when you came to help us?"

"Yeah, I knew," Bannack replied, "but the bartender said he would watch my back, if the other two started to get involved."

"Moe Price?" Emily responded. "I'm not sure you should put much faith in Moe's help, if you really get in trouble. I'm sure he means well, but my husband, Rex, says Moe has little control over what happens in this saloon."

"Sounds like it might be a better idea if you waited next time until your husband could come with you again," he commented.

"There's no doubt about that," she agreed. "I don't

think I'll ever even come to town again without my husband."

"How far do you have to go to get home?" he asked, and she said that it was three and a half miles from town. "I think it might be a good idea if I rode along with you when you go back."

"Oh, I couldn't ask you to do that," she protested, hoping with all her heart that he would. "I've already interrupted your trip more than enough."

"No trouble a-tall," he told her. "I'm not in a particular hurry to get where I'm goin', so a few miles outta the way ain't gonna make much difference. And it'd kinda set a little easier on my mind to see you get home safely." He paused. "You and old man Peter there." She hesitated, wanting to tell him yes. "What about if I do it as a favor for your husband?" he suggested.

"All right," she said, "I know he would appreciate it."

"Good," he responded. "When will you be ready to go?"

"As soon as we finish eating," she answered. That suited him. He had been glancing at the table where the three men were eating and every time he did, he met Ace Parker's eyes concentrated on them. It was difficult to tell if Ace was zeroing in on him or Emily. Either way, it meant trouble for him.

They finished their dinner, and Emily went to the kitchen door to compliment Pearl on her chicken and dumplings and tried to pay for all three dinners, but

Bannack insisted on paying for his. "If I was a perfect gentleman, I'd pay for yours and Pete's," he told her.

"If you were any more perfect, you might be sprouting a pair of wings," Emily said. "My buggy's out back, so Peter and I will go out the back door. I assume your horse is tied in front of the saloon, so we'll meet you on the street."

"Yes, ma'am," Bannack replied and walked back through the saloon and said, "So long" to Moe as he walked past the bar. Outside, he slipped his rifle back in the scabbard, untied his horses, and climbed aboard the buckskin. He wheeled away from the hitching rail and waited in the middle of the street for Emily to come from behind the saloon in her buggy. When she pulled out of the alley beside the saloon and headed north on the main street, Bannack pulled his horse up beside her.

Behind them in the saloon, Ace Parker walked up to the front window and watched their departure. He went back to the table where Short and Scully were still eating. "I'm telling you, that lyin' dog weren't supposed to meet that woman here. He's ridin' a horse and leadin' a packhorse, and she had a buggy behind the saloon. He didn't come to town with her. The two of them just made a fool outta me."

"Shoot, Ace," Short responded, "when it comes to fools about women, you already have all the parts to make one. Don't take much for anybody to put 'em together to make a first class fool. Ain't that right, Scully?"

Scully chuckled in response. "I can't argue with that.

And that feller was bigger and uglier than you, Ace, and she still picked him."

"He mighta thought he was pretty smart," Ace responded, "but he ain't seen the last of me. I don't stand for anybody trying to make a fool outta me."

"Looks to me like he's already finished that little job," Short said, egging him on. "He's done rode off with her, most likely seein' her and her young'un home."

"That mighta been his biggest mistake," Ace declared. "He mighta been better off if he'da just rode on his way and let her go on home by herself." He stormed back to the bar to confront Moe Price. "Who was that woman?" Ace demanded.

"She's just some woman who lives around here somewhere," a startled Moe Price answered. "I don't remember what her name is." Ace drew his six-shooter and pointed it directly at Moe's nose. "Emily Green, Rocking-G Ranch!" Moe blurted immediately.

Ace holstered his six-gun. "Rocking-G, I know where that is. I'm goin' after him." He looked at Short and Scully. "You goin' with me?" He started for the door without waiting for an answer.

"What you got in mind when you catch him?" Scully asked, as he and Short followed him outside.

"What the hell do you think?" Ace replied. "I'm gonna shoot him!" He stopped abruptly and did an about-face. "Are you comin' with me or not?"

"That depends," Scully replied. "You talkin' about followin' them right up to the ranch house and takin' on however many happen to be there? 'Cause that don't make no sense to me a-tall. We might as well just shoot each other right here and save ourselves a ride."

Ace hesitated when he realized he hadn't taken that into consideration. "'Course I ain't talkin' about ridin' into the ranch. You think I'm that dumb? I don't think he ever saw that woman before, so he's most likely gonna ride along with her till she gets home. Then he's gonna turn around and start back to wherever he was headed before he decided to stick his nose in my business. So are you comin'?" he asked again.

Short looked at Scully and they both shrugged. "Might as well," Scully said, "and take a look at what he's haulin' on that packhorse." He looked at Short for his confirmation, and Short made a face that said why not? So they climbed on their horses and rode out the north end of town, going about half a mile before taking the trail that led to the Rocking-G.

CHAPTER 3

Approximately a mile and a half ahead of the three drifters, Emily Green drove her buggy along a trail barely wide enough to accommodate a wagon in many places. So for the most part, Bannack rode behind the buggy, saving him from having to answer many questions. He took a look behind him frequently to make sure no one might be following them, but there was no sight of anyone all the way to the Rocking-G entrance arch. He pulled up beside the buggy to say goodbye, but she asked him to stay long enough to meet her father. "Please, John, I know I've taken enough of your time, but I would like for him to meet you because I know he would want to thank you."

"That's really not necessary," Bannack told her. "I'm just glad I could help."

"It won't take but a minute," she insisted and pointed toward the barn. "That's my father standing there in the barnyard."

George Gresham looked up to see his daughter and grandson approaching the barn from the entrance gate.

He was at once curious about the man on a horse beside her. From the look of him, he was a big man and he was leading a packhorse. Gresham walked to meet them and the closer he got, the more concerned he became. The man had an unexpressive face, as if it might have been carved from a stone. Gresham was at once cautious, wondering what form of trouble had been visited upon his daughter. He should have never permitted her to go into town. "Emily?" he questioned, waiting for her explanation while eyeing the somber stranger with her.

"Dad," Emily began, "I want you to meet John Cochran. I hate to admit it to you, but if it was not for John, I'm not sure Peter and I would have come home safely. John," she said then, "this is my father, George Gresham."

"How do you do, sir?" Bannack said respectfully after he dismounted. He shook Gresham's hand when it was offered, being careful not to squeeze too firmly. Still Gresham could not help but feel the strength in his arm, and that was enough to cause him to fear there might be an ulterior motive for his help.

Emily went on then to tell her father about her confrontation with Ace Parker and how Bannack had come to her rescue, then escorted her home to ensure her safety. Gresham was properly impressed and expressed his appreciation. "I feel like we owe you something for stepping in like you did," he said, thinking the somber-looking man might be expecting some sort of reward.

"No, sir," Bannack said, "you owe me nothing. I'm just glad I was able to help. Your daughter might have talked her way out of it, anyway." He forced a smile and nodded toward the boy. "Old man Peter would have been there to help her, too."

Gresham chuckled. "That's a fact," he said. "Wouldn't you at least like to stay for supper?"

"Thank you just the same," Bannack replied, "but there's quite a bit of daylight left. I think I'll move a little farther north before I call it a day. That trail we rode in on, is that the only trail from your ranch, here, that leads back to the north-south road we took outta town?"

"No, there's other trails from the ranch to strike the main road through Stephenville to go north or south that'll save you a little time," Gresham said. "You're headin' north, did you say?" Bannack nodded. "Then take that little path angling through those trees yonder." He pointed toward a line of trees about fifty yards away. "If you follow that path all the way, you'll strike the north road about two miles north of where you turned off to come straight to the ranch."

"That sounds like the path I need to take," Bannack said. "Thank you, sir."

"No, thank you, sir," Gresham responded.

"Thank you, John," Emily said. "I think it's a good idea you're taking another path back to the main road. I don't trust those three men."

He nodded in reply and stepped up into the saddle. *I don't either,* he thought, looked at the boy who never quit staring at him, and said, "Happy birthday, Peter."

Then he wheeled the buckskin away toward the cutoff path.

"That's a strange man," George Gresham commented as they watched him disappear into the trees. "When he rode up with you, I wouldn't have been surprised if he had whipped out a gun and demanded money for your return."

"Daddy, that's a terrible thing to say about a man as nice as he is," Emily protested. "He was nothing but a gentleman the whole time."

"I know, I know," Gresham hurried to declare. "I believe you, but that's what makes him so strange. He looks like a big mountain lion that's fixin' to rip your head off." They might have appreciated the irony of his remark had they known the name given Bannack by Judge Raymond Grant when he called him Judge Wick's panther. "At any rate," Gresham continued, "I don't know if you should tell Rex you took Peter into town today or not. He worries about you enough as it is."

"I know," she said, "but Peter's going to tell him first thing. John must have really made an impression on him. I don't ever remember Peter not making a sound for that long ever since he was born." She shrugged. "Anyway, Rex will appreciate what John did today. Just passing through town, he could have just decided not to get involved."

"Just goes to show you there are a lot of good people in the world," her father said, "but sometimes it's hard to spot 'em. And some of 'em, like John Cochran, wear good disguises."

The object of their discussion was satisfied to have escorted Emily and Peter home before the three drifters caught up with them. As he rode an alternate path back to the wagon road he intended to follow north, he had a feeling the three men were waiting for his return on the same path he took to the ranch. No doubt they were planning a nice little reception for him, and he wondered how long they would wait before they decided he wasn't coming back. Then another thought clouded his mind. What would they do? Turn around and go back to town? Or decide to ride on into the ranch? He thought back on the scene he had just left at the ranch headquarters. He had not seen another soul there other than her father. He had noticed a large house, barn, bunkhouse, stables, even a cookshack, but not another soul about. He remembered Emily mentioning her husband, Rex, and that he was not with her and the boy because he and the men were moving a large herd to new grazing. There may have been someone else inside the ranch house, but the picture created in his mind was of a defenseless target for three men of evil purpose. Ace Parker and his two friends fit that designation perfectly.

It occurred to him that he was responsible for the actions of the three men, so he could not simply ride away unconcerned. "So I reckon we'd best see what's on their minds," he informed the buckskin and turned the horse off the path to strike out in a direction parallel to the one the three were on. With no way of knowing how far along that path they might have come before they decided to stop and set up an ambush, he could only guess where he should cut back to strike that path. When he decided, he turned sharply to the south and rode a straight line through patches of stunted oaks until he came to the original path. It was easily determined by the tracks of Emily's buggy wheels. The many hoof-prints told him the three drifters had ridden at least that far, so they were somewhere between him and the short distance to the ranch. From this point on, he would have to be especially careful, so he got down from the saddle and led his horses off the path and tied them in the trees. He didn't want to take a chance on his horses greeting their horses, so he drew his rifle from the saddle and started walking toward the ranch.

He cautiously made his way along the path, trying to discover every potential spot for ambush until he stopped when about to follow the path around a sudden bend. There in the middle of the curve, he saw the three of them behind a sizable log. Two of them were sitting on the ground facing him, with their backs against the log. The other one, who he recognized as Ace Parker, was sitting on the log, watching for him to return from the ranch. Bannack noticed that not one of them had a rifle with them. Their plan was to evidently hide behind the log until he rode up beside it, then jump him before he had a chance to react. In view of that, he moved up a little closer to a sizable tree trunk, but not so close as to be in easy pistol range. He wanted to use the advantage his rifle offered.

When he was ready, he cranked a cartridge into the Henry rifle. All three men jumped upon hearing the sound of the lever cocking, looking all around them in a panic. "Just what did you boys have in mind?" Bannack asked and stepped out from behind the tree. That was the only opportunity he intended to offer them to surrender. They unwisely ignored it and went for their guns. Ace was the fastest, so he got Bannack's first shot in the chest. Scully and Short were close in reaction time, but Scully didn't clear his holster before Bannack cranked in another round and put it in his right shoulder. Short was fast enough to draw his six-gun a couple of seconds before Bannack could reload again, but in his haste, at that distance, his shot hit the tree beside Bannack before he was hit in the side. He dropped his pistol and fell back against the log, clutching his side. Bannack trained his rifle on Scully, who was making an effort to draw his pistol again. "You pull that weapon, you're a dead man," he told him as he walked toward him. Believing him, Scully sat down on the log, his right arm dripping blood from his shoulder. Bannack took the six-gun out of Scully's holster and picked up the pistol Short dropped. Then he went on the other side of the log and picked up Ace's gun. After that, he took a look at Ace and decided he was dead.

He confronted the two wounded men then. Short looked the worst but was not fatally wounded. "I don't know if there's a doctor in that town or not," he told them, "but more than likely there's somebody there that does some doctorin'. I'll help you on your horses and I'll put your partner on his and you can ride on back to town."

"What if there ain't nobody to doctor us?" Short groaned.

"Then you'll have to take care of yourselves," Bannack replied, "and maybe you'll remember that next time you decide to ambush somebody." He brought their horses up and asked who went with which horse. Then he picked up Ace's body and draped it over his saddle, using the rope to tie Ace's horse to the back of one of the other saddles. After he put the three handguns in Ace's saddlebags, he helped Scully and Short get up into their saddles. "If you don't waste any time," he told them, "maybe you can catch the doctor before he goes to supper." He gave the lead horse a smack on the rump and they headed back to town. He walked back to get his horses, trying to decide if he should go back to the Rocking-G to tell them what had happened. It had all occurred so near the ranch that they surely heard the gunshots. It might be the best thing to at least let them know there was no danger coming their way. "I've already wasted enough time," he muttered to the buckskin as he climbed up into the saddle. "What the hell," he decided, "I've killed the afternoon already." He turned the buckskin toward the Rocking-G.

* * *

"Emily, there's that man you rode home with," her mother called to her. "I wonder what he came back here for?"

Emily walked up to the parlor to join her at the window. "That's him all right," she said. "I wonder if he had anything to do with those shots we heard. But those shots came from back down the trail to town. He didn't go that way. He took the north cutoff path."

"Well, he came back from that direction," her mother said.

"He did?" She hadn't made it to the window in time to see him come off the path. "Where's Daddy?"

"He went down to the barn," her mother said. They remained at the front window, watching the big man until they could no longer see him as he rode toward the barn. Then they hurried down the hall to the kitchen, so they could continue to watch him.

"What you two lookin' at?" Ethel Bowden asked. "I know you ain't run in here to help me fix supper."

"It's that big stranger that Emily brought home with her," Alice Gresham said.

"Honestly, Mama, I didn't bring him home with me," Emily protested. "You make it sound like I did something naughty. He escorted me home for my and Peter's safety."

"And now he's back already," Ethel remarked. "Did you tell him you was a married woman?"

"Bite your evil tongue, Ethel Bowden," Emily scolded. "I was there with Peter. He could see that I had a child."

"Last I heard, you don't have to be married to have a baby," Ethel came back. "All you need is a willin' mind and a . . ."

"Never mind!" Emily interrupted. "He was nothing but a gentleman."

"Your father sees him," her mother said. "He's coming out of the barn to meet him."

Ethel crowded in between them, trying to get a better look at the stranger as he stepped down from his horse to talk to George. "I declare," Ethel blurted, "he is a big fellow, ain't he? Mr. Gresham better keep him away from the mares. You reckon I best go get the shotgun?"

"No, Ethel," Emily said, "whatever it is, he must have had a good reason to come back. I do wish Rex and the other men would get back here, though. He said most of them would get back to the ranch tonight." She gave her mother a worried look. "I wish we could hear what they're talking about."

Mr. Gresham and Bannack were talking about the shots that were fired close to the Rocking-G Ranch house. "I appreciate your coming back here to tell me what those shots were about," Gresham said. "I wondered about 'em because they were pretty close to the house and they came in a burst of shots. It wasn't like somebody shooting at a deer or something. You say it was those same three men from the Oasis, and they followed you and Emily all the way home?" He shook his head, thinking what might have been if Bannack had not happened to eat dinner at the saloon. "But how did you know they were waiting in ambush for you?"

"Well, I knew it was me they were after," Bannack explained. "It all started in the saloon with this one fellow, Ace Parker, thinkin' to have his way with your daughter. But it was me steppin' in that really riled him to the point where he was determined to settle with me. I expect he was hopin' to catch us before we got here so he could settle with both of us. And when he couldn't catch us, he decided to take it all out on me when I rode back down that trail. I've gotta be honest with you, Mr. Gresham, I don't know for sure if I never showed up, whether they would have picked up and gone back to town or not. I think your daughter will tell you these were pretty dangerous lookin' men. So after I left here, I got to thinkin' about you folks here and all your men gone. And I decided to double back on 'em and see what they were up to."

"And you found them in ambush?"

"Yes, sir, they were set up behind a log waitin' for me, but I came in behind them. I can show you where they were, if you want to see it. I gave 'em a chance to give up. I asked 'em what they had in mind. They all three just went for their guns. They didn't give me any choice."

"You killed all three of them?"

"No, sir, I killed one of 'em, the one who tried to take advantage of your daughter. The other two, I just wounded. Just tried to stop 'em, so they couldn't shoot me. They went back to town and took the dead one with 'em."

"Damn . . ." Gresham couldn't help drawling out.

"You've had quite an afternoon. And that ambush took place just a little piece down that path?"

"Yes, sir," Bannack replied. "I can show you the place, if you want to see it."

"You know, I would like to see it," Gresham said. He couldn't deny an uneasy feeling that Bannack's story didn't seem just right. "Do I need to get a horse?"

"No, sir, it's not that far. I'll just leave my horses here and I'll walk down there with you." He dropped the buckskin's reins on the ground and they turned and walked back down the trail.

Still glued to the kitchen window, the three women were at once concerned. "Where are they going?" Alice Gresham asked anxiously.

"I don't know," her daughter replied, "but I'm going to find out!" Totally convinced of the stranger's character before, she now wondered if she might have been fooled. She ran to her bedroom and got her pistol from the top closet shelf. It was kept there for times like this one when Rex was gone and her father might need help.

"What are you doing?" her mother yelled at her when she ran back into the kitchen and went out the back door. "Emily!" she yelled again when Emily didn't answer.

"I'm going to see if Daddy needs any help!" Emily yelled back at her as she ran past the two horses standing in the yard.

Her mother turned to clutch both of Ethel's forearms. "Where's Peter?"

"I don't know!" Ethel blurted. "He was with your

husband," she started, then exclaimed, "There he is!" when she saw the four-year-old come out of the barn and run after his mother. "Oh, mercy, that ain't good," she remarked.

After a walk of about a quarter of a mile, Bannack pointed to the log lying just off the trail. "That's where they were waitin' for me, right behind that log," he said and Gresham went over to the log.

"No wonder those shots sounded so close," Gresham said, his eyes fixed on the blood still evident on the log and the ground beside it. "Where were you when you fired the shots?"

"Behind that tree," Bannack said and pointed to it. He walked over to the tree and looked around on the ground until he spotted his spent cartridges. "I was pretty busy at the time. I forgot to pick up my brass."

Gresham walked over to the tree and turned to look back at the log. "You coulda got a little bit closer. What happened? They see you coming?"

"No, sir, they didn't know I was here till I called out to 'em." Then he explained that they just had their hand-guns while he had his Henry rifle. "Since they had a three to one advantage on me, I decided to get some of that advantage back by keepin' more distance between us. The third one was the only one that had time for a clear shot and he hit the tree instead of me." He showed Gresham the spot on the trunk where the bullet had ripped some bark out.

Gresham was satisfied then with Bannack's story and was about to say so when Emily suddenly appeared, carrying a revolver in her hand. "Emily, what in the world . . . ?" he started but didn't finish when he spotted Peter coming behind her. "You brought Peter, too?"

"I did?" Emily asked and looked behind her, only then realizing he was trying to catch up with her. "Come to Mama, Honey," she called to the boy.

"What's the gun for?" Gresham asked.

"Oh, that, I don't know, I just thought I'd see if you needed any help and it was handy, so I just brought it along with me." When her father rolled his eyes up toward the top of his head, she knew she had made an embarrassing mistake.

It was all pretty obvious to Bannack that his return had struck a note of suspicion about him. "I know when I'm licked," he said and grinned at Emily. "I'll go peacefully. I just wanted to let you know what happened here. I'll be on my way. There's still a good bit of daylight left."

"You know, you didn't seem to be in a big hurry to get where you're going," Gresham said. "Matter of fact, you just said you were heading west. How far is the place you're going to?"

"I don't rightly know," Bannack answered.

"What's the name of the place?"

"I don't know that, either," Bannack replied. "I figure I'll know it when I get there."

"I think you ought to wait till morning to continue your journey," Gresham suggested. "We've got empty bunks in the bunkhouse. You can stay there tonight and have supper with us. I feel like I'd like to extend some hospitality to you for bringing my daughter back to us safe and sound. I appreciate that, John. You can take care of your horses, feed them some grain, and keep them in the barn tonight. Whaddaya say, John? We got a cook that'll jump for joy if she gets a chance to feed a man big as you."

"I declare," Bannack said, "that's hard to turn down. Is that all right with you, Mrs. Green?"

"Of course it is, John. I'd be delighted if you'd stay here tonight," she said at once. "And you can stop calling me Mrs. Green. You know my name's Emily."

"Thank you, ma'am. I had to be sure though, *Emily*," he said, emphasizing Emily. "When you came runnin' up that path with that gun, I figured you weren't plannin' to use it on your father."

Gresham chuckled and said, "You never know. Sometimes I think she considers it. Come on, let's go back to the barn and take care of your horses."

When they walked back to Bannack's horses, they discovered the chuckwagon back in the barnyard. "Good," Gresham declared. "Lefty's fixing to feed the men here at supper, so I reckon they got all the cattle moved."

Emily left them and went back to the house. "You'll be eating with us, John," she made it a point to emphasize before she walked away. "I'll tell Ethel to make sure she's got plenty."

"Yes, ma'am," Bannack replied, "but tell her not

to go to any trouble. I could just as well eat with the cowhands, since we ain't givin' Ethel much notice."

"Not tonight," Emily said. "Tonight, you're our guest and we usually eat around five-thirty, so don't be late."

"Well, you now know who runs the ranch," Gresham said as he and Bannack continued on toward the barn.

Several riders rode in as they reached the barn. "We moved 'em all back on this side of the range, Boss, and Rex is doublin' the boys ridin' night herd tonight." He threw a leg over and slid down off his horse, looking the big stranger over openly.

"That's good, Willy," Gresham responded. "Maybe that'll cut some of our losses. Like you to meet John Cochran. John say howdy to Willy Crider. Willy's been with the Rocking-G ever since I brought in the first herd of three hundred cows. That was over eight years ago, and I've expected him to quit every year after that first one."

"Glad to meetcha, John," Willy said and stuck out his hand. "Are you a cattleman?" he asked when they shook hands. The question caught Gresham's interest as well, and he waited for Bannack's answer.

"No, I can't say as I am," Bannack answered. "I used to own a farm with my brother, but I left that a few years back." They waited for him to say more, but that was all he offered.

"So that tells you right there that he must be smarter than the rest of us," Gresham remarked. "John just stopped to have supper with me and the family and he's gonna bunk in the bunkhouse tonight." Talking to Bannack then, he said, "You can put your saddle and your packs in one of the stalls, if you want. Then take your saddlebags and whatever else you need and we'll go find you a cot in the bunkhouse. By the time we get that all squared away, it ought to be close to suppertime."

CHAPTER 4

After Gresham had him squared away with a bed for the night, they went into the house where Gresham introduced Bannack to Emily's mother and Ethel Bowden, the cook and housekeeper. Alice Gresham gave him a very warm welcome and expressed her deepest gratitude for protecting her daughter. Ethel openly looked him up and down, then commented, "I'm just baking some more biscuits right now." She turned around and went back to the kitchen to check on them, while they proceeded to the dining room.

Before they sat down at the table, they were joined by Rex Green, Emily's husband, who had just ridden in. A tall, slender, young man, he went first to embrace his wife before turning his attention to the stranger standing beside his father-in-law. "Sweetheart," Emily said, "I'd like you to meet a good friend of mine. This is John Cochran. John, this is my husband, Rex."

Obviously confused, since he had never heard a mention of a friend of his wife's by that name, he looked at the formidable-looking man and unconsciously tried to stand as tall as he could manage. "Pleased to meet you," he said and extended his hand, almost stumbling when his son came from behind him and wrapped his arms around his thighs.

"Likewise," Bannack replied.

When Rex looked back at his wife for an explanation, she chuckled and said, "I didn't know he was my good friend until today."

Gresham interrupted then. "John turned out to be a helluva good friend to the whole family." He went on to relate the day's events that led up to Bannack's invitation to have supper with them and breakfast as well before he went on his way.

"I am certainly in your debt, sir," Rex said to Bannack after he heard the story. "I hope you realize how much I appreciate what you did for my wife and my son. Especially on this big boy's birthday," he said and picked up Peter to give him a hug. "Of course, I reckon I should also apologize for my wife puttin' you in a situation where you had to risk your life to keep her safe."

"I knew that was coming," Emily said, "but it was Peter's birthday."

"And thanks to Mr. Cochran, here, Peter might make it to see another one," Rex remarked. "What if he hadn't been there today?"

"Children!" Gresham scolded. "Let's save the family fight until sometime after supper. I think I'd like a drink before we eat, and I know Rex needs one. How about you, John? I've got scotch and bourbon. What's your pleasure?"

"Just whichever you're trying to get rid of," Bannack responded. "I ain't much of a drinker, so one is about as good as the other."

"In that case, I'll pour you and Rex a shot of bourbon. Ain't no use wasting good scotch on two souls who don't appreciate the finer gifts of malt and grain whiskey," Gresham said. He walked over to the buffet where the two bottles were and poured the three drinks. When he returned to the table, he raised his glass of scotch and said, "Here's to those who watch over us and thanks to the Lord for sending folks who can do the job."

Bannack wasn't comfortable with the salute, which he could only assume was in honor of his actions on that day. It didn't seem right for him to drink to himself, but he took a drink anyway. It burned his throat on the way down, just as it always did, and he wondered why he never seemed to get used to it. Thankfully, Alice Gresham took over then. "All right, now everybody sit down at the table before we drive Ethel's temperature up. John, you sit down over here next to me." Everybody sat down but Emily, who went into the kitchen to help Ethel put the food on the table and pour the coffee for everyone including Peter. When everyone had food and coffee, she sat down next to her husband. The conversation shifted to the cattle then, as it normally did at mealtime, with Gresham questioning Rex about the status of the herd. Rex told him that the main part of the herd had been successfully moved to graze closer to the ranch headquarters. He said that he hoped the herd was far enough away from the Bar-W to keep their riders from rustling any small groups of Rocking-G cattle.

Then Rex asked Bannack a question. "Those three men you stopped on the trail to town, do you know who they were?"

"I have no idea," Bannack answered. "I think they were just drifters, like a lot of men you see hangin' around a saloon. The bartender knew them, though."

"So you don't remember any names?" Rex asked. He was curious to see if they were any of the known troublemakers that hung out around town and the reason he didn't want Emily to drive into town by herself.

Bannack started to say he didn't know any names but then remembered. "I do know the name of one of them, the one I had to kill. The bartender told me his name was Ace Parker."

Rex's eyes lit up. "You killed Ace Parker?"

Seeing his reaction, Bannack immediately defended his position. "I had no choice. He went for his gun, so it was either him or me." He looked around at the others. "I'm sorry, this ain't no talk for the supper table. I beg your pardon, ma'am," he said to Alice Grisham.

"No offense taken, John," Alice said. "You didn't bring it up, anyway. Rex asked the question."

"I sure did," Rex said. "Ace Parker rides for the Bar-W." He looked at Bannack and grinned. "At least, he used to ride for the Bar-W, and I expect the two fellows with him are Bar-W hands, too. I'll bet old Luther Womack is fit to be tied right now. He lost his stud horse and two of his men are crippled. I'll bet he didn't know Ace and the two men with him were in town today. I don't know if Mr. Gresham told you but we've been losing cattle to rustlers and we're pretty sure those rustlers are Bar-W hands. We just haven't been able to catch 'em in the act, so we finally moved our whole herd over on this part of our range, even though we need to be grazing that grass closer to the Bar-W range." He paused then when he realized he had taken over the conversation with a subject better saved for later between him and his father-in-law. He looked at his mother-in-law and said, "Excuse my manners, Miss Alice," which was how he always referred to her, "I'll shut up about the cows now."

"He can't help it, Mama," Emily said in his defense. "That's all he ever thinks about."

"That's the reason he's my foreman," her father remarked. "I pay him to think about the cows all the time."

When the conversation was shifted away from the cattle, it quite naturally fell upon Bannack and how he had happened to pass through their little town at the exact time when he was needed. He tried to explain that it was just happenstance. He was simply passing through town at dinnertime and he was ready to enjoy a good meal for a change. His explanation was not enough to satisfy Rex, however, for there was something about the soft-spoken stranger that suggested there was a deadly animal underneath the polite disguise. He restrained himself from questioning Bannack any further at the supper table, but he knew that Gresham would invite his guest to an after-supper drink and a cigar on the front porch. Out of respect for the ladies, Rex would wait till then to continue his interrogation.

When everyone had finished eating, the polite conversation continued until Ethel came in and pointedly started picking up the dirty dishes. Her actions were enough to cause Gresham to suggest brandy and cigars out on the porch. Bannack was not particularly inclined to have another drink, but he had never had a drink of brandy, so he decided to see what it was like. And he figured he might as well smoke a cigar, too, since it wasn't costing him any money. So when they got up from the table, he thanked Alice and Emily for their hospitality, then he thanked Ethel for his supper. "I haven't enjoyed food that good in a long time," he told her, which pleased her very much. He told himself that he was not lying because it seemed like a long time since he had eaten dinner at the Oasis Saloon.

He followed Gresham and Rex into the study where Gresham poured the brandy and brought out a box of cigars. Then they went out to the porch to sit in the rocking chairs and enjoy them. Rex excused himself briefly to speak to Willy when he passed by, then Rex resumed his questioning about Bannack's encounter with Ace Parker. "Had you ever heard of Ace Parker before you came to Stephenville?"

"Nope, can't say as I had," Bannack replied. "Any reason I should have?"

"Well, maybe." Rex hesitated. "Ace rode for the Bar-W, but he also had a little reputation as a fast gun in the half-dozen or so counties around Erath County."

"Reckon not," Bannack said. "Like I told Mr. Gresham, I'm from Waco and that's a good ways from here."

"I thought you mighta heard of Ace Parker and decided to call him out." Rex was seriously suspicious of Bannack's encounter with Parker, but he chuckled when he made the statement, as if he was joking. If Emily's hero was as deadly as he looked, it wouldn't pay to provoke him.

"Nope," Bannack responded. "Mr. Gresham said it right when he told you I came up on the backside of the ambush those three fellows had set up for me. The only reason all three got shot was because when I told them to get, they wouldn't. And they chose to draw their weapons on me, instead. Parker may have been fast, I don't know, but he was faster than the other two with him. That's the reason he got shot first 'cause he drew on a man already aiming a Henry rifle at him. I had to stop him. I had more time to place my shots on the other two, so they weren't fatal. I didn't see any sense in killin' all three of them for lettin' the one get them in trouble."

"I agree with you, John," Gresham spoke up then, anxious to put the issue to rest. "What are your plans after you leave here in the morning?"

"Just to keep on ridin' until I find a place that suits me, I reckon," Bannack replied.

"If you were looking for a job workin' cattle, you could stay right here at the Rocking-G," Gresham said. It had occurred to him that Bannack could fill the role of intimidator for the Rocking-G that Ace Parker had filled for the Bar-W. It could possibly discourage the Bar-W men's wanton practice of rustling Rocking-G cattle.

"I appreciate the offer," Bannack responded, "and if I knew the first thing about takin' care of cattle, I might jump at it. But I'm afraid I'd have to be taught so much that it wouldn't be worth whatever you paid me."

"I expect, if you worked a farm, you could soon learn to work on a cattle ranch," Gresham said. "If you change your mind, come on back. I'm sure Rex would welcome you."

"That's a fact," Rex confirmed, having had the same thoughts about the big man that his father-in-law had.

"Thanks a lot," Bannack said. "I'll surely keep that in mind." He sat and listened to Rex and Gresham talk about the cattle until he finished his cigar, then he announced that he was going to check on his horses and turn in.

"If you need anything, just tell Willy," Gresham said. "He'll take care of you, and we'll see you in the morning."

"Right. Much obliged," Bannack said, going down the porch steps. He walked in the barn to make sure the buckskin and his packhorse were both taken care of, then he went into the bunkhouse, startling most of the men sitting around on their cots. Only a few of them had seen him before he was escorted to the house for supper. Pausing for a few moments in the doorway, his head bowed slightly to avoid bumping it on the top of the door frame, he said, "Howdy, I'm gonna sleep with you fellows tonight."

"Why? What'd we do?" Gabby Daniels, the resident clown responded. The other men chuckled and Willy Crider got up from his cot to meet him.

"Come on in, John," Willy said. "Boys, this is John Cochran. He's just stayin' one night with us, so make him feel welcome." He looked directly at Gabby and said, "Ace Parker didn't make him feel welcome, so Ace's is dead now."

His remark made Bannack want to cringe. He had just as soon Willy refrained from passing on that information. As he expected, the comment got everyone's rapt attention, and the whole bunkhouse went silent as if waiting for him to address them. "I appreciate you fellows letting me bunk with you tonight," was all he could think of to say. He was happy to see that there were no questions from anyone about the confrontation with Ace Parker and the other two Bar-W riders. It didn't occur to him that his physical appearance greatly discouraged any questions on any subject. When he went to the pumphouse to clean up a little before going to bed, Willy was besieged with questions about Ace Parker, but everyone was exceptionally quiet when Bannack returned. *Good,* he thought, *they forgot all about it.*

* * *

He woke up early with the men the next morning, so he decided to eat breakfast with them in the cookshack. This was where Rex found him when he came down to get the men started for the day. "Damn, John," Rex declared, "I'm supposed to tell you that they're expectin' you up at the house for breakfast. Ethel's makin' pancakes this mornin'."

"That's all right, Boss," Gabby Daniels cracked, "I can take his place."

"I just started to eat," Bannack said, "and this looks too good to waste."

"Ain't no problem," Willy Crider said. He reached across the table, picked up Bannack's plate, and scraped the food off onto his plate. "I'll give you a hand. You don't wanna do nothin' to rile Ethel."

"Much obliged, Willy," Bannack said, then asked Rex, "When are they gonna have breakfast?"

"You can go up there anytime now," Rex said. "She won't fry the flapjacks until you're sittin' at the table, anyway. Mr. Gresham and Miss Alice are already sittin' at the table waitin' for you."

"Damn," Bannack swore and got up at once. "I'll get right up there. I'm sorry, Lefty," he said to the cook as he walked out the door. "That looked like a mighty good breakfast."

When he was gone, Gabby remarked, "It took that scary lookin' dude to stop Ace Parker. We shoulda sent Ethel after him a long time ago." The cookshack suddenly got noisy again.

With his horses already packed and saddled, Bannack led them to the kitchen door, tied them at the handrail, and knocked on the door. "Come in, it ain't locked," Ethel yelled from the other end of the room. He walked in and saw her standing in front of the big iron stove with a big mixing bowl under one arm. With her free hand, she spooned out the pancake batter and poured it on a hot skillet. "Pour yourself a cup of coffee and take it on in the dining room. There's sausage and grits on the table. These cakes will be ready in a jiffy."

"Good mornin'," he returned their greetings when he walked into the dining room. "I hope you haven't been waiting for me to get started."

"We just sat down," Alice Gresham said. "You're right on time."

He doubted that, judging by the half-eaten pancakes on everybody's plate. By the time he had served himself sausage and grits, Ethel walked in with a platter of hot pancakes. "Don't hold back," she said, "I've got plenty of batter." The breakfast was fine and he ate all he thought he could hold because, for some reason, Ethel seemed to be determined to feed him until he burst. She seemed satisfied when he finally said he was done and that he was afraid he would not be able to climb up into his saddle without some help. It dawned on him then that she had approached this breakfast as a contest between the two of them and that she had won. She had brought him to his knees.

After the eating contest was over, he lingered for only a short time finishing up coffee that he had no place to put. He thanked them again for their hospitality and they, in turn, expressed their eternal gratitude for his actions on Emily's behalf and made him promise to stop in if he was ever back this way. He was surprised when Emily stood on her tiptoes and pulled him down toward her to plant a kiss on his cheek. It was a first for him. He quickly said goodbye then and went out the back door where he apologized to the buckskin before stepping up into the saddle. It had been quite an experience. They were nice people, but he found he was more than ready to be on his way.

Once again, he was on the road, still with no destination other than *away*. He took the north cutoff that he had started out on from the ranch before. He soon came to the place where he had cut back to get behind the ambush. This time, he stayed on the narrow trail that eventually led him to the main road north out of Stephenville. He didn't know where it might take him, but there were many tracks on the road, so he figured it must lead to somewhere. The rest of the day of travel was uneventful to be sure. Early the second day, he came to a crossroad with a small store just short of the crossing. There was a crude sign nailed over the door that proclaimed it to be Rubin's Store. He decided to buy some more coffee, if Rubin wasn't too high in price, so he guided the buckskin up to the front of the store and dismounted.

"Howdy," Paul Rubin offered when Bannack walked into the little store. "Somethin' I can help you with?"

"Howdy," Bannack returned. "I'm runnin' a little short of coffee. I'd like to buy some if you ain't askin' too much for it."

Rubin looked him up and down as if he might have something more in mind than buying coffee. "If I asked too much for it, I reckon I wouldn't sell much coffee. I sell roasted coffee beans in two and five pound bags for twenty-seven cents a pound. If you want me to grind it for you, I charge twenty-eight cents a pound for it."

"That's fair enough," Bannack said. "I'll take a five pound sack of the ground coffee. Might as well sell me a small sack of sugar, too."

"All I've got is five pound sugar sacks," Rubin replied, "twelve cents a pound."

"That'll do," Bannack said. "It'll last me a while." He reached in his pocket and brought out some money to pay for it.

Rubin added up the two purchases for a total of two dollars and five cents. When Bannack put the money on the counter, Rubin called back over his shoulder, "It's all right, Mother, he's a payin' customer." A slight movement on a shelf behind the counter revealed a slot in the back of the shelf that Bannack hadn't noticed when he came in. He realized then that the movement was that of a shotgun barrel being withdrawn. Seeing the look of surprise on Bannack's face, Rubin said, "Tell you what, my wife made a pot of coffee just before you rode up.

How 'bout a cup? It's the same coffee you just bought, and we'll say that extra nickel you just paid will be for a cup of coffee."

"I knew I smelled coffee when I walked in here," Bannack replied. "A cup of fresh coffee would be to my likin' right now." Seconds after he said it, the door to the room behind the counter opened and a petite little woman entered the store carrying a cup of coffee. She walked over and placed it on the counter in front of him.

Rubin chuckled. "I knew you was gonna do that," he said to her.

"Oh, you did, did you?" She looked at Bannack then and said, "I feel so bad to think I pointed a shotgun at a perfectly innocent stranger who came into our store to trade. Please tell me you'll accept my apology."

"No need to apologize," Bannack said, "since you didn't pull the trigger. Have you been havin' trouble with robbers?"

"Just lately," Rubin replied. "There's been a couple of no accounts who've been stealin' cattle from some of the small ranchers and they hit our store last week. Came in like they was fixin' to buy something and pulled their guns on me. Emptied my cash drawer and I had over thirty-seven dollars in it. So we figured we couldn't afford many more visits like that and I cut a slot in that wall back of the counter in case we get another visit. Tell you the truth, this is the first time we got set up for a robbery since I cut that slot." There had been a few strangers in the store since the robbery, but they didn't appear especially dangerous. When they got a look at Bannack tying his horse to the hitching rail, they thought, *This one might kill us and burn the place down.* They did not share that information with the formidable-looking man, however.

While his wife ground the coffee, Rubin asked Bannack where he was heading, and Bannack told him he was just looking for a different place to settle for a while. "I noticed that east-west crossroad up ahead looks like a wider, more-traveled road. Where does that road go?"

"That's the road to Fort Worth," Rubin said, "if you go east on it."

"Where does it lead, if you take it to the west?" Bannack asked.

"Just wide-open prairie as far as you wanna go with a few small cattle farms trying to make it."

"What if I stay on this little road out of Stephenville?" Bannack asked. "Does it lead anywhere?"

"I declare, friend, you really are a stranger in these parts, ain't you?" Rubin responded. "Well, if you stay on this road, you'll eventually come to a little town called Glory."

"Glory?" Bannack questioned, thinking he had not heard him clearly. "The town's name is Glory?"

"That's right. I ain't surprised you ain't never heard of it. Back before the war, several farmers settled up that way. Then some ranchers found out it wasn't bad land to raise cattle on till eventually a fellow named Walter Glory figured there was enough folks up there to support a general store. That was the start of it. I wish I'd been smart enough to build my store up there, instead of this crossroad. Then they mighta called it Rubin." He paused and looked at his wife, shook his head, and remarked, "I never said I was a smart man when I proposed to you."

"Sometimes you say the silliest things," she replied as she emptied the last of the ground coffee in the sack. "We don't have that much to complain about."

"Anyway, Glory's a sizable town now," Rubin continued, "but I think they've got more saloons than a small town needs."

"Maybe I'll stay on this road and go on to Glory just so I can say I've been there," Bannack said. "Much obliged for the cup of coffee, Mrs. Rubin."

"What was your name?" Rubin asked.

"John Cochran," he said. "Pleasure doin' business with you."

CHAPTER 5

He crossed over the road to Fort Worth and continued on toward the town of Glory. His horses were ready for a rest, and the short time he spent at Rubin's Store was not long enough to give them what they needed. So he planned to ride only as long as it took him to find some water. Luckily, he rode only a short distance before he came to a stream strong enough to provide decent water with an abundance of grass around it. He unloaded his horses, then found enough wood to build a fire to cook some bacon and hardtack. Since he had just had a cup of coffee at Rubin's, he filled his coffeepot with just enough water to make one more cup.

When he was satisfied that his horses were rested enough, he set out again. It occurred to him then that he should have asked Rubin how far it was to Glory. As the afternoon wore on, he started thinking about resting his horses again. Far up ahead of him he saw a ribbon of trees crossing his path, which told him there was water. And from the heavy growth of trees he could determine it was probably a fairly large creek. Then he suddenly stopped when he heard a gunshot. A rifle, by the sound of it, and it was answered by a couple of shots, also from rifles. There was nothing more for a few minutes until another series of shots rang out. Somebody was under siege for certain. From the sound of the shooting, it was dead ahead on the road, so he could not avoid it, even if he was of a nature to do so. He urged the buckskin slowly along until he thought he had a picture of the encounter. Close enough now to determine between shots, he came to the conclusion that it was two or more shooters firing at a single target. He decided to turn off the road and cut across until he came to the trees behind the two shooters. It seemed logical to him that the lone shooter was most likely holding off an attack by the other two.

When he reached the trees, he found that he had been correct in assuming they lined a sizable creek, so he started following the creek back toward the road. He had one more concern now. In an effort to help the man under attack, he ran the risk of getting hit by one of his stray shots, so he dismounted and led his horses to a brace of large trees and tied the horses behind them. Then with rifle in hand, he advanced on foot, keeping as low a profile as he could. After fifty or more yards, he came to two saddled horses and one packhorse tied to some tree limbs. A little farther on, he could see the shooters. He stopped to study the situation and almost started when one of the two men he saw began to shout. "You might as well throw that rifle down 'cause we ain't leavin' till we see what you're haulin' in that wagon. If you throw it down now, we won't kill you, but if you don't, you're a dead man. And that's a promise."

What to do about it? He was close enough now to plainly see both of the men, but he was reluctant to simply execute them because they were trying to rob another man. He had to have a better reason to kill than that, so he decided to force them to run. He walked over to their horses and untied them. Then he drew his Colt .44 and fired four shots into the ground behind the horses and smacked one of them on the rump. It had the effect he desired. Squealing in fright, the horses raced through the trees and out onto the road. "What tha . . . ?" one of the robbers started. "Whoa!" the other one shouted and tried to stop the terrified horses, only to be knocked to the ground by his packhorse. When he tried to get to his feet, one of the saddled horses knocked him to the ground again. This time, he didn't try to get up but yelled to his partner that he was hurt and needed help.

His partner was oblivious to the call for help. He was busy trying to stop the horses as they galloped past him. Failing to do so, he turned and ran after his horse, following it out into the road. Seeing the man in the road, Bannack dropped his Colt back in his holster, and cocked his Henry rifle. With a clear shot now, he squeezed the trigger and knocked the man's legs out from under him. The man went down, landing heavily in the middle of the road. He reached down for his six-gun only to find an empty holster.

Back in the trees, Bannack stood over the man run down by his horses. He took his pistol and stuck it in his belt, then asked, "Can you get up?"

"Who the hell are you?" the man responded, obviously in pain.

"Never mind who I am," Bannack answered. "Can you get up?"

"No, damn it, that blame horse broke my leg." He started to say more but when he got a better look at the man standing over him, he hesitated, not certain what he was going to do.

"You oughta had better sense than to try to stand in front of a runaway horse," Bannack said. "Which one's broke?" The man pointed toward his right leg. "I'll take a look to see if it can be fixed, or if I might as well put you outta your misery." He pulled his skinning knife from his belt and stabbed the trousers right beside the injured leg, causing the man to yell in panic. "Hold still," Bannack ordered, then sliced the trouser leg apart, so he could see the broken bone protruding through the skin below the knee. "Well, you're right, it's broke for sure. I might be able to rig up some kinda splint for it, or I can put you outta your misery, whichever you want. You can be decidin' while I go take a look at your partner. I had to shoot him in the leg to keep him from chasin' your horses all the way to Glory. You ain't hidin' no more pistols on you, are you?" He grabbed him by his belt buckle and lifted him up high enough to feel all around his waist for a pocket pistol. It was enough to cause a yelp of pain. "Nothing in your boot?"

He quickly checked both boots. "I don't want to come back to help you and have you take a shot at me."

He left him then and walked out to the road, but before stepping out into the open, he called out, "You in the wagon! My name's John Cochran. I came to give you a hand. Both the men who were shootin' at you are down. So the shootin's over. I reckon you can see one of 'em layin' in the road. I'm fixin' to go out there to get him, so I don't want you to take a shot at me. Do you understand I came to help you, and you have nothin' to fear from me?" He paused to wait for some response, but there was none. "I don't blame you for bein' cautious. You don't have to show yourself. Just don't shoot at me for doin' you a favor. All right?"

"All right," a reply finally came back from the wagon parked by the creek.

"All right," Bannack repeated. "I'm comin' out in the road to get this fellow. Hold your fire." He left the cover of the trees and walked out into the road, picking up a gun he saw lying there. The wounded man was frantically looking from one side of the road to the other, wondering from which side the kill shot would come. "Where are you hit?" Bannack asked.

"Right above my knee," the man answered. "Are you a lawman?"

"Nope, I'm just somebody that ain't got much use for men like you that try to take something another man has worked for. Your partner's back there in the trees with a broke leg."

"What are you gonna do with us?" the wounded man asked.

"I'm still thinkin' it over," Bannack replied. "Easiest thing would be to put a bullet in your head. That would end your sufferin' right away and guarantee the fellow that owns the wagon you and your partner have been shootin' holes in that he'd never see you again. I think I'll see what the owner of the wagon thinks I oughta do with you."

"I think you oughta shoot both of 'em," a voice from the other side of the road announced. "But I'm willing to let 'em live, if they'll guarantee they'll get to hell away from here and leave me alone. They're about to shoot my wagon to pieces, and I ain't carrying a thing they could get any money for." There was a rustling of the bushes and a little man stepped out from behind them. "I'll tell you what those jackasses are tryin' to rob me for. A blamed barber chair, that's what they're tryin' to steal. What in the world would they do with a barber chair? And they were willin' to kill me for it. Said they was gonna kill me if I didn't tell 'em what I was carryin', and I told 'em it was a barber chair two or three times, but they kept on shootin' at me."

The wounded man looked up at Bannack and said, "You gotta admit that it didn't seem likely that he was haulin' a barber chair."

"I swear, I oughta shoot you right now!" the little man with the wagon exclaimed.

"Hold on!" the would-be robber blurted. "I guarantee you we'll go and you won't never see us again!"

Bannack looked at the irate little man. "Is that what you wanna do?"

He hesitated for a few moments. "I reckon," he said finally. "Are you gonna hang around for a while after they're gone?"

"Yeah, if you're headin' to Glory, I'll go along with you, if you want me to," Bannack assured him. "I'm not in any hurry to get there."

"Mister, I'll be forever beholden to you for what you did for me today. There ain't many people who wouldn't have just rode way around my trouble. My name's Buster Bridges, and in spite of what that fool thinks, I ain't got a lotta money to reward you for steppin' in when you did. The only thing I can offer you is a free haircut and a shave anytime you need one, and I gladly offer that."

"That's mighty generous of you, Buster, but I wasn't expectin' any reward. My name's John Cochran. I'll just see if I can't make your guests a little more comfortable, then I'll round up their horses and we'll get 'em started to their next adventure."

"That sounds like a good idea," Buster said. "You know, I've treated a few gunshot wounds in my time. I can take a look at this fellow's leg, if he wants me to."

"Bein' a barber, I reckon you have done some doctorin', if you ever had a shop in a town without a doctor. I'll tell you what, I'll go get this fellow's partner and bring him here, so I can keep an eye on 'em while you're fixin' 'em up." He went back into the trees to get his horses, then picked up the other would-be robber and lifted him on his belly across the saddle. Then took him to join his partner. After he set him down on the side of the road, he took his hand axe off his packhorse and cut a couple of tree limbs to use as splints.

Buster went to his wagon and brought back some rags he would use as bandages and ties to hold the splint on. "If you'll help me, I'll see if I can put that bone back in place first," he said to Bannack. Then to the patient, he said, "Get ready to hold on 'cause this is gonna hurt like hell. At least, I hope to hell it does." Then with Bannack to hold the man's knee, Buster grabbed his ankle and pulled as hard as he could. The patient screamed in pain until he passed out. Buster continued to pull until he was satisfied the bones were back in place. Then he wrapped it tightly before he tied the splints together while his patient was still out. He looked at Bannack and confessed, "I've got some chloroform in the wagon, but I'm savin' it to use on humans."

After his partner's visit with the "doctor," the other robber insisted he could take care of his gunshot wound himself, if Buster would give him the bandages and splash some whiskey on it. "I can dig that bullet outta there," Buster told him, but the robber pleaded to take care of it. "Suit yourself," Buster said. He watched as the man tenderly treated the gunshot wound while Bannack went to round up the horses he had scattered. When the man with the broken leg had recovered enough to stay on his horse, Bannack helped both men up into the saddle and warned them that if he saw them again, he would shoot on sight. They assured him that they were going to Fort Worth to recover. Bannack was inclined to believe them. He figured they were not in any condition to seek revenge.

"Mr. Cochran," Buster declared grandly after they had gone, "I thank my lucky stars that you came along. Those two got on my tail back on the Fort Worth road. I tried to stay ahead of them as best I could. But with me driving a wagon, they kept catchin' up. They were just waiting for me to rest my horses and finally I had to stop. They wanted to ride in, but I told 'em I druther they didn't because my wife was sick with the pox."

"Your wife is sick?" Bannack responded, immediately concerned.

"No, no," Buster quickly replied. "I ain't got no wife. I just told them fellows that. Thought maybe it would run 'em off, but they was willin' to catch the pox to see what was in my wagon. And I figured once they saw there wasn't nothin' in the wagon but my barber's chair, more'n likely they'd shoot me for puttin' 'em to the trouble. So they started shootin', and I was afraid I'd run out of cartridges before they gave up."

"I'm glad I came along when I did," Bannack said. "We could move on a little bit farther before we call it a day. I don't know how you feel about it, but I'd just as soon camp right where we are. My horses need a rest. You said your horses were tired, and it's a pretty good place to defend yourself. You've already proved that. I doubt we'll find a spot any better, and I think those two are done with us, anyway. So whaddaya say? Let's build a fire and cook something to eat."

"That suits me just fine," Buster replied. "I've got some good side meat and flour to make some pan biscuits. I'm sorry to say I'm out of coffee."

"I just bought some fresh ground coffee back at the crossroads in Rubin's Store," Bannack said.

"Hot damn!" Buster exclaimed. "I was wonderin' how I was gonna make it through the night without a good cup of coffee." They both started searching for firewood.

As a precaution, they built their fire below the bank of the creek to minimize the glow that might be seen from a distance and made their beds underneath the bank as well. As they had assumed, however, the night passed peacefully with no uninvited guests, so they revived their fire and made breakfast there before starting out for Glory. Bannack was slowed somewhat by the pace of Buster's wagon, but he didn't mind. As he told Buster the night before, he was in no particular hurry, and besides he was learning a lot about the town of Glory from Buster as he rode along beside his wagon. He learned that Buster had a barbershop in Stephenville, but on a visit to the little town of Glory, he found that he liked the idea of the town and the people who had founded it. He decided that his business would grow much faster in Glory because he thought the town itself would outgrow Stephenville. Besides, there was a widow woman who lived in Glory who had been married to the owner of the hardware store. And he had been making it a habit of sitting next to her at the church on Sunday mornings. "She don't look all that bad for wear for a woman her age and she just had one young'un. He's tryin' to run the store since his daddy died, but he's awful young and has to have her help. I kinda feel it my Christian duty to help out if I can."

"I reckon so," Bannack replied. "Ain't no doubt your heart's in the right place."

They stopped to rest the horses once more before pulling into the town of Glory a little before noon. Situated on the west side of the Brazos River, the town was a little bigger than Bannack expected and it appeared to be quite busy for that time of day. In fact, Buster was surprised by the number of people on the street. "Something must be goin' on," he said as they rode up the street past the sheriff's office. Ever since breakfast that morning, Buster had been insisting he was going to buy Bannack's dinner at Sawyer's Café. He had raved so much about the quality and the quantity of the food at Sawyer's that Bannack was building up an appetite all morning in anticipation. According to Buster, Sawyer's was a family-run restaurant owned by Russell Sawyer. Russell's wife, Effie, did most of the cooking with help from their daughter, Louella, who also helped her younger sister, Susie, wait the tables.

When they came to a new building with no sign on it, Buster said, "This is my place," and he pulled his horses to a stop. "It'll look a whole lot better when I put my sign and my barber pole up."

"You want to unload your barber chair now?" Bannack asked. "I'll give you a hand."

"I figured you would," Buster replied, "but I'm gonna feed you first. We can go down that little alley up ahead and go around to the back of my place. I'll leave the wagon there while we go up the street to Sawyer's. You can leave your horses there, too, unless you'd rather tie 'em in front of Sawyer's. I don't think anybody will bother them behind my shop."

"You're probably right, but I don't like to leave my rifle and saddlebags that far outta my sight." So they parked the wagon behind the buildings and led Bannack's horses back to the street. "Is that the place up ahead?" Bannack asked.

"Yeah, but something's goin' on," Buster answered. "I don't know what the crowd is doin' outside the café." He saw a man he knew, so he asked, "What's goin' on, Pete? What's the crowd waitin' for? Is Sawyer's closed?"

"Hey, Buster," Pete replied. "It ain't closed, but it might as well be. Virgil Dawson ran everybody out of there and says he's gonna shoot the first one that comes back in the door."

"What the hell? Is he drunk?" Buster responded. He knew Virgil by reputation as a bully.

"Yeah," Pete replied, "he got in an argument with one of the Twin Creeks hands in the saloon next door and shot him in the face. The man wasn't even wearin' a gun. Virgil walked out of the saloon then and went into Sawyer's and told everybody to get out, that he didn't want nobody to bother him while he ate. Russell told him he couldn't order his customers out and Virgil hit him upside of the head with his six-gun and laid him out cold. Then he dragged him to the door and threw him outside with his customers."

"Where the hell's Jim Bryan?" Buster asked. "Didn't anybody go get the marshal?"

"Sure," Pete replied. "Matter of fact, I ran to get the marshal. And Jim came back with me right away. He went to the door and yelled for Virgil to come outta there with his hands up. Virgil yelled back and told him to come in with his hands up. We waited to see what Jim was gonna do about that and he said he weren't gettin' paid enough to walk into a suicide. We'd just have to wait till Virgil decided to leave or passed out. So that's what's goin' on. It's just Virgil Dawson in there with the three Sawyer women."

"Well, that ain't too good for Effie and the girls is it?" Buster said. "Where's Russell?"

"He's over yonder by the saloon door gettin' his head bandaged up. Then he says he's goin' back in his place to protect his women, if the marshal won't do it."

"He'll get hisself killed," Buster said.

"That's what we've been tryin' to tell him," Pete said, "but, hell, it's his family in there with that wild man."

Bannack had heard enough. "This the place we're supposed to eat dinner?" Buster said that it was. "So this fellow is keepin' us from eatin' dinner. Is there a back door?"

"Sure is," Buster answered. "You thinkin' about goin' in?"

"I'm hungry," Bannack replied, and tied his horses to a nearby hitching rail. He made his way through the spectators gathered on the boardwalk and walked around the building to the back door. He was pleased to find it unlocked, so he went inside a covered porch with a pump and some washtubs to another door. He opened it and startled a frightened little woman, who almost cried out upon seeing him, but he held his finger to his lips to silence her.

"My daughters!" she whispered frantically. He nodded, trying to reassure her that he was there to help them. He went to the door leading to the café and edged up to the side of it to peek into the dining room. He was in luck, for Virgil Dawson was seated at a back table, facing the front door, his Colt .45 in handy reach on the table. On one side of the table, Sawyer's youngest daughter, Susie, sat looking properly terrified. Her sister, Louella, stood in front of the table, worried about the drunken monster's boast about what was in store for her sister when his dinner was finished.

"Mama!" Virgil suddenly roared, startling all three women. "If you don't get them biscuits out here right now, I'm gonna deflower this young'un right here on the table!" Susie started to jump up from the chair, but he grabbed her arm and sat her back down.

"Please, don't hurt her," Louella begged. "I'll go see if the biscuits are done." She ran to the kitchen and would have screamed had not Bannack clapped his hand over her mouth.

"Just stay right here with your mother," he whispered. "I'll take care of your sister." And when she looked at her mother, who was holding her finger to her lips, she understood.

He went quietly into the dining room then, causing Susie's eyes to open wide at the sight of the huge man. Noticing her sudden change of expression, Virgil turned to see what had caused it. "Here's your biscuit," Bannack said as his massive fist made solid contact with Virgil's face. The straight right hand landed with the force of a kick by a mule, knocking Virgil out of the chair and onto the floor. As Virgil struggled to make sense of what had happened, Bannack took his pistol off the table and stuck it in his belt. Then he reached down to offer Virgil a hand up. Totally disoriented, Virgil reached up and took the hand. Bannack pulled him up high enough to give him a hard left hook that effectively put Virgil's lights out. Holding onto the limp hand, Bannack dragged the helpless man out the front door of the café. When the door opened, the people parted to give him a path.

"What did I tell you?" Buster said to Pete. He then reached down and grabbed Virgil's boots and declared, "Let's take him to jail."

CHAPTER 6

When they got to the jail, they found Daryl Boyd there, sitting in the marshal's chair. "Where's Marshal Bryan?" Buster asked. "We've got a prisoner for him."

Totally confused, Young Boyd looked from the almost dwarf-sized Buster to the bigger, more intimidating man with him. Daryl, who helped out at the jail and was not an official deputy, had just been stunned a short time earlier when the sheriff told him he was resigning. "He said he wasn't the marshal anymore," he finally answered Buster's question.

"Well, I reckon that leaves you in charge," Buster said. "Open a cell and we'll tote him in."

"I don't know if I can do that or not," Daryl replied.

"I don't think you've got any choice," Buster told him. "This man has earned a right to be put in jail, and you've been left in charge. So it's up to you to see that he gets his right."

"I don't know, Mr. Bridges," Daryl pleaded. "I'm not

no deputy. I just clean up and run errands for Marshal Bryan. He took care of lockin' prisoners up and all that."

"Well, we can help you some," Bannack finally took over. "What's your name?" he asked, and Daryl told him. "All right, Daryl, open up that cell door." Daryl opened the door, not willing to defy the big stranger. Bannack and Buster carried the still groggy Virgil inside and laid him on a cot. When they came out, Bannack said, "Lock the cell. All right, you say you ran errands for the marshal?" Daryl nodded. "Like goin' to pick up breakfast and dinner trays for the prisoners?" He nodded again. "All right, Daryl, all you have to do is go to the same place that fixes meals for the prisoners and tell them you're gonna need meals for one prisoner. Then go pick 'em up when it's time to eat. He's got water and a thunder mug in the cell, so you're all set till tomorrow. Here's that fellow's Colt. Put it wherever the marshal put 'em. He might need some doctorin', but I wouldn't worry about that right now. I expect you're gonna hear something from the mayor or the city council pretty quick when they find out their marshal has quit. Just don't let that fellow talk you into openin' that cell for any reason." He looked at Buster then. "I'm ready to try that lady's cookin' now. How 'bout you?"

"If you're through trainin' the new marshal," Buster replied, opened the door, and held it for Bannack to pass through. Dumbfounded, Daryl Boyd stood, still unable to believe what had happened. When the door closed behind them, he just faintly heard Buster ask, "What did you hit that feller with?"

And the big man answered, "My fist."

When they returned to the café, most of the spectators were still standing around the front door, discussing the incident. "Here he comes now," Pete said, and they parted to make a path when they saw him coming. "Did you see the marshal?" Pete asked Buster when they walked past him.

"No, he weren't there," Buster answered him. "That young fellow that helps him was the only one there and he said Jim Bryan quit. Where's Russell Sawyer?"

"Couple of fellows took him to see Dr. Taylor to get his face stitched up," Pete said.

"Are they open for dinner?" Buster asked.

"I don't know," Pete answered. "Ain't nobody said." Bannack didn't wait to find out and opened the door and walked in, so Buster followed him.

Inside the café, they found the three Sawyer women huddled together near the kitchen door. They first appeared startled when they saw Bannack walk in. "Are you ladies gonna be open for business?" he asked politely.

"We hadn't decided," Effie Sawyer answered, "but we'll surely feed you, if you're hungry, Mister. And there won't be no charge. You two just sit down wherever you want. Susie, get some coffee for them while I get their plates ready." She started for the kitchen but stopped to ask, "What is your name, sir?"

"John," he said and caught himself in time to say, "Cochran, John Cochran, ma'am."

"Well, welcome to Sawyer's Café, Mr. Cochran. I can't tell you how pleased I am to make your acquaintance." As an afterthought, she said, "And of course you're welcome as well, Buster, especially if you're a friend of Mr. Cochran's."

"Why don't we go ahead and tell them outside that we're open again, Mama?" Louella asked. "Papa said to go ahead and open up when they took him to see Dr. Taylor. We especially need to feed those folks who were in the middle of their dinner when that monster chased everybody out of here." Her mother agreed, so she went to the front door to make the announcement and people started filing in the door right away. Most of them sat down at the tables closest to where Bannack was seated.

"It looks like I'm not going to have to worry about getting rid of all that food I had cooked up before that drunken monster emptied my dining room," Effie said when she brought Bannack's and Buster's plates to the table. "I hope you enjoy your dinner, Mr. Cochran."

"Yes, ma'am," Bannack replied. "Buster's already guaranteed me that I will. And why don't you just call me John?"

"All right, John, if you'll call me Effie, okay?" He nodded and smiled. "So tell me, John, what brings you to Glory? Are you gonna be with us a while?"

"No, ma'am, I'm just passin' through on my way north. I might hang around a day or two just to see what the town's all about."

"Well, I'll expect to see you back here to eat again while you're still in town," Effie said. "I'll leave you alone now, so you can eat your dinner." She went back to the kitchen.

Louella was somewhat surprised when she saw Walter Glory and Richard Prentis come in the door. Glory was the owner of Glory General Merchandise and honorary mayor, since he founded the town. Richard Prentis was the president of the Cattleman's Bank and senior member of the town council. Both men occasionally ate at Sawyer's, but this was the first time she had seen them come in together. "Good afternoon, gentlemen," Louella greeted them, "you're welcome to sit anywhere you can find a table."

"Afternoon, Miss Sawyer," Glory said as he and Prentis both looked over the dining room. "There," he said to Prentis then and pointed. Back to Louella, he asked, "That table back there, is that the man who took that drunk out of here?"

"Mr. Cochran?" Louella replied. "Yes, sir, that's him."

"Cochran," he repeated to help him remember the name. "We'd like to join him at his table, if he doesn't mind," Glory told her.

Surprised by his request, Louella could think of nothing to say other than, "I guess we can ask him." She started back to their table and the two council members followed along behind her. She stopped beside the table and said, "Excuse me, John, this is Mr. Walter Glory and Mr. Richard Prentis."

That was as far as she got before Glory took over. "Mr. Cochran, I'm Walter Glory and this is Richard Prentis. We represent the town council. Mind if we join you?"

"I reckon not," Bannack replied, genuinely puzzled since there were empty tables available. He glanced at Buster and noticed that the little man's eyes seemed to have grown considerably. It occurred to him that he might possibly be about to be invited to move on without delay because of the brutal way he had rid Sawyer's Café of its problem.

"Are you gentlemen going to have dinner?" Louella asked when they sat down.

"No, thank you," Glory said. "I would like a cup of coffee, though." Prentis said that would be fine for him also. When Louella left to get the coffee, Glory said, "I'll get right to the point, Mr. Cochran. We don't mean to pry into your business, if it's something you don't want to discuss, but can I ask you why you happen to be visiting our town?"

Still somewhat suspicious of the nature of their visit, Bannack answered simply. "I didn't come to visit your town. It just happens to be on my trail north."

"So you're just passing through Glory?" Prentis asked. "Do you mind if we ask you where you're heading?"

"I don't mind, but I can't tell you because I don't really know myself."

"Mr. Cochran." Glory looked him straight in the eye. "Are you wanted for anything by the law?"

Bannack paused to return the direct look, then said, "If I am, I'm not aware of it. Are you and Mr. Prentis telling me to get out of town?"

Glory chuckled and waited for Louella to place his coffee on the table before continuing. "No, I'm trying to offer you a job," he said.

Bannack looked from one of them to the other, trying to decide if Glory was serious or just toying with him. "A job?" he responded. "Doing what?"

"Glory town marshal," Glory said. "You probably know our marshal resigned today and you sure look like you could handle the job, based on the way you arrested that man you put in the jail. Have you ever served as a lawman anywhere before?"

"No, sir, that's one thing I have not done," Bannack answered. "So I'm not sure I'd know what to do if I was the marshal."

"From what I've been told about the incident in here today, I'd have to disagree with you. You did exactly what the marshal is supposed to do. When a killer murders a man in a card game, then terrorizes everyone in an eating establishment, a good marshal goes after that man and puts him in jail. Mr. Prentis and I were both impressed by the fact that you didn't simply shoot the man in the back but overpowered him and put him in jail."

Bannack didn't know what to think. To be offered the job of town marshal was perhaps the most remote possibility to enter his mind. His only thought up to this moment was to disappear somewhere in the event Judge Raymond Grant was successful in canceling his pardon, making him a hunted man. But instead of riding off to who knows where, would it be as effective or maybe more effective, to hide in plain sight, using a different name and an unlikely occupation? It was a lot to consider.

Up to this point, Buster had respectfully held his tongue, since it was none of his business, but it was hard not to get excited by the purpose of the mayor's visit. "Excuse me, Mr. Mayor," he interrupted, "but I think you and Mr. Prentis might be interested to know that the only reason I'm sittin' here with John is because he came along when I was jumped by two outlaws when I was on my way back from Fort Worth. Well, sir, John sent 'em limpin' off to lick their wounds and sorry for the day they thought about robbin' me."

Glory and Prentis looked at each other and nodded as if their opinion of the man was confirmed. They could both see that he was giving it serious thought, so they started to sell the town of Glory and how optimistic they were for the growth of the town. "To be quite frank about it," Prentis said, "we have not been happy with our prior marshal. Jim Bryan is a fine man, but he did not have the steel in him to deal with the likes of Virgil Dawson. I think it was a good idea for him to resign when he realized he wasn't tough enough to handle the job."

"To be completely honest about it," Glory said,

"the job as marshal of our town is not going to be an easy one. More and more, worthless drifters and outlaws on the run discover our growing town every week. We have three saloons already, but we also have a thriving church community that will support the law when necessary. You would be paid a monthly salary and provided with a free room at the Glory Hotel." When Bannack still did not say yes or no, Glory suggested that he think it over and give them a decision the next day.

"All right," Bannack said, "I'll think it over. Did they name this town after you or were you named after the town?"

Glory and Prentis both laughed, and Glory answered him. "Actually, I built the first buildings in the town. When the US Postal Service located a post office here, I had to name it something, so I named it Glory. Does that make a difference in your decision?"

"Yes it does. I've decided. I'll take the job. Any chance I can get my hotel room tonight? And I'll expect to keep my horses in the stable at no charge, too. Is that all right?"

"No problem at all," Glory replied. "I'll personally go with you this afternoon to take care of it. We should have you ready to take the customary evening patrol of the town by nightfall." He reached into his coat pocket and took out a small ring of keys and handed them to Bannack.

"What's this?" Bannack asked.

"Keys to the jailhouse," Glory answered. "And your first name is John, Marshal Cochran?"

"Yes, sir," he answered, "John Cochran." He shook hands with Glory, then he shook hands with Prentis.

"Good!" Glory announced, obviously pleased with the agreement. "We'll go now and let you finish your dinner in peace." He and Prentis got to their feet. "How about if I meet you over at the jail in an hour?" Bannack nodded. "We'll get you set up with the hotel and the stable then," Glory continued. He turned to leave but paused a moment more. "You were still giving it some thought. Why did you make a decision so fast after you asked me if I named the town?"

Bannack shrugged. "Tell you the truth, I figured any man who is vain enough to name a town after himself is gonna do everything he can to make that town live to stay on the map and grow. Might be a good place to be."

"I like your common sense, John," Glory said with a chuckle. "I'll see you in an hour." He and Prentis walked out the front door, stopping briefly on the way to offer to pay for Bannock's dinner, only to be told there was no charge for Bannack's and Buster's dinners or their coffee, either.

Back at the table, it was as if Buster had been offered the job. "Well, I'll be . . ." he started. "If that ain't the dad-blamedest thing . . . Ain't been in town a whole day yet and already hired as the town marshal." When Louella came to the table with the coffeepot, Buster asked, "Did you hear that, Louella? Mayor Glory just hired John, here, as the new town marshal." He looked back at Bannack then and said, "Sounded like he expected you to go to work tonight, too."

"It did, didn't it?" Bannack replied.

"Is that what those two big shots came in here for? Well, congratulations, John," Louella said. "I believe you'll make a good one." She went straight to the kitchen to tell her mother and her sister. They both came out to tell him how happy they were to hear it.

"I feel safer already," Susie commented.

"Maybe we better wait to see what kind of marshal I make," Bannack said. "It's something I've never done before, so I'm not sure if I'll handle it right or not." Even as he said it, he was thinking that he did have quite a bit of experience in law enforcement. He wondered how excited they'd be if they knew it was all from the wrong side of the law.

"You'll do fine," Effie said. "You just follow your conscience and do what you think is right, just like you did today."

"And like you did last night when those two outlaws attacked me," Buster piped up again. His comment caused questions, so he had the opportunity to tell his story again. "You oughta go around back and look at the bullet holes in my wagon," he concluded.

"I appreciate all your good wishes, and I wanna thank you ladies again for my dinner," Bannack said. "I have to tell you that Buster bragged on your cookin' all mornin', Mrs. Sawyer, and I didn't believe anybody's cookin' could be that good. But I do believe it was better than he said." He got up from the table. "I guess

I'd better be goin'. I'm supposed to meet Mr. Glory at the jail and I don't wanna be late and end up gettin' fired on the first day on the job. Buster, I reckon I'll be seein' you later. I believe you still owe me a shave and a haircut. If you wait till I'm finished with Mr. Glory, I'll help you unload that barber chair and carry it into your shop."

"Don't worry about that chair," Buster called after him. "You just go take care of business, and I'll see you after a while." As soon as Bannack went out the door, Buster took advantage of the women's interest in the new sheriff to embellish the details of his rout of the two attackers on his wagon. He also implied that he and the sheriff were close friends as a result of their encounter with the two bandits.

Bannack went to get his horses, then proceeded to ride back to the sheriff's office in time to encounter Jim Bryan coming out the door, carrying a sack filled with his personal belongings. He paused when Bannack stepped down from the saddle. "Are you looking for the marshal?" he asked.

"No," Bannack replied simply.

"He's the one I was telling you about," Daryl Boyd called out from the doorway to the office.

Bryan looked Bannack up and down, then remarked, "I can see why that man in the cell is in such rough shape now." He nodded toward the bag he was carrying. "These are some personal things of mine. I used to be the marshal, but I quit this morning. Whatever you need, maybe Daryl, there, can help you."

"Right," Bannack said and watched while Bryan tied the sack to the saddle horn, then climbed on his horse and rode away. Daryl backed out of the doorway when Bannack tied his horses to the hitching rail and came inside. "Did you get any dinner?" he asked the young man.

"No, sir," Daryl answered. "I didn't know if I was supposed to get dinner for the prisoner or not because he was in Sawyer's eating when you arrested him."

"I'm not talking about the prisoner. He doesn't need to get fed until supper. I'm talking about you. Did you go to get something to eat?"

"No, sir," Daryl said.

"Why not? Aren't you hungry? Where do you usually eat?"

"I usually eat at the hotel, same place we feed the prisoners," Daryl answered. "They give me a discount, same as they did for Marshal Bryan. But I was afraid to leave the jail after you left me in charge."

"Is it too late to get something at the hotel now?"

"No, sir, not for another fifteen minutes."

"Well, get yourself up there right now and get something to eat," Bannack told him. "The prisoner ain't goin' anywhere."

"What are you gonna do?" Daryl asked, obviously unsure of his obligation to watch the jail.

"I'm gonna wait here to meet the mayor," Bannack said, realizing then that Daryl was reluctant to abandon the marshal's office to the menacing-looking stranger. "I'm the new marshal."

He saw Daryl's whole body relax when he said it. "Thank goodness," Daryl said, "'cause I really didn't want to tell you to leave. I'll go eat." He headed for the door, but paused before going out. "Do I still work here?"

"So far," Bannack answered. "Have you got a key to the office door?" Daryl said that he did. "Good," Bannack said. "I may not be here when you get back, and if I'm not, I'll lock the door when I leave."

"Yes, sir," Daryl said with considerably more enthusiasm. He went out the door.

Bannack decided to look in on his prisoner to see what kind of shape he was in, so he looked in the desk drawers and found a ring of keys. After trying a couple of them, he found one that fit the lock on the door between the office and the cell room. He opened the door and went in to find Virgil Dawson lying flat on his back, his head propped up a little by a rolled-up blanket behind his neck. "Who the hell are you?" he growled between two swollen lips. His mustache and whiskers were snarled with dried blood that had run from his broken nose, the result of the two-punch combination administered by the stranger in the café.

"I'm the marshal," Bannack answered him.

"The hell you are," Virgil barked and winced when it caused his face to hurt. "I know what the marshal looks like, and you ain't him."

"Things have changed around here. I'm the new marshal, and I don't like no-good tramps like you. You and your kind are gonna have to learn that the town of Glory won't stand for saddle trash assaulting the citizens who live here."

"You just might be talkin' yourself into more trouble than you can handle, Marshal," Virgil threatened. "When are you gonna let me outta here?"

"Not for a long time, Virgil," Bannack said. He knew how the system operated, having worked for Judge Wick Justice before he died. "You'll be with us here until your trial. If it's not here, they'll send a couple of Deputy US Marshals to take you to wherever they're gonna have your trial. I'll let you know when I find out."

"What the hell are you talking about?" Virgil roared. "What trial? I got drunk and scared some people in that eatin' joint. Drunk and disorderly conduct, sober up in jail, and let me go. I'm the only one who got busted up."

"If that was all there was to it, you might be right," Bannack informed him. "I reckon that little incident in the saloon, where you shot that fellow down musta slipped your mind. A gunfight where only one man has a gun, the law calls that murder. So you'll be tried for murder in a court of law. We'll make your jail time here as easy as possible, but only if you cooperate. I'll see if I can get the doctor to take a look at your nose and maybe clean your face up a little." He figured that's what a marshal would do. He went out to the office again and locked the cell room door behind him. When he told Virgil about the Deputy US Marshals coming to transport him to the county seat and a trial, it triggered a troublesome thought in his mind. Of course, Virgil would be tried by a circuit judge, like the one he used to work for. Who would that judge be in this part of the territory? What if it was Judge Raymond Grant, the judge who was trying to have his pardon revoked? If he or that snake, Clark Spencer, who worked for him ever got a look at Marshal John Cochran, he would be on the run again. He heard Walter Glory on the steps then and figured he might get an answer to his problem right away.

"Well, Marshal Cochran," Glory said when he walked inside, "are you getting acquainted with your new surroundings?"

"Yes, sir," Bannack answered. "I was just checkin' on my prisoner, and I think I need to have the doctor take a look at his nose."

"Well, you can certainly do that," Glory said. "Dr. Weldon Taylor is his name and he's accustomed to doctoring prisoners occasionally. He'll just send his bill to the town council, and we'll pay him."

"Will a circuit judge come here, or is Virgil Dawson gonna have to be transported to the county seat for trial on a murder charge? What town does the circuit judge work out of for this county?"

"It sounds like you already know a little bit about the law," the mayor said. "Criminals arrested here in Glory are usually tried in the courthouse in Jacksboro. It's the county seat. Judge Calvin Stark travels out of Fort Worth, but he doesn't ride the circuit."

"Judge Calvin Stark," Bannack repeated. To himself he thought, *In that case, looks like I'm still the marshal here*. "What's the situation with Daryl Boyd?" Bannack asked then. "What is his job? Is he paid by the town council just like I am, or is he somebody the marshal hired?"

"He's paid by the town council," the mayor said. "He's not a deputy. He's just a handyman and does the housekeeping for the marshal. It's up to you, though, whether or not he stays on. If you want somebody else to do that job, you can let Daryl go."

"He's fine. I just wanted to be sure about what he's supposed to do."

Bannack locked the office door then and they went to the hotel to introduce him to Fred Bradley, the owner of the Glory Hotel, to check him into his room. From there, they went to Shaw's Stables, where Bannack met Clem Shaw. He left his horses there and Walter Glory made one more call with him when they stopped by Dr. Weldon Taylor's office. "Maybe I'll see you later when I make my rounds after supper tonight," Bannack said when they parted.

"Maybe so," Glory replied, pleased to hear his new marshal planned to do that. *Jim Bryan never made any rounds,* he thought, in spite of the comment he had made to Bannack earlier about customary evening rounds. *Bryan was too fearful of finding something wrong.*

CHAPTER 7

When he got back to the jail, Bannack sat down at the marshal's desk and began to acquaint himself with everything. One of the first things that caught his attention was a stack of wanted papers in the bottom left-hand drawer. He went through each one just to make sure there was not one for John Bannack. In the top drawer, he found the badge for the City Marshal. He held it in his hands and looked at it for a long time, hesitating to wear it, wondering if it might catch on fire if he pinned it on. He thought about his time when he was in the hard-work barracks at the Unit, Texas State Prison, and he was known as The Man from Waco. Life was tougher back then, but it was a whole lot simpler as he reminded himself that he had made arrangements with Dr. Taylor to treat his prisoner. "I've got to take Virgil to the doctor," he told Daryl. "While he's out of his cell, you can make sure he's got water and empty his thunder mug. Then you can take his horse to the stable. He said he left it tied in front of the River House saloon. It's a gray gelding. Tell Clem Shaw to put his saddle wherever he keeps 'em, but if there's a rifle on it, bring that back here." He paused, then asked, "Is that about what Jim Bryan usually did?"

"Pretty much," Daryl responded.

"You know I've never had a job as a marshal before, so I'd appreciate it if you let me know if I'm neglecting any of my responsibilities," Bannack said.

Daryl's face lit up with a wide smile. "Yes, sir, I surely will," he responded at once. "Do you want me to hold a gun on the prisoner while you open his cell and put the handcuffs on him?"

"Did you usually do that?" Bannack asked.

"Yes, sir, just about every time, except when it was just some prisoner sleepin' off a drunk."

"Probably a good idea," Bannack said, "but I don't think it's necessary this time." He was fairly confident that, if Virgil tried anything, he was more than likely going to end up with more injuries for Dr. Taylor to treat. He got a pair of handcuffs out of the desk drawer and went into the cell room and unlocked Virgil's cell. "Get on your feet and put your hands behind your back," he ordered him. "We're gonna go see the doctor." Virgil got slowly to his feet, watching the big man carefully. "You're thinkin' about it, ain'tcha?" Bannack asked. "Well, go ahead and make your decision." The aching in his nose and jaw reminded Virgil of the force behind the blows that caused the aching. He dutifully stood still and put his hands behind his back. Bannack closed the cuffs on his wrists and walked him out of the cell.

* * *

"Bring him right on in here, Marshal," Barbara Taylor greeted them at the door. "The doctor's expecting you." She frowned as she took a preliminary look at the patient's face. "What a mess. We're gonna have to clean you up before the doctor can even see what needs to be done." She favored Bannack with a look of disapproval. "Take those handcuffs off him, so he can lie back on the table please." Bannack did so.

"Thank you for your kindness, ma'am," Virgil uttered pitifully and laid back on the table.

"You just try to relax," Barbara told him. "The doctor will be in shortly to see you." Then she looked at Bannack and said, "You can wait out in the parlor, Marshal, and we'll let you know when the doctor's finished."

"I reckon not, Mrs. Taylor," Bannack said. "I reckon I'd best stay in here with Mr. Dawson. I wouldn't want him to leave without me."

"Very well," she said when it was plain to see he had no intention of leaving Virgil unguarded. "We'll try to make you as comfortable as possible," she said to Virgil. Then to Bannack, she asked, "What did you hit this poor man with?"

Having had enough of her attitude, he answered her. Holding up his right fist, he said, "First I hit the poor man with this, so he would turn that young girl loose. Then I hit him with this." He held up his left fist. "So I could drag him outta the café. I expect you mighta seen

Russell Sawyer's face before your husband stitched it up. That was after this poor man laid it open with the barrel of his pistol. I reckon you won't have to look at that cowhand this poor man shot in the face over a card game. A .45 bullet at close range makes a real mess of a man's face. They took him to the undertaker instead of the doctor."

She was at a loss for a response after his unapologetic explanation for Virgil's injuries, but she was still not willing to admit she had judged the new marshal by his looks. So she said, "As you wish. I must get some hot water to clean some of that blood away."

Dr. Taylor came into the room before his wife returned. "This the man you think might have a broken nose?" Bannack said that it was. "Barbara said it needed to be cleaned up and she was right, but I can still see what's happened. There's a lot of bruising and swelling in his lips and around his mouth that oughta go down in a couple of days. I'm gonna let her clean away all that dried blood and I'll close up a couple of places with some stitches. His nose just got crushed, but I can pick out some of the small bone fragments and maybe build up a little arch and let the skin grow over it. He won't have that handsome profile anymore, but at least he won't have to live with nothing but a hole where his nose used to be."

"Do you know about how long this business is going to take, Doc?" Bannack asked.

"For what I can do for him, I'd say about an hour,"

the doctor said. "Why? You got something else you need to do?"

"Yeah, I have," Bannack answered, "but I can't take a chance on leavin' this fellow unguarded. How about if I tie him down to that table? I could put the handcuffs on one hand and maybe you've got a little piece of rope or clothesline I could use to tie the other hand."

"Yes, you could do that, but I'm going to chloroform him, anyway. If I give him a pretty heavy dose of it, he'll be out for about an hour. How much time do you need?"

"That oughta be enough time to do what I've gotta do," Bannack said. "But let's tie his hands to the bed, anyway, just to be sure. I can't take a chance on losing my first prisoner." So that's what they did. After Barbara cleaned up Virgil's face, she and Doc administered the chloroform, and in a matter of minutes, Virgil was dead to the world.

Bannack was glad that Doc had not asked him what he had to do that was so important. But he had made a promise to do something, and the time was running out on him. He had said he would do it before suppertime and he didn't think he could have made it if he sat around the doctor's office, waiting for Virgil to wake up. When he got there, he was glad to see he was not too late. "Well, I'll be . . ." Buster started. "Marshal Cochran, I didn't expect to see you again today. What with all your appointments with the mayor and the doctor and all, I thought you'd be too busy."

"I told you I'd help you move that chair into your

shop," Bannack said. "So let's get her out of that wagon. I've got Virgil Dawson waitin' at the doctor's office for me to come take him back to jail."

"I swear," Buster said, "I thought you'd forget all about my barber chair, and I told you not to worry about it." He turned away to keep Bannack from seeing a tear forming in his eye. "Come on in and I'll show you where I'm gonna put it." He had figured with Bannack having landed the important job of marshal of the town, he would no longer have time to be a pal to a runty little barber like him. "Right here is where I'm gonna put it, right here beside the window so folks walking by the shop can look in and see a fellow gettin' a shave in a genuine barber chair, just like in St. Louis. It ain't gonna be easy totin' that chair in here, though. It weighs about three hundred pounds. 'Course, I don't know, you might be able to pick it up by yourself."

"I ain't so sure," Bannack chuckled. "I think I'd rather have help."

"Gettin' it outta the wagon and into the door is gonna be the hardest part," Buster said. "And I started workin' on that part of it before I even went to Fort Worth to buy the chair. I got two heavy planks at the sawmill that'll take the weight. What I hadn't figured out was who I could get that could help me slide that chair across them planks. I was thinkin' about Beulah Mae Thompkins till you came along," he joked.

"Who?" Bannack asked.

"You ain't met her yet. I was just japin'."

"Let's get that chair in there," Bannack said. "I've gotta get back to get Virgil."

The wagon was already backed up to the back door of the barbershop, so they lowered the tailgate and laid the planks from the wagon bed to the back door. They climbed into the wagon then and began to test the weight of the chair. "You sure this thing doesn't weigh more than three hundred?" Bannack asked as he rocked it back and forth in an effort to set the base up on the planks. "You shoulda greased these planks and we coulda slid this chair right across."

"I thought of that," Buster said. "Thought of greasin' the floor, too. But the trouble with that is I'da never got the grease off the base of the chair or my floor, either."

"It would be easier to set the chair on the ground somewhere and build a barbershop around it," Bannack said as he climbed up on the planks. Then with a foot on each plank, Bannack pulling and Buster pushing, they inched the heavy chair across to the door. Once it was through the door, Buster got a deer hide he had been saving for the purpose and they worked the chair off the planks and onto the deer hide.

"Now all you have to do is just slide it where you wanna take it," Buster said and picked up the edge of the hide and pulled. Nothing happened. "Just gotta get it started," he said and strained but still it didn't move. "You're standin' on the damn deerskin," he said.

"No, I'm not," Bannack said. "Let me try." He walked around to take the lead edge of the hide and put his back into it. The chair slid along the floor with only a little resistance, so he kept it moving. "Where do you want it?" Buster ran around in front of him and guided him to the spot. When he had it facing exactly the way he wanted it, they worked the chair, tilting it back and forth, until they got the deer hide out from under it.

When it was solidly located, Buster said, "Partner, I don't know how I woulda got that chair here without your help. I still can't believe how hard it was to move it on that deerskin."

"It wasn't really that hard," Bannack said. "I was standin' on the hide when you were trying to pull it."

"I knew it!" Buster exclaimed. "You son of a gun! I knew I could pull that chair by myself. Tomorrow, I'm gonna set up my barber pole and get my sign ready and Glory, Texas, is gonna have a first-class barbershop."

Bannack laughed and said, "I reckon I'd best go see about my prisoner now." He had lied to Buster. He wasn't standing on the hide when Buster tried to move it, but he thought it would be better for Buster's self-esteem to tell him that he was.

When he got back to the doctor's office, Barbara Taylor told him that Virgil was just coming out of the anesthetic. She led him back to the surgery where they found Dr. Taylor fanning Virgil to get some air into his lungs. When he was still slow in coming out of it, the doctor passed a bottle of ammonia under his nose. Finally, Virgil came to, but he wasn't sure where he was. Bannack went over beside the table and unlocked the handcuffs holding him there. The doctor had already untied the length of clothesline that had been holding the other hand. Virgil had been cleaned up and a large bandage wrapped around his head held a cocoon-like pad over the broken pieces of his nose, holding them in place.

"His nose will grow partially back," Dr. Taylor said, "but not like it was originally. At any rate, it was the best I could do for him. I had a few cases like his during the war. Some turned out pretty good. Some didn't recover at all." He turned his attention back to his patient when Virgil began stirring. "You know where you are?" Doc asked him.

"In a damn whorehouse," Virgil mumbled.

"Well, that's pretty close," Barbara said. "You're in the doctor's office, but we have a pretty good idea of what you were dreaming."

"Is he gonna be able to eat all right?" Bannack asked the doctor.

"Oh, yes, he can eat," Doc answered. "His lips are swollen, but that shouldn't keep him from eating, if he wants to. Sometimes patients coming out of anesthetics have a little nausea and don't want to eat. But if he's hungry, he can eat."

"I'll order his supper from the hotel then," Bannack said. "I wouldn't want him to be hungry." He purposefully glanced at Barbara when he said it.

"All right," she responded, "I guess I owe you an apology. I misjudged your handling of your prisoner."

"No need to apologize," Bannack said. "I must have a look about me that makes people expect the worst out of me."

Doc laughed and said, "I guess I untied his hand before I should have." His remark didn't make any particular sense to Bannack until Barbara turned around to leave the room and he noticed what looked like a dirty handprint on the back of her skirt.

Daryl was ready to go to supper when Bannack got back to the jail with Virgil, so Bannack told him to go ahead. And since the hotel provided the meals for jail-house prisoners, one of Daryl's responsibilities was to bring the prisoner's supper back with him. "Don't worry about Virgil's supper tonight," Bannack told Daryl. "Virgil's still groggy. He's gonna be a while before he wants to eat, so we might as well wait and I'll bring his supper back later. If you find the door locked when you get back, it'll be because I started my walk around town early."

"Do you want me to tell you which saloons cause the most trouble and which one attracts most of the town folks?" Daryl asked.

"No, I reckon not," Bannack replied. "I expect I'll find out for myself soon enough." He wanted to pay a visit to the River House saloon where Virgil had shot the cowhand while it was still fresh in everyone's minds. He anticipated being summoned to Virgil Dawson's trial and since he was not present at the shooting in the saloon, he thought he should at least have a pretty good picture of the crime. The River House was on his way to the hotel dining room, so after checking on Virgil again and finding him asleep, he took a little walk up that side of the street.

He took a leisurely walk along the board walkways in front of a series of small shops. His gait was reminiscent of the stride of a great cat on the prowl, no doubt the inspiration for the nickname, Judge Wick's Panther, created by Judge Raymond Grant. But Judge Wick was dead now and so was his panther, as far as Marshal John Cochran was concerned. He stopped when he saw a man coming out of a gun shop ahead of him, pausing to lock the door. "Good evenin'," Bannack said.

The man, startled, turned and froze when he saw him. He started to take a step backward but was stopped by the door he had just locked. "Can I help you?" he finally managed.

"Just good evenin'," Bannack said and pulled his vest aside to show the badge on his shirt.

The man exhaled the great gulp of air he was holding. "You're the new marshal! You scared the hell outta me."

"That wasn't my intention, even though it sounds like something that would be good for a man, doesn't it?"

"I swear, when I turned around and saw you, I thought I was . . ." He decided he'd better not finish the thought. "My name's Bill Godsey. It's Marshal Cochran, right?" He stuck his hand out. "This here's my gun shop. I sell 'em and fix 'em. Were you coming in? Because I can open up right away."

"No, sir, I was just takin' a little walk," Bannack assured him. "I'm glad to meet you, Mr. Godsey. Have a good evening." He continued his walk while Godsey went in the other direction. A short distance farther brought him to Sawyer's Café and the River House saloon next door. It was tempting to go into Sawyer's to eat supper because he knew the food there was hard to beat. But he decided to go to the hotel, since they had a special arrangement with the marshal's office and he had to pick up Virgil's supper, too. He walked on past to the saloon.

He stepped inside the batwing doors and paused there to survey the busy saloon. Even though it was just the supper hour, half of the tables were occupied with card games and drinking parties and there were half a dozen standing at the bar. He immediately captured the attention of a good portion of the customers, as he usually did, so he didn't hesitate long before walking up to one end of the bar. There was one bartender working the bar, a short wiry little man with a bald pate and a thick black mustache. He came down to the end of the bar and said, "Howdy, stranger. First time in the River House?"

"As a matter of fact," Bannack replied.

"What can I pour you? You look like a man who likes rye whiskey," the bartender said.

"Is that so? Well, pour me a rye whiskey and I'll see if you're right." He waited while the bartender poured out of a bottle of rye. Then he tossed the drink back and placed the empty glass on the bar upside down.

"One drink?" the bartender asked. "You came in for one drink?"

"No, I came in to look the place over and see if I can get some information. I just bought the drink to see if you were right, but I'm not much of a drinker, so I can't tell much difference between rye and corn. It all burns goin' down. Two bits?"

"Yeah, two bits." He waited for Bannack to drop a coin on the bar, then asked, "What kind of information you lookin' for?"

"That cowhand that was shot in here earlier today by Virgil Dawson, do you know his name?" Bannack asked.

"What do you wanna know that for?"

"'Cause I'm the town marshal and I need that fellow's name," Bannack replied.

"Son of a . . . You're that stud that dragged Virgil Dawson outta Sawyer's! I heard they gave you the marshal's job. Damn! I'd like to shake your hand. Them Dawson brothers ain't nothin' but trouble. My name's Smut Smith. I don't know that cowhand's name. They were callin' him Hurley. I know he rode for the Twin Creeks Ranch. Here, take your money back. That drink's on the house."

"What are you so excited about, Smut?" The question came from behind him and Bannack turned to confront a woman who looked almost as big as he was. She looked him up and down. "Why don't you introduce me to your friend?"

"He's the new town marshal," Smut told her. "He's the fellow who walked into Sawyer's today and dragged ol' Virgil Dawson outta there. Marshal, this little prairie flower is Beulah Mae Thompkins."

For some reason, the name sounded familiar, then it struck Bannack. It was the name Buster mentioned when the two of them were struggling with his barber chair. He couldn't suppress the grin. "Pleased to meet you," he said.

"I expect a man big as you has a hard time findin' a woman big enough to handle him," Beulah Mae said. "You came to the right place to find what you need. What's your name, Honey?"

"John Cochran," he answered. "I wish I had the time to think about a woman, but right now I've got to get up to the hotel to pick up some supper for my prisoner in the jail. Thank you for the drink, Smut." He turned and walked out the door.

"Well, damn," Beulah Mae swore, "what did he have to run off so quick for?"

"You scared the hell out of him, that's why," Smut said.

Charley Riley's first thought when he glanced up to see the intimidating figure coming in the dining room door was trouble ahead. As manager of the dining room, it was Charley's job to enforce the hotel's rule of no firearms in the dining room. And this one was not only dangerous looking, he was wearing a sidearm. With every intention of doing his job, however,

Charley came out from behind the cash register to meet the stranger. He was surprised, however, when the stranger spoke first. "Mr. Riley," Bannack said, "I'm Marshal John Cochran. They told me I should let you know who I am."

"Marshal Cochran!" Charley announced with a great sense of relief. "Welcome to the dining room. We've been anxious to meet you. You know, of course, that we have a no firearms policy, but that doesn't apply to officers of the law. You here for supper?"

"Yes, sir, I am," Bannack said, "and I'll need to take one supper back with me."

"Come along and pick out a table," Charley said. "When Jim Bryan was marshal, he always sat at a table in the back of the room, so he could watch the whole room he said."

"That sounds like a good idea," Bannack said. As they walked toward the back of the room, he noticed two women waiting tables. Charley signaled for them to come join them. Both women seemed truly puzzled but came at once.

"This is Carol and this is Dora," Charley introduced them. "One of these ladies will be taking care of you when you're here. "Ladies, this is Marshal Cochran." Both their faces came to life at that announcement.

"Well, I wondered," Dora responded. "I was afraid we were getting robbed when you walked straight back through the room."

"I declare, Dora, what a thing to say," Carol scolded.

"Welcome to Glory, Marshal Cochran. Dora and I will try to take good care of you and I think you'll find our cook is the best in the county. Her name's Evelyn James and I'm sure she'll be out here to meet you before you leave. You're lucky you got here tonight. You'll get to try Evelyn's meatloaf. Now, what do you want to drink? I'm guessing coffee." He answered with a nod, and she went at once to get him a cup.

He was well taken care of while he ate his supper and as Carol had predicted, Evelyn James came out to meet him and ask if he enjoyed the meatloaf. He told her that he had been skeptical about Carol's claim that it was the best in the county. But after having it, he found he couldn't dispute her claim. He didn't tell them that the fact of the matter was that, after five years of prison food, everything he ate was excellent. He figured that was one of the few, if not the one, benefit of having spent time in prison. When he finished eating, he was satisfied with the arrangement the town had worked out with the marshal's office. Evelyn brought him a tray with Virgil's supper on it and he walked it down to the jail. Behind him, Charley and the women joked about the difference in the old marshal and the new. The women laughed when Charley said he told Cochran that Jim Bryan always sat in the back of the room so he could watch the whole room. "I didn't tell him we were pretty sure he sat back there, so he could slip out the back door if any real trouble showed up."

"We're being pretty hard on poor Jim," Carol said. "He knew he wasn't cut out to do the job of marshal, but he stuck it out for better than three years."

Virgil was ready to eat something by the time Bannack returned to the jail, and Daryl had made a pot of coffee. So Bannack finished his walk around town to make sure the shops were locked up tight for the night but primarily to let the other two saloons in town know there was someone in the marshal's office. The evening passed peacefully in spite of the trouble that had happened in the River House saloon and Sawyer's Café that day. Someone could have told the new marshal that the reason was because no one at the Dawson cabin was aware that Virgil was not coming home that night.

CHAPTER 8

"Where's Virgil?" Henry Dawson demanded when he looked around the table at his sons attacking the supper his woman, Berta, had prepared. None of the three boys lifted their heads out of the bowls of beef stew in front of them. Like hogs at the trough, they gulped, grunted, belched, and groaned as if in a competition to finish first. Not until the old man picked up the empty bowl and threw it in the middle of the table to get their attention did they pause. "I asked you a question," he roared. "Where's Virgil?" Again, no one answered. "If one of you sorry hogs don't answer me right now, I'm gonna get my axe handle and use it on the lot of you."

"He rode into town, Pa," Junior, his eldest said. "I told him you was gonna raise hell if he weren't back before supper. He knows we're supposed to go after them Twin Creeks cows tonight. He said he'd be back."

"The hell he did," Henry fumed. "You know he ain't got no sense when he gets a little likker in him. You shoulda stopped him. I oughta whip you for lettin' him go."

"I didn't take him to raise," Junior protested. "You oughta stomped him when he was born."

"He ain't the only one I shoulda stomped," Henry fumed. "If he ain't back here by the time we go to get them cows, he'd best not come back a-tall."

"He mighta got into some trouble, Pa," Gilbert said.

"I guarantee you he got into trouble," Johnny declared. "That's what he goes into town to do. He might be in the jailhouse."

"If he is, he musta broke in," Junior remarked. "Either that or he drank till he passed out 'cause that's about the only way that chicken-livered marshal would try to arrest him."

"It don't make no difference," Henry said. "I ain't waitin' for him. We've gotta ride six miles to get to that bunch of cows Johnny found this side of the creek. Then we'll need to rest our horses a little while before we get that little herd started north and drive 'em all the way back to our valley. So finish up with your supper, it's time to get started."

They saddled their horses and taking nothing other than their guns, canteens, and whips, they started out just as the last rays of the setting sun were doused by the faraway hills to the west. Johnny led the string of riders since he was the one who found the bunch of about thirty head of cattle that had gathered next to a branch of Twin Creeks. Henry was happy to see that Johnny had not exaggerated the number of strays and that they had not been found by their owners yet. After a short rest for the horses, the Dawson gang started moving the herd of cows away from the creek in a northerly direction. There was little need for instructions from Henry, for his sons were well practiced. Cracking their whips, instead of their guns, they put the reluctant cows in motion. Once started, the cattle moved slowly through the night under the light of a rustler's perfect moon, a little past three-quarters full.

It was just about breakfast time when the stolen cows were left to rest by the creek that ran down the middle of the valley where Henry Dawson's cabin was built. Already up, with a fire going in her stove, Berta heard the cows when they entered the valley, so she started rolling out her biscuit dough. Henry was going to raise hell when he found out that Virgil still had not come back from town. She wished he would find something to throw at the boys other than her big serving bowls. Otherwise, he was going to have to give her some money to go into town and buy some new bowls.

In a few minutes, Henry came in the back door, leaving the boys to take care of the horses. "Where's Virgil?" he demanded as soon as he walked into the kitchen.

"He ain't never come back," Berta answered, her tired, unemotional response evidence enough that she didn't really care if he had or not. She had never had much use for Virgil. She had no affection for Henry's other sons either, but she could tolerate them. Virgil was different, however. He had a knack for irritating people.

"Whaddaya mean, he ain't never come back?" Henry insisted. "He ain't come back a-tall?"

"Not so's I'd noticed," Berta responded.

"Johnny mighta been right," Henry said. "Virgil mighta got hisself so drunk that he got throwed in jail. If that yellow-bellied sheriff put one of my boys in jail, I'll personally stick a boot up his behind. Hurry up and fix me some breakfast."

"You goin' into town?"

"That's where the blamed jail is, ain't it?" he roared back. "'Course, I'm goin' into town."

"You said last night if Virgil didn't come back, then he could just stay gone and good riddance."

"I never said that," he claimed. "I'd had a few drinks. Hell, he's my son."

"If you think so," she responded. "But last night, that's exactly what you said. If he weren't back by the time you and the other boys was ready to ride, he could just keep on goin'."

"You must be gittin' old, old lady. You're startin' to hear things that ain't been said."

Junior walked into the kitchen then. "I smelled that coffee boilin' from out on the back steps, Berta."

"If you and your brothers want some breakfast, one of you better go in the barn and find me some eggs," Berta told him. "I got biscuits ready to go into the oven in about five minutes and bacon ready to go in the skillet."

"I'll get you some eggs," Junior said. "I expect we'll have steak for dinner. Ain't that right, Pa? We usually butcher a steer when we adopt a new bunch of cattle."

"I expect so," Henry said. "You pick one out. You know what to do. I'm gonna take a little ride into Glory to see if Virgil's in that jailhouse."

"He never came back?" Junior asked a stupid question. He never caught on even when they both just stared at him. "I'll go find you some eggs, Berta, and while I'm at the barn, I'll throw your saddle on a fresh horse, Pa. Which one you want, Brownie?"

"Yeah, Brownie'll do," Henry replied.

"You want some of us to go in with you?"

"No, I don't need nobody else to scare the trousers off that sheriff," Henry answered.

"Invite him out here to dinner, Pa," Junior said. "We'll feed him a fresh steak."

It was about the middle of the morning when Henry Dawson rode down the main street in Glory on his way to the jail. He decided to make that his first stop because it didn't make any sense that Virgil could be anywhere else, unless he was dead. He had already made up his mind that he was going to scare the trousers off Jim Bryan. And if that didn't work, he considered taking Virgil by force. He pulled the bay gelding named Brownie up to the hitching post in front of the jail and stepped down. He adjusted the gun belt and holster he was wearing on his hips until they rode where he wanted them. He walked inside to find Daryl Boyd sitting on a stool at one end of the sheriff's desk. "Can I help you, sir?" Daryl asked politely.

"Yeah, son, have you got a prisoner in here name of Virgil Dawson?"

"Yes, sir, we do," Daryl answered.

"Well, I'm here to pick him up," Henry declared.

Daryl was plainly confused. "What do you mean?" he asked. "Who are you?"

"I mean I'm here to take him outta this piece of crap you call a jail. I'm his father, and I'll be takin' him home now, so get him out here."

"You can't do that, sir," Daryl insisted. "Virgil Dawson has to go on trial in Jacksboro."

"What are you city folks tryin' to pull?" Henry demanded. "You don't do nothin' to drunks and hellraisers but keep 'em in jail for a day or two. You've had my son in your jail overnight, so now I've come to take him home. And if you don't get him here pretty damn quick, I'm gonna tear this place apart. Do you get my message, Sonny?"

"You better talk to the marshal," Daryl said, completely intimidated.

"You're damn right!" Henry ranted. "I need to talk to the marshal. Where is he? Get him out here 'cause you're just wastin' my time!"

"He's in the back fixing a door," Daryl said. "Just wait right here, I'll get him." He hurried to the cell room door, opened it, and called, "Marshal! There's a man up here who wants to see you!" Then he remained there holding the door for the marshal.

Henry Dawson squared his stance to face the door. He set himself as if ready to draw his weapon, his intention to frighten the cowardly marshal. He froze in that position involuntarily, however, unable to move when the intimidating figure of John Bannack filled the doorway. He was holding nothing in his hand but a hammer, but in his hand it looked like a deadly weapon. Expecting Jim Bryan, Henry Dawson's bravado drained into his boots. "You wanted to see me?" Bannack asked.

"No, I mean, yes," Henry stammered, his tone considerably milder than that he had used with Daryl. Then realizing that this was so, he tried to regain some of the tone he had cowered Daryl with. "My name's Henry Dawson. I understand you're holdin' my son in there."

"That's right, Mr. Dawson," Bannack replied calmly, "he's being held on primarily a charge of murder, along with some minor charges of disturbing the peace, assault, and accostin' three females."

"Murder?" Henry questioned. "Who did he murder? And who saw him do it?"

"He murdered a cowhand who rode for the Twin Creeks ranch and everybody in the saloon saw him do it," Bannack said.

"In a saloon?" Henry responded. "Over a card game, I'll bet. Two young fellers face off against each other and you people are callin' it murder. It ain't murder if one of 'em gets killed. It's a duel."

"I had to explain the same thing to your son, Mr.

Dawson. It ain't a duel when the victim doesn't even have a gun. Your son called the cowhand a cheater. The cowhand said he wasn't cheating, so then your brave son drew his gun and shot the cowhand in the face, killed him instantly. In the state of Texas, that's called murder. I hope that clears it up for you. I made the arrest but only after he left the saloon and went next door to a café where he chased all the customers out and threatened to shoot anyone who came in. Then he proceeded to assault the owner and terrorize the women working at the café. Yes, sir, Mr. Dawson, you've got a son you can really be proud of. Anything else I can help you with?"

Henry was left speechless for several long moments as he tried to decide what he should do. Finally, he asked, "Can I visit him, long as I'm here?"

"Sure you can," Bannack answered. "I'll take you back there to talk to Virgil. I'll have to ask you to take off that gun belt and leave it here on the desk, and I'll have to check you for pocket weapons. Then you can talk to him for fifteen minutes. I'll strap on my .44 just as a precaution and I'll sit in a chair in the back corner of the cell room, just so I can see you. But I'll be far enough away that I can't hear what you're sayin'. If you keep your voice down, I won't be able to hear your escape plans, and it'll be a fair game for all of us. All right?"

Henry was astonished. He didn't know what to say, or if he should protest, so he just echoed, "All right."

And he stood there until Bannack reminded him to remove his gun belt.

When he did so, Bannack patted him down, removed a pocket pistol, then led him into the cell room and announced, "Virgil, you've got a visitor. Your father's here to see you." He left Henry at the cell door while he continued on to the back corner of the room and sat down in the chair sitting there.

"Pa?" Virgil responded and walked up to the cell door. "I thought that sounded like you out there."

"What in blazes happened to your face?" Henry asked when he got a look at his son's face through the bars. He lowered his voice to make sure Bannack didn't hear him. "Did that brute do that to you?"

"He done that when he arrested me," Virgil answered. "It looked worse than that before he took me to the doctor. Right now, a bump I got on the back of my head hurts just about as bad as my face does."

"What the hell did he hit you with?" Henry asked, still appalled by the damage done.

"His fists," Virgil replied. "I got the bump on my head when he dragged me outta the café and my head bounced on the step down to the street."

"Where's Jim Bryan?" Henry had to ask next, since he was still not over the shock of meeting Bannack. "When did they make that gorilla the marshal?"

"When I refused to come outta Sawyer's and dared anybody to come in to get me," Virgil said. "Jim Bryan was there, but he had better sense than to come in there after me."

"And they fired Bryan?"

"No," Virgil said, "he quit."

"This feller they got now," Henry asked, "are they gonna keep him as the new marshal or is he some gunslinger who's just passin' through town?"

"He's the new marshal," Virgil said. "I think he was just passin' through town, but he decided to take the job." He gave his father a helpless look and remarked, "Maybe he'll change his mind before they take me to trial and go back to driftin'."

"When are you supposed to go to Jacksboro for trial?"

"They don't know yet. They're waitin' for word from the judge." He looked at his father, hoping for some sign of encouragement and seeing none, he made a suggestion. "Maybe we could talk this big cat into lettin' me go, if we pay him a fine or something."

"I swear, Virgil, sometimes I can't believe you're dumb enough to get yourself in a fix like this one. But when I hear you come up with an idea like that, I can see that you really are that dumb."

"We don't know that he wouldn't take the money and move on outta Glory," Virgil insisted. "From what that Daryl feller said, it sounded to me like this new marshal was a drifter, just passin' through Glory. He ain't gonna make a lot of money bein' the marshal. He might take the money and go on driftin'. It's worth a try, ain't it?"

"You've got about three more minutes to visit,"

Bannack called out from the far corner of the room then.

"All right," Henry called back to him, then to Virgil, he said, "That ain't enough time to tell you how dumb you are. Accordin' to what that young feller in the office said, they've already contacted the judge for the trial, and they're just waitin' for the date. Then a couple of Deputy US Marshals will be down here to get you. Besides, have you got a big pile of money hid somewhere that me and your brothers don't know about?"

"I figure you could use the money from sellin' them cows you and the boys stole last night," Virgil said. "If there was as many as Johnny said there was, that oughta make a good payoff."

"I'm hopin' to sell them cows for enough to support all of us for a little while, till we can line up something bigger. We can't keep goin' after Twin Creeks stock. They're gonna start gittin' better about watchin' their stock, and we're gonna start rustlin' cattle a farther ways from home. Uh, oh, the big cat is gittin' up outta his chair. I reckon he's fixin' to run me outta here."

Virgil began to panic. "Hell, Pa, you ain't gonna just leave me to rot in here, are you?"

"I reckon I oughta, anybody dumb enough to get hisself in a fix like this, but it ain't the Dawson nature to turn on one of their own. We'll try to come up with somethin'. We'll try to visit you right regular, so you can tell us what's goin' on here. You keep your eyes open, too, and if you get a chance, take it."

He turned and headed for the door when Bannack approached him and led him out the door into the office. Daryl handed him his gun belt and Henry waited for Bannack to close the cell room door before speaking. "I reckon I owe you an apology for comin' on so strong when I came in here, but I didn't know my boy was arrested on such a serious charge."

"No problem," Bannack replied. "I can understand how you felt."

"I hope you'll let me visit him again while he's still here in the Glory jail."

"I don't see why not, long as you go by the rules and don't stay too long," Bannack said and walked to the door with him. He turned and walked back into the office when Henry rode away.

"He turned out to be a much different man than he seemed like when he first walked in here," Daryl commented.

"Don't be fooled by his polite attitude when he left," Bannack cautioned. "The Henry Dawson who first walked into the office is the real Henry Dawson. You'd do well to always remember that. As rotten a human being as Virgil is, his pa is gonna try to break him outta here. Our job is to make sure we don't make it easy for him. And I don't want anything to happen to you 'cause you make better coffee than I do. So when he comes to visit Virgil again, he might bring one or more of his other sons with him, and I want to make sure you find me."

"Don't worry, I'll find you as quick as I can," Daryl said.

They were interrupted then when a young boy came into the office. He was carrying an envelope, and since he knew Daryl, he immediately handed it to him. "Thanks, Sammy," Daryl said and opened a drawer of the desk and pulled out a nickel for the boy.

"Thank you, sir," Sammy said, although he never took his eyes off Bannack.

"This is Marshal Cochran, Sammy." Daryl handed the envelope to Bannack and said, "Sammy is the son of Sam Peters, who runs the telegraph office. He always makes sure we get any important wires right away."

"Good to meet you, Sammy," Bannack said.

"Yes, sir," Sammy said and went out the door.

"So that's what that little cup of nickels is for," Bannack said.

"Yep," Daryl replied. "Marshal Bryan started that not long after he took the job as marshal. He thought it would insure our getting telegraphs as soon as they came in."

"I expect he was right," Bannack said as he opened the envelope and read the telegram. "There will be a Deputy US Marshal named Bill Clayton and a Deputy US Marshal named Conrad Priest arriving in Glory sometime in the afternoon day after tomorrow." He paused to check the calendar. "That's Wednesday. They're planning on takin' Virgil back to Jacksboro the next day. They will need reservations made for two rooms in the hotel." He paused to think about that. "What do they need two rooms for?"

"In case they might have an overnight guest after they visit the saloon that night," Daryl answered his question.

"Oh, right," Bannack said. "All right, two hotel rooms for Wednesday night, I believe that's your department, Daryl."

"Yes, sir," Daryl acknowledged. "I'll make 'em tonight when I go to supper."

Bannack thought about the message. He was glad the deputies were coming to get Virgil in two days. He had been concerned that Virgil was going to be a resident of the Glory jail for longer than that, giving his father and brothers more time to plan his escape. He was convinced that the Dawson family would make some attempt to free Virgil, although he had nothing to base it on other than a gut feeling. He decided to fetch his bedroll and sleep in the office that night and Tuesday night just as a precaution. He first considered sleeping on one of the cots in one of the other two cells, but he wouldn't be able to see the street in the cell room. There were no windows in the cell room. He didn't care much for sleeping back there with Virgil, anyway. So he would get his bedroll and his saddlebags from his hotel room when he went to supper that night. And to give himself a small measure of comfort, he would take a mattress off one of the cots in the cell room and bring it into the office.

CHAPTER 9

Henry Dawson rode the poor bay horse named Brownie unmercifully the whole eight miles back to the valley where he had made his home. All the way back from Glory, he thought of different ways to free Virgil from a jail that was considered a joke while the mild-mannered Jim Bryan held the job of town marshal. He would have considered simply riding into town and raiding the jail and releasing his son, and God help anyone who got in his way. Still suffering from the shock of confronting the new marshal, however, he was not sure what options were his. Thinking of the mess that was now Virgil's face, he figured that surely Virgil was mistaken when he said the big man hit him only twice, once with each fist. He must have had some weapon that Virgil did not see. He recalled the mental picture of Bannack coming in the door, holding a hammer in his hand. That would better explain the damage done to Virgil's face. But he attacked Virgil in the café. One of the three women present should have seen the hammer or whatever weapon it was, if in fact there was one. He'd have to ask.

When the exhausted bay gelding finally pulled up in front of the cabin, Junior and Gilbert walked out on the front porch, took one look at Brownie, and assumed the worst. "Who's chasin' you, Pa?" Junior exclaimed. Both sons peered back at the trail that led into the valley.

"Ain't nobody chasin' me," Henry answered gruffly. "Your brother has got hisself into one helluva lot of trouble, and it ain't gonna be easy gittin' him out of it."

"You saw Virgil?" Gilbert asked.

"I seen him and I talked to him there in the jail where they've got him locked up. The damn fool shot an un-armed man in the River House Saloon and killed him. And then he went into that eatin' place next door."

"Sawyer's Café?" Junior asked.

"Yeah, that one," Henry continued. "He started shootin' that place up, ran everybody out except the three women. He swore he was gonna kill the first man who tried to come in."

Johnny walked out on the porch in time to hear the last statement. He laughed and said, "Leave it to ol' Virgil to keep the three women."

"You think that was funny?" Henry asked sarcasti-cally. "There was some oversized hombre who looks like he was born in a cave somewhere that walked in that eatin' joint and knocked Virgil out, then dragged him outta there all the way to the jail. Virgil's face is swollen all up and he's got a bandage tied over his nose.

Now comes the good part. Jim Bryan ain't there no more. That big stud is the marshal now."

"Damn," Junior swore. He could see that his father was really concerned about this new marshal. "What are we gonna do, Pa? We gonna ride in there and get him, ain't we?"

"Yeah, ain't no doubt about that," his father answered. "I just ain't figured out the best way to do it yet."

"Just ride into town with our guns blazin'," Gilbert said. "Them people in that town will be runnin' over each other tryin' to keep from gittin' shot."

"We ain't gotta worry about the rest of the people in that town," Henry said. "We only got one man to worry about, that big cat wearin' the marshal's badge now. We go ridin' in there like you say and I expect he'll just knock us outta the saddle, one by one. We've got to come up with some way to hit him when he ain't lookin'."

"Maybe you're right, Pa," Junior said. There was no doubt that this new marshal had his father worried. "How are we gonna do it, though?"

Trying to remember everything he had learned on his visit to the marshal's office, Henry shook his head perplexed. Then he remembered what Daryl Boyd had said before he was confronted with the image of the new marshal. "That young feller that works for the marshal said they was gonna take Virgil to Jacksboro to stand trial for murder. He said the court would send somebody from there to take Virgil back for trial. That might be the best chance we have to spring Virgil loose." They talked it over then until Junior expressed his concerns that if they ambushed a couple of Deputy US Marshals, the whole family would be wanted by the state of Texas. "We'll have to think on it some more," Henry said. "Take care of my horse," he said to Johnny. The front door opened then, and Berta stuck her head out far enough to declare that she was fixing to throw a pile of steaks out if somebody didn't come to the table right away.

"She's just ornery enough to do it," Junior said, so they filed in the door behind her, all except Johnny, who led his father's horse to the barn, complaining all the way that it was always him that had to do the chores.

They assaulted the freshly butchered beef steaks in their usual animalistic style until everyone's gut was sufficiently packed to the point where they could take time to talk between bites. The conversation was a continuation of the previous discussion on ways to free Virgil from the arms of the law. One thing that was decided right away was that one of them should visit Virgil every day, so they could find out when he was going to be transported to Jacksboro. At least that would tell them when they had to attack the jail. By suppertime that night, it was decided that Junior should ride into town the next morning to visit Virgil.

Like his father the day before, Junior rode into Glory after breakfast and asked to see Virgil. He found that his father had not exaggerated when describing the new marshal. Following his father's advice, Junior was very respectful when requesting to visit his brother, and the marshal was cooperative. Consequently, Junior had plenty to tell his father and brothers when he returned to the little valley, based on what Virgil told him and what he observed on his own.

"Tomorrow?" Henry repeated, surprised. "They're takin' him to Jacksboro tomorrow?"

"That's what Virgil said," Junior answered. "He said they told him to get ready to take a ride tomorrow. Two Deputy US Marshals are supposed to show up this afternoon sometime and they'll stay in the hotel tonight, then take him back tomorrow."

"They drivin' a jail wagon?" Henry asked.

"No, they're just gonna take him back on horseback. That marshal told him he'd be ridin' his own horse. It ain't but one prisoner, so I reckon they don't wanna mess with a jail wagon."

"Damn," Henry swore. "That don't give us much time to break him outta that jail. We're gonna have to do it tonight."

"And that ain't gonna be easy," Junior declared. "That big cat they hired as marshal is sleepin' right there in the jail. He's got him a mattress and blankets in the office." Gilbert and Johnny exchanged questioning looks, and Henry clenched his teeth.

"That could cost us plenty," Henry confessed.

It was Berta who inspired the battle plan. Listening to all the talk at the dinner table, she finally had to comment. "That sounds like a really dumb thing to do. If that cat is half as tough as you and Junior say he is, he'll most likely shoot half of you, if not all of you, before you set foot in the door. And even if you got away with it, everybody would know who it was that broke him outta jail. That's just stupid."

"Oh, yeah, big mouth," Henry reacted. "What would you do, just let 'em take Virgil to the gallows?"

"Hell, no," she said. "The smart thing to do is just rob the two deputies takin' him to Jacksboro."

"Now, that sounds like somethin' a fool woman would come up with," Henry said. "Rob the Deputy US Marshals. Rob 'em of what? Their guns?"

"Why not?" Berta responded. "There's four of you and ain't but two of them. Rob 'em of their guns and whatever else they've got, includin' their horses."

Henry inhaled a big gulp of air, preparing to advise her to tend to the cooking and cleaning and keep her mouth shut when the men were making plans, but Junior interrupted. "Wait a minute, Pa, she's makin' good sense! There ain't nothin' that says you can't rob a lawman. They're just makin' a one-day ride to Jacksboro, but you know they're gonna stop somewhere and rest their horses. So if we show up while they're restin', they sure as hell won't be expectin' to get robbed. We'll be wearin' masks and pretend we don't know who Virgil is and take their guns and any money they've got and leave 'em on foot. They won't know we're his brothers. They'll just think tomorrow is the unluckiest day of their lives."

"What if Virgil gives it away when he sees us?" Gilbert asked.

"Shoot him," Johnny answered him.

"I don't know, though," Henry hesitated. "Robbin' 'em still seems like a crazy thing to do when it would be a helluva lot easier to just wait for 'em and shoot 'em."

"Then there wouldn't be no doubt in anybody's mind who done it," Berta said, "and they'd have the Texas Rangers and everybody else comin' after you. If they just got robbed, then we'd just have to hide Virgil when they came lookin' for him."

"Damn, Berta," Junior said, "I gotta hand it to ya. That's a damn good idea, and there ain't no way those two lawmen can say it was us that done it."

"And you thought I was just another pretty face," she said.

"You musta guessed what I was thinkin'," Henry said to her. "Women do that sometimes."

"Right," she said and winked at Junior, who grinned in response.

The next few hours were spent discussing what had to be done to prepare for the planned robbery. They knew the road to Jacksboro, but they had to guess where the two lawmen might decide to stop to water and rest the horses. There was a good campground used by a lot of folks coming to Glory, but it was only five miles from town, too soon to make a stop, if you were leaving town. From the valley where their cabin was, they could ride at an angle to intercept the Jacksboro road north of Glory. With that in mind, Henry said, "I'll tell you where to wait for 'em. If we take that trail from here like we was goin' to Jacksboro, we'd strike the Jacksboro road about a mile or so short of Razor Creek, about halfway between Glory and Jacksboro. That's where they'll stop to rest their horses. There ain't a better spot to rest 'em."

"I'm thinkin' they most likely found out Razor Creek was about halfway when they rode down to Glory," Henry said. "There's a pretty good chance they'll just stop there on the way back when they figure that out."

"Reckon how early in the mornin' they'll head out?" Johnny asked.

"Ain't no worry there," Junior answered him. "Virgil said them two deputies weren't leavin' till after breakfast. They didn't bring no jail wagon with a cook for that short a trip, so they'll eat a big breakfast and make it last till Jacksboro."

"Well, we got us a plan, and I believe it's a good'un," Henry declared. "The only thing we need to do now is make sure we mask up and make sure nobody can identify us."

It was in the middle of the afternoon when deputy marshals Bill Clayton and Conrad Priest pulled up to the hitching post at the Glory marshal's office. Bannack had hung around the office ever since dinnertime so he would be there to welcome them. He met them at the door and introduced himself as Marshal John Cochran. They shook hands and he introduced them to Daryl Boyd. "You wanna see your prisoner?" Bannack asked and they said they might as well, so he led them inside the cell room. "Stand up and let them take a look at you, Virgil," Bannack said, and Virgil got up from his cot. The deputies took a quick look and turned around to leave.

Back in the office, Priest said to Clayton, "He doesn't look like he'll be much trouble." Then he lowered his voice so Bannack wouldn't hear him. "From the looks of his face, it looks like he's already been saddle broke. Probably more'n ready to get outta this jail." To Bannack, he said, "I assume he's got a horse and saddle in that stable we passed on the way into town."

"That's right," Bannack said. "Clem Shaw is the owner of the stable, and he knows you'll be stayin' overnight and takin' Virgil's horse with you tomorrow. We reserved two rooms in the hotel for you. Anything else you need, just let me know."

"'Preciate it, Marshal," Conrad Priest said. "Here are the papers authorizin' us to take possession of the prisoner. We'll pick him up after breakfast in the morning, so make sure he gets breakfast. Otherwise, he won't get anything to eat till we get to Jacksboro tomorrow except a cup of coffee and maybe a piece of jerky."

"I never been to Glory before," Bill Clayton said. "Where would you send a man to get himself a good supper?"

"Two places in town will serve you a good supper," Bannack replied. "One is the hotel dinin' room and the other is Sawyer's Café. I don't think you'd be disappointed at either one."

"All right, then," Priest replied, "I reckon we'll see you after breakfast in the mornin'."

Bannack walked outside with them and waited while they climbed on their horses and rode up the street toward the stable. "Where do you eat breakfast, Marshal?" Clayton called back to him.

"Hotel dinin' room," Bannack answered him as they rode away.

The rest of the afternoon passed without incident enough to complain to the marshal's office, so Bannack let Daryl go to supper a little bit earlier than usual. "You can bring Virgil's supper back with you," he told him. "I think I'll take supper at Sawyer's tonight. I ain't ate there in a while and every time I see one of 'em they wanna know why. They know I get a big discount when I eat at the hotel, but they don't ever offer to match it." He couldn't tell Daryl the real reason was that he preferred not to eat with the two deputies and he figured they would likely eat in the hotel dining room. Considering the two marshals had never heard of a lawman by the name of John Cochran, Bannack was afraid it might be the natural tendency to ask a lot of questions regarding his history before Glory. He didn't want to concern himself with remembering what he made up to tell them.

When Daryl returned with Virgil's supper, Bannack locked the marshal's office and walked up the street to Sawyer's. Russell Sawyer greeted him cordially when he walked in the front door. "Evenin', John," Russell asked, "you gonna take supper with us tonight?"

"I thought I might," Bannack returned, "if you're not too particular who eats here."

Sawyer laughed. "I'd get my brains beat out by three women, if I ever turned you away. And besides, I wanna thank you for sending those two deputy marshals here to eat. They said you recommended us."

"You're welcome" was all Bannack could think to say at the moment, since he had come to Sawyer's to eat to avoid eating with the two deputies.

"I reckon you want to join them," Sawyer said. "They've got a pretty good head start on you."

"No, I can't join 'em right now," Bannack responded, trying to think of a reason. "I've got something I've got to take care of before I can eat, so I just stopped by to let them know I couldn't make it."

"Oh," Sawyer replied, obviously disappointed, "I thought you were going to eat with us tonight."

"Oh, I am," he said at once, surprised by Sawyer's show of disappointment. "I'll be back to eat supper. You'll be open for another hour, won't you?"

Sawyer cheered up right away. "Yes, we'll be open, but you come on in even if the closed sign is up. My girls would never forgive me if you missed your supper."

Being a man of few emotions beyond caution and anger, Bannack was not certain how to handle Sawyer's expression of gratitude. So when the café owner pointed to the table where the two deputies were eating, he said, "Right, I'll just go tell 'em."

Since a man of his size never walked through a crowded room unnoticed, Clayton and Priest noticed him approaching when he was still a good distance away. When he got to the table, he was glad to see the two lawmen were well along the way toward dessert. "Well, Marshal Cochran," Conrad Priest greeted him, "if we'd known you were gonna join us, we would have waited before we started eatin'."

"I'm glad you didn't wait for me," Bannack replied. "I had something I had to attend to and I wasn't sure if I was gonna be held up or not. I've still gotta go back to the office, but I thought I'd drop in here on the way to make sure you boys were gettin' taken care of all right." He was aware of Susie standing behind him then, so he turned to address her. "Make sure these gentlemen get plenty to eat, Susie. They're here on important business."

"She's takin' good care of us," Bill Clayton offered. "We can wait for you, if you want."

"No, I'd rather you go ahead and enjoy your evenin' in Glory," Bannack insisted. "Your prisoner's eatin' his supper now, although it doesn't look as good as that on your plate. And he'll be ready to go in the mornin'. I expect I'll see you at breakfast." Both men nodded in agreement, apparently not particularly interested in waiting to spend their evening with the marshal.

Susie, on the other hand, looked disappointed as she walked with him when he left the table. "Aren't you going to eat here tonight?"

"Yes, ma'am, I sure am. I told your papa I'd be back before you close."

"You promise?"

"I promise," he said, amazed that she cared that much. She turned back to take care of her tables then, and he went out the door. "I'll be back in thirty minutes," he said to Russell Sawyer when he walked by his desk.

He joined Priest and Clayton for breakfast in the hotel dining room the next morning. They both looked a little worn and in need of strong coffee. He was not concerned as much about joining them for breakfast as he had been for supper. Unlike supper with the whole evening to follow to enjoy yourself, breakfast was something that had to be done in a timely fashion because there were things to prepare for a journey. There was no time for idle chatter. Bannack and Daryl got Virgil fed, then waited while the deputies got their horses as well as Virgil's horse from the stable. Virgil held up pretty well until the two lawmen pulled the horses up in front of the jail. At that point, he began looking all around him as if expecting help coming from any direction. He had been confident that his father and his brothers would make some attempt to rescue him. They had not tried to break into the jail that night. *So it will be when they take me out of the jail and put me on my horse,* he thought. So he made no attempt to resist when told to walk out of his cell and put his hands behind his back. He didn't even flinch when Deputy Priest locked the cuffs on his wrists. He looked up at Bannack and smirked when Priest walked him past the marshal on his way to the door. *Come on, Marshal,* he thought. *Don't lag behind in this office. Get your big behind outside where you can be seen.* With a deputy on each side of him, leading him with a hand on each arm, they stepped out the door onto the boardwalk. He tensed, anticipating the shots, but none came. He panicked and yelled out, "What are you waitin' for? Shoot!" All three of the lawmen reacted to the cry of alarm, drawing their weapons and looking all about them for signs of attack. But there was none. Virgil went limp and would have sagged to the ground had he not been supported by the two deputies. "Papa . . ." he moaned pitifully.

"I reckon this just ain't your day, Virgil," Deputy Clayton said as he dropped his sidearm back in his holster. They led him to his horse, but he made no attempt to climb up into the saddle. "You might as well get this straight," Clayton told him. "You might not wanna take this ride, but you're gonna. Now, you can make it easy on yourself or make it hard. Either way, you're gonna end up in a cell in Jacksboro before the day is over and the courtroom tomorrow mornin' to set a trial date." He picked up his leg and shoved his foot into the stirrup, then he and Priest lifted him up to sit in the saddle. Clayton tied his boots together under the horse's belly. "You fall outta that saddle and we'll haul you upside down all the way to Jacksboro," Clayton threatened.

"All right," Virgil finally relented, "I won't cause you no trouble. You can take these cuffs offa my hands."

Clayton smiled. "I reckon not. You just set there in that saddle and we'll take a nice easy ride."

CHAPTER 10

Berta fixed another big breakfast of stolen beef for the Dawson men before they set out to rescue Virgil. "Don't let on you know who Virgil is or they'll know who you are," she reminded them. "Then you'll have to kill 'em and as sure as you do, you'll all be marked men."

"Damn it, Berta, don't you think we know that?" Henry replied, tired of hearing her go on about her brilliant idea. He knew they had a head start on the two lawmen transporting Virgil to Jacksboro, so they set out at an angle to strike the road to Jacksboro and then continued on to Razor Creek.

It was not a ride of more than about three miles before they struck the Jacksboro road south of Razor Creek. Once they got to the road, they turned their horses toward Jacksboro and followed it the short distance to the creek. The spot they decided on looked to be a perfect choice. Henry estimated it to be about halfway between Glory and Jacksboro where a wide stream crossed the road as it ran through a thick grove of trees. "I wouldn't be surprised if them two lawmen mighta stopped here on their way to Glory," Henry said, repeating his thoughts of yesterday. That inspired a close inspection of the little grassy clearing close to the stream, which resulted in some recent hoofprints as well as recent ashes. "This is the spot," Henry declared. "They stopped here on the way down. They'll stop here on the way back. We'll set up a little reception for 'em, and if they don't stop here, we'll just follow 'em till they do stop and jump 'em wherever that is."

"Our biggest problem is gonna be Virgil," Gilbert said. "I don't care how good our masks are, he's gonna know it's us."

"Maybe so," Junior said. "If we have to, we'll just outbluff him."

They picked their hiding places, all centered around the recent campfire remains, then Henry told Johnny to take their horses far enough downstream to keep them from giving the ambush away. "Then you ride yours back here 'cause you're gonna be our scout." When Johnny wanted to know what his father meant by that, Henry explained. "You ride back toward Glory for about a couple of miles. Find you a place where you can see the road for a good distance, but make sure you stay hid so they can't see you. Then as soon as you see them come into sight, hightail it back here so we can all get ready for 'em."

"Right," Johnny said, excitedly and jumped on his horse again.

"Don't let 'em see you!" Henry reminded him again as he galloped away from the clearing. As soon as he was gone, Henry continued to rehearse his other two sons on their parts in this sham holdup.

"Hell, Pa," Junior complained, "this ain't our first holdup."

"It's the first one on two Deputy US Marshals," Henry came back. "So I don't want nobody to slip up and let 'em know who we are."

"We ain't gonna slip up," Junior said. "Remember, if you have to shoot one of 'em, just try to wound him."

It had been a good half an hour or more before Gilbert exclaimed, "Here he comes!" They looked back toward Glory to see Johnny coming up the road at a full gallop. They grabbed their weapons and ran out to the road to meet him.

"They're comin'!" he exclaimed. "Two of 'em! One of 'em's leadin' a packhorse and the other one's leadin' Virgil's horse."

"Did they see you?"

"No, Pa," Johnny answered impatiently. "They didn't see me. They ain't in a hurry, just walkin' their horses. It'll be a few minutes before they get here."

"All right," Henry said, "take your horse downstream with the others and get back here in your hidin' place. The rest of us can get to our spots and wait for me to spring the trap. Just don't go jumpin' the gun on me.

Let 'em get their horses watered and get started with whatever they're gonna do. The more comfortable they are, the easier it'll be to take 'em."

Conrad Priest led Virgil's horse into the clearing and stopped. "Might as well build a fire right where we built the last one," he said to Bill Clayton as he rode in behind him and dismounted. He let his horse go to the water but held the packhorse until he got a coffeepot, some coffee, and some jerky out of the packs. Priest stepped down from the saddle and helped Virgil dismount.

"How 'bout takin' these handcuffs offa me so I can pee," Virgil said.

Priest unlocked his wrists, then pulled them around to handcuff them in front of him. "Now walk over to the edge of the clearin' to them bushes over there and just pee into the bushes," he told him. "Remember, I'll be holdin' this Winchester rifle aimed right on the middle of your back till you turn around and come back to this spot right here."

Close enough to hear everything said by the two lawmen, all four Dawsons froze when they heard what Priest said. *The place the deputy had pointed to for Virgil to relieve himself was the bank of bushes Johnny had picked to hide behind.* Their elaborate robbery plan was shot down immediately. There was to be no choice but to execute the two deputies. Still, they held their positions, for no one was eager to fire the first shot to officially destroy their plan. Unaware of the drama he had created with his need to answer nature's call, Virgil walked up to the bank of bushes and was in full stream before he was suddenly aware of some movement behind the bushes. A small rodent of some kind, he thought, until he heard a whisper. "Virgil, it's me, Johnny."

"What?" Virgil started before he could stop himself.

"Virgil! Don't say anything!" Johnny whispered desperately. "It's me, Johnny. We've come to get you, but you gotta pretend you don't know who we are."

"You say something?" Priest asked.

"I belched," Virgil answered him.

"Hurry up," Priest said.

"I'm hurryin'," Virgil said. Then back to the bush, he asked, "What are you waitin' for? Shoot them before they find out you're here."

"No," Johnny whispered. "You don't understand. We've got a plan, and you've got to pretend like you don't know us. Don't let 'em know who we are. No matter what, you just play like you never saw us before. And we'll do the rest. Understand?"

"Yeah, I don't know you," he whispered, "but you better get me outta here."

"Go on back and do whatever they tell you. We're gonna free you."

Feeling confident again, he went back to the center of the clearing where Clayton was already building a fire. "Hey, I ain't gonna cause you no trouble. How about takin' these handcuffs off?"

Ignoring his question, Priest led him over to the other side of the little clearing and handcuffed his hands around a small tree. "That's so we don't have to watch you while we're makin' some coffee and fixin' a little jerky to eat with it." Anticipating Virgil's next complaint, he said, "You can eat with your hands cuffed together with no problem." He went back to get the coffeepot then and took it to the stream to fill while Clayton built the fire.

In a short time, there was a good blaze going, and the coffeepot was set in the edge of the fire. Huddled close to the fire to watch its progress, Priest was suddenly startled by the voice behind him. "Howdy, couldn't help smellin' your smoke on the road back yonder. Whatcha cookin'?"

"Damn, where'd you come from?" Priest replied as he turned to face the voice. His hand dropped automatically to his holstered .45 when he saw the bandanna around the man's face."

"That'da be a big mistake if you was to draw that weapon," Henry said. "Then I'd have to put a hole in your brain."

"Bill!" Priest yelled to alert his partner, but Clayton was looking into the barrel of another rifle as Junior eased out from behind a tree trunk.

"Suppose you just back over there by your partner," Junior told him. "What are you carryin' on that packhorse?"

"Hey, Boss," Gilbert called out to Henry, "there's another one handcuffed to a tree over here."

"You men are makin' a helluva big mistake," Priest said. "We're Deputy US Marshals, transporting a prisoner to Jacksboro. You picked the wrong people to rob."

Henry acted surprised and turned to look at Virgil. "So that's why you locked him to a tree. What did he do?"

"He shot a man in cold blood," Priest answered, then jumped when Johnny lifted his handgun from his holster. Then Johnny relieved Clayton of his weapon.

"How 'bout it, young feller?" Henry asked. "Did you do it?"

"Hell, no, I didn't, but they won't listen to me," Virgil answered.

"Give my partner the key to those cuffs, deputy, I've decided that feller is tellin' the truth," Henry said.

"I can't do that," Priest said. "He's under arrest."

"You're gonna be the first lawman I ever shot," Henry said. "As a rule, I don't shoot folks I rob, but I'm gonna make an exception outta you if you don't give my partner the key to them cuffs. I despise handcuffs. And I'm already gettin' pretty irritated that you two turned out to be lawmen." Priest still hesitated, so Henry cocked his rifle and put a bullet in the deputy's shoulder. He cocked it again and aimed it at Priest's head.

"For God's sake, hold it!" Clayton shouted. "Here's my key! Unlock them with it!"

"Looks like your partner is a helluva lot smarter than you are," Henry said. Johnny took the key from Clayton and unlocked the handcuff, freeing Virgil from the tree.

"Much obliged," Virgil said to his father.

"Right," Henry replied. "You're free to go, young feller. You got a horse?"

"Yes, sir," Virgil said, playing along with the ruse.

Henry looked at Junior and said, "Give him a gun belt and a pistol." Back to Virgil, he said, "Jump on your horse and get outta here."

"I was thinkin' maybe I could ride with you and your men," Virgil said.

"I'm not takin' on anybody else," Henry answered. "You're a wanted man, and everybody in Texas will know your name. My advice to you is to head for Oklahoma Indian Territory. So you better get started." He winked, so Virgil did as he was told, climbed on his horse, and started up the road toward Jacksboro. When he was gone, Henry watched the two lawmen while his three sons searched through the packs on the packhorse, then through their saddlebags.

"There ain't much here, Boss," Junior said.

"Well, their weapons and horses will bring a little something," Henry said. "Empty your pockets," he ordered then, which they did.

"Don't take our horses, man," Clayton begged. "I've got a wounded man here I need to get to a doctor. How can I get him to a doctor if you don't leave us at least one horse."

"Hell, walkin' ain't crowded," Henry responded. "That's the reason I shot him in the shoulder instead of his leg, so he could walk back to Glory. There's a doctor there. Most fellers in my business ain't that thoughtful about folks they rob. Look at the bright side, at least you won't have to fool with walkin' that prisoner back to Glory. But you better get started, it's gonna take you a while to walk back to Glory. Come on, boys," he yelled out to his sons. "We've got a long ride ahead of us." He got on his horse and kept his eye on the two lawmen until his sons rounded up all the horses. Then they rode out to the road and turned toward Jacksboro, riding until well out of sight before leaving the road and cutting back toward their little valley. "Turn them three horses loose," Henry ordered then.

"Pa," Junior objected, "them's three good horses!"

"We can't take a chance on some lawman findin' them horses with us. That would blow up our whole story."

Junior nodded thoughtfully. "Right, I didn't think about that." They released the horses.

Virgil and Berta were sitting on the front porch of the cabin when Henry and the boys rode into the north end of the valley, firing their weapons into the air in celebration of their victorious attack on the deputy marshals. They rode into the small barnyard, whooping and hollering about how they pulled the wool over the eyes of the law. Virgil jumped off the porch and ran to the barn to join in the fun. "There he is!" Gilbert exclaimed. "He oughta be on the stage, as good an actor as he is."

"You reckon we oughta let him join up with us, Boss?" Junior japed.

"Hell, I changed my mind," Virgil japed back. "I don't believe I wanna join up with a gang of outlaws that ain't got no better sense than to pull a holdup on two Deputy US Marshals. You can't make a livin' that way."

"Our little ol' plan worked like a charm, didn't it?" Henry shook his head when he thought about it. "Virgil, you coulda blown the whole plan to pieces when you saw Johnny in them bushes."

"He gimme a scare," Virgil admitted. "When I saw somethin' movin' in them bushes, it liked to backed my water up all the way to my throat. But when I saw it was Johnny, I just tried to go ahead and pee on him."

"I swear, I think he did," Johnny declared. "I was fixin' to shoot him if he did, too, and that woulda took care of the whole deal."

"Take care of them horses," Virgil said, "and come on up to the house. Berta made a big ol' apple pie for dinner."

"We oughta ride into town, so we could buy them deputies a drink when they get to town," Gilbert said. The japing and the celebrating would continue on for quite some time.

* * *

"What in the . . . ?" Clem Shaw started to express his disbelief. Standing out in front of his stable, talking to Buster Bridges, he had to be sure it was who he thought it was. "Look," he said then and pointed up the north road out of town. "Ain't that them two deputy marshals that just took Virgil Dawson to Jacksboro?"

"Where?" Buster asked, looking for men on horses. "I don't see nobody."

"Yonder," Clem said, "walkin'."

"Yeah, I see 'em now. It does look like those two fellows, but what in the world are they doin' walkin'?"

"And where is Virgil Dawson?" Clem asked. They continued to stare at the two men and when they were a little closer, Clem said, "One of 'em's actin' like he's hurt. I better go give him a hand." He had just started to unhitch his wagon when Buster stopped to talk to him, so he climbed up into the seat. "Hop on," he said to Buster.

"You go," Buster replied. "I think I'd better go get Marshal Cochran."

"That's a good idea," Clem said, gave his horse a slap with his reins, and started up the road toward the two lawmen. When they saw the wagon coming to them at a trot, the two deputies stopped and waited for it, as if too tired to take another step. "Lord a-mercy," Clem exclaimed when he pulled the wagon to a stop in front of them. "What happened to you boys?"

"He's been shot," Clayton said. "I need to get him to the doctor."

"Just crawl in the back of the wagon and I'll take you to see Doc Taylor. You need any help gettin' him in there?" Clayton said he could manage. He lowered the tail gate and helped Priest to climb on it. Then he climbed on beside him and signaled Clem to drive. Clem drove the wagon through the middle of town and when they came to the marshal's office, they found Bannack and Buster waiting out front for them. Bannack walked along beside the wagon and Buster followed.

"What happened?" Bannack asked Clayton.

"We got ambushed," Clayton said. "Back at that creek, we stopped to rest the horses and we got robbed."

"Robbed?" Bannack started to question, but Priest groaned and interrupted him.

"It makes me feel like a damn fool, but Bill's right, we got robbed by a gang of four men, all wearin' masks. Let him tell it." So Bannack just walked and listened while Clayton gave him a complete picture of the whole incident. But he never doubted who the four men were, in spite of the two lawmen's insistence that they were robbers. By the time they reached Dr. Taylor's office, he was convinced that Henry Dawson and his sons freed Virgil.

While Priest was being treated by Doc Taylor, Bannack continued to question Clayton. "And these men set Virgil free?" Bannack asked.

"It was like I told you," Clayton insisted, "they were wearing masks. Virgil didn't know who they were and they sure didn't act like they knew him. They set him free because he was an outlaw, same as them. I would have been surprised if they hadn't set him free. He even said he'd like to join up with them, but they said no. So he left on his own, headed for Indian Territory, if he took their advice."

"After they set you and Priest on your way on foot, which way did they go?"

"They went north, toward Jacksboro," Clayton answered. "Their boss told them they had a long ride ahead of them."

Not as long as you might think, Bannack thought. "So what are you and your partner gonna do now?" Bannack asked.

"I don't know," Clayton answered. "I ain't ever been ambushed and robbed while I was transportin' a prisoner before. I reckon I need to get to the telegraph office and let my boss know what happened." He paused to shake his head. "And ain't he gonna be happy to hear the news? He just might fire me and Conrad, if he answers my wire at all. Here we are, back in Glory, without no horses or guns."

Bannack thought about it for only a moment before deciding. He didn't like the idea of Virgil Dawson getting away with his senseless crime of murder and his actions upon the people in Sawyer's Café. And he surely didn't like the bold robbery hoax Henry Dawson got away with. "Maybe your boss won't fire you if you tell him you've got a pretty good idea who robbed you and where your prisoner is and you and your partner are goin' after him."

"Maybe not," Clayton replied, "but I don't know any of those things."

"I do," Bannack said. "That gang of four outlaws that robbed you are Henry Dawson and his three sons. And I'll bet Virgil went right back home with 'em."

"I don't know, Marshal," Clayton replied, not so sure. "Like I said, they were all wearin' masks. And even if they hadn't been, I never saw 'em before, so I couldn't say it was them or not, if it went to court. And Virgil didn't act like he knew them, either. Besides, Conrad's hurt. He ain't gonna be in no shape to take on that whole family, especially if what you say is true."

"I'll take Conrad's place, if you really want to take your prisoner to jail," Bannack said. "I don't have any jurisdiction outside the city limits of this town, but I'll go with you as a posse member. Clem's got a couple of horses that belong to the marshal's office we can fix you up with. Right, Clem?" Clem nodded. "The only thing I can't help you with is where Dawson's place is. I'm still new in town, myself."

"I can help you with that, too," Clem volunteered. "I can tell you how to find his cabin."

"If he can't, I can," Buster spoke up. "He took over a farm in a little valley with a creek runnin' up the middle of it, Tyson's Creek, named for the man who built the cabin."

"That's a fact," Clem said, "and according to Dawson,

him and his boys found old Tyson layin' in the bed dead one day, so they buried him and took over the farm."

"Well, I'll swear, I didn't know that," Buster said.

"I'm thinkin' we might as well go and get your prisoner back, Deputy. Whaddaya say?" Bannack asked. "As soon as Doc finishes up with your partner, you can send your telegraph. Then we'll fix you up with a horse and a gun, and we'll go see if Virgil Dawson really is dumb enough to go back home."

"I can't believe you folks are willing to go to so much trouble to help me and Conrad after we got played like idiots."

"Don't be too hard on yourself," Bannack told him. "The fact that they were playin' a trick on you ain't got nothing to do with it. You got surprised by four outlaws who wouldn't hesitate to kill. There wasn't much you could have done about it. That was a real bullet they put in your partner's shoulder. There wasn't any trick about that."

"I reckon the most important thing is for us to get our prisoner back," Clayton said. "But even if he is there, we've got no evidence that his father and three brothers were the four outlaws."

"You're right," Bannack agreed, "but it would help if your horses are there, since you said Virgil didn't take 'em with him."

"Damn, that's right," Clayton said. "Virgil just got on his horse and took off up the road to Jacksboro. They gave him a gun, but they didn't give him an extra horse.

So if we find our horses at Dawson's place, that pretty much tells the story."

"'Course, if we don't find your horses at Dawson's, it just might mean he was smart enough to cut your horses loose. Either way, my money's on Dawson and his boys to have pulled that ambush on you."

CHAPTER 11

Barbara Taylor walked out the front door to deliver the news that her husband had successfully removed the bullet from Conrad Priest's shoulder. "It went very well," she declared, and the patient should be recovering from the anesthesia in about twenty minutes."

"Thank you, Mrs. Taylor," Bannack said politely. "We'll be back to pick him up." He turned to ask Clem, "You don't mind if we use your wagon long enough to carry him back to the jail, do you?"

"No, sir," Clem replied. "I'll do the drivin' for you. There ain't no hurry for me to get back to the stable."

"'Preciate it, Clem," Bannack said. "Hop on, Bill, and we'll take you to the telegraph office."

"I'll go with you," Buster said. "There weren't nobody sittin' in the barbershop when we rode by." He crawled up in the wagon, and they pulled away from the doctor's office and went to the telegraph office where Clayton jumped off and went inside. Bannack went in behind him to tell Sam Peters to charge the wire to the marshal's office. On Bannack's advice, Clayton advised his boss of the situation and told him what he was going to do, instead of asking if it was all right to do it. That way, Bannack told him, he wouldn't have to wait around for his boss's reply, and they needed to get started pretty quickly.

Clayton sent his wire, and the posse went back to get Priest. He was awake when they returned, and he was in the process of trying to explain to Doc that he had been robbed and couldn't pay his fee. Bannack volunteered to pay for him, so Doc told him to forget about it, and Priest promised to send him the money when he got back to Jacksboro. Again, Doc said to forget it, ignoring Barbara's frown.

"All right," Bannack said, "next stop the jail." They helped Priest up on the wagon and having seen the frown, Bannack slipped the four-dollar fee in Barbara's hand before he jumped on. When they got to the jail, they helped Priest inside to the marshal's office where they were met by a totally confused Daryl Boyd. "Your job is to make sure Deputy Priest is comfortable while I'm gone," he told Daryl while he got a gun belt and handgun plus a rifle out of the cabinet for Clayton. "We're gonna be gone for a good while, so at suppertime, go up to the hotel and get your supper and order another one just like you do for a prisoner. Can you do that?"

"Yes, sir," Daryl answered. "I'll take care of him. You are coming back tonight, aren't you?"

"We plan to," Bannack replied. They left the jail then and went back to the stable where he saddled the buckskin and Clem saddled a bay for Clayton's use. Buster saddled his horse as well. "Why are you saddlin' up?" Bannack asked the little man.

"Because you don't know how to find Tyson's Creek," Buster answered.

"Couldn't you just tell me how to get there?"

"I could, but it'd be easier to show you," the little man replied. "And that way, you won't be stumblin' around when it gets dark wonderin' how you got lost."

"All right," Bannack said, "but if you get shot, don't blame me. Me and Clayton are paid to get shot at."

"Any shootin' starts, I'm gonna stand behind you," Buster remarked.

They rode until they came to a gentle creek Buster said was Tyson's Creek. They struck the creek where it came out of a narrow pass that led to a small valley. Buster had been correct in suggesting that showing was better than telling the way, for there were a couple of places where it was necessary to leave one trail and pick up another. It was beginning to look more like a hideout than a working farm, the closer they got. "How'd you ever find this place?" Bannack had to ask.

"Henry Dawson sold me a cow one time," Buster replied. "He said he'd sell it to me cheap, if I came to get it. He didn't wanna bring it to town."

"You buy cows from Henry Dawson?" Bannack asked.

"Not no more," Buster quickly answered. "I just bought that one cow. I didn't buy no more after I figured out where he got 'em." They rode a little farther, and Buster cautioned them. "See up ahead where the creek turns, the whole valley turns, and when we get around that curve, you can see Dawson's place right beside the creek."

"Then I reckon we better be a little more careful," Clayton said. "I don't know what you've got in mind, Marshal, but I ain't sure I want to get into a gunfight against all five of 'em. My interest today is to recover one prisoner, if possible."

"I understand that, Deputy," Bannack replied. "I don't want to fight the whole bunch of 'em either. If it's possible, I'd like to get close enough to spot Virgil, if he's there. Then maybe we can find some way to catch him apart from the rest of them." He looked at the sky at the western end of the valley. The afternoon was getting along toward suppertime. It was still plenty light, but it would not be long before the sun sank beneath the sides of the narrow valley.

When they reached the little curve in the creek, they could see the open mouth of the valley to the west. They also picked up the sound of cattle, most of them beyond the small cluster of cabin, barn, outhouse, and smokehouse, some seventy-five yards away. "They've got a nice little place there," Bannack commented. "They've got a little herd of cattle, too. If we're gonna get any closer, though, we're gonna have to take to the timber on the side of the valley," he said pointing toward the pine forest that covered the slope. "If we stay quiet, we oughta be able to get pretty close to that cabin. Whaddaya think, Deputy?"

"You seem to know what you wanna do," Clayton replied. "Least, I hope to hell you do. Right now, I don't know how we're gonna separate our man from the rest of those gunmen, but you call the shots, and I'll try to back you up."

"All right," Bannack said. He looked at Buster then. "Buster, like I said before, ain't nobody payin' you to get shot at. You can stay here and watch for us to come back and maybe make it hot for anybody that's chasin' us."

"The hell I will," Buster replied. "In for a dime, in for a dollar. I'm comin' with you." Bannack shrugged and started up through the trees on the slope. Clayton turned his horse to follow and when he passed Buster, Buster said, "Don't worry about it, Deputy. I've seen him in action."

They moved on farther along the slope until Bannack decided it best to continue on foot before their horses might start to communicate with the horses in the corral. A few minutes later, the sun suddenly dropped out of sight, painting the dark sky with a splash of fiery red before fading away to leave the little valley in darkness. "You two stay here, and I'll slip down across from that cabin and maybe I can see if Virgil's in there." Neither Clayton nor Buster protested, so Bannack hurried off along the slope on foot. When he got to a point where he was directly opposite the front of the cabin, he cautiously moved down the slope until he was looking straight across the creek at the open door of the cabin. *This ain't such a good idea,* he thought. *I'm gonna have to have some luck because it's too dark to see into that cabin.* He couldn't blame Buster and the deputy for staying with the horses, but he thought he might see Virgil walking around inside the cabin. He was thinking about sneaking across the creek to try to look in a window when Junior Dawson walked out the front door, walked over to the side of the little porch, and proceeded to relieve himself of the coffee he had consumed. Bannack recognized him from his visit to the jail to see Virgil. A few seconds later, Virgil walked out the door and went to the other side of the porch. He was easily recognized by the bandage still wrapped around his face. *I appreciate it,* Bannack thought silently.

He knew now that his thinking had been correct. Virgil was there. Now, the bigger problem was how were they going to snatch him away from the other four Dawsons? As quickly as he asked the question, the answer came to him. So he backed away from the creek and retraced his path back to Buster and Clayton. "He's in there, all right," he announced.

"How the hell are we gonna get him outta there without startin' a war?" Clayton asked.

"We're gonna rustle their cattle," Bannack answered. "There's a little herd of about twenty-five or more on the other side of that cabin. I'm figurin' on waitin' a little while until it gets hard dark. Then I'm gonna stampede those cows down that valley. When they come out of that cabin and chase 'em, I'm hopin' to get a chance to catch Virgil when he ain't lookin'. He'll be easy to spot 'cause he's still got a bandage wrapped around his face."

"What's gonna keep the rest of those boys from comin' after us?" Clayton asked.

"I figured I'd leave that up to you and Buster," Bannack answered. "I figure that once we stampede those cows down the valley, you and Buster can just let 'em go, and you can hightail it out of the valley. Anybody sees you and follows you, use your rifles on 'em, and I'll see you back in town. But I expect they'll try to stop their cattle before they chase you."

"You know, Marshal, you're sure as hell stickin' your neck out, tryin' to get this piece of dung back under arrest, and it ain't even under your jurisdiction. Don't you think it might be better to come back here with half a dozen deputy marshals?"

"Probably less risky," Bannack replied, "but Virgil might not be here by the time you came back. I ain't gonna take any big chances, but I'd like to take a shot at catchin' him. I just don't like the son of a gun. But it'll help me out if I know you two are out of danger, so all I have to worry about is me."

"All right," Clayton said, "we'll do it your way."

They led their horses through the trees on the slope until they were past the cabin and the barn. Below them, on the other side of the creek, they could now see the dark forms of the cattle huddling together for protection. "I reckon it's dark enough now," Bannack said. "We better get goin' before the moon comes up."

* * *

Inside the log cabin, the Dawson men were lying around the fireplace, their bellies full from another heavy meal of beef and their brains numbed by corn whiskey. Henry Dawson was feeling self-satisfied, his boots extracted by Berta, still enjoying the charade he and his boys performed on the two Deputy US Marshals. He had no doubts but that the law would be visiting him within the next few days, looking for Virgil. But Virgil wouldn't be there, and his escape from the two deputies would be big news to him and Virgil's brothers. *Hell,* he thought, *me and the boys mighta been famous thespians if we'da gone on the stage, instead of robbing it.* His thoughts were interrupted then when Berta asked, "What are you chucklin' about?"

"I was just thinkin' about the look on them two deputy marshals' faces when . . ." That was as far as he got before their quiet was shattered by the sudden sound of hell breaking loose outside. Multiple gunshots exploding confused them all for a few moments as they all scrambled for cover. Then they realized none were hitting the cabin, and Henry roared, "The cattle! They're rustlin' the cattle!" There was no need for any further orders. They all snatched up their gun belts and ran for the barn to saddle their horses to go after their cows as quickly as they could. Henry ran to the corral, still with his boots off. Realizing that, he stopped and yelled encouragement to his sons. "Catch 'em before they drive 'em across the river! Don't let 'em across!" It no longer sounded like a big gang of rustlers. Judging by the sounds of gunfire he now heard, it sounded like only two or three rustlers. And if his boys could catch up with them on this side of the river, there was a good chance the cows would get confused in the thick growth of trees and bushes on the near bank, effectively stopping their stampede. "Then we'll deal with the rustlers," he said to himself.

The four Dawson brothers rode in hot pursuit after their cattle. The darkness of the night made it difficult to pick out individual riders, and Junior shouted out orders to be sure before shooting. "Me and Virgil will go up this side!" he shouted. "Johnny, you and Gilbert go up the other side! It don't sound like there's more'n two of 'em, so let's keep 'em between us." They chased the herd into the heavy growth on the riverbank and as Henry had thought, the cows began to scatter in many different directions. The brothers tried to turn them all toward the center, but it was hard keeping track of one another.

For a few seconds, Virgil lost sight of Junior, so he swung wide around a large clump of bushes where he had last seen him. He was relieved to hear him then. "Virgil, over here!" He gave his horse a kick and followed the voice until he saw him in the dark shadows, bending over examining his horse's hoof.

"What happened?" Virgil asked as he pulled up beside him. "Did he go lame?"

"Yeah," he said, swinging his rifle like a club as he straightened up. The rifle caught Virgil beside his ear, knocking him out of the saddle to land on the ground unconscious. Wasting no time, Bannack took a quick look around to make sure Junior wasn't coming back that way, then he tied Virgil's hands together with one end of a long piece of rope. He picked him up, much like he would pick up a deer carcass, and laid him across his saddle. Then he reached under the horse's belly and pulled the rope under it and tied it around his boots. He then climbed aboard his horse and led Virgil's horse over the slope and started back the other side. As he rode away, he could hear mumbling sounds that told him Virgil was coming to. *I reckon you ain't dead, anyway,* he thought. Behind him, on the other side of the ridge, he could hear Virgil's brothers calling out to each other in the dark. The voices became more and more faint as he followed the ridge, so he was satisfied that they were not following him. Figuring he was in the clear, he relaxed, only to suddenly start when he detected a motion in the darkness ahead of him.

"Don't shoot, John," Buster called out. "Did you get him?"

"Yeah, I got him," Bannack answered, close enough to see both of them now. "What are you doin' here? I thought you were goin' back to town."

"We waited for you, so you wouldn't get lost," Buster said. "We didn't come this way."

"Is he alive?" Clayton asked when Bannack pulled up before them.

"I think so," Bannack answered. "I heard him make

some mumblin' noises a little while ago. I know he can't feel too good, though. I didn't have time to try to talk him into surrenderin'. Did you boys have any trouble?"

"Nope," Clayton replied. "We shot up a lot of ammunition and made a helluva lot of noise. I expect we said goodbye to the herd at the same little gap in this ridge that you crossed over." He clinched his lip and shook his head and commented, "Conrad Priest ain't gonna believe the way we got our prisoner back. I just hope he's still able to stand trial."

"Hey, what the hell?" Virgil suddenly groaned.

"Yeah, he's still alive," Clayton said. "It's a damn miracle, though."

Back behind them, on the other side of the ridge, Virgil's three brothers were trying to keep the cows from going into the river. Having not seen hide nor hair of any cattle rustlers, they figured they had successfully prevented the attempted theft of the herd they had stolen from Twin Creeks Ranch. "Let's drive 'em outta these trees," Junior told Gilbert and Johnny. "Get 'em up to our end of the valley where they belong."

"They ain't gonna go nowhere," Gilbert said. "Why don't we just wait and move 'em back in the mornin' when we can see if we got all of 'em?"

"You know Pa's gonna raise hell, if we don't drive them cows back close to the house," Johnny answered him. "We leave 'em here and those rustlers will most likely say, 'thank you kindly' and come back and get 'em."

"Where the hell is Virgil?" Junior asked. "We could use a little help."

"He was followin' right behind you," Gilbert said. "He mighta seen one of them rustlers and went after him."

"His horse mighta stepped in a hole or something and throwed him off," Johnny said. "We oughta go look for him. He might be layin' up somewhere with a broke leg. Pa will raise hell if we don't find him."

"Yeah, I reckon we oughta," Junior said. "But if we waste half the night out here lookin' for him and find out he just went home, I'm gonna kick his butt."

They split up then and started riding back and forth through the woods and along the riverbank, but there was no sign of Virgil, even now with the help of a full moon. Finally, they came to the conclusion that he wasn't there. He had ridden off somewhere, following one of the rustlers possibly, and maybe his body was in the river somewhere. "He ain't here," Junior declared. "Ain't no sense to keep lookin' in the same places over and over. He ain't here, and it ain't no fault of ours. We might as well go tell Pa Virgil's gone again." So they started rounding up the cows and moving them back to the other end of the valley.

Once they got the cattle back where they were supposed to be, they went to the barn to see if Virgil's horse was there. When they found that it wasn't, Junior said, "Better not take our saddles off yet. Pa might send us right back out to look for Virgil." So they left the horses saddled while they went into the cabin.

"I shoulda gone with you," Henry complained upon hearing that Virgil was missing.

"It wouldn'ta made no difference, Pa," Junior told him. "It was so dark down there near the river, you couldn't see twenty feet in front of you. Virgil was followin' me, then I don't know where he went. After we ran those rustlers off, we went back over them woods by the river and we couldn't find no sign of him."

"Saddle my horse," Henry said, "we'll look one more time." He was not convinced that their search had been as thorough as they claimed. And he was concerned that Virgil might be lying out there in a gully with a broken bone or a cracked skull. After another search of the ground between their cabin and the river, Henry decided to check the other side of the river, so they forded the river. As soon as he came out on the other side, something he saw struck him as odd. There in the sand at the water's edge, the tracks of each one of their four horses were plain to see in the moonlight. But there were no other tracks. He dismounted and started walking along the edge of the water. Why, he wondered, were there no other tracks coming out of the water? If the rustlers got away by crossing the river, why were there no tracks? It occurred to him then that their visitors might not have been after the cows. They were after Virgil and that would explain why his sons decided there were only two rustlers. Maybe those two deputy marshals got horses and figured Virgil would come home before he went anywhere else. He was surprised the one he shot in the shoulder would be capable of pulling it off. And how the hell did they know where this valley was? But if he was right, even if they did just slip in here to snatch Virgil, that didn't mean they didn't believe the ruse they pulled about being robbed by someone other than the Dawsons. There was no proof they were there and that meant he and his other sons had nothing to fear regarding the ambush of the two lawmen. Therefore, he wouldn't hesitate to ride into town in the morning to see if he could find out what happened to Virgil.

CHAPTER 12

It was well into the wee hours of the morning when the weary trio rode down the deserted main street of Glory, Texas, on their way to the marshal's office and jail. When they came to the barbershop, Buster said, if he wasn't needed for anything else, he thought he would get some sleep and see them later on. Clayton thanked him for his participation in the retrieval of the missing prisoner and Bannack told him it could not have been done without his help. Bannack and Clayton continued on to the jail where they found a lamp still burning in the office. They dismounted and Bannack went to unlock the door. When he opened it, he paused for a few moments before walking quietly over to the desk and moving the shotgun out of the sleeping Daryl's reach. "Daryl," he said softly a couple of times, not wishing to alarm the young man, until Daryl finally jerked back in the chair, his hand automatically closing on the shotgun that was no longer there.

"Marshal Cochran!" Daryl exclaimed when he was

finally awake. "Boy, am I glad to see you! Did you find Virgil?"

"Yep, we found him," Bannack replied. "He's right outside. Did you have any problems?" he asked, wondering why he had been sitting there with a shotgun on the desk.

"No, sir," Daryl said. "Deputy Priest is sleeping in the first cell. Do you want me to wake him up?"

"No, let him sleep. We'll put Virgil in the second cell, then I think Deputy Clayton will probably use the other cot in the first cell. Then maybe you and I can catch a few hours in the third cell, unless you'd rather go home now."

"No, sir," Daryl said. "I'd rather stay here."

"All right, then," Bannack said, "open up cell two and three. I'll go out and help Clayton get Virgil off his horse."

When he went back outside, he found Deputy Clayton standing watch beside Virgil's horse, but having made no move to get him off the horse. "Cut me loose!" Virgil squawked. "My head's about to explode and this jackass won't cut me loose."

"I was waiting for you," Clayton said to Bannack. "I wasn't gonna take a chance on losing him again. I don't care if his head falls off."

"It's a lot easier when two of us get you off that horse, anyway," Bannack said sarcastically. "That way we can be more careful to see that you don't have any discomfort." He looked at Clayton and suggested, "I tell you what, why don't you just let me get him off and you take your six-gun out and if he tries anything, put a bullet in his head. If anybody has any questions about it, I'll verify that he was shot while trying to escape."

"You almost busted my head, you big ape," Virgil said. "They take me to court and the judge is gonna say you ain't got no jurisdiction to arrest me outside this town."

"Listen to that, Deputy," Bannack commented. "Virgil has been doin' a lot of thinkin' while he was ridin' upside down. Must have gotten some blood to his brain. I don't know, Virgil, maybe that's the way you should have always rode on a horse. But I wasn't trying to arrest you. I was just helpin' you dismount. Deputy Clayton arrested you. Now, we're gonna get you off that horse and put you back in your cage. Deputy, keep your six-gun on him while I cut him loose."

"I'll be glad to," Clayton replied, "and I hope he tries something. I'd be more than happy to shoot the SOB."

Bannack untied the rope around Virgil's boots and threw the loose end back under his horse's belly. Then he grabbed his belt and pulled him off the horse. Virgil would have fallen on the ground from riding so long with his head hanging down, but Bannack spun him around and threw him over his shoulder. He stepped up on the porch then and carried him in the door like a sack of fertilizer. Daryl was standing there holding the cell room door open for him, so he carried Virgil on into the second cell before putting him down and untying his hands. The bandage wrapped around his head was soaked red on the side of his face, a result of the blow from Bannack's rifle that knocked him off his horse. "We'll take a look at that in the morning and see if the doctor needs to look at it." Once Virgil was locked in his cell, Bannack and Clayton took the horses to the watering trough in front of the general merchandise store. Then they led them around behind the jail and tied them there, because Clem Shaw wouldn't open the stable until five o'clock. Since there was nothing else they could do until morning, they all tried to get a few hours' sleep.

With the coming of daybreak, Deputy Clayton was anxious to get to the telegraph office as soon as it opened, so he could report to his boss that he and town marshal, John Cochran, had recaptured their prisoner. He had already reported the loss of their horses and the fact that Deputy Priest was wounded. Sammy Peters found Bannack and the deputies eating breakfast and delivered a return wire instructing Clayton and Priest to stay there and that two deputies and a jail wagon would be there the next day. "Damn," Clayton exhaled after he read it, "we're done for. Me and Conrad are gonna be servin' subpoenas, summonses, and warrants for the rest of our lives. Might notta been so bad, if we hadn't lost our horses and everything." His lament caused a spark in Bannack's mind that continued to burn after breakfast when the two deputies went to reserve another room for the night in the hotel. He told them he had some business to attend to and he would see them for dinner. He was not sure enough of a possibility that had occurred to him to even suggest it, but it interested him enough to explore it, himself. So when he got back to the jail, he told Daryl he would be gone for a while and told him to remember the prisoner's dinner. Then he left before Daryl started to ask questions.

He hurried up to the stable then and saddled his horse, telling Clem there was something he had to check on, again leaving without giving details. Once again on the road to Jacksboro, he said to the buckskin, "I hope you're rested enough because we've got to make another quick trip." His mind was still working on the fact that the only way to tie the Dawson men to the ambush of the two deputies was if they had possession of the three missing horses. It had been too dark the night just past to identify the three horses, even if they had been in Dawson's corral with the other horses. It was not out of the question to assume that Henry Dawson was smart enough to have let the deputies' horses go free. So when he left the camping spot, he might have had to discourage the three horses from following him and possibly leading the law to his farm. Bannack couldn't resist checking on the possibility that what he thought possible may have really happened. Left alone, it would not have been that unusual for the horses to wander back to the campsite.

When he arrived at the creek where Clayton and Priest had stopped to rest their horses, there was no sign of the three missing horses. He rode into the little clearing where the two lawmen had built a fire. Maybe that means Dawson didn't release the horses after all and now they might be used as evidence against him. Verifying that Dawson had possession of the horses still might be difficult to prove. *I had to take a look, even though what I don't see doesn't prove anything, one way or the other,* he thought. Suddenly, the buckskin whinnied and was immediately answered by another horse farther down the creek. Bannack immediately followed the sound and rode down the creek about thirty yards where he met the three horses coming to meet him, two of them saddled and one still carrying a packsaddle. Bannack almost laughed. They wouldn't testify to Dawson's part in the holdup hoax, which Bannack was now sure of, but Priest and Clayton would be mighty glad to see them. Planning to make good time back to Glory by trading off on the horses, he tied them on a lead rope, climbed up into the saddle on Clayton's horse, and started back to Glory.

It was well into the dinner hour by the time he got back to the stable with the horses. Clem found it a miracle that he had recovered them. He told Bannack he would take care of the horses and for him to hurry to get something to eat while Sawyer's was still serving dinner. "Sawyer told the two deputies to come there for dinner and he wouldn't charge them, since all their money was stolen."

"'Preciate it, Clem," Bannack said and hurried down to the café.

"Speak of the devil," Clayton cracked when he

walked in, "here he is now. We were wonderin' when you were gonna show up again."

"Is that right?" Bannack replied, then asked Louella, who was standing beside their table, "Am I too late to get dinner?"

"Marshal Cochran, you're never too late to get dinner," she said. "If Mama's already thrown it to the hogs, I'll cook you something, myself." She pulled a chair out for him. "Sit yourself down and I'll get you some coffee."

"Thank you, ma'am," Bannack said and sat down.

"Your whole town has been mighty generous to us," Deputy Priest said. "Mr. Porter over at the hotel told us there was no charge for our rooms for the extra night tonight. And you know the doctor wouldn't charge anything for taking that bullet out of my shoulder."

Bannack smiled and replied, "I remember."

"They sure think a lot of you," Clayton commented.

"You think so?" Bannack responded. "I haven't been on the job but a short time. I don't think I've met enough of the people for them to decide if they like me or not. I think the man I replaced was so bad that anybody would have done better."

"I don't know, John," Clayton said. "You must be doin' something to impress them. Even the mayor, himself, was in here a little while ago lookin' for you."

"What did he want?" Bannack asked. "He mighta wanted to remind me that I don't have any jurisdiction outside the town limits. I hope you told him you were keepin' an eye on things till I got back."

"No, he wanted to tell you that you did a good job,

putting Virgil Dawson back in jail after we let him get away. I shoulda told him that we have the authority to deputize you to make arrests out in the county. Where were you, anyway? That young fellow in your office, what's his name? He didn't even know where you were. We took Virgil to the doctor so he could take a look at his head, so he's got a new bandage on it."

"I went to get your horses," Bannack said so casually that they didn't understand what he meant.

"How's that again?" Clayton asked.

"Your horses," Bannack repeated. "I rode up to that creek to get your horses. I figured you might want 'em back." He immediately had their attention.

"You got 'em?" Conrad Priest demanded. "You got our horses back? Where are they?"

"I took 'em to the stable," Bannack answered. "Clem's takin' care of 'em." He paused then to let Louella set a plate of food in front of him. "Thank you, ma'am." Back to the two deputies who were exchanging looks of disbelief, he said. "'Course, that makes it kind of hard to prove that Virgil's pappy and brothers were the four men that stole the horses."

"You got our horses," Conrad said again, this time not a question but a statement of amazement.

Bannack went on to tell them that it was a matter of curiosity that prompted him to see if their horses were set free and, if so, would they return to the creek they were taken from. "I gotta give my horse the credit for findin' 'em, though. I was about ready to turn around and come back, but my horse knew they were there, and he announced it. They answered him. So maybe you want to call on your boss again and tell him they don't need to send extra horses."

Neither one of the deputies spoke again for a few brief moments as they both thought about that recent turn of events. Finally, Clayton spoke. "It depends on how Priest feels, since he's the one who's shot, but I'm thinking about wiring the boss and tellin' him to forget about sendin' anybody with a jail wagon. And me and Conrad will bring the prisoner back, ourselves, just like we were assigned to do." He looked at his partner. "What do you think, Conrad? Are you up to it?"

"Well, he shot me in my right shoulder," Priest answered. "I reckon he didn't notice I'm left handed and I still got my gun hand. I ain't feelin' too bad right now, but I'm afraid you'd have to do most of the work. It might be too much for you to keep track of and do all the work, too."

"Yeah, it might be a little too much, if we're ambushed again," Clayton allowed. "'Course, that would really be bad luck to get ambushed again. If we weren't, it wouldn't be that much of a problem. You could watch the prisoner while I make the camp. It would make it a lot easier if we had one more man with us. Then let 'em try that again and we'd be ready for 'em."

It was rather obvious what they were hinting at, but Bannack didn't take the bait. "If you need an extra man, I reckon the county would pay him the same mileage rate there and back it pays a deputy marshal, right?"

"Oh, yes, sir," Clayton quickly agreed. "He'd be paid the same as we're paid."

"Well, that would help a little," Bannack said. "I'll ask Daryl if he'd like to pick up some extra money. He might be interested because Lord knows he doesn't make much workin' for me." When both Clayton and Priest started rapidly shaking their heads, Bannack spoke again. "No? Well, you could check with Buster. For a barber, he's a pretty good volunteer for anything risky."

"All right," Clayton said. "You know damn well who we're interested in, so whadda you say? I don't expect to see that bunch that attacked us again, but if you were with us, I wouldn't care if we did. And that's the fact of the matter. Right, Conrad?" Priest nodded to confirm it.

"I'll tell you the truth," Bannack told them. "I wouldn't mind takin' a ride up to Jacksboro with you, since you're shorthanded. But I've got a job here as the town marshal. And that job is to keep this town safe. I'll remind you that I just got this job, so I don't know what the men on the town council who hired me would think about me leaving the town without a marshal for a whole day. So what I'm tellin' you is you're askin' the wrong person. I work for the mayor and his council. Ask him, and if he says yes, I'd be happy to go with you. If he says no, then I expect I'd best keep my job and wish you boys the best of luck."

"We'll go talk to Mr. Glory right now while you're eatin'," Clayton said. "Come on, Conrad. It'll help for him to see you're wounded." He got up from the table.

"Thank you, kind ladies for that wonderful dinner." He and Priest thanked Russell Sawyer on their way out the door, then hurried down the street to talk to Walter Glory at Glory General Merchandise.

Bannack finished his dinner and prepared to pay Russell, but Sawyer said it wasn't fair to charge him for his meal when they let the two deputies eat free. Bannack insisted on paying, however. "I didn't have all my money stolen," he said. "There ain't no reason to let me eat free."

"I got three women in here that think I oughta let you eat free anytime you come in here," Sawyer said, "and I find it hard to disagree with 'em. I'll tell you what, I'll give you a special charge of half-price anytime you eat here. Is that fair enough?"

"That's mighty generous of you, Mr. Sawyer. I thank you very much." He paid half-price for his dinner and left to go to the jail.

He paused outside the café to let a lady and her daughter pass by him on the boardwalk. The lady looked up at him with a warm smile and said, "Good afternoon, Marshal Cochran."

Her greeting caught him by surprise. He wasn't expecting it. Most often, a woman and her young daughter would have a tendency to shrink back against the building to give him plenty of space. He was well aware of the impression he made when first met by strangers. "Good afternoon," he returned as friendly as he could make it sound. It was a brief encounter, but he found that he liked it. Maybe being a marshal in a small town wasn't a bad way to make a living. As he walked across the street toward the marshal's office, he looked down the street to see if Clayton and Priest might be on their way back. There was no sign of them, so he figured they didn't get a quick answer from Walter Glory.

When he walked into his office, Daryl jumped up to greet him. "I'm glad to see you back," he exclaimed.

"Why?" Bannack asked. "What's wrong?"

"Nothing," Daryl answered. "There was just a lot going on and I didn't know where you went and people would ask me. Deputies Clayton and Priest didn't even know where you were. They had to go get Dr. Taylor to take a look at Virgil's head."

"Well, they should have," Bannack said, "he's their prisoner. Did you get him fed?" Daryl said he did. "Did you get dinner?"

"Yes, sir, and they went to Sawyer's for dinner, but I don't know where they are now." He looked as if he was about to wring his fingers in frustration.

"Everything's all right," Bannack said. "You did your job. I saw Clayton and Priest over at Sawyer's, and they went up to Glory's store. They'll most likely be back here pretty soon." He went on then to tell him where he had been all morning and that the deputies had recovered their horses. "So they might be at the telegraph office now, wiring Jacksboro not to bring any horses down here tomorrow."

He was in the cell room taking a quick check on Virgil when the two deputies came back to the jail, so he went back to the office to hear how their request to

Walter Glory had fared. "He didn't think much of the idea," Clayton said. "He took us to the bank to talk to Mr. Prentis to see what he thought about you leaving for one whole day. Prentis was dead set against it. They said they finally had a marshal they could count on to protect the town and that meant every day." Clayton shook his head then. "I've gotta wire my boss about the horses, and I can't decide to tell him to send a wagon or not."

"You got any objections about ridin' at night?" Bannack asked him. Clayton didn't answer right away. He looked at Priest instead to see his reaction. Bannack didn't wait for an answer. "It seems to me that's the easiest way to get around this whole problem. If you want to do that, I'll go with you. We'll just wait till the town's all closed down for the night. Then we'll load Virgil up on his horse and head for Jacksboro. We can ride as far as you like before stoppin' to rest the horses. Stop at the same place you got robbed, if you want to. We ain't likely to run into anybody in the middle of the night. Then when we move on from there, and get a little closer to town, I don't see any need for me to go all the way into Jacksboro with you. I don't know if Henry Dawson is crazy enough to try to rescue his son again or not. But if he is, he's gonna figure you're gonna leave in the mornin' after breakfast, just like before. And when he and his boys leave the cabin to go to the ambush spot, you'll already be in Jacksboro."

"I'm a hundred percent in favor of that plan," Clayton responded. "How 'bout you, Conrad?" Priest just grinned and nodded his head. "Whadda you reckon your mayor will say about that?" Clayton thought aloud.

"I doubt he'll think about it at all, if we don't tell him," Bannack replied. "Like I said, I'll close up the town for the night, just like I always do. I just won't go to bed. I'll be back when the town's wakin' up again. We'll just have to gamble on the chance there won't be a fire or bank robbery in the middle of the night, and it seems to me that's worth gambling on."

"I swear, John Cochran, you're one helluva town marshal," Clayton said. "I've worked with a few, and Conrad will tell you this, there ain't none of 'em that'll stick their neck out to help like you have."

"I just ain't got much use for Virgil and the rest of his family, I reckon," Bannack said. "I don't wanna see him miss out on his chance to stand trial."

"I'm sure I speak for Conrad as well as myself when I say thank you for all your help, everything you've done, to put two ol' deputy marshals back in business. I'm going back to the telegraph office and send the wire to tell headquarters we'll be droppin' off our prisoner early tomorrow mornin' at the county jail."

"I'll go talk to Clem to let him know we're going to be comin' for our horses just before he closes tonight," Bannack said. "I'll tell him to keep it quiet, we don't want anybody in town to know we're leavin' tonight. I didn't check your packhorse to see what was left in your packs, if anything was. I know you don't have any money to buy any coffee or bacon or something to get you through the night. I'll see what I've got in my packs.

We've got some coffee here in the office, but that's about all we've got. Clem stays there at the stable pretty late, so we'll just leave the horses behind the jail after we pick 'em up."

"Well, ain't he got a lotta nerve?" The words dropped out of his mouth before he realized he was saying them out loud.

"Ain't who got a lotta nerve?" Smut Smith asked as he poured Buster Bridges another shot of whiskey.

"Henry Dawson, that's who," Buster said. "Sittin' back there at that table like a judge or something. Ain't that the same table that sorry son of his was sittin' at when he pulled out his pistol and shot that cowhand in the face?"

"The one next to it," Smut said. "I heard this mornin' that Virgil Dawson is back in the Glory jail."

"That's a fact," Buster said. He wanted to tell Smut how he knew it was a fact, but John Cochran had sworn him to secrecy.

"I can't figure how they got him arrested again so quick after that gang ambushed those two lawmen and stole their horses," Smut said. "I'd like to hear that story."

"Yep, that's mighty peculiar, all right," Buster remarked while feeling like he was going to bust if he didn't get to tell it soon. But Bannack had told him he had to keep shut about it until Virgil was safely in the county jail in Jacksboro. He continued to stare at

Henry Dawson and suddenly another thought struck him. *Maybe Henry doesn't know if his son is in the jail or not!* All he probably knows is that Virgil is missing. He never showed up last night. He's in town for no other reason than to find out if it was the law who kidnapped his son right out of his own backyard. He couldn't help chuckling over the thought of it.

"What's so funny?" Smut asked.

"Some days, everything is," Buster replied. "You just gotta see the humor in it." He placed some coins on the bar for his whiskey. "I better get back to my shop. Somebody might be waiting for a haircut." He started for the door but paused, unable to resist the urge, so he turned around and walked back to the table where Dawson was sitting. "He's in the jail, if that's what's eatin' you." Then he turned around and walked out of the saloon.

"Why, you sawed off little . . ." Henry started to get up and go after him but decided this was not the time to call attention to himself. If Virgil was, in fact, back in that jail, then there was no attempt to rustle his cattle. And he was in no mood to appreciate the irony of a fake cattle rustle to recapture Virgil after his fake robbery to free him. Of one other thing he was also certain, the deputy marshals might have been involved in the snatching of his son last night, but the man who actually did the deed had to be Marshal John Cochran. It just seemed to be his style. Buster Bridges was probably right when he said Virgil was back in jail, but Dawson had to be sure of it, so he could decide what to do about it. One way to find out was to go to the jail and ask to see his son. There was no reason why he couldn't. No one had approached him to question him and his other sons about the fake holdup and without anyone who could identify the robbers, Cochran had nothing to go on. When he thought about it, he decided that was what an innocent father would do. He got up from the table and with the bottle of whiskey he had just bought in hand, he walked out the door and headed for the jail.

CHAPTER 13

"Hey, Marshal Cochran, you ain't gonna believe who's coming to see us," Daryl said. He was standing by the door, looking out at the street. When Bannack didn't seem interested enough to ask who, Daryl said, "Mr. Henry Dawson is coming this way and he's carrying a bottle of whiskey."

That was enough to capture Bannack's attention. He got up and walked over beside Daryl to see for himself. Henry Dawson was in fact walking in their direction and when he turned directly toward their door, Bannack said, "Well, let's make him welcome." And he went back and sat down at his desk. Daryl opened the door for Dawson. "Well, Mr. Dawson," Bannack greeted him. "I didn't expect to see you today."

"I don't know why not," Dawson replied. "I heard you've got my boy in jail again."

"Is that so? Where'd you hear that?"

"Buster Bridges," Dawson answered.

"Buster Bridges," Bannack repeated. "He seems to

know just about everything that's goin' on in Glory, doesn't he?"

"Too much to suit me," Dawson said, "but is he right? Is Virgil back in this damn jail again?"

"Yes, sir, he sure is, but he just came back for a short visit. We're only gonna keep him for a couple of days till they can send a jail wagon down here to take him back. You see, he still has to go to that murder trial in Jacksboro. As you know, he got delayed yesterday because some two-bit outlaws attacked the two deputy marshals who were transportin' him up there. They shot deputy Conrad Priest and stole their horses. I'll bet you were surprised when he showed up at your house yesterday. I was kinda surprised, though, that a man of your integrity didn't bring him into the jail yesterday to set an example for the rest of your fine sons."

"I expect if I was to ask him who arrested him this time, he'd most likely say it was you again, wouldn't he?" Dawson asked. "The first time you arrested him, you broke his nose and damn near crushed his face. I suppose he got hurt this time, too."

"Not too bad," Bannack said. "I think he bumped his head when he fell off his horse. That was about it."

"And you ain't got no jurisdiction outside the town limits," Dawson said. "You ain't supposed to make any arrest out in the county."

"Actually, it wasn't my arrest. It was the deputy marshal's arrest. He deputized me to work in the county, so I just went along for the ride. They didn't need my help."

Dawson favored him with a knowing smile. "Right," he said. "So, whadda you say? Can I visit my son?" He held up the half-empty bottle of whiskey. "I thought I'd like to have one last drink of likker with him before they take him to that trial. Any harm in that?"

"I reckon not," Bannack said. "That sounds like a fine way to wish your boy luck. Same rules as before, though. Leave your weapons out here and a fifteen-minute limit on the visit." Dawson unbuckled his gun belt and handed it to him. "It's easy to forget about that little pocket pistol a lot of men carry," Bannack reminded him.

"Yes, it is," Dawson agreed and pulled his out of his vest pocket. "I forgot I had it."

Bannack placed the weapons on his desk and told Daryl to open the cell room door. "You want me to go sit in the cell room?" Daryl asked.

"No, I don't think that will be necessary," Bannack told him. "We'll just leave the door open so we can see them talkin'." Daryl opened the door between the office and the cell room and told a surprised Virgil Dawson that he had a visitor. Virgil got up from his cot and came to the cell door as soon as he saw who it was.

"Papa!" Virgil exclaimed. "I didn't think they'd let you come to visit me this time."

"Why not?" Henry responded in a show of bravado. "Hell, I told that damn crazy marshal I wanted to take a drink of likker with my son before they haul you outta here again." He held the bottle up for him to see. "Hell, maybe he'll let you keep the bottle. Then if you don't drink it all, you could take a drink with your brothers tomorrow, if they come to see you." He passed the bottle through the bars, and Virgil took it.

"Ain't gonna be no use for anybody to come to see me tomorrow," Virgil said. "I ain't gonna be here."

"Why ain't you?" Henry asked. "He said you was gonna be here a couple more days till they send a jail wagon down here to take you back."

"I don't know why he told you that," Virgil said. "Daryl told me to be ready to go after breakfast tomorrow mornin', 'cause them two deputies are takin' me to Jacksboro tomorrow. They got their horses back and the one you shot said he was ready to ride."

"How the hell did they get their horses back?" Henry asked. "We turned them horses loose after we turned off the Jacksboro road."

"I don't know," Virgil replied. "The marshal brought 'em back. I don't know how he found 'em."

"That lyin' son of a . . ." his father started. "He didn't know that sissy feller, Daryl, told you you was leavin' here tomorrow. He told me you was gonna be here for two more days, just to make sure I didn't try anything tomorrow when they take you to Jacksboro. He knows damn well it was me and the boys that sprung you loose the first time. He just can't prove it." He lowered his voice, even though he knew they couldn't hear him in the office. "This time, it ain't gonna be no robbery. You might have to take a little trip for a while, but there ain't gonna be no witnesses left to point a finger at us. And

Marshal Cochran will know who set you free, but he still won't be able to prove it."

After approximately fifteen minutes had passed, Henry walked to the door and asked, "My time's about up. Is it okay if I leave what's left in this bottle with Virgil?"

"Yeah, I don't care," Bannack answered, "as long as there ain't enough in it to get him drunk."

"That's mighty considerate of you, Marshal," Henry commented as he put his pocket pistol away in his vest and strapped on his gun belt. "I don't know any other sheriff or marshal that is as considerate as that."

"Might as well make his last few days with us as comfortable as possible," Bannack said.

"Good day to you, Marshal," Henry said smugly and walked out the door. He could imagine he could feel Bannack's frustration over having no strong evidence to place him under arrest. It added to his sense of control.

"Mr. Dawson," Bannack replied, politely.

The rest of the afternoon was spent making sure everything was ready for their departure that night, especially the horses. Taking no chances, Bannack took Virgil's horse to Jake Tracey, the blacksmith, to replace the shoes on the horse's front feet. They were worn so badly that he was afraid the horse might throw a shoe. The two deputies returned to the hotel to again thank Fred Bradley for offering the two rooms free of charge for the night, but they told him they had decided to sleep in the jail. They were careful not to admit that they were not really going to sleep in the jail but were going to leave town in the middle of the night and take the marshal with them. As much as Marshal Cochran had done for them, they surely didn't want to cost him his job. However, they did accept the hotel dining room's offer of supper at no charge.

Bannack sent Daryl to the dining room as soon as they opened, so he could eat supper and bring Virgil's supper back for him. Then Bannack and the two deputies went up to the hotel to eat. He was no longer concerned about questions they might have about his past. There were too many other subjects more important to discuss. Charley Riley welcomed them warmly and Carol and Dora both gave them plenty of attention. "I'll tell you one thing," Dora remarked. "If anybody's ever thinking about trying to rob the dining room, I hope it's tonight. We got three lawmen sittin' here waiting for trouble, even though one of 'em's got a crippled wing."

"I declare, Dora," Carol said, "sometimes you say some of the dumbest things." She filled their coffee cups for the third time. "You boys are sure drinking a lot of coffee. You might not be able to go to sleep at all tonight."

All three men laughed. "Maybe not," Clayton replied.

After supper, they returned to the jail to wait out the evening. Bannack suggested the two deputies could catch a few hours' sleep in one of the cells, but neither one felt the necessity. "I'm sorry we can't start out right now," Bannack told them, "but I feel like I have to make sure the town's all right before I leave it for the night. I'm about ready to make my early walk around while the shops are closin' down, and I can take a look in the saloons to see if there looks like any potential trouble."

So he went back outside and took a casual walk from one end of town to the other, checking to see if doors were locked or if anybody was working late. He walked into the River House saloon, the town's busiest, to find a modest crowd, mostly made up of local men, stopping in for a drink on their way home. Buster Bridges was standing at the bar, talking to Smut Smith, the bartender. "Howdy, Marshal," Smut greeted him. "Pour you a drink?"

"No, thanks, Smut," Bannack replied. "I reckon not."

"What's the matter, John?" Buster asked. "You gettin' short on cash? I'll buy you a shot."

"Thanks anyway, Buster," Bannack replied. "I just ain't cravin' one right now."

"I saw Henry Dawson in here earlier this afternoon," Buster said. "Did you get a visit from him over at the jail?"

"Yes, I did, and I'd bet that you mighta had something to do with his decision to come visit his son."

"He already had an idea Virgil was back in your jail," Buster said. "All I did was tell him I'd heard the same thing somewhere."

"He had a nice visit with his son," Bannack said. "Brought a bottle of whiskey with him, and father and son had a quiet drink together. It'll give them something to remember after Virgil's gone off to prison or the gallows and Henry's sittin' at home by the fire with all the grandchildren his other three sons have fathered."

"I swear," Buster said, "you're in a downright cynical mood tonight, ain'tcha?"

"Nope," Bannack said. "I was just trying to paint a pretty word picture for you, so you wouldn't think bad thoughts about the Dawsons. Anyway, things look peaceful enough here in the River House saloon, so I think I'll go check on the other two saloons." He turned around and walked out.

"I'll tell you what," Smut said after Bannack went out the door, "I feel one helluva lot safer at night ever since the town council hired that grizzly bear as the town marshal."

His comment prompted Buster to once again tell the story of how he first met John Cochran before anyone else in Glory knew him. "I was haulin' my barber chair here from Fort Worth, and I stopped to rest my horses. And these two jaspers had been followin' me ever since the Fort Worth road, wantin' to see what I was haulin'. I told 'em it weren't nothin' they'd be interested in. So they decided they was gonna have a look, anyway, and started pepperin' my wagon with rifle shots . . ." Smut stopped listening at that point. He'd already heard Buster's story enough times to know it word for word.

Bannack made brief stops at the Lucky Sixes and Riker's saloon at opposite ends of the street and found them to be relatively quiet as well as the River House. *So far, so good,* he thought and hoped that the evening would continue that way. He returned to the jail then, where he found Clayton and Priest killing time playing penny ante poker with Daryl. "I thought you two might be getting a couple hours' sleep," Bannack said.

Priest said he laid down on one of the cots and tried to sleep, but he wasn't successful. "I didn't even try," Clayton said. "I knew I wouldn't be able to go to sleep. I'm too anxious to get on the road. I'll sleep after we get that jasper to Jacksboro."

"I reckon we can walk on up to the stable and get the horses now, anyway," Bannack suggested. "Clem oughta be gettin' ready to close up for the night any time now." His suggestion was met with a considerable measure of enthusiasm from the two deputies, such was their boredom with the waiting. He was tempted to tell them it wasn't necessary to wait any longer, but he wasn't willing to leave the town until he saw the saloons closing down for the night.

Clem Shaw greeted them when they came into the stable. "Evenin', fellows," he said. "Still plannin' on takin' that ride tonight?" When Bannack answered that they were there to get the horses, Clem said, "Well, they're all ready to go. Fed, watered, and that roan of Virgil's is wearin' new shoes. Jake brought him back a couple of hours ago."

"Much obliged," Bannack said. "We'll take 'em off your hands now." They led the horses out and picked up their saddles. "Let me give you a hand," he said to Priest, who still had his right arm in a sling.

Clem saddled Virgil's horse and Clayton saddled the

packhorse. "I see you added some more chuck to what we had, John," Clayton said. "I'm especially glad to see the coffee. I'm tempted to start a fire in this hay in Clem's barn and build a pot right now."

"I needed to get that coffee out of my packs and use it in the office, but I kept forgetting to do it. It oughta still be good. It's some I bought just a little while back. At the time I bought it, I had no idea I'd be wastin' it on a couple Deputy US Marshals," he joked.

When all the horses were saddled, they led them out of the stable and Bannack reminded Clem that he didn't want the word to get out that they were taking Virgil out of the jail that night. "And whatever you do, if you see Buster tonight, don't tell him. He's liable to come after us if he finds out." Clem laughed and told him there wasn't much chance he'd see Buster tonight because he was going to go straight home. He wasn't going to drop in at the River House for a nightcap. So they said goodnight to Clem and rode the horses back to the jail where they led them around behind the building and tied them. The town closed down very quickly soon after that with only a couple of places with lights still on, since Riker's saloon had closed earlier than usual. When Bannack returned to the jail after making his final round of the town, he reported everything was peaceful.

"What the hell?" Virgil protested when he was rousted out of a sound sleep by Deputy Clayton. "What are you doin'?" He squawked when the deputy rolled him over on his cot, pulled his hands behind his back, and clapped the handcuffs on him. "What's goin' on?"

"We're gonna take a little ride," Clayton told him. "It's a nice cool night out with the moon still almost full. It'll be a perfect night to take a ride."

"I don't wanna take no damn ride," Virgil insisted. "Where's that big cat? You ain't supposed to disturb my sleep!"

"Oh, don't worry," Clayton said, knowing who he was referring to, "he's goin' with us. Matter of fact, takin' a midnight ride was his idea."

Virgil wasn't convinced that there was no evil intent on the part of the deputy marshals. His first thought was the taking of revenge for the ambush his father and brothers had staged to free him and the wounding of Deputy Priest and the theft of their horses, weapons, and money. He rolled off the cot, onto the floor, then tried to roll under his cot. When Clayton had a hard time getting him untangled from the cot, Bannack walked into the cell, picked the cot up off Virgil, then grabbed his belt and jerked him up on his feet. "What the hell's the matter with you?" Bannack demanded. "We're goin' to Jacksboro to take you to the county jail. If you don't behave yourself, we'll let you ride belly down on your saddle, like you rode into town."

"I'll behave! I'll behave!" Virgil pleaded. "I thought they was fixin' to hang me."

"That would be a whole lot easier than havin' to haul your no-good butt all the way to Jacksboro," Bannack said, "but they are officers of the law, so they play by the rules. That's something you and that den of wolves you come from don't understand."

Now that he was reasonably sure they were not taking him outside to hang him, Virgil let himself be led outside the jail by Deputy Clayton. Deputy Priest followed along behind him, his revolver drawn and trained on Virgil's back. Bannack waited a couple of minutes to talk to Daryl. "You gonna be all right here till I get back in the mornin'?" Daryl thought that he would. "'Cause you can go home if you'd rather. Just lock the place up."

"What time do you think you'll be back?" Daryl asked.

"Well, if things go as I expect them to, I'm plannin' on gettin' back here in time to go to breakfast with you," Bannack told him.

"I'll just stay here tonight, then," Daryl decided.

"All right," Bannack said, "I'll see you in the mornin'." He went outside to join the others, finding them in a minor standoff behind the jailhouse. "What's the problem?" he asked, since no one was on a horse yet.

"I gotta pee," Virgil answered, "and they won't let me."

"That ain't so," Clayton declared. "We told him to go ahead and pee."

"They got my hands behind my back," Virgil complained. "I can't do nothin' with my hands behind my back. I asked 'em to help me out, but they won't help me."

"Hell, no, I ain't helpin' him," Clayton said. "He can just pee in his pants."

"Look, Deputy, why don't you just cuff his hands in front of him for this trip?" Bannack suggested. "Then he can take care of business without anyone's help. It'll make it a lot easier for him to ride, so we can make better time. One of us will be leading him with his horse's reins, so he can't do nothing but sit there. And one of us can ride behind him, too, to shoot him if he does try something."

Clayton looked at Priest and they both shrugged. "I reckon that would work all right," Clayton said and unlocked Virgil's wrists, then cuffed them in front of him. Virgil promptly took care of business, then dutifully climbed up into the saddle. When he was comfortable, Clayton took a short piece of rope, tied one end around one of Virgil's boots, then pulled it under his horse's belly and tied it to his other boot. "I was transportin' a prisoner from Austin to Waco one time," he said. "Had his hands cuffed behind his back. We was ridin' along the top of this ridge and all of a sudden, he jumped off his horse, landed on the downslope of that ridge and tumbled all the way to the bottom. Broke his shoulder when he landed on that slope. I've been tyin' their feet together ever since."

"Interestin' story," Bannack remarked. "This is your parade, deputies. How do you want to do it?"

"Well," Clayton responded, "it don't make a lot of difference, I reckon. Why don't we start out with you takin' the lead, Marshal, and you can lead our packhorse. Then I'll come behind you, leadin' the prisoner's horse. And ol' one-wing Priest can bring up the rear and watch Virgil's back. Is that all right with everybody?"

No one objected. "We can switch around after a while if you want to."

Bannack climbed up into the saddle. "Everybody ready?" Everybody was, so he guided the buckskin gelding out from behind the jail and led the somber procession up the deserted main street, heading for Jacksboro.

CHAPTER 14

As Deputy Clayton had remarked earlier, there was still most of a full moon hovering over the Brazos River when they passed Clem Shaw's stable again and left the sleeping town of Glory behind them. Bannack was able to see a good distance down the road before him as he held the buckskin to a comfortable lope, intent upon eating up the miles in a hurry before easing him back to a walk. As a result, in good time they approached the creek where Clayton and Priest had been ambushed. Since it was an excellent place to rest the horses, they decided to stop there again, in spite of the deputies' experience there before. There was almost a zero possibility that the Dawsons would anticipate the night trip to Jacksboro. There was also the presence of Marshal John Cochran, which both deputies felt added to their defensive prowess. As far as Bannack was concerned, he felt certain Henry Dawson would not be there before nine or ten o'clock the next day. So, with an eye on Deputy Priest's watch, they watered and rested the horses at the creek and made a pot of coffee to help them all stay alert.

"This is one creek I'll always remember," Conrad Priest announced. "Has it got a name?"

Bannack shrugged before he answered. "Buster Bridges told me the local folks call it Razor Creek." When Priest asked why they called it that, Bannack said, "Supposedly because it cuts such a sharp line through this heavy growth of trees."

"I can see that," Priest said. "It's a good name for it."

"I reckon," Bannack replied. "Keep in mind, I said Buster told me that."

They left the creek and pushed on until they were within two to three miles of the town limits of Jacksboro, which prompted Bannack to pull his horse to a stop. "I don't think even Henry Dawson is crazy enough to come this far to ambush you again," he told Clayton. "So I reckon I'll turn around here and go back to my little town. I'll tie your packhorse on behind Deputy Priest's horse."

"Marshal Cochran, Conrad and I owe you one helluva lot," Clayton said. "And I hope you know how much we appreciate it."

"That's a fact, John," Priest said. "There ain't no way a town marshal or sheriff could do as much as you did to recover and replace so much of what Bill and I lost on this damn prisoner transport. It looks like we just wasted your time on this midnight ride tonight, but it woulda been pretty rough on the two of us, if we had guessed wrong and you hadn't come with us. I know you've got to get back to Glory, otherwise, I'd invite you to come on into town with us, so we could buy you a big breakfast before you ride back."

"Ain't you forgot?" Clayton asked Priest. "You're broke. Virgil's pappy stole all our money."

"Hell, that's right. I forgot about that. Anyway, it's the thought that counts. Ain't that right, John?"

"You're absolutely right," Bannack said.

"But I know I'm gonna let everybody in headquarters know what a fine job you're doin' as marshal in that town," Priest said. "You're doin' one helluva job, and it won't hurt to let 'em know your name."

"I 'preciate what you're sayin', Deputy, but I don't need to get my name too well known. First thing you know, I'd have gunslingers comin' to Glory to look me up." He shook hands with both of them, then turned the buckskin around and started back the way they had come. According to Priest's watch, he had plenty of time to get back before Dawson set up an ambush, if he had one in mind.

It was still fairly early in the morning when Bannack reached Razor Creek again, but he approached it cautiously just the same. There was no one there, as he expected, and his horse deserved a stop for water and a little grazing. However, Bannack saw no sense in tempting fate. He was dealing with a crazy man. That much he was certain of, so he continued on to the smaller creek that was only about five miles from Glory. It was not as nice a camping area, but it had water and grass, so he would rest the buckskin there and then ride on into town.

It was close to seven-thirty when Bannack finally rode into town, so he stopped as soon as he came to the stable. "You just gettin' back in town, Marshal?" Clem asked when Bannack stepped down from the buckskin.

"Yep, I thought I'd get back before you opened, but I got to feelin' sorry for my horse and let up on him."

"Virgil and the two deputy marshals get where they wanted to go?"

"Well, I reckon the deputies got to where they wanted to go," Bannack answered. "I don't know about Virgil. I expect he had half a dozen places he'd rather have gone to."

Clem chuckled. "I expect so. Just want you to know, though, I ain't said a word about you boys haulin' Virgil outta town in the middle of the night. Not to nobody."

"'Preciate it, Clem. I figured I could count on you."

He left the stable and went to the jail where he found Daryl in the office. "Mornin', Daryl," he said when he walked in the door, "sorry I didn't get back in time for breakfast with you."

"Morning," Daryl returned. "I didn't eat yet. I was waiting for you to get back."

"Well, let's get on up to the hotel," Bannack said. "The dinin' room ain't closed yet, but it will be if we

don't hustle up." They locked the office and left right
away.

"Good morning, Marshal, Daryl," Charley Riley
greeted them both. "I was wondering if anybody from
the marshal's office was gonna show up this morning.
You're running a little later than usual."

"Yes, we are," Bannack responded. "We don't have
a prisoner to feed this mornin' and I reckon we were
just not noticin' how late it was gettin'."

"Carol's already gone to fetch your coffee," Charley
said, having noticed the young girl turn and head for
the kitchen when she saw them come in the door. They
walked on back to the table they usually occupied,
close to the kitchen door, and Carol brought the coffee.
She looked at Daryl and asked, "The usual?"

"Yes, ma'am, I reckon," Daryl answered.

"One order of hot cakes coming up," Carol replied.
"How 'bout you, Marshal? What you gonna have this
morning?"

"Hot cakes sound good this mornin'," Bannack said.
He was hungry after riding all night. "But I'm gonna
need some eggs and bacon with that."

"I was gonna say the same thing," Dora said as she
came out of the kitchen. "A man your size needs more
than hot cakes."

Carol hoped Dora would restrain from her usual
playful remarks until they all got to know Marshal John
Cochran a little better. The man's solemn expression
was almost menacing, and yet he was always polite and
patient. Carol remembered Dora's comment after the

first time he came into the dining room to eat. She said she knew how the man at the circus felt when he had to feed the lion. "How do you want those eggs, Marshal?" Carol asked.

"Scrambled," Bannack answered. "I like the way Mrs. James scrambles them."

Carol smiled. "I'll tell Evelyn you said that."

Bannack formed a smile in return. He liked Evelyn's scrambled eggs because they were done the same way Lottie Grimsley prepared them when he was living at Judge Wick Justice's house in Austin. It now seemed a hundred years ago. He realized his mind was wandering back before he was John Cochran when Daryl asked him about the trip to Jacksboro. "It was totally uneventful," he told Daryl. "I didn't go all the way into town with them, and then it was just a ride straight back here. No trouble a-tall."

There was trouble, but it was just in the beginning stages of forming as Henry Dawson led his three sons to Razor Creek at the Jacksboro Road crossing. "Papa, don't you think it'd be a better idea to ambush 'em somewhere else?" When his father asked why, Junior said, "'Cause this is where we robbed 'em last time. They might be extra careful when they ride through here."

"We're waitin' for 'em here because this place has the best cover for us to hide behind," Henry told him. "It don't make no difference if they're spooked ridin' through here or not. They still gotta ride past us and we're just gonna shoot 'em down before they know what hit 'em. Just be sure of your target and make sure you don't shoot your brother."

"I don't know, Pa," Gilbert japed. "This might be a good opportunity to get rid of a lot of trouble at the same time, if we shoot ol' Virgil and the deputies, too."

"Don't talk like that about your brother," Henry scolded. "What if it was you in that fix?"

"Only Virgil gets hisself into fixes like this," Gilbert said. "He oughta have to git himself out of 'em."

"Quit your bellyachin' and find you a spot to shoot from and don't get directly across from none of the rest of us," Henry said. "They told Virgil to be ready to ride right after breakfast. I expect they'll be showin' up here before very much longer. So pick your places and get ready to wait." Once he saw each of his sons in a good place to shoot from and he was satisfied that they wouldn't be shooting at each other, he picked his spot. Then he made sure they all knew where he was, so the targets would be lawmen and not Dawsons. Now there was nothing to do but wait. So wait they did, one hour, two hours. No one but an old man driving a two-wheel cart, drove past the creek during that time. All three sons laid their front sights on the old fellow. They were tempted to pull the trigger, just to break the monotony.

Another hour passed and Junior stood up from the screen of bushes he had hidden behind. "They ain't comin', Pa! And I'm 'bout to starve to death. Who told you they was takin' Virgil to Jacksboro today?"

"Virgil did!" Henry yelled back. "He said they told him to be ready to ride right after breakfast 'cause he was goin' to Jacksboro."

"Well, they woulda sure as hell been here by now," Junior said. "They lied. They ain't plannin' to take him nowhere today."

"Get the horses," Henry ordered. "We'll ride on into town. If we meet them lawmen comin' outta town, we'll shoot 'em down right there in the road. If we don't meet 'em, I'm gonna pay that marshal a visit and find out what's goin' on." They came out of their hiding places and went to get their horses, all except Johnny. "Where's Johnny?" Henry asked. Junior and Gilbert both shook their heads, so they walked back to the trees he had chosen to protect himself and found him fast asleep, a half-empty whiskey bottle still in his hand.

When they reported it to their father, he said, "That sorry, no-good drunk. Just leave him be. He weren't gonna be no help, anyway." So they left him sleeping, got on their horses, and headed toward Glory. When they got a little closer to the town, they met a two-horse wagon driven by a farmer who gave them a wide berth and a nervous nod in passing, which pleased the three of them. But there was no sign of the two deputies and their brother. It was well past dinnertime when they finally rode into Glory, so they were too late to eat at the hotel or Sawyer's Café. Of the three saloons in town, only the Lucky Sixes had a full-time cook, a bony woman named Corena. With nothing else to choose from, they tied their horses in front of the Lucky Sixes and went inside.

"Howdy, boys, what's your pleasure?" Burt Williams, the bartender greeted them. He knew who they were but pretended he didn't.

"You still got that old hag that used to cook here?" Henry asked.

"You mean Corena? Yes, sir, she's still here. You fellers lookin' for something to eat?"

"You still sellin' that God-awful stuff you call corn whiskey?" Henry asked then.

"We still sell corn whiskey," Burt replied. He was thinking that with such a low opinion of the saloon, why didn't they just take their business somewhere else. But he knew their reputation as hell-raisers and was bent on saving the saloon from destruction.

"We'll take a shot of whiskey and whatever she's got cooked up," Henry said. "What is it, anyway?"

"Beans and rice," Burt said.

"Well, that suits my taste," Junior declared.

"Me, too," Gilbert said and Henry nodded his approval, so Burt experienced a slight feeling of relief. He poured three shots of corn whiskey, then went to the kitchen door to tell Corena to bring three bowls of beans and rice.

The Dawsons sat down at a table and awaited their food. In a few minutes, the skinny little woman came out of the kitchen carrying a tray with three bowls and one plate with cornbread on it. "I got coffee that ain't too old," she said. "You want that, or you want some water?" They all decided to gamble on the coffee, so she went back to the kitchen to get the pot and three cups.

They were all hungry enough to eat the beans and rice fast enough to avoid wasting time to evaluate the taste. It was more an exercise of filling an empty space as rapidly as possible. After the space was filled, there was time to consider the quality of the bulk just ingested, primarily by the aftertaste delivered in the resulting belches. "Damn," Henry swore after a hearty belch singed the hairs in his nose, "I coulda lit a cigar with that one." They drank another cup of coffee, then he announced that he was going to the jail to visit Virgil. Then just to be sure, he asked Burt, "Is that new marshal in town today?"

"Marshal Cochran?" Burt replied. "Yes, sir, he's in town. I saw him walk past the front of the saloon about an hour ago."

"Good," Henry said. "I'll go see if he's in the office, and I'll find out why them deputies didn't take Virgil today." He paid Burt for the whiskey and the food with some of the money he had taken from Clayton and Priest. "You wanna go see your brother?" he asked Junior and Gilbert, "or are you gonna sit here?"

"You go on, Pa, and we'll come along later," Junior answered. He looked at Gilbert then and said, "I wonder if Johnny's woke up yet. Where did he get that bottle of whiskey?"

"Danged if I know," Gilbert said, "probably outta the old man's trunk."

"Uh-oh," Daryl uttered, then said to Bannack, "Henry Dawson is marching up the street and it looks like he's coming straight to the jail."

"I'm not surprised to see him come callin'. Didn't think it would be this quick, though," Bannack said.

Daryl stepped back away from the door when he was sure Dawson was coming to see them. Dawson charged into the office like a man on a mission. "Afternoon, Mr. Dawson, what can we do for you?" Bannack greeted him politely.

"I want to see my son," Dawson demanded. "I want to talk to him."

"Why, sure, you can certainly try to talk to him, but it might be kind of difficult," Bannack said.

"Whadda you mean by that?" Dawson responded.

"You'll see," Bannack said. "Same old rules, I'll have to have your handgun and that pocket piece you carry." With a show of irritation, Dawson took off his gun belt and took the pocket pistol out of his vest pocket. Daryl opened the cell room door for him and he charged through it like a bull.

There was no sound for a few seconds, but then they heard a yelp as if he had been stung by a bee. "Johnny!" he blurted, confused, but it was not enough to awaken the man sprawled on the cot in cell one. "What the hell?"

He turned to face Bannack, who was now standing in the doorway. "What the hell?" he repeated.

"Don't worry," Bannack said. "He ain't dead, if that's what you're worried about. He's just dead-drunk. That's a bad habit to get into with a boy that young."

"How did he get here?" Dawson asked, still demanding in his tone.

"You know, drunk as he is, I was wonderin' that myself. Daryl can tell you, we were here in the office a little while ago, and he came bustin' in here, just like you just did, yellin' something about seein' his brother. So when we told him his brother ain't here, he acted like he didn't know what to do. So I decided to arrest him for drunk and disorderly conduct and let him sleep it off, then let him go in the mornin'. It sure makes my job easier when the drunks come right to the jail to get arrested. I didn't expect you to be in town today, though. But I'm willing to release him in your custody, if you want to take him home."

"Never mind him!" Henry exploded. "Where's Virgil? I came in here to see Virgil."

"Oh, Virgil," Bannack responded casually. "If you wanna see Virgil, you'll have to ride up to Jacksboro to the county jail to visit him."

"They weren't supposed to take him up there until today," Dawson protested.

"Who told you that?" Bannack asked.

"My son, Virgil," Dawson fumed. "He said they told him to be ready to travel today after breakfast."

"That's true," Bannack said. "But last night was such

a nice night, they decided to go ahead and take him to Jacksboro at night. They figured there'd be less chance of trouble. You know, like the last time they started up there with Virgil and one of 'em got shot." He paused then to watch Dawson's reactions, and he decided that the irate man was beginning to realize he might be painting himself into a corner. So he continued, "Like I said, I didn't expect to see you in town to visit Virgil today, since I knew he probably told you they would be transportin' him today. And you said he did," he reminded him.

Dawson forced a smile. "That's a fact," he said. "Me and my other two sons had to come into town today, lookin' for Johnny who got away from the house this mornin' with a bottle of my whiskey. I thought as long as I was in town, I'd check by the jail just to make sure Virgil was gone. I reckon I got all confused when I saw Johnny in there layin' on the bed."

"You want to take him home?" Bannack asked, thinking to save the town the cost of Johnny's meals if he kept him overnight.

"Yeah, I'll take him off your hands," Dawson replied. "How much is the fine?"

"I won't charge a fine, since I didn't really have to go arrest him. There might be a stable fee for takin' care of his horse. Clem Shaw might not charge you anything since you're getting' the horse so soon after we gave it to him." He watched Dawson as the father stared at his youngest son, still passed out on the cot. Henry's stare reminded him of the kind of look you saw on a man's face when he's deciding whether or not to put a crippled horse out of its misery. He was tempted to offer to do it for him. Instead, he said, "We might wanna see if we can sober him up enough to ride. You say your other two boys are in town?" Henry said they were. "You can have them carry him across the street to the waterin' trough and try to sober him up."

"Yes, that's what I'll do," Dawson said. "I'll get my boys and we'll take care of Johnny. I'll be right back." He went out of the cell room, took his weapons from Daryl and went out the front door.

Daryl followed him to the door and remained there to watch him as he walked back down the street. "Here come his other two sons coming up to meet him," he reported. "They're leading the horses."

"All right," Bannack said, "come give me a hand with Johnny."

Daryl hurried back to the cell room as Bannack was lifting Johnny up from the bed. "Where do you want me to grab him?" Daryl asked.

"I got him," Bannack replied and picked up Johnny to lie across his shoulder. "I want you to pick up that thunder mug and hold it under his mouth while I carry him outside. I don't want whatever he's got in his stomach to go down my back."

"Right," Daryl said, "I understand." He picked up the chamber pot and held it against Bannack's back and followed right behind him as he walked out the office door to the street.

"Well, I'll be . . ." Junior started when he saw Bannack walk out of the jail with Johnny draped across his shoulder like a sack of cornmeal. "What did he do to him?"

"He ain't done nothin' to him," Henry said. "I told you, Johnny's still dead-drunk. You and Gilbert take him to that water trough and see if you can wake him up enough to ride home."

"Where's his horse?" Gilbert asked and was told it was at the stable.

"I felt him startin' to move a little bit," Bannack said when the three Dawsons got to the jail. "Maybe he can stand up." He took him off his shoulder and held him up with a hand on each shoulder to hold him steady. Johnny gave his brothers a silly grin, then proceeded to empty the contents of his stomach into the street.

"Take him," Henry ordered, and Junior and Gilbert took him from Bannack and walked him to the watering trough. Henry stood there and watched them until they reached the trough, then he turned back to Bannack and said, "I'll bid you good day, Marshal." Bannack nodded in return, then Henry walked away to join his sons, feeling the total defeat of the day. Virgil was in the county jail in Jacksboro, and the thorn in his side that was Marshal John Cochran was still festering. He was certain that the marshal knew he and his sons were the "robbers" who attacked the deputy marshals and freed

Virgil. And he knew after today that the marshal knew he and his sons were waiting in ambush to kill the deputies and free Virgil. And he also knew that the one wildcard he held in the game between them was that knowing and proving were two different things. And Cochran had no proof.

CHAPTER 15

"I can't understand how a man that big can just disappear," Judge Raymond Grant complained. "There has not been one response from those Wanted Posters since they were sent out."

"He must be hiding out in the woods somewhere, living off the land," Clark Spencer remarked. "I went down to Judge Wick's place and those people who are still livin' there said when Bannack left, he just said he was headin' west. And I believe them because I think Bannack is smart enough not to tell anybody where he was goin'. I think he knew you would get that pardon of his revoked and he'd be an escaped prisoner."

"I want that miscreant back in a prison cell where I put him," the judge fumed, "and I want Judge Wick Justice to somehow know I put him back in prison, wherever that old buzzard is spending eternity. I'm gonna have wanted posters sent out on Bannack again and I'm gonna put you on a special assignment. You've tracked men down for me before, Clark, but this one is the most important job I've ever sent you on. I want you to find John Bannack and arrest him if you can. Kill him if you can't arrest him. I want him rotting in that prison or dead. I'm going to make it well worth your effort. You'll be well paid for your success, and I'll stake you to plenty of expense money while you're searching for him."

"I'll find him if he's still alive," Clark said. "I'll leave in the mornin'." He had been planning to suggest that to the judge, anyway, knowing he would be more than generous in compensating him. "I'll start with his brother's farm near Waco where he was arrested. I don't know where Bannack might have headed, but I'm willing to bet he went back there first thing to see his brother. Maybe I can get an idea which way he went from there. A big man like that ought to be easy to track. If we're lucky, he might even still be there, but I wouldn't count on it."

"Good idea," Judge Grant said. "That's a good place to start, and if they want to know by what authority you're asking questions, you tell them you're a special investigator for the governor."

"Right," Spencer said, "special investigator, I like that. If you don't need me here at the office for anything this afternoon, I'll go get my horses ready to travel and buy the supplies I'm going to need, so I can start early in the morning. This may take a while. I'll try to keep you posted on my progress whenever I'm near a telegraph." The judge wished him good hunting and told him to pick up anything he thought he might need at the general merchandise store and put it on his account.

* * *

"Pa, look yonder," Tommy Bannack called to his father, who was unhitching the mule from a plow. When his father looked at him, Tommy pointed toward the path that led from the main road. There was a rider approaching the house, leading a packhorse.

"Looks like we've got company," Warren Bannack said, but it didn't look like anyone he knew. Since he had time, he finished unhitching the mule and told Tommy to let it in the corral, then he walked out into the barnyard to meet the stranger. The closer he came, the more convinced Warren was that he was someone he had never seen before. His first thought when Tommy called his attention was a drifter looking for a free meal, but the closer the stranger came, he decided he was wrong. His next thought was that he looked like a tax collector, and he was not aware of any taxes that he owed, so he said, "Howdy. Can I help you?"

"Howdy," Spencer returned politely. "Are you Warren Bannack?"

"Yes, I am," Warren replied.

"Good," Spencer replied, "I wasn't sure I had found the right place. My name's Clark Spencer. I'm a special investigator for the judicial branch of the governor's office. And I'm trying to get in touch with your brother, John. I was told that he had returned to his home here on the farm. I wonder if I might speak with him."

"I'm sure he'd be glad to speak with you, if he was

here," Warren said. "I'm afraid you made a trip for nothing, Mr. Spencer. John doesn't live here, anymore. I'll invite you to step down for a drink of water or water for your horse, but whoever told you John was livin' here gave you some bad information."

"Thank you, sir," Spencer replied and stepped down from his horse. Warren noticed that he wore a Colt six-shooter in a position for swift withdrawal of the weapon if needed in a hurry. He wouldn't brand him a gun-fighter, maybe, but it was not typical for a government official, either. "I just stopped at the river before I got here, but I would enjoy stretchin' my legs a little," Spencer continued as he grinned at Tommy, who came back from the corral to join them. "This your son? He looks like he could do a man's work."

"Yes, sir," Warren answered. "This is Tommy."

"Glad to meet you, Tommy. My name's Clark Spencer. I'll bet you miss your Uncle John, don't you? A man that size is like havin' an extra mule, ain't it?"

"I reckon," Tommy said.

"I expect it's kinda hard for Tommy to remember much about John since it's been over five years he was gone. Tommy and his brother were just little fellows when John went off to prison. Then when he came by here, he wasn't here long enough for them to get to know him again."

"So he didn't stay here long enough for you and your brother to get to know him again?" Spencer repeated to Tommy.

"No, sir," Tommy answered. Warren suspected Spencer's question was designed to trick the boy into a response that would contradict his father's statement.

"You know, Mr. Spencer, I'm gonna level with you," Warren said. "When John came here after the judge he worked for died, he stayed here one day and one night. I tried to talk him into comin' home for good, but he said he couldn't do that because there was a judge who would work night and day to revoke his pardon and send him back to prison. And he said he wasn't going back to prison, no matter what. Right now, I suspect that is exactly what happened and I believe if you'll be as honest with me as I'm gonna be with you, you'll admit that you're lookin' for John so you can put him back in prison or kill him for some reward money. Now, is that pretty much the way things really are?"

Spencer couldn't suppress an impish grin. "Well, there ain't much sense in tryin' to play any more games about it, is there? The truth is your brother was dead right on his guess that his pardon would be lifted and he'd be a wanted man again. There is a reward out for him already, dead or alive, but I'm not workin' for a reward. I'm a special investigator for Judge Raymond Grant, and my job is to find your brother and return him to finish his sentence. By helpin' me find your brother, you'd be helpin' him because, if I find him first, it could save his life."

"I reckon it's a good thing for you that you ain't a bounty hunter, 'cause the whole time we're standin' here talkin', Tommy's brother has been layin' up in the hayloft with his Winchester rifle trained on you. One little hand signal from me and you'd get to see how good that boy can shoot. Ain't that right, Tommy?" Tommy smiled and nodded his head, at the same time hoping that Billy didn't come running out of the house to join them.

"There's no need to spill any blood over this," Spencer quickly pleaded. "Like I said, my primary mission is to keep John from being cut down by some ruthless bounty hunter. So I was hopin' you'd understand that and help me out. You say your brother ain't here, and I believe you. Just tell me where he went when he left here and I'll be on my way."

"He went west," Warren said, "and that's as much as he could tell me because he said he didn't know where he was going, that he would know it when he got there and that's where he would stop."

"You sure he didn't say south, or southwest toward Mexico?" Spencer pressed. "I'm trying to help your brother stay alive."

"He said he was gonna take the road to Stephenville, and when I asked him, he said he wasn't goin' to Stephenville, he would just start out on that road and go west. Now you know everything he told me when he left here."

"All right, Mr. Bannack, I'll say I believe you. What I know about John Bannack would lead me to believe he wouldn't tell his own brother where he was going.

Because he knew if he didn't tell you, nobody could beat it out of you. The road to Stephenville is a start in the right direction, so that's where I'm headin'." He climbed back up into the saddle. "And by the way, your other son ain't in the hayloft. His head's in the window of the front room of your house beside his mother's. Good day to you." He wheeled the gray gelding back onto the path he rode in on and left at a trot.

Peaceful days followed the failed plan to assassinate Deputy Bill Clayton and Deputy Conrad Priest. Marshal John Cochran received a wire from Jacksboro summoning him to appear in court as a witness in the murder trial of Virgil Dawson, since he was the arresting officer. Since the scene of the actual murder was in the River House saloon, next door to the café where the arrest was made, the presiding judge wanted witnesses to the murder. But there were no names of the several cowhands and drifters who saw the shooting. Smut Smith, the bartender, witnessed the shooting but claimed to be unable to travel to Jacksboro for the trial for health reasons. He was amenable to signing a statement saying Virgil Dawson shot Twin Creeks ranch hand, Hurley No Last Name. Another witness, Beulah Mae Thompkins was willing to testify but had no transportation to the trial, so she also signed a statement. The marshal was obliged to deliver the statements to the court. Bannack couldn't help wondering why a circuit judge could not come to Glory and hold the trial there. He was told that Judge Calvin Stark was the presiding judge and he did not ride the circuit. All trials in the county under his jurisdiction were now held at the county seat.

"Lonnie George said this packet of papers has been there at the post office for a while," Daryl said when he walked in the marshal's office, just having been to breakfast. "You want me to start checking the post office every day?"

"We don't get that much mail," Bannack said, taking the packet from Daryl. He pulled out his pocketknife and cut the string holding it together. "It's just a new batch of wanted posters." He sat down at the desk and started leafing through them. Many of them he had already seen. Then one new one stopped him. He read it slowly. *Wanted: Escaped Prisoner John Bannack: Armed and Dangerous: Approach with Caution*. He read the description written there and realized it was a description of John Cochran, too. He quickly pulled out another poster and covered the damning one. He feared that anyone who saw it would immediately know it was talking about him. *Damn Judge Raymond Grant and damn Clark Spencer, the snake that works for him.* Even after Judge Wick Justice's death, it wasn't satisfaction enough for the vengeful judge, Raymond Grant. He didn't stop until he successfully used his influence with the new governor to revoke Bannack's pardon. And he wasted no time in creating a manhunt for him, determined to make him serve the remaining fifteen years of his twenty-year sentence. It had been a gross injustice to sentence him for a crime that should not have called for more than the five years he served. The fact that it was his brother who actually committed the crime made it even harder to stomach. He remembered then the glowing praise that Deputy Priest had heaped upon him when he said goodbye to him and Clayton at Jacksboro. He sure hoped Priest didn't brag about him like he threatened. Now that what he feared might happen had actually happened, marking him as a wanted criminal, he could not welcome any attention focused upon Marshal John Cochran.

"Are you all right, Marshal Cochran?"

Bannack's head recoiled slightly. "What? Oh, I'm sorry, Daryl. I got lost there for a moment. I think I ate something at breakfast that ain't settin' right in my stomach. Did you ask me a question?"

"I asked you when you have to go to Jacksboro to deliver those witness statements."

"Sunday, so I can be in the courtroom Monday mornin'," Bannack said.

"At least you won't have to sneak up there this time to keep the town council from knowing you're gone," Daryl joked. "This time it's a court order. We're all still gonna be on pins and needles till you get back."

"You shouldn't be worried," Bannack said. "We've got some pretty good men in this town I like to think we could count on if we needed them. Jake Tracy comes to mind. Clem Shaw and Bill Godsey, don't you think those men would pick up a rifle if they needed to?" He paused to think of someone else. Then he joked, "'Course it goes without sayin', Buster Bridges would be there to lead 'em. And I expect you'd be there as well."

Daryl slowly shook his head. "Oh, I don't know how much good I'd be if the going really got rough. I've never been much of a fighter, and I'm not a very good shot with a rifle or a pistol."

Bannack realized how little he knew about Daryl Boyd beyond the fact that he had worked for Marshal Jim Bryan as a caretaker and errand runner. When he accepted the job as marshal, he had no idea if he would be in it for very long. So when he was asked if he was satisfied to retain Daryl, he said he was. He saw no reason to fire the young man when his tenure as marshal was in question. The town wasn't paying Daryl enough to matter, anyway. "Let me ask you a question," Bannack said. "Why did you get a job workin' for the town marshal's office?"

"I don't know," Daryl answered. "I guess I just thought it would be a good place to learn to be stronger and learn more about weapons and such." He shrugged. "But I guess I didn't learn much working for Marshal Bryan except how to clean up the jail and keep the water buckets filled."

Bannack stroked his chin and looked at Daryl as if seeing him for the first time. "How old are you, Daryl?"

"Seventeen next month," he answered.

"That's just about the age I quit being a boy and started to become a man. I think it's about time you started your change, and I think I can help you." Daryl's eyes began to grow wide and he wasn't sure if he wanted to hear any more or not. "But first you have to decide that's what you want, because I've learned that you're not going to become a man until you decide you're ready to do it. So when you decide it's time, let me know and I'll help you." Then he turned his attention back to the packet of papers that came in the mail, pretending to be interested in them.

"I guess it's time," Daryl said after a few minutes of silence.

"Did you say something?" Bannack shot back. "Speak up!"

"I said I'm ready!" Daryl almost shouted.

"Damn, there is a voice buried inside you, after all. Now, when you talk like that, I know you're in the room. It's the same with the rest of your body. You got strength in you that God gave you. If you don't use it, then you're wastin' your life. You're as big as anybody seventeen years old, bigger than a lot of them that age. The only ones that seem bigger are the ones that know they've got more than that inside, fightin' to get out." He paused for a moment to study Daryl's reactions to his comments. He turned his chair to reach in the cabinet behind the desk and took out a rolled-up gun belt and holster holding a Colt .45 revolver. He drew the weapon out and checked to make sure the hammer was resting on an empty cylinder. Then he put it back in the holster and handed it to Daryl. "Here, strap this on. It belonged to Virgil Dawson. See how it feels. Maybe you could put it to some good use for a change."

Daryl hesitated. He had never before worn a sidearm, afraid that if he wore one, he might be forced to try to use it. "You want me to put on Virgil's gun?"

"Yeah, put it on," Bannack encouraged. "The gun ain't got no conscience. It ain't good or bad. It's the person who uses it that's good or bad." He watched as Daryl reluctantly strapped the gun belt around his waist and buckled it over his other belt. "That ain't gonna be very comfortable," Bannack said. "Let it out a notch or two and let it ride more on your hips."

Daryl did as instructed, caught up now in this first-time experiment. "It feels heavy," he answered when Bannack asked him how it felt.

"You just ain't used to it yet," Bannack said. "Wear it for the rest of the day, and you'll forget you're wearin' it. Now, let your arm drop to your side. That's about right, your hand falls right on the handle of that Colt. If you needed it in a hurry, all you'd have to do is close your hand and pull it out of the holster. Face the cell room door and try it a couple times, just don't cock it or pull the trigger. Just draw it like you're gonna shoot the door." Daryl tried it. The first time was slightly awkward, as was the second, but the third and fourth looked a lot more natural. "That's not bad at all," Bannack encouraged him. "You might be a natural. The only thing that slows it down and makes it harder is when it's a man with a gun you're facin' instead of a door." He suddenly had an idea. "You know, the town seems pretty quiet this mornin'. I think it'd be a good time for you and me to take a little ride up the river. Have you got a horse?" It occurred to him that he had never seen Daryl on a horse.

"No, sir," Daryl answered, "but Mr. Shaw has one that he lets me ride when I have to have one."

"All right then," Bannack said, "we'll lock the office door and go saddle up our horses." He got up from the desk and picked up his rifle.

"Yes, sir," Daryl replied, "let me put Virgil Dawson's gun back in the cabinet."

"Whoa," Bannack said. "Don't take that gun off. That's your gun now. You've got a full cartridge belt, but I'm gonna take a few extra cartridges, so we don't empty your gun belt." Daryl didn't say anything else, but his wide-open eyes told Bannack that he was overcome with excitement. He further confirmed it when he had some difficulty inserting the key in the office door to lock it.

"Mornin', Marshal. Mornin', Daryl," Clem Shaw greeted them both when they went in the stable.

"Mornin', Clem," Bannack returned. "Daryl and I are gonna take a short little ride up the river a-ways to do a little target practice. I expect you'll hear some shots, so you'll know that's just us makin' life miserable for some trees. Have you got a horse Daryl can borrow for a short ride?"

"Sure do," Clem replied. He looked at Daryl and said, "Take that paint you rode last time. You know where his saddle is."

"Yes, sir. Thank you, sir," Daryl said respectfully and went to fetch a bridle and saddle.

Clem walked with Bannack when he went to saddle his buckskin gelding. "You takin' Daryl out for some target practice, you say. I noticed he was wearin' a gun. Don't believe I've ever seen Daryl wearin' a gun before."

"I'm glad to see he can saddle a horse," Bannack said.

"Yep, I taught him how," Clem said. "Showed him one time, and he did it every time after that. He's a smart enough young man, but he ain't never had a man in his life to teach him what a man's supposed to know. If you don't mind me sayin', it tickles me to see you takin' the time and the interest to teach him a few things. I was hopin' Jim Bryan would work with him some, but Jim wasn't much better than another woman."

"I haven't really done much for him, either," Bannack said. "Up to now, I didn't have the time. I don't even know where he lives. Dependin' on what's goin' on at the jail, sometimes he went home, but sometimes, like the night we took Virgil to Jacksboro, he stayed at the jail all night. And as far as I knew, he never got in touch with anybody to let 'em know if he was stayin' or comin' home."

"Well, he didn't have nobody but his mama," Clem said, "and she died about a year ago. They lived in a little shack 'bout a mile south of town. Just the two of 'em, they lived in that shack ever since Daryl was about twelve years old, that's how old he was when his old man ran off and left them." He shook his head sorrow-fully and said, "That big strapping young man, raised by his mama and her sick in bed the last couple of years of her life. That's a fine thing you're doin', Marshal, takin' an interest in that boy."

They turned to see Daryl leading the paint gelding saddled and ready to go. He had a look on his face that Bannack could not recall having seen before. He hadn't planned the making of a man out of the mild, apologetic boy, but now he felt justified in accidentally taking on the task. "I'd better get movin'. I'm holdin' things up," he declared as he threw his saddle on the buckskin's back. "'Preciate the information, Clem."

They climbed on their horses, and Bannack led them out to the north on the Jacksboro road. When they came to the little creek about five miles from town, he left the road and followed the creek back to the point where it emptied into the river. "This oughta do," he said, "no houses or fields nearby." They left the horses there by the creek and walked up the river a little way before the training began. "To start with," Bannack instructed, "I want you to draw your weapon and get the feel of it." He watched as Daryl drew the Colt six-gun and passed it back and forth from one hand to the other. "That's it. Now, pick out a tree. That one right there. Cock your gun and shoot that tree."

That's how the lessons started. Bannack found Daryl to be fairly well coordinated when it came to drawing his weapon and firing, most of the time hitting within his target. He was not what gunfighters would refer to as a natural, born with lightning-like speed. But he had the ability to improve his speed if that was a burning desire for him. At his present stage, he held no such desire, even though his confidence seemed to be increasing daily. There were several rifles in the gun cabinet so Bannack told Daryl to pick the one that suited him best and Daryl picked a Winchester 66, which used the same .44 cartridge Bannack used in his Henry rifle. He had become so familiar with his Colt that he continued to use it, even though it fired a .45 cartridge. After the second lesson, Bannack told Daryl there was little more he could do for him. "How good you get with your weapons depends on how much time you want to devote to practicing alone."

"I might have created a monster," Bannack muttered as he watched Daryl walking toward him from the stable. There was a look of confidence in the young man's stride that wasn't there before. Bannack was sure of it, noting the tip of his hat when he passed a lady and her two children, instead of his prior tendency to cross the street to avoid eye contact. "If he keeps it up, though, I might convince the council to make him a deputy and give him a raise."

"You fixin' to leave now?" Daryl asked when they met in front of the River House saloon.

"Yep," Bannack replied. "I'm on my way to the stable now. I locked the office door."

"In that case, I'll walk back to the stable with you," Daryl said. "It's been a rather quiet Sunday," he commented.

"The kind we like, right?" Bannack said.

"You have any idea how long they'll keep you up there for that trial?"

"No, I don't," Bannack replied. "I don't see how the trial could take more than one day in court. You never know with some of these judges, and I don't know anything about Judge Stark. But I'll get back here just as soon as it's over. You can count on that."

"I'll try to hold it all together till you get back," Daryl said.

"I know you will," Bannack declared. "That's all the town can ask." *He's ready to try to hold it all together,* he thought. *Instead of being on pins and needles the whole time I'm gone. That's the difference a little self-confidence can make.*

"I saddled your horses," Clem Shaw told him when he and Daryl walked into the stable. "You might wanna check your cinch. He blew his belly out a little when I tightened it." Bannack checked and tightened it a notch. Clem lowered his voice when Daryl walked to a stall and led Bannack's packhorse out. "You did a helluva favor for that kid."

"He did it all, himself," Bannack said. "He just needed someone to tell him he could do it." He climbed aboard the buckskin. "Well, I hope to see you gentlemen Monday night or Tuesday mornin'.

"We'll take care of the town while you're gone," Daryl called after him as he rode out of the stable toward the road to Jacksboro.

Lord, I hope so, Bannack thought. *I sure hope you don't get your first test while I'm somewhere I can't help you.*

Bannack decided to stop to rest his horses at Razor Creek and eat a dinner of coffee and cold biscuits and ham that he brought from the hotel dining room. All the bad luck that had happened at that campground had no effect on his conscience. He wasn't expecting any bad luck on this trip and it was the best place to rest the horses between Glory and Jacksboro, so he took a nice long break there before continuing on to Jacksboro. It was another town he had never been to. He didn't count the night he rode with the two deputies and their prisoner because he didn't actually go into town. In a message from the US Marshal's Office, he was told he had a room reserved in the Jacksboro Hotel and to report to the marshal's office at eight Monday morning. He wondered if the marshal and all the deputy marshals had looked through the latest wanted posters. It occurred to him that this was the first time he had spent any worrisome thoughts about anyone discovering his true identity since he had introduced himself as John Cochran.

Luckily, there was no picture or artist's drawing of him on the wanted paper, only an estimate of his height and weight. He was still thinking about that when he rode into Jacksboro.

The hotel was in the middle of the main street, a plain two-story building with nothing but the word HOTEL on a sign on the handrail of the second floor porch to identify it. Bannack reined the buckskin to a stop and dismounted. He tied the horses to the hitching rail, then paused to take a look around him before walking into the hotel. His first impression of Jacksboro was that it didn't look as big as Glory, but it seemed to be more active, even on a Sunday. He decided that was because it was the county seat. He walked on inside to what appeared to be a registration desk with a staircase behind it. There was no one at the desk, but over in a corner of the room, a young man and a woman were sitting at a table, drinking coffee. The man got to his feet and hurried over to the desk. "Are you Marshal Cochran?"

"Yes, I am," Bannack replied, surprised. "How'd you know that?"

"They told me I'd recognize you," he said. "My name's Bobby Nance, I'm the hotel clerk. We've reserved a room for you upstairs on the front. Is that all right with you?"

"If it's got a bed in it, I expect it'll be fine," Bannack said and signed the register when Bobby turned it around for him. "Where's a good place to get some supper?"

"We like to think our dining room is the best place to

eat in town," Bobby said. "But if you don't want to eat here, there's two saloons that serve food, Murphy's and Crowder House."

"I didn't think you had a dinin' room," Bannack said. "I didn't see a sign outside."

Bobby laughed. "We try to keep it hid," he joked. "It's behind the hotel. You can get to it if you go through that door and go down the hall. There's an out-side entrance from the street running right behind the hotel. Molly Mayes is the cook and we're proud of her cooking."

"I'll give her a try," Bannack said.

"I don't think you'll be disappointed," Bobby pre-dicted. "They'll be open for supper in about thirty min-utes. I expect they told you the court is paying for your room." Bannack nodded. "They musta forgot to tell you that includes your dining room expenses, too." Bannack nodded again. "I expect your next question is gonna be, where's the stable, right?"

"Right."

"It's on the same street that runs behind the hotel," Bobby said. "Just follow it toward the north end of town till it runs into Main Street and you'll see it, Fowler's Stable. Jim Fowler's the owner. Here's your key. You're in room six, last room at the end of the hall."

"Much obliged," Bannack said. "I'll just get my saddlebags and my rifle off my horse and put them up in the room. Then I'll take my horses to the stable."

He went upstairs and left his things in room six, then left his horses at the stable in Jim Fowler's care. By the time he returned to the hotel, the dining room was open, so he used the outside entrance and was met by the manager, Robert Fraiser. "Good evening, sir. Are you dining alone this evening?"

"Sorta looks that way," Bannack replied. "Want me to go eat in the kitchen?"

"Not at all, sir," Fraiser quickly assured him. "I was just going to ask if you wanted a private table or if you wanted to sit at the big table, family style where you might enjoy some conversation with other single diners."

"All the same to you, I think I'd rather have less conversation," Bannack told him.

"Very well, whatever you prefer," Fraiser said. "Right this way." He led him to a small table close by the kitchen door. "Lucy will be taking care of you. I hope you enjoy your supper."

He sat there for a few minutes while several servers went in and out of the kitchen door, still setting all the tables. Finally, a middle-aged woman, lean of face and figure, stopped in front of his table. "Hey, darlin', what did you do to get sent to this table?"

"Nothin' I know of," Bannack replied. "Why? What's wrong with this table?"

"Nothing, I guess, if you don't mind hearing all the kitchen noises and the people going in and out like you're settin' in the middle of a herd of cattle. The good part about it is that I'm your server. My name's Lucy and I get a lot of you drifters. You campin' over by the creek and decide you'd come get a good supper?"

"No, I'm stayin' in the hotel," Bannack said. "I'm in town for a trial tomorrow." He pulled his vest aside to expose his badge. "I'm the town marshal of Glory, Texas."

"Whoops!" she exclaimed gleefully. "Ol' Fraiser stepped in it this time. I can't wait to tell him!" She motioned for him to get up when he didn't understand, she told him, "Get up from there. I'm gonna move you to a better table."

"Oh, that's all right. I don't mind sittin' here."

"Well, I mind," she insisted. "I wanna rub ol' Fraiser's nose in it. Get up!" He shrugged and got up from the chair. "Damn!" she blurted. "You just don't stop getting up, do you? Come on!" She grabbed his hand and led him to a small table farther away from the kitchen. "Now, that's better. You want coffee with your supper?"

"Yes, ma'am, I do," he said obediently.

"The special tonight is roast beef. If you don't want that, Molly will fry you some ham."

"I'll take the roast beef," he said.

She disappeared into the kitchen, and he heard her yell, "Robert! You ain't got the brains God gave grasshoppers!" She was back in a couple of minutes carrying a plate of roast beef and a cup of coffee. "Here you go, darlin', this will get you started. Biscuits will be out of the oven in five minutes."

He thanked her and went to work on the plate piled

high with beef, potatoes, and beans. In fact, he was so intent upon his supper that he paid no attention to the two men who came in the door from the hotel and were involved in conversation with Robert Fraiser. He still paid them no mind until they appeared to be marching toward him. He dropped his knife and fork when he recognized the grinning faces of Conrad Priest and Bill Clayton. "You never know who you're liable to run into in these fancy hotels, do ya?" Bannack joked.

"Howdy, John," Priest greeted him. "We figured you might be in the hotel."

"Yeah," Clayton said, "we checked with Bobby Nance at the desk, and he said you were most likely in the dinin' room."

"I see you got your arm outta that sling," Bannack said to Priest.

"Yesterday," Priest said.

"You boys wanna join me for supper?" Bannack asked. "It's roast beef, and it's mighty good."

"That was our plan," Clayton said as they both pulled out a chair and sat down, "'cause we figured we owed you a big supper. We just told Robert Fraiser we wanted to pay for your supper, and he said the hotel's takin' care of it with the courthouse."

"Seems to me, since the US Marshal Service is payin' the bill, that's the same as you and Conrad payin' it," Bannack said. "I hope they didn't give you any trouble about that robbery business when you lost ol' Virgil the first time." He knew they had been really worried about how it would look on their record.

"Not a bit of trouble," Clayton replied. "In fact, they used the whole business as an example to the rest of the deputies of what it means to never give up and determination to do your duty, no matter what. Made regular heroes out of us. It added to the story when Conrad got shot." He suddenly turned serious for a moment. "You know, John, it might help your stock go up, if we was to tell the straight of how we got Dawson back and our horses, too."

Bannack shook his head and created a smile. "I like it better the other way," he said. "Walter Glory don't want me to bring any attention to his little town."

"I swear, Bill," Priest remarked, "it looks like we're at least gonna have to buy him a drink after supper."

"Just one," Bannack said, "then we'll be square."

Their conversation was interrupted then when Lucy Webb returned to the table. "Well, forever more!" she exclaimed when she saw the two deputies. "Are these two friends of yours? If I had known they were coming to join you, I wouldn't have moved you over to this table," she japed. "I'da set you up on the back steps."

"We shoulda known they'd stick you with Lucy Webb." Clayton chuckled. "You musta gave ol' Fraiser a hard time."

"Are you two eating?" Lucy wanted to know.

"That's what this place is supposed to be, ain't it?" Clayton responded. "An eatin' place?"

"If we don't get served pretty soon, we're gonna take our complaints to the manager, Mr. Robert Fraiser," Priest japed. "Then you'll find yourself back out on the street."

"He can kiss my foot," Lucy responded. "I'm the only thing holding this place together." She did an about-face and went back to the kitchen to get them started.

Chapter 16

Bannack found it very interesting to see the difference between the two deputy marshals who rode into Glory to transport a prisoner to the county jail and the two wise-cracking good ol' boys who welcomed him to Jacksboro. The back-and-forth banter between them and Lucy Webb was harsh at times but always good-natured. She always gave as good as she got. When they finally called it quits, and prepared to adjourn to the Wildflower Saloon for that drink of whiskey they promised him, he was surprised when she grabbed Clayton by the sleeve. "You'd better not show up at my door drunk and smelling like that cheap perfume those sluts at Wildflower bathe in. You'll find the bar on my door."

"You got no cause to say that," Clayton replied. "John ain't much for drinkin', and we've gotta be in court in the mornin'. I'll be home early."

Bannack was surprised even more when she caught his arm as he started to follow them out. Turning serious for a moment, she said, "Bill told me you saved his and Conrad's necks down in Glory. Thank you for that.

I'm glad I got to meet you." Her frank statement left him speechless. Seeing him trying to think of how to respond, she said, "You don't have to say anything. I understand."

When they left the hotel, they walked a short distance up the street to the Wildflower Saloon. They paused before going inside when Priest pointed to a large single-story wooden building with a two-story wing on the back. "That's the courthouse," he said. "That two-story part on the back is the jail. That's where Virgil Dawson is. I reckon they told you to report to the marshal's office at eight or eight-thirty, right?" Bannack said that was so. "That's just to kinda officially tell you what to do and where to go when the trial starts at nine o'clock." He pointed to another small building next to the larger one. "That's the US Marshal's Office. That's where we'll be in the mornin', and we'll go to the courthouse with you."

"Right," Bannack replied. That settled, they went inside the saloon and walked up to the bar.

"Howdy, boys," Gus Welch, the bartender greeted them. "Where'd you two get this big ol' feller? I hope you ain't arrested him 'cause if you're fixin' to buy him some whiskey on the way to jail, he's liable to tear this place down if he gets drunk."

"You talk too much, Gus," Clayton said. "This is a friend of ours from Glory and we'd like to buy him a drink of your good rye whiskey." He paused then to check with Bannack. "Rye whiskey all right, or do you prefer corn?"

"One's about as good as the other to me," Bannack answered. "Just pour me whichever one you're drinkin'." He really wasn't much of a drinker, never had been. Whiskey just wasn't available to him when he was growing up. On the one occasion when he and his brother decided to see what it was like to really get drunk, it turned out to be a very unpleasant experience. He didn't like the way he seemed to lose control of his muscles, and it was much worse later on when he seemed to have lost control of his stomach and his bowels. It was effective enough to cure both him and his brother from ever wanting to be that way again. As he grew a little older, he found that he could enjoy a drink but never more than two. He didn't care to lose that control of his body again.

Gus poured three shots and Priest picked his up and said, "Here's to stompin' snakes like Virgil Dawson. I hope they hang his sorry behind."

"I'll drink to that," Clayton said and tossed his down, too.

"Amen," Bannack said softly and took his drink in one gulp as well. But while Clayton and Priest slammed their glasses down hard and upright, signaling for Gus to pour again, he seemed distracted.

"You really gonna stop after one drink?" Priest asked.

"No," Bannack answered, still distracted, "I'll have one more, but that's all." *Maybe one more will clear my vision,* he thought and put his glass on the bar for a refill. But the second drink was no help.

"Is something eatin' at you?" Priest asked.

"I'm lookin' at that table over in the dark corner. If I ain't mistaken, I think I'm lookin' at the man who shot you, Conrad." Both Priest and Clayton braced immediately, both dropping their hands to rest on their six-guns.

"Where?" Priest asked.

"Don't shoot anybody," Bannack said, "in case I'm wrong. But I'm lookin' at four men sittin' back there at that table in the corner. The one facin' this way looks like Henry Dawson. The other three are his sons, Junior, Gilbert, and Johnny."

"Are you sure?" Clayton asked, he and Priest having never seen their faces. "What the hell are they doin' here?"

"I'm sure now. They came to go to Virgil's trial," Bannack replied.

"That was dumb on their part," Clayton said. "We can arrest 'em right here."

"Arrest 'em for what?" Bannack asked. "This is the first time you've ever seen their faces. You can't identify them as the men who attacked you."

"Hell, maybe not," Priest said, "but you can identify 'em."

"I didn't see 'em shoot you," Bannack said. "I wasn't there. I just know in my gut that they are the four men who attacked you. I can't prove it, neither can you. I know we found Virgil at his father's house, but that just proves he went home. I found your horses wanderin' near Razor Creek, not at Dawson's farm. And that's why they're sittin' up here waiting to go to his trial. They know we can't prove they had anything to do with it."

"Why are you sure the father is the one who shot me?" Priest asked.

"Just goin' by what you said," Bannack answered. "You said that one man gave all the orders and the other three called him Boss. It just makes sense."

As tense as the situation was for the three men standing at the bar, it was even more tense for the four men seated at the table in the corner. Feeling trapped and naked due to a ban on the wearing of guns on Sunday as well as on weekdays when the court was in session, they sat helpless. This was especially so when the three men that captured their attention were all wearing sidearms. "They're all wearin' guns," Johnny Dawson declared. "Why is that? We can't wear no guns."

"Because they're all three lawmen, dummy," Junior told him.

"We're in trouble," Gilbert warned. "How are we gonna get outta here?"

"Just sit still, damn it!" his father ordered. "The law ain't got no reason to bother us. They can't prove we ever done anything. They know we wouldn'ta come to this town full of lawmen if we was guilty of anything, so don't act like a dog caught in the henhouse. The one I'd really like to catch out by himself is that big devil, Cochran. He knows it was us that sprung Virgil loose. I'd like to tell him he was right, we done it, just before I blow a hole in his head."

"Pass that bottle back over here," Johnny said.

"Yeah, Pa, pour Johnny another drink," Junior said. "Maybe he wants to get likkered up enough to go over there and say howdy to his old friend, Marshal Cochran."

"You go to hell, Junior," Johnny responded. "You act like you ain't never got drunk."

"I ain't never got so drunk till I staggered into the jailhouse and said, 'Lock me up!'"

"Shut up! Both of ya!" Henry Dawson snapped. "Let's get outta here. We'll take the bottle back to camp and you can finish it there. I wanna go to that jailhouse and see if we can talk to Virgil. When we walk outta here, act like you ain't got nothin' to worry about, 'cause you ain't." He got up then and started for the door.

"I know what you're thinkin'," Clayton quickly warned Priest when the four Dawsons got up and approached the bar on their way out. "But you just hold steady and let 'em go. You'll be in a world of trouble if you do anything right now. It could cost you your job."

"Evenin', Marshal Cochran," Henry said as they walked past the three lawmen while pretending not to know the two men with him. "I reckon you're in town for the trial."

"Mr. Dawson," Bannack acknowledged but offered nothing more.

When the Dawsons went out the door, Priest turned back to the bar at once and said, "Pour me another one, Gus." Then, with his hand trembling with rage, he tossed it back.

"I reckon I'll see you in the marshal's office in the mornin'," Bannack said. "I'm gonna go see how that bed in my room sleeps. I wanna be sure I'm rested up good for that trial. I hope the judge wants to get it done as fast as I do and I can get on back to Glory." He thanked them for the drinks, bade them a goodnight, and walked back to the hotel. Priest and Clayton carried their drinks to a table and sat down. In a few minutes, a couple of the wildflowers sat down to join them.

On the opposite side of the courthouse from the hotel, Henry Dawson and his three sons walked in the fading evening light around behind the two-story wing that was the jail. They called out Virgil's name until they were answered from one of the windows upstairs in the middle of the wall. "Hey, Pa, you come to bust me outta here?"

"Hey, Pa, bust me outta here, too," an unfamiliar voice called out, followed by the sound of chuckling.

"Shut your damn mouth," Virgil threatened, "or I'll shut it for you! Move over this way, Pa. I see you. You got the boys with you, too. If you'da brought a long ladder and something to break these bars out of this window, I'd come down to see you."

"They treatin' you all right?" Junior asked, for want of anything else to say.

"Yeah," Virgil replied. "They're a little bit skimpy on the food, and I'm used to eatin' fresh beef. Seems like the only animal they ever heard of here is a pig. You and the boys gonna be at my trial?"

"Yep, we'll be there," Henry said. "We're camped

over by the creek, and every time we come into town we have to turn our guns in at the sheriff's office." He figured Virgil already knew that, but he wanted to tell him again in case he was expecting him and his brothers to try to break him out of there. At this point, he didn't know what he was going to do to save his son from prison or possibly hanging. If there was an opportunity at any point in the trial or during the trip when they were transporting him to prison, he was bound to try. But there had to be a good chance to succeed. He wasn't ready to commit suicide in an effort to save his son.

"I ain't never seen so many lawmen in one place before," Virgil said. "But the one that done it all to me is that damn town marshal in Glory. I don't know if you know it or not, but it was him that came out to our place that night and knocked me off my horse. Them two deputies didn't have nothin' to do with that. And he's the one that told them to sneak me outta that jail and go to Jacksboro in the middle of the night, and he went with 'em."

"I suspected that," Henry responded, "and we waited half a damn day for them to show up when he said they was gonna take you up here."

"Pa," Virgil said, "if you don't get a chance to help me, please promise me you'll square things up for me with that meddling marshal."

"Don't worry about that," Henry said. "I promise you he ain't gonna die of old age."

"I gotta go now," Virgil said. "It's time they do their

head count for the night. I'll see you in the courthouse in the mornin'."

"Good morning, Marshal Cochran," Robert Fraiser greeted Bannack when he walked into the dining room for breakfast. "Your server last night, Lucy Webb, asked to serve you this morning when you came in for breakfast."

"She did?" Bannack asked, quite surprised. "Well, that's a first."

"Is that all right with you?" Fraiser asked.

"Sure is," Bannack replied. "I'd be glad to have her wait on me." He suspected, however, that it was more likely that she was assigned to take care of him because she was tough enough to handle the drifters and the untamed-looking creatures. When she first saw him at supper, she even mentioned the fact that she waited on a lot of drifters. He didn't care. He was accustomed to women giving him a wide berth. Fraiser showed him to the same table he had eaten supper on.

When Lucy came out of the kitchen and saw him there, she grinned, spun on her heel, and went back for the coffeepot and a cup. When she came back out, she widened the grin and put the cup on his table and filled it. "Good morning, John Cochran. Did you get a good night's sleep?"

"I did," he answered and tried to copy her smile. She smiled even wider at his obvious effort, thinking a welcoming smile just looked pitifully out of place among those chiseled features. "How 'bout yourself?"

"Oh, yes," she answered, this time with a little more impudence in her smile. "I always get a good night's sleep." She motioned toward his coffee. "If I remember correctly, you take it just like it comes out of the pot, right?"

"That's a fact," he said. "I reckon that's because I never seemed to have any milk or sugar to put in it. I reckon I just got used to it."

"Bill said you didn't hang around the Wildflower very long last night."

"No, ma'am, I reckon I didn't. I was anxious to try out that bed in my room, and it didn't disappoint me. I woke up with an appetite. What have you got to take care of that?"

She laughed at his enthusiasm. "How do you feel about a stack of flapjacks, scrambled eggs, and link sausage with some genuine blueberry syrup."

"Sounds perfect to me," he responded. "Can't think of a better way to start the day than that."

"They'll be right up," she said. "And Bill said to tell you he'll see you at the marshal's office. He had to be there early this morning."

"Did he eat breakfast?" Bannack asked.

"Yes, he came with me to open up this morning. You didn't miss him by much when you came in. And Conrad eats breakfast at the boarding house he lives in, if you're wondering about him." She went to the kitchen then to give Molly Mayes his order. When she returned with it a few minutes later, she heated his coffee with some fresh made. When he commented that it looked like a lot of food, she said, "You're a lotta man to fill up. I bet you can handle it." She started to walk away then but stopped to say one more thing. "Bill said you were the finest lawman he's ever seen, and he's known quite a few."

"He's being overly generous, I reckon," Bannack remarked, thinking Clayton was genuinely impressed by his assistance in recapturing their prisoner when, as a town marshal, he was under no obligation to do so. It was obvious that both Bill Clayton and Conrad Priest seemed to be intent upon building a reputation for him. And a reputation was something he did not want. With wanted papers out on John Bannack, he didn't like the prospect of law officers starting to compare John Cochran to descriptions of John Bannack. It might be too easy for some inquisitive marshal or ranger to check into John Cochran's past history and find there was none before Glory, Texas.

The thought caused him to question his decision to hide in plain sight when the town marshal's job was so openly handed to him. Maybe the best thing for him right now was to hand the signed witness statements to the judge, then get on his horse and continue on to the northwest. Luckily, he had spent a little time rubbing some of the peach fuzz off Daryl Boyd. Maybe Daryl was ready to grow into the marshal's job. He shook his head, knowing Daryl was not ready to have that responsibility dropped in his lap. It might destroy the young man. *Ah, hell,* he thought, *I can't leave the town without a marshal again. I just need to get back down there as quick as I can get away from here, and keep my head down.*

"What were you thinking about?" Lucy asked. "You looked like your mind was a hundred miles away."

"What?" He recoiled slightly and recovered. "I was wishin' I didn't have to go sit in a courtroom all mornin'. I need to get back to my little town. But if I know what's good for me, I reckon I'd best get on over to that marshal's office before they send Bill back here to arrest me. I wanna thank you for that fine breakfast. The flapjacks were perfect, and the service wasn't bad." She laughed and warned him not to drift off to sleep while the judge was talking. "I ain't gonna guarantee it," he said.

US Marshal Calvin Turner stood up and extended his hand across the desk to shake Bannack's hand when Bill Clayton escorted him into his office. "Damn, Clayton, he's as big as you said he was." He grinned at Bannack then. "Marshal Cochran, it's a pleasure to meet you. Deputies Clayton and Priest tell me they might not have gotten back with the man they're tryin' today without your help."

"I'm mighty glad to meet you, sir," Bannack said. "I just tried to help Clayton and Priest any way I could.

But I think the reason they got back here with Virgil Dawson was because they refused to give up when they ran into some real bad luck."

"I expect they might have been a little modest in their report," Turner said. "They're good men. I understand you have a couple of written witness reports with you, signed by the witnesses."

"Yes, sir."

"And verified authentic by a notary," Turner continued.

"Yes, sir."

"Good, you just hand those over to the judge when he asks for them. You'll also be called to the witness stand to testify, since you are the arresting officer. Just answer the prosecutor's questions truthfully, and that's all you have to do."

"Yes, sir," Bannack replied respectfully. He could have told Turner that he had participated in many court trials while in the employ of the late Judge Wick Justice, back before he was John Cochran.

"Have you got any questions?"

"No, sir," Bannack answered, so he and Clayton did an about-face and left the office.

"We might as well go on over to the courtroom," Clayton said to Conrad Priest, who was waiting outside Turner's door. "I don't know how much the judge will want from you and me, just the part about resistin' arrest, I reckon. John, you're the one who made the arrest both times, in the café and at the house by the creek. So they oughta be questioning you the most."

"Reckon so," Bannack replied. "I just hope they get this thing done quick. I need to get back to Glory. Daryl might be havin' the nervous sweats if I'm gone much longer."

"John, you ever think about movin' up to a higher job in the law business?" Priest asked.

Here it comes, Bannack thought. "You mean try to get hired as a Deputy US Marshal like you and Bill? I ain't sure I'd be any good in a job like that. I kinda like stayin' in one spot like Glory."

"I swear, John," Priest insisted. "I don't think a little town like Glory can hold you for very long. I ain't ever seen a man go after a criminal like you went after Virgil Dawson. You could be doin' the county and the state a lot more good, if you were authorized to go anywhere."

"I gotta agree with him, John," Clayton said. "You might find out you like bein' able to cover more ground, instead of bein' tied down in that little town. You oughta talk to Calvin Turner to see if they're lookin' for more men right now."

"I 'preciate what you're sayin', and I'll think it over. Maybe I'll talk to Calvin Turner before I go back to Glory," he told them, although he had no such intention.

They walked around the jail and entered the court-house through a back entrance into the single story part of the building. They followed a hallway, past an entrance to the two-story jail wing, and Clayton said, "That's where they'll bring Virgil out of the jail. They'll take him right down this hall to the courtroom." They continued down the long hallway, passing several doors until reaching an open door that led into the courtroom, which reminded Bannack of the courtroom in Austin. The two deputies were very instructive in educating him on the way the courtroom was set up, what each section was called, who sat where and so on, everything that he was already well familiar with. He accepted the education politely and refrained from telling them that he had often set up a courtroom where there was none, when he worked for Judge Justice.

CHAPTER 17

Shortly after they sat down, several other people came into the room. Two of them were obviously lawyers, and they paused to have a quick conversation before moving on to sit down at two separate tables. Bannack figured one was the prosecutor and the other was a public defender representing Virgil. There was no one in the jury box because there was to be no jury. Judge Calvin Stark would hear the arguments by the two lawyers and decide the verdict. A few visitors came in the front door and sat down, simply spectators with nothing else to do. Most of them had absolutely no knowledge about the crime or the person who was being tried for it.

A few minutes before the hour of nine, Henry Dawson and his three sons walked into the courtroom. Bannack watched as a guard checked to make sure they were not wearing guns before he allowed them to find seats. When they sat down, he told Clayton, who was sitting next to him, "You might want to tell that guard that Henry Dawson carries a pocket pistol inside his vest."

Clayton was immediately concerned. He got up and went to the guard right away to tell him what Bannack had told him. The guard reacted just as Clayton had and went at once to address the four Dawson men. "Sir, I'm gonna need to have you stand up," he said to Henry.

"Why?" Henry reacted. "What the hell for?"

"Just stand up," Clayton told him.

Henry looked around him at the other deputy, the other court guards, Bannack, and now even the bailiff, who just walked in. They were all focused on him, and they were all armed. Resisting the guard's instructions was out of the question, so he got to his feet and stood quietly while the guard checked inside his vest. "Sir, what is this?" the guard asked when he felt the derringer in Henry's vest. He drew it out and held it up before him. "Do you know it's against the law to carry a weapon into this courtroom? I'm gonna have to place you under arrest for carrying a concealed weapon into a court of law."

Cochran, Dawson thought and looked at once in the Glory town marshal's direction to discover Bannack looking at him. "Whoa!" he blurted. "Wait a minute! I forgot that was in my pocket," he pleaded. "I just carry it for emergencies. We turned all our weapons in at the sheriff's office. I just forgot I had this one in my pocket. I don't even know if it's loaded."

"It's loaded," the guard said and backed two rounds

out of the pocket pistol. "I'm gonna have to ask you to leave the courtroom."

"I can't do that!" Henry pleaded. "That's my son who's on trial this mornin'. These boys are his brothers; he needs to see that we came here to try to support him. You can keep the doggone derringer. I don't want it, anyway."

"These three are your sons, too?" The guard nodded toward them. "You boys, get on your feet. Hand over your pocket pistols," he ordered.

He received nothing but blank stares until Junior spoke. "Ain't none of us got one of them little ol' guns. We ain't got no use for a gun you can't hit the side of the house with."

"We didn't come here to cause no problems," Henry begged. "We just want my son to know we cared enough to come to his trial."

The guard looked at Clayton for help, but Clayton knew them for what they were, and knew if he had any evidence to back him, he'd throw them all in jail. Instead, he just shrugged and left it up to the guard. At that moment, two guards brought Virgil into the courtroom and delivered him to the defendant's table. Another moment saw Judge Calvin Stark enter the courtroom, and the bailiff ordered all to rise. He then introduced the judge, and Stark told everyone to sit down. Flustered, the guard told Henry, "I'm gonna let you stay. I'll turn your pistol over to the sheriff. Sit down and don't disturb the proceedings and you can pick it up with your other weapons."

Judge Stark had the bailiff read the charges against Virgil Dawson, the primary one being a charge of the murder of one, Hurley No Last Name, in the River House saloon in Glory, Texas, as witnessed by two witnesses who could not attend the trial but were represented by signed and verified statements. There were secondary charges filed for resisting arrest, terrorizing the customers and staff of the café next door to the saloon, assaulting the owner, plus attempted escape. Judge Stark turned it over to the prosecutor to make the case for the county. The prosecutor maintained that it was a simple case of blatant disregard for human life and the county was seeking the death penalty.

Virgil's lawyer, a public defender named Wiley Pitt, insisted that the taking of Hurley No Last Name's life was a simple case of two young men, impaired by an overindulgence of alcohol. According to Pitt, the two young men came to an impasse over a card game. They resolved to settle their dispute with the use of firearms. "It was just the victim's poor luck that my client, Mr. Virgil Dawson, was quicker to draw his weapon and fire. So it was simply a duel, a fast-draw contest that happens too often in our saloons, but is not a case of murder. Consequently, Your Honor, we ask that the case be reduced to drunk and disorderly conduct."

The prosecutor walked up to the bench and handed the judge the two witness reports that Bannack had brought with him. "Your Honor, what Mr. Pitt said could have been a fast-draw contest if Hurley No Last Name had a gun. According to what both of these eyewitness reports state, Hurley wasn't wearing a gun and he held both hands up in front of him to indicate he wasn't armed. But Virgil Dawson drew his revolver from his holster, pointed it directly at Hurley No Last Name and fired a mortal shot into his face. When the patrons in the saloon showed their hostility for his cowardly actions, he retreated to Sawyer's Café next door and threatened the customers there and finally chased all of them out except the three Sawyer women. When Russell Sawyer tried to intercede on behalf of his wife and daughters, Virgil Dawson struck him with the barrel of his pistol, opening a gash on the side of his face that required stitching up by the doctor."

It was during that part of his prosecution that he called Bannack to the witness stand. "Now, Marshal Cochran, would you explain the circumstances under which you came to meet with the accused, Virgil Dawson?" Bannack explained how he happened to make a citizen's arrest of Virgil because he was holding the three Sawyer women hostage in the café. He didn't go into any detail of the actual procedure. And when he was asked why he used the term "citizen's arrest," he explained that he was not the town marshal at the time. "But you were the town marshal when you arrested him the second time at the Dawson farm after his escape from the deputies transporting him to Jacksboro, right?"

"That's right," Bannack answered. "You might say I assisted Deputy Marshal Clayton in that arrest since Deputy Priest was wounded."

The prosecutor said that was all he wanted to ask the witness, so Judge Stark asked Virgil's lawyer if he wanted to cross-examine. "Yes, sir, I would, Your Honor," Wiley Pitt replied and got to his feet again. "Marshal Cochran, you're the town marshal of Glory, Texas. Is that right?" Bannack said that it was, so Pitt asked, "Does your jurisdiction extend beyond the city limits of Glory?"

"As town marshal, no, sir, it doesn't," Bannack answered.

"Virgil Dawson told me that while he and his brothers were trying to stop a stampede of their cattle in the middle of the night, you came upon him and knocked him from his horse and placed him under arrest. Is that a fact?"

"Yes, sir, I reckon it is," Bannack answered.

"Marshal Cochran," Wiley Pitt asked, "isn't it a fact that the Dawson farm is outside the city limits of Glory, where you would have no authority whatsoever to arrest Virgil Dawson?"

"Ordinarily, that would be the case," Bannack answered. "But Deputy Marshal Clayton is empowered to deputize someone, and he deputized me. I reckon, officially, it was his arrest, anyway. I just helped him make it."

When Pitt just stood there with obviously nothing left to question, Judge Stark asked him if he had any further questions for the witness. Pitt said he didn't, and the judge told Bannack, "You may step down, Marshal." The whole picture was plain to see in Bannack's opinion and he felt certain the judge had already ruled on it in his mind. He figured Judge Stark was only trying to decide how severe the punishment should be, death or twenty years or life imprisonment. Actually, he was right, but for a show of impartiality, Judge Stark announced that there would be a thirty minute break, during which he would review the testimony. "The court will reconvene at ten-fifteen for the verdict and sentencing thereof," he announced.

The bailiff called for all to rise, and the judge left the bench. The two guards with Virgil marched him out to a holding cell, and the two opposing lawyers walked out of the courtroom while in a conversation with each other, as they had before the trial. Bannack couldn't help wondering if this whole business of deciding the rest of this man's life was little more than a game they played against each other.

"What are we gonna do, Pa?" Gilbert Dawson asked. "It don't look too good for Virgil when you hear them tell about it."

"There ain't nothin' we can do," Henry told him. "We ain't even got our guns and everybody else in here is armed to the teeth. We'll just have to wait to see what that judge decides to do with him. Maybe they'll send him over to Huntsville to the prison there and we might get a chance to cut him loose like we did before. We'll just wait and see what happens, then we'll see what we can do. One thing I know for sure, though, Marshal John Cochran is a walkin' dead man, and he don't even know it. Don't matter what they do to Virgil, I'm gonna kill that devil."

Judge Stark took the full half hour to have his coffee, then he returned to the courtroom to render the verdict he had decided upon before the break. The guards paraded Virgil back into the courtroom, and the bailiff announced the judge once again. "Will the accused rise," the judge ordered, then pronounced, "Virgil Dawson, this court finds you guilty of murder in the first degree. You shall be hanged by the neck until dead. You will be incarcerated in the Jacksboro jail until a date of execution has been decided upon."

"Damn!" Henry Dawson gasped aloud before he could stop himself. He jumped to his feet and started after the two guards leading Virgil out of the courtroom but was stopped by the guard who had taken his pocket pistol from him.

"Mister," the guard told him, "you can't follow them through that door. If you want to see your son, you have to wait till he's back in the county jail. Then you can visit him there. That's where they're takin' him right now."

"But that judge said they was gonna hang him," Henry protested.

"That won't be for a while yet," the guard said, now feeling a hint of compassion for a father's grief for the hanging of his son. "It usually takes a little time to schedule the hangman to perform the execution, and he has to come over here from Fort Worth. So you'll have some time to visit your son before then. They're usually pretty good about letting your family members visit you when you're waitin' for the hangman."

"All right, 'preciate it," Henry said, much to his three sons' relief, for they were greatly outnumbered by the armed lawmen in the courtroom. He came back to the row where they were sitting. "We'll go visit Virgil in the jailhouse after they get him back in a cell. And while we're there, we'll pick up our guns and then we'll decide what we're gonna do."

"They won't let us have our guns back as long as we're in town, will they?" Johnny asked.

"That's only when court's in session," Henry said. "Least, that's what the sign says. We'll go to the jail first and see if they'll let us see Virgil."

They went around to the front entrance to the jail where there were two guards sitting at a long desk. When Henry told the guards who he was, he was surprised by their courteous response to his request to see his son. One of the guards got up from the desk and said, "Follow me and I'll take you upstairs to see your son."

"Just me," Henry asked, "or all of us?"

The guard asked, "These three, his brothers?" Henry and all three boys nodded, so the guard said, "All of ya."

"That's mighty neighborly of ya," Henry said. "When we'd go to see him in the jail at Glory, they'd always make us take our guns off."

The guard smiled at him and said, "You ain't wearin' any guns."

"Oh, that's right," Henry said, "I forgot about that."

The guard unlocked a door at the bottom of the stairs, then led them up the steps where he unlocked another door at the top of the stairs. Then he led them down a narrow corridor between rows of several cells, most of which were occupied by prisoners, all of them staring at the four visitors. When Virgil, in the end cell on one of the two rows, saw them coming down between the cells, he got up from his bunk and came to the bars. "Dawson, you got some visitors," the guard called out.

"Howdy, Pa," Virgil greeted him casually, in an attempt to show an attitude of indifference for his situation. "I thought you and the boys would drop by, but I was hopin' you would bring a couple of guns with you."

"We almost got throwed out of the courtroom because of Pa's little pocket pistol," Junior said. "All our guns are in the sheriff's office."

"When are they gonna hang you?" Johnny asked. "I thought when that judge said you was gonna be hung, they'd throw a rope around your neck and drag you out to the first tree they could find."

"No, you dummy," Gilbert said. "They gotta do a legal execution, with a hangman and somebody sayin' some official words before he swings." He looked back at Virgil and asked, "How you doin', brother?"

"How you think I'm doin'?" Virgil came back sarcastically. "I'm just havin' a helluva good time. Why don't you ask them if you can take my place?"

"Ain't no reason to get your bowels all in an uproar," his father said. "It ain't Gilbert's fault you're settin' where you are." He looked around him to make sure no one could overhear what he said next. "We got you loose the first time they tried to bring you up here. It ain't nobody's fault but yours that John Cochran knocked you off your horse and put you back in jail."

"And that's something else that riles my blood," Virgil responded. "Why the hell ain't nobody shot that big ox? If they hang my butt, I wanna see Marshal Cochran in hell when I get there."

"I done told you we'd get Marshal Cochran," Henry said, lowering his voice again for fear of being overheard. "That's a promise, but our best bet is to catch him on his way back to Glory and we don't know when your hangin' is scheduled. Did anybody tell you when they're gonna do it?"

"He ain't gonna wait around here to watch me swing," Virgil said. "That fool they gave me for a lawyer told me they don't know when the hangman can get over here. He said it would most likely be a couple of weeks, maybe more. Cochran ain't gonna wait for that. He'll head back to Glory right away." The thought of it caused Virgil's already threadbare anger to rise to the point where Henry had to warn him to keep his voice down. "All right, Pa," Virgil said, his voice lower but the tone still angry. "But you and the boys go take care of that devil before he gets back to Glory where it'll be a lot harder for you to do it and get away with it. Then come back and tell me all about it. I don't know if I'll get a chance to get free or not, but if I don't, I want the satisfaction of knowin' he's dead, too."

"You know we ain't give up on the chance to set you free. Ain't that right, boys?" He looked at his other three sons, who all nodded vigorously. "But I reckon if we're gonna settle with John Cochran, you're right, the best chance we've got is to get him on his way back home. So if we're gonna do that, we're gonna have to get our eyes on him right now. He might already be startin' out for Glory while we're standin' here talkin'."

"It's gittin' close to dinnertime," Junior said. "Reckon he might eat dinner before he starts out?"

"I know I would," Gilbert declared. "We oughta go see if we can find him and keep an eye on him till he leaves town."

"We gotta go to the sheriff's office to get our guns before we do anything," Johnny said.

"I swear, I forgot about that," Henry said. "That's what we'll do right now." He gave Virgil what he hoped was a sincere look of faith and said, "We'll be back to see you as soon as we take care of John Cochran. Don't you give up hope." They filed out of the cell room and called for the guard to come unlock the doors to let them out.

They went directly to the Jacksboro sheriff's office to get their weapons and dutifully asked a deputy there if it was lawful to wear their guns in town, now that the court was no longer in session. They were told that the council was considering making it unlawful at all times, but so far the law had not been passed. Henry told him that they were soon going to be leaving town, anyway, but they wanted to be sure they weren't breaking any laws. After leaving the sheriff's office, they got their horses and packhorses ready to ride and tied them in front of the Wildflower Saloon where they could keep an eye on them.

John Bannack met Bill Clayton and Conrad Priest at the Wildflower Saloon for a final drink to celebrate the conclusion of the Virgil Dawson trial. It was a rare occasion when John was anxious to take a drink of whiskey. But after the trouble it had been to finally bring Virgil to trial, he was anxious to celebrate the occasion. In fact, Clayton and Priest talked him into having another before he begged off for good. "I know you said you're anxious to get back to Glory," Clayton said, "but you ain't thinkin' about headin' back tonight, are you?"

"As a matter of fact, I was," Bannack answered. "But I'm thinkin' about changin' my mind and just start back in the mornin' after breakfast. I've got a room that's paid for tonight and supper and breakfast free. I think I'll feel more like ridin' back to Glory in the mornin'. If I'm lucky, nothin' will happen today or tomorrow in my little town, and Daryl will do just fine without me."

"Now, you're talkin' some sense," Priest commented. "I'll have supper with you in the hotel dinin' room, and I expect Deputy Clayton might join us."

"That sounds like a good idea," Bannack said. He suddenly realized Conrad and Bill had become his friends and he could never really remember having a couple of friends before. Certainly not in prison, where he was known simply as The Man from Waco who seldom spoke to anyone. It was the same during the period of time he worked for Judge Wick Justice. He was personal protection for the judge and his clerk, Elwood Wilson. They were both kind and friendly toward him, but they were never really friends. He was just an employee, although he owed Judge Wick more than he could repay him for freeing him from prison. But Conrad and Bill were friends who wanted him to join them in the US Marshal Service as a deputy. It gave him a good feeling but for only a brief moment before a mental picture of their reaction upon discovering his true identity came to his mind. "I expect I'll take advantage of that hotel room and get a good night's sleep, so I can get breakfast as soon as the dinin' room opens in the mornin'," he announced.

"I swear, he sure is anxious to get back to Glory, ain't he?" Clayton commented.

"It must be one of those little gals in Sawyer's Café," Priest replied. "Or maybe one of those two in the hotel dinin' room, most likely Dora. How 'bout it, John?"

Bannack could only smile at the possibility when he

thought about the typical look of caution on the faces of most women meeting him for the first time. "I can understand why you might suspect something like that," he responded to Conrad's question. "But the fact of the matter is, the town council gave me the job of protectin' their town, and I don't think Daryl is ready to handle any real trouble yet. And I need the money they're payin' me as marshal, so I need to get back to my job."

"Looks like we ain't gonna talk him into getting good and drunk tonight, Conrad," Clayton declared. "I swear, I don't know if you can trust a man that don't like likker. At least, we got him to take two drinks today."

"I expect we'd best get back to the office now, since the trial's over," Priest said, "or Calvin Turner's gonna wanna know who gave us the afternoon off."

"Yeah, you're right," Clayton said, and all three got up from the table. "We'll see you at supper, John." The three of them walked out of the saloon together, then the two deputies headed back toward the courthouse while Bannack went to the stable.

"They're comin' out of the Wildflower!" Johnny Dawson exclaimed to his father. The two of them were standing beside a tree near the blacksmith shop. "Them deputies went back to the courthouse, but it looks like he's headin' toward the stable."

"Yeah, he's headin' to the stable," Henry Dawson agreed.

"You reckon he's gittin' ready to leave town?" Johnny wondered. "Want me to signal Junior and Gilbert?"

"No," his father told him. "He ain't leavin' town. He ain't carryin' no saddlebags or nothin' and he would be if he was fixin' to get on his horse and leave. Junior and Gilbert will let us know if he leaves town and, if he does, we'll bring the horses."

Junior and Gilbert were sitting out in front of Garner's Saloon, which was the closest saloon to the stable. "Look comin' yonder," Junior said. "He's headin' to the stable. We better get ready to signal Pa and Johnny."

"He ain't carryin' nothing with him," Gilbert, like his father, pointed out. "Let's wait and see if he comes out on his horse." Their plan, as their father told them, was to keep an eye on Bannack, since they had no idea when he might start back to Glory. Then when he did leave, they would follow him and blow the lantern out in his head. They didn't really care if he was heading back to Glory. They just wanted him out of Jacksboro with all its lawmen in town, anywhere where there were no witnesses. So they continued to sit in front of the saloon and watch the stable while Bannack was inside telling Jim Fowler that he planned to come get his horses in the morning after breakfast.

"I 'preciate you takin' care of my horses for me," Bannack said to Jim Fowler.

"No trouble a-tall," Jim replied. "I'll give 'em a portion

of grain in the mornin', since you're gonna ride back to Glory tomorrow. Maybe I oughta give that buckskin a little more than that, since he's totin' a pretty good load," he japed in reference to Bannack's size.

"You sure I don't owe you a little extra for that?" Bannack asked.

"Yes, sir, I'm sure. It's all paid for by the county, just like your hotel bill and your meals," Jim said. "I give 'em a lower rate than I usually charge, so everybody's happy."

"Are you a drinkin' man?" Bannack asked.

"Why, sure, ain't every man a drinkin' man?"

"Well, I ain't goin' to the saloon tonight, but I'd like to buy you a couple of drinks. I think my horses would like to thank you for the good care you gave 'em." He reached into his pocket and pulled out some change. Then he picked out three quarters and handed them to Jim. "Here you go, the buckskin wants to buy you a drink, the sorrel wants to buy you one, and I wanna buy you one."

"Why, hell," Jim responded, "you didn't have to do that, but I'll thank you kindly, and I'll drink to your health and a good ride home."

"I'll see you in the mornin'," Bannack said and walked out of the stable feeling like a big shot. He walked on down to the hotel, unaware of the two men following along behind him on the busy street and without a notion that anyone would be following him.

Junior and Gilbert followed the big man down the

street until they got to the Wildflower Saloon where they had left their horses tied. They stopped there and watched until Bannack continued on to the hotel and went inside. Their father and their younger brother joined them at the horses shortly after. "He went back in the hotel," Junior said when Henry and Johnny walked over to them. "He sure ain't actin' like he's fixin' to ride outta here tonight."

"I don't think he is gonna go back tonight," Henry said. "He's gonna stay here in that hotel tonight and ride back to Glory in the mornin'."

"How you know that, Pa?" Gilbert asked. "He rode up here to Jacksboro in the middle of the night when him and them deputies brought Virgil up here."

"He had a reason that time," Henry said. "He knew we'd be waitin' for him if they rode up here in the daylight. He ain't got no reason to start back at night this time. And if he was in a hurry to get back, he's go right now, but he don't act like he's in a hurry to get goin'. Nah, he ain't goin' back tonight. He's gonna have hisself some supper, go to sleep in a nice bed, and have his breakfast in the mornin', then he's headin' back to Glory. So he better enjoy it because he ain't gonna like what's waitin' for him on the road to Glory."

"That sure makes sense to me," Junior said. "That's what I would do, if I was him."

"If you was him, I'd put a bullet in your head right now," Johnny japed.

"So we're gonna climb on our horses and head outta

town and make camp for the night," Henry said. Before they started to question him, he continued, "We'll ride down the road to Glory, till we find a good spot to wait for Marshal Cochran. This time, we're gonna get the job done right and we'll come back here and let Virgil know we done what he wanted." He got a serious nod of commitment from each of his three sons, then they climbed on their horses and backed away from the hitching rail and rode out the south road.

CHAPTER 18

Clark Spencer was familiar with Stephenville. It was on Judge Grant's circuit. The judge had tried a murder case there about a year and a half ago, which turned out to be a duel and the judge had to rule in favor of the accused. There were so many eyewitnesses that testified that the young man who died should not have challenged the accused to face him in the street. A foolish young man, the judge had decided, he deserved to get shot for challenging a known gunslinger. Spencer tried to remember the name of the accused who was acquitted on the ride from Warren Bannack's farm to Stephenville. It came to him on the second day, Ace Parker, and he could picture the big swaggering bully who had gained a reputation as a fast gun.

He rode into the town of Stephenville at dinnertime. He was ready for a good meal cooked by a real cook, and he remembered where the only place to get one was located. It was a saloon called the Oasis and they had a helluva good cook. He hoped she was still there. As he rode along the one short main street, it appeared that nothing had changed since he had last been there. So he pulled up to the hitching rail and dismounted, tied his horses to the rail, and went inside. When he walked up to the bar, Moe Price, the bartender, gave him a concentrated look before greeting him. "Howdy, what can I pour for you?"

"Give me a double shot of rye whiskey," Spencer said, "and then I'm going to go back to your dinin' section. Is Pearl still doin' the cookin'?"

"Yes, sir, she sure is," Moe answered. "I remember you now. You was with that Judge that comes here when we have a court case. You was with him when they tried to hang ol' Ace Parker for shootin' Billy Douglas in a face-off in the street."

"That's a fact," Spencer said. "Is Ace Parker still around?"

"No, Ace is dead," Moe said. "Just a short while ago."

"He ran into somebody who was a little faster than him, I reckon," Spencer speculated.

"Well, I don't know about that," Moe replied. "He ran into somebody a whole lot bigger and somebody who backed him down. It was right here in the Oasis." Moe went on to tell Spencer about the incident when Ace tried to force himself on a lady and her child when they were eating dinner. "Well, like I said, this big stranger moved in on Ace and backed him down. It got away with Ace so bad that he and two of his friends followed the woman and the stranger out to her ranch and set up an ambush for the stranger on his way back.

But the big feller outsmarted 'em. He went around the ambush and came up behind 'em. He just wounded the other two fellers, but he killed Ace."

Spencer was intrigued. "When did all that happen?"

"I don't remember exactly," Moe said, "but it wasn't that long ago."

"And you say this was a big fellow, bigger than Ace Parker?" He was getting more and more interested in the story. In fact, he decided, it couldn't have been anybody else but John Bannack, and it confirmed what Warren Bannack had said. He knew now he was heading in the right direction. "Do you happen to remember this fellow's name?"

"No, sir, I don't," Moe answered. He stroked his chin and gave it some thought. "Matter of fact, I don't believe he ever said his name the whole time he was in here. He mighta said it to Emily Green when he sat down at the table with her but not no other time."

"The name, John Bannack, sound familiar?" Spencer asked. Moe shook his head and said that it did not. "Well, I'll see what Miss Pearl has cooked up for dinner," he said, tossed his whiskey back, and headed for the tables set aside for dinner customers.

"Pearl!" Moe yelled. "Dinner customer!"

Pearl Simpson came to the kitchen door in time to see Spencer pulling a chair out at one of her tables. "Are you gonna want coffee?" the tiny woman asked. He said that he would, so she continued on out the door with the cup of coffee she had already poured. "Beef stew today," she said when she placed the coffee before him. "If you don't want that, I can fry you a slice of ham."

"I'll take the stew," Spencer said. "It's been a pretty good while since I've been back here. You probably don't remember me."

"I don't remember your name," she said, "but you're the fellow who came in here with Judge Grant."

Surprised, he said, "Well, you sure do have a good memory. I'll bet you remember the name of that fellow that shot Ace Parker. You know, that big man that sat down with the lady and chased Ace away."

Pearl paused for a few seconds as if trying to recall. "Come to think of it, I never heard his name. I expect he told Emily Green his name but not when I was around."

"Doesn't matter," he said. "I was just curious."

"Let me go fix you up a plate of beef stew," she said then. "You want some honey for your biscuits?" He said that would be nice, so she retreated to the kitchen again, thinking she had a funny feeling about the man. He was polite as could be, but for some reason she had decided not to tell him that she heard the man who shot Ace Parker tell Emily his name was John Cochran.

Spencer took his time to enjoy the generous meal Pearl served him because he couldn't remember a town between Stephenville and Rubin's Store. He intended to stay on this road because, so far, indications seemed to prove that Bannack had definitely gone this way. He was bothered somewhat, however, by the fact that Bannack would involve himself in the troubles of people like Emily Green. His picture of Judge Wick's panther was one of a heartless ex-convict with animal-like instincts who cared not a fig for Emily Green's problems. With those thoughts in mind, he left Stephenville and rode until his horses began to show signs of needing a rest. He pushed them a little farther until reaching a stream that offered a good camping spot, both for him and his horses. So he decided to stop there for the night, thinking he might not find another as good.

Since he had time to do it, Bannack decided to take advantage of the hotel's washroom and take a hot bath and shave. It would cost him fifty cents, but he thought he could afford one on this occasion, so he paid the attendant to heat the water and get him a towel. The attendant, a young man of sixteen, took one look at him and decided it would take two towels. He also provided a razor and shaving soap for his use. *If I was back in Glory, I'd go to Buster's and let him shave me and give me a haircut, too,* he thought. It took a little maneuvering to fold most of his body into the tub, but he got enough in it to enjoy the hot soak. Afterward, he felt rejuvenated and eager to meet his friends for supper. He put on his clean shirt and pronounced himself ready. It was still a little too early for the dining room to open for supper, so he decided to pass some time riding one of the two big rocking chairs on the hotel porch.

When he went out on the porch, he found both the

two big rockers occupied, one by a lady, the other by a small boy, obviously her son. There were several other chairs on the porch, all smaller, straight-back chairs, so he looked them over to see which might be the sturdiest. The woman watched him with interest for only a short time before she said, "Ricky, come over here and sit beside me. Let the gentleman have that big chair." The boy got out of the chair and went over to sit down in the chair his mother indicated.

"Oh, you don't have to do that, ma'am," Bannack was quick to insist. "I don't want to chase the boy outta the rocker. There are plenty of other chairs."

"He doesn't mind, do you, Ricky?" He didn't answer, only slowly shaking his head and his eyes growing larger as he gazed up at the man towering over them. "Besides," the woman said, "I wasn't sure I was going to be able to help you up, if one of those smaller chairs collapsed under you."

He laughed with her, then said, "Well, Ricky, I appreciate you givin' up your chair for me. And I thank you, ma'am. It's usually the other way around, though. A gentleman is supposed to give up a chair for a lady, but I have to admit, I ain't ever been mistaken for a gentleman."

She smiled at him and said, "It's not always easy to recognize one by the outside wrapper he comes in. Are you waiting for the stagecoach?"

"No, ma'am, I'm just killin' some time until the dinin' room opens. Are you and Ricky waitin' for the stage?" He didn't see any luggage, if they were going somewhere.

"Yes," she answered. "My husband's on the stage from Fort Worth, and Ricky and I haven't seen him in almost two months. My name's Mary Davis and my husband, Wilbur, is the loan officer in the Jacksboro Citizen's Bank. That's my buggy tied at the end of the rail there."

Wilbur Davis, he thought and wondered why it somehow had a familiar ring to him, but he couldn't associate it with anything. "Almost two months, huh? Well I expect you'll be glad to see him. He was in Fort Worth, was he?"

"No, not really," she said. "That's where he got on the stagecoach. He was actually in Waco all that time. He's been down there substituting for the president of the First Bank of Waco while he was recovering from some complications after catching pneumonia. My husband used to work at that bank as a teller years ago."

Bannack suddenly felt as if he had been struck in the chest with a blunt object as it all came rushing back to him. The First Bank of Waco, the bank his brother robbed for which he went to prison. Wilbur Davis was the bank teller who testified at his trial and was so anxious to step forward when Judge Grant asked him to identify the bank robber. He remembered Wilbur Davis pointing his finger at him and testifying, "That's the man who robbed the bank and threatened to shoot us." Bannack went stone silent for a few minutes while he gathered his wits again. Then he realized that Mary Davis had asked him a question, so he asked her to repeat it.

"I asked you what kind of business you are in," she said.

"I'm the town marshal in Glory, Texas," he answered. "John Cochran's my name. I had to come up to Jacksboro to testify at a trial."

She started to make another comment but was interrupted by the sound of the stagecoach coming up the middle of the street. She sprang up from her chair and, grabbing Ricky's hand, hurried down the steps to the street to wait on the boardwalk. Curious to get a look at the man who had identified him as a bank robber after so many years, Bannack got up and walked to the edge of the porch. When the coach came to a stop, an elderly couple got out before Wilbur Davis stepped down to be greeted warmly by his wife and son. Standing at the edge of the porch, Bannack recognized the younger man now wearing the signs of almost six years of aging. He felt no hostility for the younger Wilbur Davis who had condemned him. Although he had been wrong, he didn't know it at the time and Bannack knew he would have been convicted with or without Davis's testimony.

Whereas he could recognize Wilbur Davis, Bannack wondered if Davis could recognize him. He knew that prison had changed him drastically. He was still growing when he was incarcerated and physically, he had become twice the size of the boy who was sent to the prison hard-labor camps. When he saw Davis pointing to a trunk on top of the coach that he couldn't reach, he decided to see if he recognized him. He stepped down from the porch, walked up to the stage, and said, "Let me give you a hand." Then he reached up, took hold of the trunk, and pulled it off the stage. "On your buggy, Mary?"

Surprised, Mary responded, "Why, thank you, John. Yes, on the buggy. How nice of you."

"No bother," he said, "I owe you that for the rockin' chair." He took the trunk and placed it on the back of the buggy.

When he came back to the hotel steps, she said, "Wilbur, this is John Cochran, he's the town marshal in Glory."

Wilbur was not quite sure what to think, so he extended his hand and said, "Thanks for your help, sir."

"Don't mention it," Bannack replied and trapped the soft hand of the banker in his rough paw, but only squeezed hard enough to let him know it was captured. "Have a pleasant evenin'." He nodded to Mary and went back to the hotel porch and sat down in the rocking chair again, amazed by the obvious fact that he had changed so much since Wilbur Davis had last seen him that Wilbur didn't know who he was. He chuckled when he saw Wilbur and Mary having what looked like a heated conversation as they climbed aboard the buggy. They were too far away for him to actually hear it.

"How the hell do you know that scary-looking man?" Wilbur asked in a rather demanding tone.

"We just met him, Ricky and I," Mary answered. "He was a very nice man. Wasn't he, Ricky? I don't know why you're so upset."

"You really don't, do you?" Wilbur responded. "Any woman with any sense at all knows better than to just let any stranger start up with them. You're just lucky the stage got here when it did. From the looks of that fellow, he could have been a bank robber or worse."

"Oh, fiddle," Mary responded, "he was the town marshal of Glory."

"Sure he was," Wilbur replied. "I bet he even had a badge to show you, too."

"If he did, he didn't bother to show it to me," she said. "I wish to hell I had invited him to supper with us. Maybe I could have some polite conversation tonight. Welcome home, by the way."

Sometimes this world doesn't make a damn bit of sense, Bannack was thinking when he walked in the dining room and saw Conrad Priest and Bill Clayton sitting at a table back near the kitchen door. They both signaled him as soon as he came in the door. Lucy Webb was standing beside the table, talking to them, and when they signaled, she turned and flashed a big smile when she saw him. Robert Fraiser was at his usual post and he said, "Your friends are waiting for you."

"Evenin', Robert," he said and walked on back. He had friends waiting to have supper with him and they were both lawmen. And he had just come from meeting again a man who had testified in the trial that branded him a criminal for life. He wondered what would happen if Wilbur Davis walked in and pointed at him and said, "That's John Bannack, bank robber, alias the man from Waco, alias Judge Wick's panther." He realized again how fragile the world was that he lived in, and he couldn't help but think he might be making a mistake by returning to Glory. His best course of action might be to keep going northwest, or at least to get out of Texas. Thinking again of the coincidence with Wilbur Davis, he wondered how long it might be before someone who knew he was John Bannack might drop in on him in Glory. As he approached the table, he decided to enjoy the supper and the evening and decide whether or not to return to Glory in the morning when he picked up his horses.

"What are you looking so serious about?" Lucy Webb asked him when he pulled a chair back to sit down.

"Was I lookin' serious?" Bannack replied. "I reckon I've been worryin' about my reputation if I keep eatin' with these two deputies. I don't want it to get back to the folks in Glory."

"I don't blame you," Lucy said. "Set yourself down and we won't tell anybody you ate with 'em. I'll get you some coffee."

It was an enjoyable supper and they lingered over it

for quite a while. Afterward, Conrad and Bill tried talking Bannack into one more drink at the Wildflower before retiring for the night. "I already said I wasn't gonna go to the saloon tonight," he reminded them. "Besides, you boys have to go back to work in the mornin', and I don't want you blamin' me for the way you feel tomorrow."

"We need to have a drink for good luck," Clayton said.

"One drink," Bannack relented, "and that's it for me."

"Why the hell don't you come in tomorrow and talk to Calvin Turner about joinin' up with the marshal service?" Priest asked. "I know damn well he'd love to sign you up."

"I would, Conrad, but if I did, the town of Glory would dry up and blow away. And I can't have that on my conscience," Bannack answered. He looked at Lucy and said, "Before you know it, they'd turn me into a drunk, too."

"Then you better go on back to Glory," she joked.

In spite of what he had told Jim Fowler, he went to the Wildflower with his friends and had their farewell drink, two in fact. Then they finally said goodnight, planning to meet for breakfast in the morning. Bannack found himself worrying more and more about those wanted posters. It would be pretty tough to handle if his two friends found out about him and were given the job to arrest him, because he was not planning to surrender to any law enforcement officer. Some of his last thoughts before finally falling to sleep that night were that it might be best to keep traveling far away from there. And if worse came to worse, and a shoot-out occurred, at least it wouldn't be against his friends.

CHAPTER 19

Waking at first light the next morning, Spencer saddled his horses and set out on Bannack's trail once again. When he came to a sizable creek after riding a good distance, he decided he'd best not pass it up. So he stopped to rest and water his horses and make some breakfast for himself. Ready to ride again, he was back in the saddle but only rode about five miles when he saw Rubin's Store up ahead. It had been a while since he and the judge had traveled up this far on this road, but he remembered it. The building was a store and just beyond the store, there was a crossroads. And if he turned east at the crossroads, that road would take him to Fort Worth. To the west, he was not sure where the road would lead. Not to any town that he knew of, that much was certain. And that option might have been the one that Bannack thought to be his safest bet. There was a good chance that Bannack had stopped at the store, and if he had, the owner of the store would surely remember him. Spencer could only hope that Bannack might have given the owner some idea as to which road he would take at the crossroad.

"Rubin's Store," Spencer read aloud, remembering the old man who owned it. He pulled up to the hitching rail and stepped down from the saddle. When he climbed the steps to the porch and walked inside, he caused a tiny bell on the top of the door to announce his entrance.

"Howdy," Paul Rubin sang out as he walked in from the door to the storeroom. "What can I do for you?"

"Howdy," Spencer returned. "I thought you might have some smokin' tobacco. I'm plumb out, and I need to get some coffee. I'm fixed up pretty good on everything else." He didn't actually need tobacco and coffee, he had plenty of both, but he thought Rubin might be more forthcoming with information if he bought something.

Rubin went about the business of showing Spencer the package sizes the coffee and tobacco came in, and Spencer made his selections. "I recollect you was in here before," Rubin said, "but I can't remember when."

"I was in here with Judge Raymond Grant last time," Spencer reminded him. "I'm a special investigator for the governor. Clark Spencer's my name. This trip, I'm on a special assignment to try to catch up with an escaped convict named John Bannack. He might have stopped in here on his way to wherever he's goin'. I think you'd remember him if he did, great big fellow, looks like he could fight a bear."

Cora Rubin walked into the store in time to hear Spencer's description of Bannack. "There was a gentleman in here that sure fit that description. Wasn't there, Rubin? I don't think he ever said his name, but I don't think he was the man you say you're looking for. He certainly didn't act like an escaped convict. Just a really nice man, do you remember his name, Paul? Did he ever say?"

"He might have," Paul answered, "but if he did, I forgot it."

Once more, Spencer was confused, John Bannack, a gentleman? Judge Wick's panther, a really nice man? But it had to be Bannack, going by the physical description. "Did he say where he was going?"

"I don't remember if he said or not," Paul said, "but I was out on the porch and watched him ride away. He got to the crossroads and went straight across, headin' for Glory."

Well, that's where I'm going, then, Spencer thought. "Much obliged for the information. I reckon I'd best be movin' along."

"You're welcome and thank you for the business," Rubin said. He stood there for a while, watching Spencer ride toward the crossroads. In a few minutes, he said, "He went to Glory."

Cora moved up to stand beside her husband. "Do you think John Cochran is who that man says he is?"

"Hell, no, but I worry about him a little bit 'cause I don't think that feller is who he says he is."

* * *

Walking down the hallway, Bannack passed Lucy Webb's door just in time to bump into Clayton coming out of her room. "Lucy ain't here," Clayton said without thinking. "She's already gone to work. I just told her I'd check her room. She was afraid she'd forgot to blow her lamp out."

"I swear, Bill, that wasn't bad, considerin' you only had a couple of seconds to come up with it," Bannack said. "We sure wouldn't want the hotel to burn down."

"Well, doggone it," Clayton declared, "I don't want to do nothin' to soil Lucy's reputation."

"Lucy strikes me as not givin' a damn what anybody thinks about her reputation," Bannack said. "But you don't have to worry about me. I ain't got anybody to tell." They walked up the hallway to the dining room entrance and walked in just as Robert Fraiser was turning the sign around to the OPEN side.

"Good morning, gentlemen," Robert greeted them formally. "Your colleague, Deputy Priest, awaits you. He arrived five minutes ago." They returned his greetings and proceeded to the usual table.

"I was beginnin' to think you two were gonna skip breakfast this mornin'," Priest said. "I've been sittin' here half an hour. You know that's a sign you're gettin' old when you can't get outta bed in the mornin'."

"When you get where you can't tell time, that's

another sign you're gettin' old," Clayton replied. "Robert said you got here five minutes ago."

"That lying son of . . ." Priest started but was interrupted when Lucy popped out of the kitchen with the coffee.

"Good morning, boys," Lucy greeted them cheerfully. "Did everybody have a good night?"

Bannack and Priest returned her greeting, but Clayton grinned and said, "I reckon, but I tossed and turned a lot before I finally went to sleep."

"I'll bet you did," Lucy came back, under her breath before asking, "Ham and eggs, everybody?" She got an affirmative on that and got their preference on how they wanted the eggs, then went to the kitchen to give Molly the order.

Breakfast was good with fried potatoes and biscuits and honey to go with the ham and eggs. They did not linger over it as they had at supper the night before because Clayton and Priest had to report to headquarters on time. When they finished, they shook hands with Bannack and again expressed their appreciation to him for saving their butts on the arrest of Virgil Dawson. Bannack said it was a pleasure working with them and told them to take care of themselves. When they left, he thanked Lucy and Robert for their hospitality, then went back to his room to get his saddlebags and rifle before checking out of the hotel.

"Mornin'," Jim Fowler greeted him when he walked into the stable. "I got you all ready to go. You might

wanna check the cinch on your saddle. I tightened it to
the notch that looked like it was the one you used. I
put your packsaddle on just like you left it."

"I 'preciate it, Jim," Bannack responded. "Thanks for
takin' good care of my horses while I was here. I feel
like I owe you a little extra to add to what the county
pays you."

"No, not at all," Fowler insisted. "Weren't no trouble
at all and I'm gonna have a couple of drinks of likker
tonight, thanks to you, so let's call it even. You headin'
back to Glory this mornin', I reckon. Looks like you got
a nice day to travel."

"Yes, it does, don't it?" Bannack replied. He glanced
at his packhorse, trying to remember what supplies
he was carrying that would still be good for a long
time. Thinking about it now, he wondered why he had
brought his packhorse with him to Jacksboro, since it
was not that long a ride. Maybe his subconscious had
already figured he wouldn't be returning to Glory when
he was finished here. Having made that very decision,
he climbed up into the saddle and wheeled the buckskin away from the stable. "So long, Jim," he said and
started out toward the road leading north, hoping it
would lead him to a place unlikely to ever see a wanted
poster. He still had a little bit of money, but he was
going to have to find a source for more, since there
would be no more marshal's salary. He would most
likely seek some employment as a ranch hand. He had

no real experience working cattle, but surely some ranch might have use for a man of his size.

When he was passing behind the jail, he reined the buckskin to a stop to look at a couple of workers repairing the gallows. He wondered how long it would take before Daryl Boyd was ready to deal with men like Virgil Dawson. It might still be a while, he thought. He recalled the occasion of his meeting Buster Bridges near Rubin's Store and the fight with the two outlaws to save Buster's new barber chair. The chain of events after that meeting seemed an unlikely path to the job of town marshal in the little town of Glory. It was a story that would in all likelihood send Judge Raymond Grant into a fit of hysterics. "Hell," he declared when it struck him that he could not leave that town now with no marshal. "I might have done just enough work with Daryl to get him killed. Damn the Wanted Posters!" He wheeled the buckskin around and started back to Glory.

It was close to dinnertime when Spencer rode into the town of Glory. He had never been in the little town before. When he was in this part of the territory, traveling with Judge Grant, that crossroads behind him at Rubin's Store was where they had always taken the east–west road that led back to Fort Worth. Now seeing the town for the first time, he was surprised to discover it was this big. He slow-walked the gray gelding along the street until he came to the town marshal's office. And just beyond it, across the street, he saw the River

House Saloon and next door, Sawyer's Café. They might answer his two needs of the moment, a drink of whiskey and some dinner, so he pointed the gray in that direction and tied him at the hitching rail.

He walked inside, paused a few seconds to look the place over, then walked over to the bar where he saw a short little man talking to the bartender. Smut Smith interrupted the conversation with Buster Bridges to greet the new customer. "Welcome to the River House. Whaddleya have?"

"I'll have a double shot of rye whiskey," Spencer replied.

"There's a man who gets right down to business," Smut said as he poured the whiskey. "Ain't seen you in here before."

"Ain't been in here before," Spencer said. "Not a bad lookin' little town."

"You lookin' to do some business here, or just passin' through?" Smut asked.

"I'm lookin' for somebody," Spencer answered, "and I'm thinkin' I might find him here in Glory."

"You a lawman or something?" Buster asked.

"I'm a special investigator for the governor, and I'm lookin' for a man who escaped from prison. His name's John Bannack. I think he mighta showed up here." Smut and Buster looked at each other and shrugged. "This fellow is hard to miss," Spencer went on. "Stands about yea-high"—he held his hand up high over his head—"and built like a brick outhouse." Buster and Smut both laughed. "What's so funny?" Spencer asked.

"You just described our town marshal," Buster said. "He's the only man I've ever seen around here who fits that description. Ain't that right, Smut?" Smut agreed.

"What's the marshal's name?" Spencer asked.

"Cochran," Buster answered, "John Cochran, and he's a stud horse like that fellow you're huntin'. But I hope that fellow you're lookin' for ain't here in town right now 'cause John's outta town." Spencer asked where he was, and Buster said, "He's up in Jacksboro. That's the county seat. He's up there for a murder trial for a fellow who killed a cowhand right here in this saloon."

"That's right," Smut confirmed, "feller named Virgil Dawson, but Marshal Cochran arrested him at Sawyer's next door when Virgil holed up in there holdin' the Sawyer women as hostages. John weren't marshal then, but he went in there and drug ol' Virgil out and took him to the jail."

Spencer could feel his pulse quicken in response to hearing that. "So this Cochran fellow wasn't the marshal then? And now he is?"

"That's right," Buster said. "The fellow who was the marshal quit when Virgil was holed up in Sawyer's and dared him to come get him." Buster paused to chuckle. "But John was hungry and Virgil was holdin' up supper. The town council hired him as the new marshal on the spot."

I found him! Spencer told himself. *He didn't get any farther than Glory,* he thought smugly. To further verify it, he said, "When I stopped at a little store called

Rubin's, back at the crossroads of the Fort Worth road, the fellow who owns that store described a man like your marshal in his store about a little while back. You reckon that mighta been your marshal?"

Buster hesitated only a second to recall the time before answering. "Yeah, that was John," he said with certainty.

"How do you know that?" Spencer asked.

"'Cause I was with him up that way," Buster answered. "John helped me bring a barber chair for my shop back to Glory." Cocksure a moment before, Buster's statement now gave Spencer pause. According to what he had pieced together up to now, Bannack was traveling alone from Stephenville, just following the road to Glory. He stopped briefly at Rubin's Store before continuing on to Glory. Now this little half-pint is saying he went back down that road with Bannack, or Cochran, whoever the hell he was. Did that mean Bannack had been in Glory before that time, or not at all, and this Cochran fellow is just another man the size of John Bannack. *Nah, it has to be him,* he decided.

"Who's watchin' the town while your marshal is in Jacksboro?" Spencer asked. "Is there a deputy marshal?"

"Nah," Buster answered, "there ain't no deputy. There's a young feller that works for the marshal, but he ain't no deputy."

"He's come a long way since Cochran started workin' with him, though," Smut offered in Daryl's defense. "When he worked for Jim Bryan, Daryl didn't do nothin' but clean up and keep the water buckets full. But if you see him lately, he's wearin' a gun, and Clem Shaw says the marshal's been teachin' him how to handle it. He's gonna make a sure-enough deputy out of Daryl before he's done."

"When is Marshal Cochran supposed to be back in town?" Spencer asked.

"I asked Daryl that this mornin'," Buster replied. "He said he weren't sure, but he said he'd be gettin' back here as soon as the trial was over. He went to Jacksboro on Sunday 'cause the trial was set for Monday mornin'. Daryl said John didn't expect the trial to take long, so he expected him back yesterday."

"Yesterday?" Spencer echoed. Suddenly, he wondered, *What if maybe Bannack decided it was time to move on?* He wasn't very happy with that thought, since he was sure he had run him to ground. What to do? Wait for him to show up? He could have been delayed for any number of reasons. Or should he climb back on that gray gelding and head for Jacksboro? *Damn!* he thought. Then he told himself that Bannack had built a new identity for himself here in Glory. Surely, he wouldn't abandon it so easily. So the smart thing to do would be to wait him out. He might be taking advantage of Jacksboro's saloons and brothels. He decided he would wait. "How's that place next door for dinner?"

"You can't go wrong at Sawyer's," Mutt answered. "That's as good an eatin' place as you'll find. The hotel dinin' room ain't bad, either."

"Well, I think I'll try 'em both," Spencer said. "I'll have another double shot of rye and go next door to

Sawyer's for dinner. Then I'll see if I can get a room in the hotel and I'll try their dinin' room for supper. And maybe I'll see you later on tonight." He looked at Buster and asked, "How 'bout you, neighbor? You ready for another drink? I'm buying."

"I can always take another drink," Buster replied, "'specially when it's my favorite kind, the kind somebody else pays for." They all chuckled and Smut poured himself one as well. They tossed them back, and Spencer walked out of the saloon and went into Sawyer's Café. "I swear," Buster said after he was gone, "he's sure 'nough a sport, ain't he?"

Russell Sawyer welcomed him into the café and told him to sit wherever he liked, so he sat down at a table by a window. Maybe it was the rye whiskey, Spencer couldn't say for sure, but he had a good feeling about this town of Glory. He liked the idea of making himself comfortable and just waiting for Bannack to come to him. He was looking forward to Marshal *Cochran's* return from Jacksboro, and he felt positive that he would be returning. "Well, from that expression on your face, you look like you're already pleased with your first visit to Sawyer's," Louella said interrupting his thoughts. "That's the kind of expression we hope to see after you've eaten."

He gave her a good-natured chuckle. "I guess you caught me thinkin' about something that always pleases me. And now, you and your cook are gonna have to work real hard to keep that expression on my face."

"Well, we're sure gonna try to do that very thing," Louella said. "Do I start you off with coffee?"

"Yes, ma'am, you sure can," he replied. "What's the special today?"

"Effie's meatloaf and baked beans," Louella answered, "guaranteed to set you free."

"That sounds like just what I need," Spencer said. *Might set part of me free for sure,* he thought. Louella was back right away carrying a plate of meatloaf and baked beans in generous portions as well as a plate with a couple of fresh baked biscuits. Right behind her, her sister, Susie, came with the coffeepot and a cup. While Susie poured his coffee, he sampled the meatloaf and was pleased to find it as good as the bartender next door said. *Yes, sir,* he thought, *I'll sit right here and wait for Bannack to come back to me.* He decided to check the marshal's office after he finished dinner to make doubly sure Bannack hadn't come back to town.

When he had finished his meal and was drinking one final cup of coffee, he engaged Louella in conversation when she came to pick up his empty plate. "I understand you have a new town marshal," he said.

"That's a fact," Louella said, "John Cochran and he's a good one. Everybody feels safer since the town council hired John to take that job."

There was little wonder why Bannack decided to stop in this little town, instead of continuing on to the wilds of the northwest territory. The temptation was too strong to settle in as the local hero. He had a paying job and no doubt any number of extra benefits that came with it. *It's a downright shame to have somebody like me come along and blow all that dream of his to hell,* he thought sarcastically. If it were up to him, he would simply shoot Bannack on sight, rather than risk dealing with him as a prisoner. But Judge Grant wanted Bannack to suffer the years away in prison. Death would end his suffering too quickly. Spencer could understand that, and if it proved possible, he would honor the judge's wishes. But if he did capture him, he planned to cripple him with wounds to his shoulders and legs to immobilize him, then transport him in chains back to prison. The thought of it brought a smile to his lips.

"Ah, there it is," Louella said when she walked by his table, "that smile of satisfaction. You must have enjoyed your dinner."

"That's right," he said at once. "You caught me at it, didn't you?"

He paid Russell for his dinner and walked out of the café. Across the street, at an angle, he saw the town marshal's office and jail, so he walked directly across the street first in case Bannack was back already. Wick's panther would recognize him immediately and he wasn't comfortable with the thought of being seen as he walked diagonally across the middle of the street. Now, on the same side of the street as the jail, he walked close to the faces of the shops between him and the jail. When he stepped up to the door of the marshal's office, he looked through the glass to see Daryl sitting at the desk and no sign of Bannack. So he opened the door and walked in.

Daryl looked up from the desk to greet the stranger. "Can I help you, sir?"

"Are you the town marshal?" Spencer asked, playing dumb.

"No, sir, I'm Daryl Boyd. I work for the marshal," he replied. "Marshal Cochran ain't here today. He had to go to court in Jacksboro. Is there anything I can help you with?"

"Nothing important," Spencer said. "I'm gonna stop in your town for a day or two and I always like to let the local law enforcement know when I'm in town." He could see that he had sparked Daryl's interest with that, so he continued. "My name's Frank Johnson." He decided he'd best make up a name. "I'm a special investigator for the state's judicial department. I've heard of Marshal Cochran, so I was hopin' to meet him while I'm in town. When do you expect him back?"

"I expected him back yesterday," Daryl answered. "So he could show up at any time now. The trial he was attending could have gone longer than they expected."

"I'm investigating the case of an escaped convict," Spencer said. "A dangerous man who was serving a sentence of twenty years down in the Huntsville Unit of the Texas State Prison. He's only served five years of that sentence and we've had reports that he was seen over in this part of the state. I've got a copy of his wanted poster right here. You've probably seen it already." He handed it to Daryl. "His name's John Bannack."

Daryl took it and briefly looked it over. "Yes, sir,

I've seen it. He's a big fellow, almost as big as Marshal Cochran. We haven't seen anybody that size come through Glory except Marshal Cochran." He smiled and added, "I told Clem Shaw about that poster, he owns the stable, and he said that fellow better not come through Glory because we've got a marshal as big as he is."

Spencer couldn't believe what he was hearing. He had to restrain himself from slapping the young man in the back of the head. Instead, however, he started asking questions, hoping they would cause a ray of doubt to enter Daryl's brain. "Marshal Cochran ain't been here very long, has he?"

"No, it hasn't been very long, I reckon," Daryl answered. "He was just passing through Glory at the time. Jim Bryan was the marshal then." He proceeded to tell Spencer the story of how John Cochran got the marshal job then.

"Where did he come from?" Spencer asked then. "Where was he before he rode into Glory that day?"

"I swear, he told me, but I've forgotten," Daryl said, "a cattle ranch somewhere, I think."

Spencer was just before telling Daryl that John Cochran was, in fact, John Bannack, the man he had come there to find, but he stopped himself just in time. The young man was so in awe of Bannack he might warn him. "Well, like I said, I like to let the local law know when I'm in their town. I might or might not still be here when your marshal gets back. If I am, I'd enjoy talkin' to him. It was good to meet you."

"Yes, sir," Daryl responded. "It was good to meet you, too."

Spencer went to the hotel next and got a room. To keep his story straight, he registered as Frank Johnson from Fort Worth. At his request, Bobby Nance gave him a room upstairs on the front, overlooking the street. From his window, he could see the marshal's office. Thinking about his visit there, he had to wonder if Daryl Boyd was that naive, or was he pretending to be. He might warn Bannack that someone was looking for him. *No,* he decided, *the kid was too good at it to be fakin' it.* He would have to set him straight as soon as Bannack returned, however, because he planned to keep Bannack in one of the cells until he had him ready to transport.

CHAPTER 20

Jim Fowler was right when he said it was a good day to travel. He had plenty of time to make the trip from Jacksboro to Glory, so he let his horse set the pace. The buckskin must have felt as good as he did, now that a final decision had been made and acted upon, for he maintained a spirited walk. "We'll stop at Razor Creek and rest a little while," Bannack said when he approached the creek. Despite the bad history with that creek, it was still an ideal place to rest, drink water, or camp. He decided to make some coffee when he stopped. He had some jerky he could satisfy himself with, and he would be in Glory by suppertime. He felt in a mood to take supper at Sawyer's. Those thoughts were occupying his mind when he was slammed in the chest and almost knocked out of the saddle, then hit in the shoulder a split second after. He wasn't even aware that he had been shot until he heard the reports of the rifles half a second after the impact. Now, he found himself in a blistering rain of gunshots, with bullets snapping as they passed all around him, and he fell forward on the buckskin's neck and dropped the packhorse's reins. He jerked hard on the buckskin's reins in an attempt to escape into the trees beside the road as he felt the impact of the bullets on his leg and his back. Then he heard the buckskin cry out as first one, and then another bullet struck the confused horse. Straining to escape the torment of the snapping death all around them, the gallant buckskin plowed through the thick bushes beside the creek before crashing to the ground, unable to go on. Trying to hold on as his horse tumbled on its right side, Bannack was thrown off the horse's left side. Knowing he was dying, he was determined to make his death costly for his assailants. With every move of his limbs now torture, he reached for his six-gun and found the holster empty, so he struggled to get to his rifle in the saddle scabbard. With bullets still flying all around him, now that his attackers were blindly shooting up the bushes that hid him, he dragged himself painfully toward his horse. He found his six-gun on the ground before he reached the dying buckskin. Grateful for that small measure of encouragement, he forced himself onward in an effort to get to his rifle.

He supposed that he had been lucky not to have been pinned under his horse, but his Henry rifle had not been so lucky. It was trapped underneath the horse, and Bannack could not pull it out of the scabbard. He had ridden blindly into an ambush and he was bleeding freely from wounds he could not count, but his anger and his grief were because of the senseless shooting of the buckskin horse. The shooting continued, even though it was no longer near them. The suffering horse tried to get up but could not. And then, in one final attempt, it managed to raise its body a few inches off the ground, giving Bannack the opportunity to yank the Henry rifle from under it. He was convinced the horse knew what it had to do, and his final effort was to free the rifle. Then it lay quiet, its eyes rolling sadly toward Bannack, asking for his help. Bannack had no choice but to end the horse's suffering. He rubbed the buckskin's face softly one last time before holding his six-gun to the back of the horse's head and pulling the trigger. "Don't go far, horse," he whispered. "I think I'll be comin' along pretty soon, too. But if I can, I'll bring some of them with me. I promise you that."

The senseless firing started up again, the bullets ripping through the bushes and trees closer to him now, the shooters having heard Bannack's farewell shot to his horse. *I gotta move from here. I ain't got a chance to get more than one of 'em if I stay here. And that horse is worth more than one of 'em.* He strained to drag himself backward, away from his dead horse and over the bank of the creek. There was no effort to try to disguise his trail. His efforts to escape were blatantly obvious. Still, he struggled to move his body, his clothes now soaked with the blood from many wounds. He tried to use his rifle butt to help push him along, down to the water's edge. When he felt the water coming up around him, he held his weapons up out of the water, one in each hand, and pushed himself across the shallow stream with his feet.

Once he reached the other bank, he found it was all he could do to drag himself up it, and he knew he could go no farther. Looking around behind him as best he could lying on his back, he saw his best defense. Right at the top of the creek bank, there was a large oak with a double trunk forming a shape like a Y. That was where he would fight. So he tried to take a deep breath and gather the strength to drag himself behind the tree. Only a little bit farther, he told himself over and over until finally making it to the other side of the tree. The base of the tree came up from the ground only about two feet before it forked to form the Y, with two large trunks growing straight up from it. His intent was to rest his rifle in the fork of the Y, for a steady platform to shoot from. Before he could do that, however, he had to turn over on his belly, an accomplishment that seemed impossible in his present condition. He laid there trying to catch his breath when he suddenly realized the shooting had stopped. That meant they would be coming to look for him! He had to make himself turn over, so he forced himself to roll over, almost blacking out with the pain from his chest wound. After a few moments, his vision cleared enough to see again, so he rested the barrel of his rifle in the fork of the tree and pulled his pistol out and placed it on the ground beside him. He was not sure he could be very effective because of the strain required to raise his body enough to aim and fire. And he had no chance at all if they came up behind him, but he was determined to make the taking of his life costly, if he could only hang on long enough. He now heard the sound of voices from beyond the bushes on the other side of the creek.

"Yonder!" Johnny Dawson blurted and pointed toward another clump of bushes. "That looks like a horse layin' on the other side of them bushes!"

"Damn," his father swore, "I wanted that horse. Be careful. Junior, do you see him?"

"No," Junior answered from several yards off to his right. "He can't be far, though. I think we got him with those first two shots. He almost came off that horse when my shot hit him in the chest."

"That was my shot that hit him in the chest," Henry said. "You hit him in the shoulder."

"I don't think so, Pa," Junior said. "I fired the first shot just a hair before you pulled the trigger and I saw him fall back like he was fixin' to come off that horse when your shot caught him in the shoulder."

"I'll be damned . . ." Henry started to disagree before Gilbert interrupted.

"I swear, everybody put a bullet in him," Gilbert said. "I put one in his back that mighta killed him. Let's just make sure he's dead. Like Pa said, be careful. I don't trust that man. He might be layin' behind that horse waitin' for us."

Taking his advice to heart, the four of them moved cautiously through the trees and bushes, approaching the body of the horse from both sides until they closed in on it. "He ain't here," Johnny exclaimed.

"Yeah, but he can't have got very far," Henry said, pointing to the obvious blood-splattered trail leading away from the dead horse.

"Look at that," Johnny said. "He's so full of holes, he had to drag hisself away from here. He ain't gonna be hard to find."

"He ain't gonna get very far, either, losin' all that blood," Gilbert predicted. "It's too bad we killed that buckskin he was ridin'. That was a nice lookin' horse, but at least we got the packhorse. I hope we can sell it for enough money to pay for all the bullets we shot up in them bushes." That statement brought a hearty chuckle from all four of them.

"It looks like he drug hisself into the creek," Henry said as he followed the bloody trail to the creek bank. "Maybe he's tryin' to let the creek float him down to the river, since he can't go very far draggin' hisself on the ground."

"No, he ain't," Junior said, pointing. "He went across. There's his trail on the other side!"

Like hound dogs chasing a fox, they all splashed across the creek, anxious to be the one to put the final nail in Marshal Cochran's coffin. Making sport of it, Gilbert and Johnny ran ahead of Henry and Junior, reloading their six-guns as they raced along the bloody trail leading to the forked tree. Suddenly, the tree erupted with two cracks like lightning and both men crashed to the ground to tumble over a couple of times until lying dead. Startled, Henry and Junior stumbled over each other in a panic to find cover with Junior catching a shot in the arm as they scrambled into the bushes near the creek bank. A fourth shot went whistling through the trees, a result of the fork of the tree being too restrictive to permit Bannack's rifle to follow them. "I'm shot, Papa," Junior moaned, confused by the sudden turn of events. "Johnny and Gilbert . . ." he started but was too stunned to understand how things had turned upside down. He peeped around a tree at the two bodies lying motionless in front of the tree. "They're dead. He killed 'em."

His father, having been stunned, as well, was fighting the natural urge to run, for he knew he would be stamped with the coward's image for the rest of his life as long as Junior lived. "He weren't as near dead as we thought," he finally spoke. "Gilbert and Johnny ought notta been runnin' blind after him like that. We can't let him get away with that. The damn devil is still dyin', but we're gonna have to make sure he finishes the job and gets good and dead." He was thinking how this turnabout had been possible and it was plain to see now. "We can get him, you and me, if we do it the smart way. He's dyin', layin' up behind that tree, 'cause he's gone as far as he can make it. There ain't no tellin' how many bullets he's got in him, and he's already lost a helluva lot of blood. We could just wait him out, and he'll be dead before dark. It'd make me feel better about myself if I circle around behind him and send him to hell straight away for killin' your brothers. I don't know how bad your arm is, so I'll leave it up to you if you wanna go with me."

"My arm hurts," Junior said, "but it ain't my gun hand. If you just wrap my bandanna around it, it oughta be all right to go take care of that devil."

"I knew I could count on you," Henry said. "We'll make sure that Marshal Cochran gets a front-row seat on the train to hell today." He took his time wrapping Junior's bandanna around the bullet hole in his arm, thinking it a good possibility that Bannack's last moments were even now running out. "All right," he finally said, "let's go finish what we started out to do."

Back at the forked tree, Bannack made the best use of the time the Dawsons spent deciding what their next move would be. Right after he was given the two easy targets to take out, he sank down on the ground when Henry and Junior fled for cover. He thought he might have hit Junior, but he wasn't sure. When he had seen Johnny and Gilbert charging the tree, he had somehow generated the adrenaline to defend himself. He had to thank the oak tree for providing the solid support for his rifle that allowed him to take dead aim for two lethal shots. After the rush of adrenaline, however, he had to sink back to the ground and get back to the business of dying. He was sure that the tree was of no further use to him. They knew he was behind it, so they would now circle around behind him to catch him unprotected. The thought of lying there awaiting execution, hoping he would die of his wounds before they came to him was repulsive to him. *So I'll move from here, or die trying,*

he thought, and still on his belly, he grabbed a handful
of prairie grass and pulled on it until he moved his body
a few inches forward. He holstered his six-gun and let
his rifle rest across both arms. Then he started pulling
himself through the grass, one hand at a time, reaching
for a handful of anything rooted in the earth to pull himself away from the tree.

He had no idea how long he had been straining to
pull his body toward a clump of berry bushes, but it
seemed an eternity with the expectation of a fatal bullet
in the back of his head at any minute. He never made
it to the berry bushes, for there was a gully before he
got to them and he rolled into it, ending up on his back.
Exhausted, he gave up and sank back against the side
of the gully. *To hell with it,* he thought, *this is where I
make my stand.* He didn't have to wait long.

"He's not here," Junior said as he suddenly appeared
on the other side of the Y-shaped tree. "He's gone."

"Whaddaya mean, he's gone?" Henry asked. "How
can he be gone? He's damn near dead and he can't even
walk. Look on the other side of that tree."

Lying in the gully, some twenty feet away, Bannack
realized he had passed out briefly. For he awoke with
Henry and Junior standing behind the tree. So he said,
"Hey, Dawsons, over here." They both jumped, startled,
but not quick enough to avoid the two rapid shots that
cut them down. He continued to watch them for a while
until there was no doubt that they were both dead. He
told himself that he was satisfied that he had avenged
the buckskin gelding that he had never been able to

christen with a proper name. He could stop fighting it
and go ahead and die, for there was no way he could
help himself. It was one thing every man had to do,
he decided. So he closed his eyes and within minutes, he
was gone.

Just as he had told Buster Bridges and Smut Smith
he would, Clark Spencer ate supper in the Glory Hotel
dining room where he was quick to make the acquaintance of Carol and Dora. He found the food quite well
prepared, just as Buster and Smut had suggested. As he
had at Sawyer's, Spencer told the ladies his story about
being a special investigator for the governor and easily
engaged them in a conversation about their new town
marshal. "I was lookin' forward to meeting Marshal
Cochran. I hoped I might buy him a drink after supper,
but you say he ain't been in for supper tonight."

"No, he hasn't," Dora said. "We expected to see him
before suppertime. He lives here in the hotel and we
thought he'd be back yesterday, but we haven't seen
hide nor hair of him. I expect he'll show up later tonight
or first thing in the morning. He's pretty reliable."

Yep, Spencer thought, *except when he's skipping town
for good.* He was beginning to think he might be wasting valuable time waiting there while Bannack was
piling up the miles between them, and no telling in
which direction. "Well, if he shows up, send him on
over to the River House and I'll buy him a welcome
home drink."

"I'll tell him," Dora said, "but from what I hear, Cochran ain't much of a drinker." She stood beside the table and watched Spencer as he walked out the door before she started picking up his dirty dishes. Carol paused on her way back to the kitchen with a stack of dishes when Dora commented, "He sure acts like he really wants to meet Marshal Cochran."

"There's something about that man that bothers me," Carol said. "I bet there ain't no such a-thing as a special investigator. I don't know, I just don't trust that man."

"Hell," Dora replied, "if you're smart, you don't trust any man." She picked up the silverware and followed Carol into the kitchen. "All except one," she said. "I trust Marshal John Cochran. Anything he says, I believe."

CHAPTER 21

"Where are you going?" Sadie Cord asked her husband when he drove the wagon past the trail he should have turned onto to go home. "You wanna drive us up to Jacksboro?"

"Sure," he japed. "Why not?" Then he laughed and said, "I just thought I'd go on up to Razor Creek and water the horses, so Tim and Mercy can play in the water a little bit. It's right up the road, and you know it's one of Tim's favorite spots."

"Ron, look yonder," Sadie said pointing up ahead after they drove a short distance.

Ron looked to where his wife pointed and saw a saddled horse standing close to the side of the road, but there was no rider. "I'll swear," he said, "looks like somebody's lost a horse. I'll bet somebody made camp and don't know they got a horse runnin' loose." He no sooner said it when another saddled horse popped out of the trees on the bank of the creek.

"I declare," Sadie commented, "if they're asleep in

there somewhere, ain't they gonna be in a fix when they wake up and find out they're on foot."

"Look, Papa," his son, Tim, called out from the back of the wagon, "there's a horse with a packsaddle."

Ron and Sadie looked at each other, questioning. "I better take a look down that creek," Ron said. "Somebody might be in trouble. I don't see no smoke from a campfire, do you?" Sadie shook her head. He pulled the wagon to a stop and reached under the seat for his shotgun. When he saw Sadie's worried look, he said, "Just in case, won't hurt to have it with me. You young'uns stay with your mama."

"I can go help you, Papa," Tim said.

"I tell you what you might do," his father said, "walk up the road there and get them two horses and lead 'em back here to the wagon. Maybe the packhorse will follow 'em. I'll go see if I can find out who they belong to." Tim jumped down and ran toward the stray horses.

"Ron, you be careful," Sadie said. She wasn't worried about Tim. At thirteen, he had handled horses before. "You stay in the wagon, Mercy," she told her eleven-year-old daughter.

Ron didn't go far off the road before he was stopped by what appeared to be a horse lying beyond a clump of bushes before him. He hesitated before continuing on, looking all around him before pushing on through the bushes to discover the horse was dead, shot several times it appeared. He unconsciously tightened his grip on his shotgun when he saw the bloody trail leading away from the horse. Once again he hesitated, thinking it might be best if he just backed away from there because something bad had happened in those woods and it wasn't any of his business. Still, his curiosity was almost compelling when he thought about the stray horses and the possibility that something more of value might have been left behind, as well. So, holding his shotgun ready to shoot, he followed the bloody trail to the creek, where he stopped.

He could see where the trail came out of the water on the other side. The question now was whether or not he wanted to wade across the creek to continue. He didn't hesitate long before going on across. Going up the opposite bank, he didn't walk very far before he was stopped by the sight of two bodies sprawled in awkward positions of death. "Oh, my Lord," he murmured under his breath, and he looked all around him to be sure he was alone before he approached the bodies. "Damn . . ." He drew out slowly when he recognized the bodies as a couple of the Dawson boys. Well familiar with the Dawson gang, like everyone else who had a homestead near Tyson's Creek, Ron knew them for what they were, thieves of the lowest order. Even now, one of the Dawson boys was in jail for murder.

He looked up ahead and thought he saw two more bodies, so he started to go forward but halted when he heard Tim calling for him from the other side of the creek. "You stay back there, Tim!" he yelled at the boy. "I'm all right! I'll be back in a minute!" He hurried on to the other side of a forked oak tree to look at the other two bodies. It was old Henry Dawson and another one of his sons. It struck him that this was the entire family wiped out, except for the one in jail, and if he was found guilty of murder, they'd probably hang him. Ron felt no guilt in thinking *good riddance*. His thoughts turned toward what might be gained by this discovery, since it appeared he was the first to come upon the scene. He should find all their horses and collect anything of value before someone else happened upon the scene. He needed to let Sadie know what was going on, thinking she must be getting pretty worried already.

He turned to retrace his steps when it suddenly occurred to him that someone else had to leave the bloody trail, and the Dawsons were probably chasing him. He had to be the one who killed all four of them, and he might be drawing a bead on him right now. He started to quickly retreat but stopped when he caught sight of someone lying in a gully not far away. With his shotgun ready to fire, he advanced toward the gully, only to find another body. A big man, whose body was covered with blood. The Dawsons must have been after him, Ron figured, and it looked like they shot him full of holes before he killed every one of them. "Sadie's gonna come in after me if I don't get back there and tell her what's goin' on," he murmured and headed back to the wagon.

He met Tim when he crossed over the creek again. "What are you doin' in here, boy? I mighta shot you."

"I've been lookin' for horses," Tim said. "There's one layin' dead over there closer to the road. Somebody shot him. But I found four horses with saddles on 'em and three carryin' packsaddles. Did you find anybody?"

"Yeah, I found 'em," Ron replied, "all five of 'em, and they're all dead."

"I knew it!" Tim exclaimed. "When I found that dead horse and them others tied on a rope line, I knew somebody got ambushed. Where are they? Across the creek?"

"You don't need to see 'em," Ron told him. "We need to go back and tell your mama what's goin' on. Come on." They went back through the woods to the road.

"I was wondering if I was gonna have to go in those woods to find you," Sadie said when the two of them came back to the wagon. "Have you been wadin' in the creek? You're wet up to your knees."

"You ain't gonna believe what I found in them woods," Ron told her. "There's five dead men layin' back there and four of 'em are Henry Dawson and his three sons."

"My word!" Sadie gasped, horrified.

"I don't know who the other fellow is, but it looks like he's the one who killed the Dawsons, and they shot him full of holes before they died. I'm gonna let Tim take these horses he tied up to the wagon over where he found the others on a rope line. Then if somebody comes along before I get back, you can just tell 'em your husband had to answer a call from nature."

"Why are you goin' back?" Sadie asked. "Are you gonna bury 'em? You don't even have a shovel. Let's just get outta here."

"No, I ain't gonna bury 'em. Let the buzzards have 'em." He nodded up toward the sky. "There's already a couple circlin' up there. But I ain't gonna drive off and leave a bunch of good stuff for somebody else to find. They might have some money on 'em, but even if they ain't, there's guns and ammunition that's worth something. I'd take the saddle off that dead horse if I thought I could get it off of him."

"I'll help you, Papa, after I take these horses," Tim volunteered. "I ain't scared of lookin' at dead people."

"I might need somebody to help me carry some things," Ron said, "so you go ahead and tie them horses. Then just follow that trail from the dead horse across the creek. It'll lead you right to me."

Tim untied the horses from the wagon and led them into the woods. Mercy climbed up on the wagon seat beside her mother. "I don't wanna see any dead people," she stated, emphatically.

After wading across the creek, Tim sat down, put his shoes and socks back on, rolled his trouser legs back down, and followed the trail to the first two bodies. He took only a few minutes to stare at the grotesque expressions of surprise already permanently in place when he saw that his father had already searched them. Going forward, he found his father relieving the bodies of Henry and Junior Dawson of their gun belts, so he stared at those two corpses for a minute before asking, "Where's the other one?"

"Over there in that gully," his father said.

So Tim ran over to the gully to look at the body.

"He's a big one," he remarked. Thinking he could help out, he unbuckled the belt and tried to pull it out, but no matter how hard he pulled, it wouldn't come. He pulled the coat back out of the way, and when he did, it revealed the mangled badge where a bullet had struck. *He was a lawman!* Tim reached up and touched the badge very carefully where the bullet had almost struck it dead center. "Waugh!" He yelped involuntarily and jumped backward when the eyes opened and seemed to be looking right at him. He backed farther away and yelled, "Papa! This one's still alive! And he's a lawman!"

Ron came to him at once and knelt beside the gully. "How do you know that?" he asked, and then he saw the badge. "I'll be . . ." he started, "so that's what happened. He was chasin' them and they ambushed him. But why do you think he's alive?"

"When I touched that badge, his eyes opened and he looked right at me," Tim said.

Ron looked at the man, whose eyes were closed now. "I don't think he's alive, son. That was most likely some reaction from rigor mortis settin' in. Things like that happen after a man's dead."

"Well, it's happenin' again," Tim said and pointed back at Bannack.

Ron looked at him again and the eyes were open. It was disconcerting even though he thought it a natural occurrence after death. To test it, he moved to one side. The eyes followed him. When he moved back, the eyes moved back with him, seemingly wary of his every move. He pulled the jacket back and laid his ear down on Bannack's chest and listened. After a long few seconds, Ron raised his head and declared, "You're right. He's alive." He was not sure that was good news. Before that discovery, he was content to take anything of value he found and leave the scene for the buzzards to clean up. Trying to be a God-fearing, honest man, setting an example for his children, he said, "We've got to see what we can do for this poor man. It looks like he's pretty much on the way to dyin', though. It might be a whole lot easier if he weren't so doggone big. Let's see if we can get him outta that gully."

Ron tried to take hold under the wounded man's arms and pull him out of the shallow gully, but he was unsuccessful. So Tim grabbed the gun belt and pulled with his father. They barely moved Bannack a couple of inches. "This ain't workin' worth spit," Ron declared. "I'm goin' to get one of them horses you tied up to pull him outta there. And we'll tell your mama what's goin' on. Might as well carry this stuff I took off the bodies back to the wagon, too."

When they got back to the wagon and dumped the weapons and other things they thought useful into the back, Ron explained the latest discovery. "He's alive?" Sadie asked. "Then we have to put him in the wagon and take him home with us and do what we can for him."

"It ain't as easy as that," Ron said. "He's so big I can't pick him up to bring him to the wagon. Me and Tim together couldn't pull him out of a gully he holed up in. That's why I've gotta take one of those horses back in there."

"What? Is he just big and fat?" Sadie asked.

"No, he ain't fat, is he, Tim?"

"He's just big," Tim said.

"I'd better go in and help you," she said, not at all satisfied with their reporting of the situation. But Ron said he didn't want to leave the wagon unattended and certainly not with only Mercy left there. "You can back the wagon a little way in the trees," Sadie said, "far enough to get it behind those first trees there. Then we would at least hear somebody messing with it. Which side of this creek is the man on? I'll back the wagon on that side. I don't want to wade across it."

Ron went to the place by the creek where Tim had found the horses tied. He picked one that looked a little better than the rest and rode it back to the wagon where he turned it over to Tim to lead, then he drove the wagon as far into the woods as he could. When Sadie saw the problem, she understood why Ron needed a horse and she was horrified to see how many wounds the man had suffered. That he was still alive must surely be a miracle. "That badge might be the only reason he's still breathing," Sadie said. "It mighta stopped that bullet from going in too deep. What kind of lawman is he?"

"I don't know," Ron replied. "The badge just says marshal. He might be a US marshal or a deputy marshal, or he might be a town marshal. If he was on Henry Dawson's trail, he might be ridin' outta San Antonio. Henry and the boys did a lot of business down that way."

Sadie waited until Mercy was out of earshot before she made her next comment. "Ron, Honey, I know what you're thinking, and I don't think you need to be worrying. There ain't any way they can connect you to this thing. It's been over thirteen years since you walked off that road gang in San Antonio and I was carryin' Tim in my belly. You've worked hard ever since to make us a home and lead an honest life. So we'll just do the right thing, do what we can for this lawman to try to help him make it. And there ain't any reason why you would be suspected of being anything but the decent hard-working man you are."

"You're right," he said. "We'll take him home and do what we can for him." He went back to the gully and tied a rope around Bannack's chest. Then he tied the other end around the saddle horn on Henry Dawson's horse. "All right, Tim, when I signal you, I want you to lead this horse real slow and your mama and I will try to help this feller come outta there in one piece."

"Yes, sir," Tim said, and they dragged Bannack's body out of the gully. Then they tested the load to see if Ron and Tim, with a little help from Sadie, could carry the dead weight back through the bushes. If they couldn't, the horse would have to drag him all the way. They found out that as big as he was, the Cord family was up to the job, so they picked him up and carried him to the wagon.

"Now, I reckon we'll take him home and see if Dr. Sadie can take care of all those wounds," Ron said.

"I wish we coulda thrown him in the creek and washed all that blood and dirt off him," Sadie remarked.

"Ah, come on, Dr. Sadie," Ron japed. "He can't be no harder than a horse to doctor." When they got Bannack settled in the wagon, with the supplies they had just bought in town and the things they had acquired at the scene of the ambush packed around him, they started out for home. On a lead rope behind the wagon, four saddled horses and three packhorses followed. Tim sat in the saddle on one of the horses and Mercy rode the one behind him.

It came as a relief to both Ron and Sadie that they met no one else on the journey back to their homestead near Tyson's Creek. So they were spared the problem of explaining their sudden wealth of horses and what appeared to be a dead man in their wagon. As soon as they got home, they put all the horses in the small corral and unloaded the wagon of everything except the body. Sadie built a fire in the stove and started heating water by the bucket full. "We'll get him out of his clothes and clean him up right here on the wagon," Sadie said. "I ain't gonna take him into my house like that. It's a good thing the weather's warm. Go ahead and pull his boots and his pants off while I go pump some more water."

"You figure on you and me strippin' all his clothes off and washin' him?" Ron asked, with a definite lack of enthusiasm for the job.

"Did you think Mercy and Tim were gonna do it?" Sadie asked sarcastically. "He's got bullet holes all over his body, and he's a bloody mess. We'll have to strip him to see where all the wounds are."

"I reckon you're right," Ron surrendered.

She couldn't suppress a chuckle. "Don't worry, we'll cover him where it's necessary. Maybe we can cut away his underwear except over his private parts, and if he's got any wounds in that area, you can fix them."

"I feel sorry for him, if I have to operate on him with my clumsy fingers," Ron said. "It's gonna be rough enough for him with your fingers, without no chloroform or nothin'."

"I guess he's lucky he ain't really come to yet," she said, "and he might not ever. So we best work as fast as we can and maybe we can save him some pain."

"You thinkin' about workin' on him out here on the wagon after we clean him up?"

"Goodness, no," she answered. "After we wash all that mess off, he might die of pneumonia, if we don't get him in the house pretty quick."

"Where we gonna put him?"

"We don't really have a place to put him, except the front room," she said, "unless we put him in Tim's room with him. He's so doggone big, he'll fill up Tim's room. We don't have another bed. I'll have to make one with some quilts on the floor. I don't reckon he'll complain, but Tim might."

Working together, Ron and Sadie hurried to clean up their patient as quickly as possible, while Tim kept the fire in the stove going and the hot water in good supply. Mercy cooked some bacon and the beans that

Sadie had left to soak that morning before they drove into town. Concerned about the barbaric surgery she was going to have to perform, Sadie was anxious to get started while Bannack still seemed to be in a state of unconsciousness. After he was cleaned up, they counted five bullet holes. The two they figured would likely be the more serious was the one that smashed into his badge on his chest and the other was a wound in the back, a little above his waistline. There was a bullet in his left shoulder and one in the back of his right leg, above the knee, and a grazing shot in his right side.

When she was ready for surgery, Sadie got an oil-cloth sheet they had used to protect some furniture they brought in the wagon when they built the house and spread it over the bed of quilts. It took the whole family to carry Bannack into the house and lay him on the oilcloth. Then with a supply of rags, old bed sheets, and her scissors and sharpest knives, she attacked the wound in his chest. He responded to the first thrust of her tweezers with an almost violent arching of his back, but not a sound came out of his mouth. He relaxed his back then and sank back flat on the oilcloth while a fresh trickle of blood flowed from the aggravated wound. Since he did not try to pull away, Sadie continued her probe and soon struck the lead slug. "I think that badge might have saved his life," she said. "It must have kept the bullet from going in deep enough to get to his heart or his lung." So she kept probing until she managed to get enough grip on the bullet to pull it out, along with a fresh stream of blood. The patient's only response was a grunt. "That's one," Sadie said.

"He felt that," Ron said. "Why don't he make more noise than just a grunt?"

"I don't know," Sadie replied. "Maybe he's lost so much blood that he's in shock or something, but I'm gonna keep going while he's still unconscious or wherever he is. Help me turn him over and let's see if we can get to that one in his back." She continued working on him throughout most of the evening, never stopping when Ron and Tim and Mercy ate the bacon and beans that Mercy cooked. "If I get through this, I don't know if I'll ever be able to eat again," she complained as she cut and probed in the helpless patient's wounds.

It was well past the normal bedtime for the Cord family when the weary Sadie announced to Ron that she had done all she could do for the wounded lawman. "Now," she said, "it's up to him to decide if he's going to come back or not. I made a mess of his shoulder wound, even if I did get the bullet out. And I couldn't get the bullet out of the back of his leg. That's gonna take a real doctor to get that out. To tell you the truth, he may not come back from all the cutting and prodding I did on that poor man."

"Ain't nobody coulda done any better," Ron told her. "I know I'm hopin' we can bring him back to good health 'cause I don't wanna have to dig a grave big enough to hold him."

A different thought crossed her mind then. "What if he starts getting better and wants to raise hell about the butchering I did on his body? A man like that, who kills four men while they're shooting him to pieces, might go wild when he gets a good look at himself."

"That's when I'll shoot him and dig that big grave," Ron said with a chuckle.

"I hope we're all awake when he does wake up," Sadie said, "if he wakes up. I think it was a good idea to tell Tim to put his mattress on the floor in Mercy's room tonight."

They sat up a while longer before going to bed. When they finally did, Ron slept on the side of the bed nearest the door, Sadie's usual side. And he placed his shotgun beside the headboard where it would be handy, if needed.

It was difficult for both of them to fall asleep. When they finally did, it was a deep sleep for both of them, resulting in the kids awakening the next morning before either of their parents. The first in the house to awaken, however, was the patient lying on the floor in Tim's bedroom.

He opened his eyes and realized he was lying on his back. He blinked his eyes several times to be sure he was looking at a ceiling. The last thing he remembered was looking up at a clear sky above him. But now, he was looking at a ceiling, so he was inside a building. How he got there, or where it was, he had no clue. So he started to get up but was stopped by the sudden stab of pain that shot through his entire body. He lay back, only then realizing all the bandages wrapped around him. His hand instinctively went to his chest, bringing a sharp pain from his left shoulder. And when he tried to sit up, he got a warning stab of pain from his chest. He soon realized that he was helpless, so he tried to relax and be still. It occurred to him then that he was alive, for he could feel the pain of it. His last conscious thought was that he was lying in a gully, and he was in the process of dying. Maybe, he thought, he was still in that process. He wasn't sure, but he knew he was helpless to do anything but lie still, so he closed his eyes again and waited for whatever his fate was to be.

"Is he dead?" Mercy Cord asked her brother, Tim.

"I don't know," Tim answered. "Mama and Papa ain't up yet, and I ain't been in my room. I'm gonna sneak in there and take a look at him."

"Me, too," Mercy whispered and grabbed the back of his shirt and followed.

The bedroom door was only halfway open, so they were careful not to touch it for fear of causing it to squeak. They sneaked inside the room and tiptoed over to the motionless body lying under a blanket, with only a head sticking out of the top and a huge pair of boots standing guard at the bottom. "I swear, he's big," Tim whispered.

"Is he dead?" Mercy asked again. "I ain't ever seen a dead man." She leaned over a little closer to get a better look. "He just looks like he's asleep," she whispered and giggled. Suddenly, his eyes opened to stare right at her, causing her to squeal uncontrollably. She jumped back, almost knocking Tim down and they both ran out of the room, only to run into their father with his shotgun.

"What is it?" Ron demanded, prepared to protect his children. "What happened? Is he up? Get around behind me!"

"Wait, Pa!" Tim exclaimed. "He ain't up. He just opened his eyes and scared the daylights outta Mercy."

"What were you two doin' in there, anyway?" Ron asked, irritated and relieved at the same time. He turned to tell Sadie, who was coming from the bedroom, still getting her robe wrapped around her, "It ain't nothin'. They just went in and woke him up." Turning back to Tim then, he asked, "Did he say anything?"

"No, sir," Tim answered. "We didn't give him any time to say anything. Mercy liked to knocked me down when she headed for the door."

"The poor man," Sadie said. "He ain't suffered enough? He had to wake up to two young'uns starin' at him?"

Ron took the shells out of his shotgun and put it back over the fireplace where he usually kept it. "I expect we better go in and see how he's doin'," he said to Sadie. "Tim, get a fire goin' in the stove, if you want any breakfast this mornin'." He looked back at his wife again and they exchanged questionable expressions, both wondering what to expect.

They went into the bedroom to find Bannack still lying under the blanket, but his eyes were open and obviously focused on them as they approached him. Since Bannack was lying flat on the floor, Ron took a knee beside him, so he wouldn't be towering over him. "How are you feelin', partner?" Ron asked.

"I've felt a lot better," Bannack answered. "I don't know where I am or how I got here, but I expect I owe you folks all my thanks, because I know where I was."

Ron looked up at Sadie and smiled, knowing she was just as relieved as he was to hear the man talking normally. "You're at our farm near Tyson's Creek, if that'll help you any. My name's Ron Cord and this is my wife, Sadie. She's the one who operated on all your bullet wounds for most of the night last night. Those two young whippersnappers that came in here to disturb you this mornin' are Tim and Mercy.

"They didn't really disturb me," Bannack said. "I'd been awake for a while before they came in. I wanna thank you for your doctorin', ma'am. I know I took a few hits."

"Five to be exact," Sadie remarked. "I'm afraid I had to leave one bullet in your leg, but I managed to get the others out. As soon as you get on your feet again, you need to go see a doctor and let him look at your wounds. We think the one that could have been the worst was the one in your chest. But you were wearing a badge and the bullet hit it, and the badge kept it from going in deep enough to damage any organs."

"Is that a fact?" Bannack asked, finding it ironic.

"Are you a lawman of some kind?" Ron asked.

"I'm the town marshal of Glory. My name's John Cochran."

"Well, how 'bout that?" Ron responded and looked

at Sadie, knowing she was relieved to find he was not a US marshal. "I thought Jim Bryan was the town marshal."

"He was," Bannack replied, "but he quit." Changing the subject, he asked, "What about the four men back at Razor Creek? You must have come along pretty soon after that ambush. Did you find four dead men at the site?"

"You mean the Dawsons?" Ron asked. "Yep, we found 'em, and they were all sure enough dead."

"So you knew who they were?" Bannack asked.

"Everybody who lives near Tyson's Creek knows Henry Dawson and his boys. And I'm afraid you ain't gonna be able to find another solitary soul who regrets their passin'."

"I'm relieved to hear you ain't thinkin' about revengin' their deaths," Bannack said. "They ambushed me when I was on my way back to Glory, and they didn't give me much choice in the matter. I have to admit I was pretty mad when they killed my horse."

"Do you think you can eat something?" Sadie asked. "You've lost an awful lot of blood and you need to start building it up again."

"You need plenty of beef," Ron said, "and I know where I can get some fresh beef. Henry and his boys just drove about thirty head of cattle into that pasture behind his place near the river. Everybody knows they stole 'em. They've been tryin' to sell 'em. I think it's only fair if I was to ride over there and cut out a couple head of those cows to get you back on your feet again."

"Ron Cord," Sadie scolded, "are you telling the town marshal you're gonna go steal some cows?"

"The more I think about it, the more I like it," Ron declared. "What about it, Marshal? If I go take a couple of those cows, would you arrest me?"

"Lyin' here helpless on my back, it doesn't look like I could do anything about it," Bannack said. "And even if I was able to do something about it, I don't have any jurisdiction outside the town limits of Glory, so it sounds like a good idea to me, if you're sure it won't be any danger for you."

"You'll be lucky if Berta Trammel doesn't take a shot at you, if you go poking around that place," Sadie said.

"Tell you the truth," Ron confessed, "I figured I'd take a couple of those horses we brought home with us and give 'em to Berta for a couple of cows. Maybe I'd leave the gun belts on the saddles, too, and tell Berta they was all we found." He looked back down at Bannack. "I don't think it's a good idea to let anybody know you're stayin' here till you get back on your feet. I don't think Berta cares a whole lot for Henry or his sons, but ain't no sense in puttin' it out there."

"Well, instead of standin' around here gabbing about getting you back on your feet, I'd best get out to the kitchen and rustle up some breakfast or we're all gonna be helpless."

"We need to talk about that," Bannack stopped her. "When I first woke up this mornin', I tried to get up from here and I couldn't do it. I will do it, but it's gonna take a little time. I ain't sure how long, but I plan on payin' you for helpin' me. I've got some money in my pants pocket, and if you took the saddlebags off my dead horse, there's some money there, too. I don't want it to cost you money to get me on my feet again."

"That's more than fair if you wanna pay for some of the fixin's Sadie needs to cook with and coffee and such, but I'll get us some beef. I gotta tell you, though, we brought your saddlebags back with us, but there wasn't no money in 'em and believe me, we looked. Somebody musta got into them in the stable or somewhere."

"Did you look in the strap that holds the two bags together?" Ron shrugged. "I'll bet you didn't," Bannack continued. "There's a double fold on the underside of that strap and you ought to find three twenty dollar bills layin' inside that fold."

Ron chuckled. "I'll look."

"I'll go get breakfast started," Sadie said and started for the door. Ron told her to send Tim out to the barn to get the saddlebags that were on the dead horse.

After she left the room, Bannack said, "I need one more thing, if you don't mind. Have you got an old fruit jar I could use?"

"A fruit jar? Whaddaya need a fruit . . . Ohhh . . . Right. I reckon you do need something for that. I'm sorry we didn't think about it before. Yeah, Sadie's got a bunch of old jars she uses for picklin'. Can you wait till Tim gets back?"

"Yeah, I ain't in trouble yet," Bannack said.

When Tim came back with the saddlebags, Ron took them from him and said. "Now, I need you to do something else and this is something that's just us men's business. We don't want your mama and Mercy to know anythin' about it. Understand?" Tim nodded very deliberately. "You know those jars of pickles your mama makes?" Tim nodded again. "Well, the marshal needs one of those jars to pee in while he's layin' on his back."

Tim nodded again, this time more slowly as he thought about it. "Won't that hurt the pickles?"

"An empty one, Tim, for Pete's sake," Ron blurted. "Bring one of the empty jars and don't tell your mama or Mercy what it's for." Tim left immediately. Ron took the saddlebags and turned them upside down. He didn't see anything unusual, so Bannack told him to run his finger along what looked like a seam. When he did, he found that the seam was not stitched and he was able to pull it apart revealing the sixty dollars. "Well, I'll be . . ." he said. "That's a pretty good idea."

"You keep that to pay for whatever I cost you while I'm here," Bannack told him. "I don't plan to be here long, but I can tell I ain't gonna be able to be on my feet today and maybe not tomorrow. I don't know, but I'll do the best I can to ride out of here."

"You want me to ride into Glory and tell the people where you are, since they're most likely wonderin'?" Ron asked.

"No," Bannack said. "I thought I would ask you to do that, but then I got to thinkin' it over and I decided I'd rather just let them wonder till I get back. The reason is this. I've got a young man workin' for me in the marshal's office that I've started workin' with to try to make a deputy out of. He's got the potential to be a good law officer, if I can keep workin' with him. And I think it might be a good thing for him, if he has the whole responsibility of policin' that town dumped right in his lap. It might be just the kind of trainin' he needs." He paused to think for a couple of seconds. "Or break him from ever wantin' to be a sheriff or town marshal ever again. Whichever, it ought to cause him to make up his mind right quick."

Ron decided he'd best talk about the horses and other personal belongings he had taken from the scene of the ambush, especially since he had mentioned using a couple of the horses to buy some cows. "What are you gonna do about the other horses and stuff I brought back here from that creek?"

"Whaddaya mean?" Bannack asked. "I ain't plannin' to do anything about it. One of those packhorses belongs to me. He's that sorrel with the white stripe on his face. And I'm gonna need one of the saddle horses to ride back to Glory. It doesn't matter to me which one. I'm gonna have one helluva time replacing that buckskin they shot. I thought an awful lot of that horse." He paused when Tim returned with an empty fruit jar. Bannack reached up and took it from him and quickly put it under the blanket. "Much obliged," he said to

Tim. Back to Ron, he said, "As far as the rest of that stuff, I don't know what it was and I don't care what went with it."

"That's mighty generous of you," Ron said. "Now, I know I'm gonna go get you a cow."

CHAPTER 22

Spencer was not the only person in the town of Glory who was concerned about the whereabouts of Marshal John Cochran. Daryl Boyd was already nervous about another evening with no sign of the marshal. So far he had been lucky the whole time Marshal Cochran had been gone, with no real disturbances of any kind. The marshal left Sunday morning for the Monday trial. Daryl had counted on his return late Monday or by Tuesday afternoon, but when he was not back, even by Tuesday night, he thought surely he would be back on Wednesday. Now Wednesday had come and gone and still no Marshal Cochran. It was time for panic as suppertime drew near on Thursday. It didn't help when Mayor Walter Glory stopped by the marshal's office on his way to supper. "Still no word?" Mayor Glory asked when he came in the door.

"No, sir, Mr. Mayor," Daryl answered. "I finally sent a telegram to the US Marshal's office in Jacksboro this afternoon. I expected an answer back this afternoon, but there hasn't been one so far."

"There is something drastically wrong," Mayor Glory remarked. "That trial couldn't have taken that long. We've been damn lucky we haven't had any real trouble since he's been gone, but I don't know how long we can count on that continuing." He remembered then that the marshal had been training Daryl for a future deputy's job. "No reflection on you, Daryl, the marshal says you show great promise. I'm sure he would want to work with you quite a bit more before handing a desperate situation over to you."

Before Daryl could answer, the door opened and Sammy Peters walked in. "Telegram, Mr. Boyd." Daryl opened the desk drawer, took out a nickel, and gave it to the boy. "Thank you, sir," Sammy said and went back out the door.

Mayor Glory stepped up to hover over the desk, looking as if he was about to snatch the telegram out of Daryl's hand. Daryl read it, then handed it to the mayor without comment. "The trial was over Monday," he read aloud. "Marshal Cochran left Jacksboro to return home Tuesday morning." Mayor Glory slammed the telegram down hard on the desk. "I knew something drastic had happened. I trusted that man with this all-important position in our town. I blame myself for not checking into his background before I gave him the job."

Daryl was shocked. "Do you think he's just jay-birding it somewhere, instead of coming back here like he said he would?"

The mayor could see that Daryl was staggered by his reaction, so he quickly said, "No, no, of course not.

I didn't mean that at all. I'm just afraid he's run into some bad luck somewhere. We'll just have to deal with whatever the situation is." He just stood there for a few more seconds, obviously perplexed before finally saying, "I'm going to supper now. If Cochran happens to come in right away, send him to the hotel dining room to see me." He turned around and headed for the door.

"Yes, sir," Daryl responded. "I'll tell him." He walked to the door after him and closed it after the mayor walked out. Then he returned to the desk and sat down to continue to wait for some word that might explain the absence of Marshal Cochran. It was no more than half an hour when Bill Godsey, the owner of the gun shop, burst through the door in a panic.

"Is the marshal back yet?" He gasped, breathless and looking all about him. When Daryl, startled by Godsey's desperation, could only shake his head in answer, Godsey groaned, "Oh, Lordy, I was afraid of that!"

"What is it?" Daryl asked. "Is it something I can help you with?"

"No, I need the marshal!" Godsey blurted, still excited. "Razor Creek! Henry Dawson and his three sons! All dead! I was on my way back from Jacksboro and when I got to Razor Creek, I could see a circle of buzzards over the creek. I was wonderin' what they found to eat, so I went down the creek a-ways and saw a bunch of 'em fightin' over a dead horse. I thought that was it, but I could hear more of 'em raisin' hell on the other side of the creek, so I rode across to take a look. I liked to messed my britches up. There was four bodies layin' there and the buzzards were goin' after them somethin' awful. I could tell who they were, ol' Henry Dawson and his boys and they were all shot."

Marshal Cochran was Daryl's first thought. "You didn't see any other body for sure?"

"I didn't hang around long after I found those four bodies, but I didn't see any others," Godsey confessed.

"You didn't see any other horses except that one dead one?" Daryl asked then.

"Not a one. I reckon the buzzards musta scared 'em off, or the shootin' that was goin' on."

"Did you see what kind of horse the dead one was?" Daryl asked. "Was it a buckskin?"

"I don't know," Godsey said. "It coulda been. I couldn't really tell with them big birds all over it and it was tore up pretty good by then."

"I gotta go tell Mayor Glory what you just told me," Daryl said. "Like I said, Marshal Cochran ain't back from Jacksboro yet, but I really hope he'll show up soon." He was afraid Bannack's body might eventually be found at Razor Creek, too. He headed toward the hotel to see if the mayor was still in the dining room, while Godsey headed toward the saloon to spread the news.

While he hurried along the street toward the hotel, Daryl tried to think of what he should do, if anything, since Razor Creek was not in the city limits of Glory.

But his concern was for Marshal John Cochran, so he decided he should go to Razor Creek and look for the marshal. His mind made up, he found the mayor still in the dining room, drinking coffee with Richard Prentice, the manager of the bank. They stopped talking when they saw Daryl come in the door and start toward them. "Sit down, Daryl," the mayor invited. "Have you heard from Cochran?"

"No, sir, but I just got some news I thought I oughta pass on to you right away." He told them what Bill Godsey had just told him. As he expected, they were both concerned that the incident had something to do with their missing marshal. Then he told them what he had decided to do. "While there's still enough daylight left, I think I'll ride up to that creek and do some lookin' around for any sign of Marshal Cochran."

"I think that's a good idea," the mayor said, and Prentis agreed. "He might be lyin' up there severely wounded. Don't delay, Daryl, go at once. I'll be at the River House when you get back. If I'm not there, come by the house."

"Yes, sir," Daryl responded and left immediately. He gave Clem Shaw a quick report of the incident while he saddled his horse.

"You be careful you don't run into an ambush, yourself, roamin' around in them woods," Clem called after him when Daryl rode away. He had some concern for the young man, and he owned the horse and saddle that Daryl borrowed.

* * *

It was late by the time Daryl returned to town, almost time for the marshal's usual last walk around town. But on this night, there were still quite a few customers in the River House saloon, the mayor, the manager of the bank, plus several other members of the town council. There was also one visitor who was as much interested in hearing Daryl's news as anyone there. Clark Spencer sat at a table alone, slowly nursing a bottle of rye whiskey, paying little attention to the chatter and speculation around him. He waited to hear the fact that Bannack was dead and if he was told that fact, he would still have to verify it to satisfy Judge Raymond Grant.

When Daryl walked into the saloon, the steady drone of barroom conversation ceased immediately, and the patrons drew closer to the table where Glory and Prentis sat. There was one groan in concert from the many voices when Daryl announced that he had been unable to find any trace of Marshal John Cochran. There was only one face with traces of a faint smile. While the citizens of Glory, Texas, were left to speculate on the fate of their marshal, the one stranger in the saloon knew for certain that their marshal was not dead. He had no doubt that it was their marshal who killed the four men, and he knew for certain their marshal was John Bannack. *So once again Bannack is in the wind,* Spencer thought. But if he was running, why did he come back to this creek that's only a few miles from Glory? And from the description of the scene Daryl found, it sounded more like an ambush that went bad for the assailants. He was not convinced that Daryl could be much of a scout. He seemed young and as innocent as a puppy. He got up from the table and headed for the door.

"You fixin' to turn in for the night, Mr. Johnson?" Smut Smith said to him when he walked past the bar.

"Looks like you ain't never gonna get to buy that drink for Marshal Cochran," Buster Bridges remarked from his usual place at the end of the bar.

"It is beginning to look that way, ain't it?" Spencer replied. "Maybe next time I'm through here." He walked on out the door.

"If that man's a special investigator for the governor, then I'm a garter inspector for the ladies' church choir," Buster said to Smut. "I don't know what he's up to, but it don't smell right to me."

"I wonder if he's still hangin' around Glory 'cause he's interested in a job as town marshal," Smut said. "Maybe we ought notta told him how John Cochran got hired. I notice he wears that gun where he can get to it pretty fast."

"I noticed that myself," Buster said. "Remember that story he told us the first time he came in here? Said he was a special investigator for the governor and he was just passin' through town on the trail of an escaped convict. And here he is, still stuttin' around the town, talkin' about buyin' a drink for John Cochran. I don't know how fast John is on the draw. You reckon he's got a name as a gunslinger in some other part of the state? And that Johnson feller is just lookin' to add John's name to his kills?"

Smut slowly shook his head. "I don't know, Buster. John don't seem like that sorta feller. We'da noticed it by now, if he was. He's so damn big that half the time he don't need a gun."

"I think it'd be a good idea to keep an eye on that Frank Johnson, or whatever his name is," Buster decided. He suddenly threw his hands up in surrender then. "Well, that's it for me tonight. I got things to do in the mornin'. Goodnight, Smut." Smut said goodnight and watched the little fellow walk out the door, taking strides that were about two and a half times longer than a natural stride for one his height.

The morning brought a promise of a cloudless, sunny day for the little town of Glory. It was one of those days that Mayor Glory liked to call a Glorious day. He was generally excused for his poor attempt to be clever. For Buster Bridges, it was a day of growing concern for a man he counted as a close friend. John Cochran, a total stranger at the time, came to his defense when he was under attack by two men determined to kill him and take possession of his wagon. Ever since that day, Buster had tried to support the new town marshal in any way he could. Because of that personal commitment, Buster turned the OPEN sign around and closed the barbershop this morning while he did some investigating. He started with the marshal's office.

A greatly concerned Daryl Boyd told him that there was still no sign of the marshal, and he was afraid the mayor had given up hope on his return and was already talking about hiring a new marshal. That was all Buster needed to know before he saddled his horse and rode up to Razor Creek to investigate the carnage described by Bill Godsey the night before. Everybody in Glory knew about the hatred the Dawson men held for Marshal Cochran, so Buster was certain they had waited in ambush to kill him at that creek. And he would bet his soul that John had killed all four of the Dawsons, so there had to be some trace of his body, as well.

When he reached the creek, there were still some buzzards picking at the leavings of their feast, so he got a pretty good idea where the bodies were from the sound of their squawking and fighting over in the trees that lined the creek. There was a smaller bunch of buzzards nosily working at a site north of the creek, so he figured that was probably where the one horse was killed. He guided his horse off the road and made his way to the spot where he found what was left of a horse. The buzzards still there challenged him, and he dispatched one of them with his pistol, causing the others to back away. The saddle was gone, but the bridle was still on and the horse's belly had been opened and the organs and other guts scattered on the ground. He considered trying to remove the bridle, but the smell was almost overwhelming just standing there. He was afraid the smell of dead horse would remain with the bridle forever. What was now mostly a collection of hooves and bones had enough hide to tell him the horse might have been a buckskin. Whoever took the saddle was going to have a hell of a time getting the stench out of it. Thinking a person would now be able to smell Razor Creek from a mile away, he forced himself to scout the bushes and ground until he found the rider's trail away from his horse.

Following the trail that Ron Cord had followed, he found the four bodies of the Dawson gang, although by this time the buzzards had made it more difficult to identify them. He searched the area around the scene of the feast but found nothing that indicated the shooter had been there until he found some empty shell casings in a gully not far from the four bodies. Looking at the edge of the gully he found definite marks in the dirt left by a heavy object being dragged from the gully, an object as heavy as John Cochran. "But, who dragged him out?" he asked aloud, certain now that it was John and that someone had dragged him out of the gully.

He followed the trail the body left, a trail that went in the general direction of the road and then it stopped. *Maybe they threw it on a horse,* he thought. He searched a little farther, looking for hoofprints, but then he saw the distinct tracks of wagon wheels. That meant he was alive, but where did they take him? In a hurry now, he followed the obvious wagon tracks back to the road where they turned toward Glory. This caused him to pause. If they knew who he was, why didn't they turn up in Glory? He continued to follow the wagon tracks for about a mile trying to make sense out of what the wagon tracks were telling him. Then one other possibility occurred to him and that would only require his riding about a hundred yards farther. So he gave his horse a little kick to cover the distance quickly. It proved to be a good idea, for the wagon turned off the road onto the trail toward Tyson's Creek. "Hot damn," he muttered. "I almost went back to Glory to search door to door!"

There were quite a few families with little patches of land they were trying to make a living on around Tyson's Creek. Buster didn't know any of them with the exception of Henry Dawson and his boys. And that was because he had once bought a cow from Henry, only to find out later that Henry and his boys were in the business of cattle rustling. Buster remembered a woman who lived with Henry. Her name was Berta. He wondered what would happen to her, now that there wasn't a man in the house. That might be the place to go to get an idea where to look for the driver of that wagon, he decided.

"Hello, Miz Berta!" he yelled when he pulled up in front of the front porch. There was no response to his yell, so he yelled again, "Miz Berta!"

Finally, the front door swung open and the wiry little woman stepped out onto the porch, holding a shotgun.

"Who the hell are you?" she yelled. "Whadda you want?"

"Ain't come to cause you no trouble, ma'am," Buster said. "I thought you mighta remembered me. I bought a cow from Henry a while back. But I just heard about what happened to Henry and his sons up on Razor Creek, and I wanted to stop by and tell you how sorry I am for the loss of Henry and the boys. He was a good man."

"He was trash, but ain't we all?" Berta said. "You're the first one of my neighbors to offer any kind words for Henry and the boys' passin'. You wanna get down off that horse and come in for a cup of coffee? I was just fixin' to have myself a cup and maybe a biscuit to go with it when you rode up."

"Why, that's mighty neighborly of you, ma'am," Buster replied. "But I wouldn't wanna put you to no trouble durin' your time of grievin'."

"Ain't no trouble a-tall," she said. "I'd appreciate a little visit at a time like this."

"Well, then, I'll stay for just a cup of coffee. I don't want to intrude on your remembrance of your family." He stepped down from his horse, thinking the tough-looking little woman wasn't wasting any time scouting out replacements for Henry and his sons.

"I'm sorry I mighta seemed a little rude when you rode up," Berta said. "But I've already had some people around here thinkin' I'm gonna abandon this house just because Henry and his sons are gone. They're surprised when they find out that me and Henry owned this house together," she lied, "and I ain't got no reason to leave it. I was the cook and housekeeper for the Dawsons and nothing else." When he walked up on the porch, she looked him directly in the eye and asked, "You know what I mean?" Then she said, "I swear, you ain't no taller than I am, are you? Well, come on in the house and we'll have a cup of coffee."

He followed her into the kitchen where she poured him a cup of coffee from a pot that had been sitting on the stove since breakfast. There were a couple of biscuits on a plate on the table. She shooed the flies off of them and offered him one. He figured, *What the hell?* And he took one. "That coffee might be gettin' a mite strong. Too much of coffee that strong will stunt your growth. But I reckon I don't have to tell you that."

He took a sip and clinched his teeth when he swallowed it. It was more like taking a drink of likker. "When did you find out about Henry and the boys gettin' killed?" he managed to ask after a bite of the cold biscuit.

"The other day," she answered, "when Ron Cord brought two of the horses back. He found 'em on that creek where Henry and the boys were killed. He said they was the only ones they found. So he brought 'em to me and I swapped him two cows for 'em. He said he needed to feed his boy a lotta beef to build his blood up."

"I don't believe I know Ron Cord," Buster said. "He live near you?"

"About a mile from here, close to the river," Berta answered. "He's married and has two young'uns, a boy and a girl. I reckon the boy has weak blood or something." She fashioned a sweet smile for him and said, "You oughta find you a place here around Tyson's Creek."

He felt a chill between his shoulder blades as she continued to stare at him like she was looking at a fresh plum. "That might suit me just fine," he said, "but my wife's a city gal, so I'm afraid I'm stuck in Glory."

"Oh, you're married? Well, good for you. I 'preciate you stoppin' by. I hope to hell you ain't rode all the way out here from town just to console me. Are you a preacher?"

"Yes, ma'am, and I hope you will find peace with the Lord." He figured two lies weren't much worse than one lie. He wasn't married and he wasn't a preacher, but he figured he might need both lies to save himself. "I'll be takin' my leave now, Miz Berta. Lord's blessings on you."

A preacher, she thought as she watched him ride back along the creek. *Now, ain't that just what I need?*

Buster followed the creek until he came to a cabin he estimated to be about a mile from Dawson's place. There was a woman in the yard splitting up firewood, and she stopped to stare at him as he approached. "Howdy, ma'am, I'm lookin' for Ron Cord's place."

"Next house you come to," she said without emotion and continued to stare at him.

"Thank you, ma'am, and good day to ya," he said. She said nothing in response but continued to stare, her face expressionless.

He continued on for less than a quarter of a mile before coming to a fairly substantial-looking log house. Looking the place over as he approached the front porch, he noticed a small barn and a corral that looked a little cramped for the number of horses inside it. He had an idea that he was looking at the rest of the Dawson horses as well as the wagon he had followed from Razor Creek. He could also see smoke from a fire behind the house somewhere, but he couldn't see the fire. He dismounted and walked up beside the porch steps and rapped on the porch floor. He waited for a few seconds before rapping again, harder than the first time. In a couple of minutes, the front door opened and Sadie Cord walked out on the porch, leaving the door open behind her. "Mrs. Cord?" Buster asked. She answered only with a nod of her head. "I wonder if I might speak with your husband?"

"He ain't here," Sadie said.

"Reckon that might be him behind the house, tendin' that fire you got goin' back there?" Buster asked politely.

"It's all right, Sadie," a man's voice came through the open door. "He doesn't mean any harm. He's just naturally nosy."

"John!" Buster blurted. "Is that you? Thank the Lord! I thought you was dead for sure!"

"I thought I was, too," Bannack said as he stepped into the doorway but stopped there, so he could hold onto the doorjamb for support. "And if it wasn't for this kind lady and her family, I expect I would be. Sadie, this is Buster Bridges, and I shoulda known if anybody came lookin' for me, it would be him. Buster, this fine lady is Sadie Cord. She and her husband found me at Razor Creek and brought me here where she sewed up my bullet wounds and got me back on my feet yesterday. Her son, Tim, cut me a long walkin' stick to hold onto, and I've been walkin' around a little bit better today."

After his first wave of sheer joy upon finding Bannack alive, Buster was struck by a second wave of pure shock when he saw the weakened condition of the indestructible man. When Sadie saw his apparent loss of voice, she said, "He was shot five times and lost an awful lot of blood. But he's coming back strong. When we first brought him home, he couldn't even raise up from the floor."

"I thought I might be able to ride back to town to-morrow, if I can get back on a horse," Bannack said. "How's Daryl holdin' up without me?"

"He's doin' the best he can and he's been walkin' the town a couple of times a night like you do. He's been lucky that there ain't been no real trouble a-tall. 'Course, I've been keepin' an eye out in case he needs help. But you need to get back as soon as you're able 'cause the mayor and the rest of the town council are already talking about havin' to find a new marshal. And right now, it ain't gonna be Daryl Boyd."

"I reckon you can see why I never came back from Jacksboro," Bannack said. "I was careless. I thought Henry Dawson and his three sons were still in Jacksboro when I left there, but they were set up in an ambush, waiting for me. I managed to do for all four of 'em, but it cost me. And if Sadie and her husband hadn't found me lyin' in a gully, I reckon I'da been on the same train to hell as the Dawsons. You see all these bandages, Sadie pulled most of the bullets outta me and plugged up the holes, but it was her cookin' that saved my life. I can feel my body comin' back from wherever it went."

"It's all that fresh beef we've been eating," Sadie said. "Ron and Tim are out behind the house smoking some of it for jerky. You're just in time for dinner, Mr. Bridges. We've got plenty of fresh beef and you're welcome to join us."

Buster looked at Bannack, and Bannack nodded. "Why, thank you ma'am," he said. "I'd be plumb tickled to join you."

"Good," Sadie replied, then said, "Mercy, run tell your pa we've got company."

Buster heard the sound of tiny feet running away from the door and Bannack was still standing, holding onto the doorjamb. "How'd you know she was back there?" he couldn't help asking.

Sadie laughed. "She's always behind John. She's his private nurse." Buster laughed, but he was thinking to himself that he didn't think he would tell that to any-body. It might hurt the marshal's reputation. He likened it to a mountain lion being tamed by a child and not the image a town wanted for its marshal.

CHAPTER 23

"How about another steak, John?" Ron Cord asked. "Somebody's gotta eat all this meat I cooked up, and you gotta build your blood back up. That's what your nurse says. Ain't that right, Mercy?" His daughter nodded her head vigorously. "Cooked outside over an open fire, too, just like us cattle rustlers like it. Right, Marshal Cochran?"

Bannack came as close to chuckling as he ever did and remarked, "If I don't leave this place pretty soon, I won't be able to climb up on a horse."

"You were mighty lucky these folks came along when they did," Buster commented.

"Yes, I was," Bannack replied. "It was the one good thing about that ambush, but I have to admit I'd rather have just met these folks on a Sunday at a picnic." He turned solemn for a moment and said, "The worst thing that happened is losin' my buckskin gelding. They don't make many horses like that."

"That's right," Buster said, "you ain't got a horse." He

thought of the last time he saw Bannack's buckskin but decided not to mention it.

"I've still got my packhorse," Bannack said, "or at least, Ron says I do. And he's willing to let me take one of the horses he brought back from Razor Creek to ride back to Glory."

"I expect that's about the least I can do for you," Ron declared. "You're the one who killed all four of the men who attacked you. I just happened to come along after it was all over to collect all the spoils of the fight."

"That may be," Bannack reminded him, "and you could have just left me there to die. So I figure you earned anything you found at the scene. Besides that, I didn't have any other way to pay you and your family for savin' my life." He paused, then added, "And all the beef I've eaten."

"If you say so," Ron japed. "You're too big to argue with."

"That reminds me," Buster remarked. "Do you know anybody named Frank Johnson?"

"Can't say as I do," Bannack answered. "Who's Frank Johnson?"

"He's some feller that's been hangin' around town ever since you've been gone. He said he's a special investigator for the governor of Texas. And you ain't never heard of him?" Bannack shook his head, so Buster continued, "When he first hit town, he said he was just passin' through 'cause he was on the trail of some feller that escaped from prison. Said he was a big feller about your size. He told me his name, but I forgot it.

Daryl had a wanted paper on him. Anyway, this Johnson feller was tellin' me and Smut Smith that he'd heard about you and wanted to buy you a drink of likker when you got back from Jacksboro. And day after day went by and you ain't come back. The whole town was worried, and this feller is still here. Something just didn't smell right about him. Me and Smut got to talkin' about it one day and we got to wonderin' about him. He wears a Colt six-shooter in a fast-draw holster, and I wouldn't be surprised if he was a fast gun who heard about you since you've been in Glory. And he's hangin' around, waitin' to try you out."

Clark Spencer, Bannack thought, *Judge Raymond Grant's gunman. It didn't take him long to get on my trail.* Buster and Smut were halfway correct in their assessment of Spencer. He was fast with a gun, but he had not tried to build a reputation for it. It would not have been appropriate for the judge's assistant to be a fast gun. Consequently, most of Spencer's kills came under the category of murder. What if it wasn't Spencer? Maybe it was some would-be gunslinger out to build a reputation for himself. In that case, he would handle it in his usual fashion without facing him in a quick-draw contest. The problem with that was the timing. He was still extremely weak from his loss of blood, not really halfway toward recovery. He thought about that possibility for a moment, then rejected it. Frank Johnson was not a would-be fast gun. He was Clark Spencer and he had come to take him back to prison or kill him.

The question was whether he should run or attempt to resolve the issue now, in Glory, and be done with it.

Knowing Buster was waiting for his response, Bannack said, "It's hard to say if you and Smut pegged this Johnson fellow right or not. I'd appreciate it if you could do something for me, though. When you go back to town today, would you tell Daryl and Mayor Glory, too, that I'll be back there tomorrow?"

"Why, sure, I'd be glad to," Buster replied at once, delighted to be the one to give the town the news. "I'll let 'em know you're comin', and it'll be mighty welcome news. I can tell you that."

"You sure you'll be ready to ride tomorrow?" Sadie asked, concerned that he was still holding onto things for support. "You know, most people would still be in bed recovering from all the wounds you have."

"I expect it's all because of your expert doctorin' and all that fresh steak," Bannack said. "I'll be ready to go back to work." He knew he had to go back. If it was Spencer, he was going to have to settle it sooner or later. It might be better to settle it sooner.

Buster lingered over another cup of coffee after dinner was finished, but then he said he'd better get back to town, since his barbershop had been closed half a day already. "I'd hate for folks to think I've gone outta business. If I ain't back pretty soon, they're liable to think the same about me as they've been thinkin' about John," he joked. He thanked Ron and Sadie for their hospitality and told Bannack he'd see him tomorrow. Bannack knew the little man was mostly anxious to get back to tell everyone that he had found their missing marshal and that he would be back tomorrow.

"Odd little man," Sadie remarked as she stood beside Bannack, watching Buster ride away. "He must think a lot of you to go to all the trouble he went to trying to find you." She turned to Ron and asked, "Can you believe he followed our wagon wheels back to Tyson's Creek and kept looking till he found us?"

"Buster's a good friend," Bannack told them. "Sometimes he wants to help more than he's needed, but he's a good friend."

As Bannack suspected, Buster pushed his horse a little harder than usual in his hurry to ride back to Glory. Just as Bannack had instructed, he went first to the marshal's office to give Daryl the welcome message. Daryl made no attempt to hide the sense of relief he experienced upon hearing the marshal would be back the next day. In a slight display of superstition, he knocked on the wooden desk and hoped no one in town would shoot somebody or rob somebody for at least one more night. As instructed, Buster went from there to the Glory General Merchandise Store to give Mayor Glory the message that the marshal would be back the next day. Walter Glory was even more relieved than Daryl had been, but still showed some concern when told of the reason Bannack had been missing for so many days and questioned Buster about the marshal's recovery. "Well, he's the toughest man I've ever known," Buster said. "He was ambushed on his way back here by that Dawson gang, and he was shot five times, but he killed all four of 'em before he was left to die. And I expect he mighta died, too, if a fellow named Ron Cord hadn't found him and took him home with him. And he says he's gonna ride back here to Glory tomorrow afternoon. I expect you can count on it."

His obligation to Bannack fulfilled, Buster went from there to the River House saloon to enlighten the drinking citizens of the town on the status of their marshal. He at once confirmed what many of them already thought when he told them that it was Marshal Cochran who killed the four Dawson men after they had ambushed him on his way back from Jacksboro. It was welcome news to all in the saloon to hear that Marshal Cochran would be returning to Glory tomorrow afternoon, even though he was still healing from five bullet wounds. It was of particular interest to one, Mr. Clark Spencer, who smiled in anticipation of meeting the town's marshal, convinced he had run John Bannack to ground. "Bartender," he called out to Smut Smith, "pour Mr. Bridges a double shot of rye whiskey and put it on my bill."

Buster saluted him and said, "Much obliged, Mr. Johnson!"

"That's for your good work in finding the marshal," Spencer said. *And for flushing Judge Wick's Panther out of his hole,* he thought. *Tomorrow's going to be a good day for one of us.*

John Bannack woke up stiff and sore the next morning to the sound of Tim Cord milking the cow below him in the barn. He knew that after milking the cow, the boy would look for eggs in the nests in the small barn and take the milk and eggs into the house to his mother. It had taken quite a bit of persuading to convince Sadie Cord that he would be comfortable sleeping in the hayloft the last night of his stay with them. She was not willing to believe him when he said he always slept in the hayloft at one place he had worked before coming to Glory and was quite content with the arrangement. He couldn't tell her that it was during the period he worked for Judge Wick Justice, so he said it was at a large farm. The only difficult part of it was climbing up the ladder to the hayloft, but he only had to do that once. He couldn't use his left arm to climb, but he managed with just the right one. At any rate, Tim never complained, but Bannack knew the boy was glad to get out of his sister's bedroom.

After Tim went to the house, Bannack dropped the few belongings that had survived the ambush down from the hayloft, then suffered a mildly painful descent down the ladder. He picked up the saddle he had selected and with a painful grunt, threw it on the back of the dun gelding he had chosen to ride back to Glory. He would let Ron or Tim put his packsaddle on the sorrel since the packs were mostly empty. He then left the horses in the little corral and went to the kitchen, knowing from the sounds that Sadie was already cooking breakfast.

"Good morning," Sadie sang out cheerfully to him when he walked in the door. "You sleep all right up in that little loft?"

"Like a baby," Bannack answered her.

"Guess what you're having for breakfast," she teased.

"I don't know," he said. "If I had to guess, I'd say steak and eggs."

"Well, that was a pretty lucky guess," she said and placed a cup of coffee on the table for him, so he sat down at the table.

Ron came in the back door then. "I see you already got that dun saddled. I was gonna do that for you, but you beat me to it. I was checkin' on that ol' sow to see how she's doin'. She's gonna have pigs any day now." He poured himself a cup of coffee and sat down at the table. "You sure you feel strong enough to ride back today. You know you're welcome to stay as long as you need to. Ain't that right, Sadie?"

"Yes, indeed it is, John," Sadie said. "You're no trouble a-tall, and you've been way too generous with your money."

"I owe you for my life," Bannack said. "It wouldn't have been fair to give you less."

After breakfast, the Cord family gathered in the backyard to say goodbye to their patient. Bannack thanked them all individually, expressing his appreciation to

Mercy for being his private nurse and Tim for sacrificing his room. "Come to see us any time you're out this way," Ron invited. Bannack thanked him again and said goodbye. They watched him ride away. "Yonder goes a man with a date with destiny," Ron said to Sadie. "There ain't much chance he'll die of old age."

"I expect you're right," Sadie said, thinking of the scars she saw that looked like old bullet holes when his shirt was off.

He followed Tyson's Creek for about a mile before he left that trail and cut over to strike the trail to Razor Creek. He wanted to see the site of the ambush before he went back to Glory. Specifically, he wanted to see the remains of his buckskin horse to see if there was anything left for him to keep as a remembrance of that faithful horse. A piece of bridle, a buckle, a saddle ornament, anything to remember the buckskin by. The horse had meant a lot to him. It was the closest thing to family and it was difficult to think there would ever be anything to replace it. So he rode the dun that one of the Dawson men had ridden and guided it toward Razor Creek.

When the breeze brought him the smell of death, he was still at least a mile away from the spot where the road crossed the creek. The dun snorted his report of the odor but Bannack chose to ignore it. He continued on until he came to the creek, then he looked for the spot where the first shots hit him. He saw the tracks where the buckskin swerved off the road into the brush and trees, and he guided the dun to follow them. It was hard to remember much of the attack beyond the swarm of bullets flying about him and the sting of those that found his body. Then the dun reared back suddenly when it came to the remains of the buckskin. He grabbed the saddle horn to keep from coming out of the saddle.

Once he calmed the dun, he realized he was too late to retrieve any mementos of the buckskin and he told himself he didn't really expect anything to be left. He was disappointed but not surprised. After this many days, there was no telling how many people looked to see what the buzzards had feasted upon. So he decided to follow the trail he had left to the shoot-out with the four Dawsons, since it was still obvious. He rode across the creek and up the other bank, and he remembered the Y-shaped tree he took cover behind. *Wasn't a helluva lot of cover,* he thought, but at the time, that was all there was. He stepped down from the saddle and looked at the base of the tree, remembering how he had to steady his rifle in the fork of the tree to shoot the first two of the four. Then he walked over to the gully where he had retreated when the other two circled around behind him.

"I figure they musta followed that trail you left from your horse over to this side of the creek and that's where you shot two of 'em." The voice, coming from behind him, was like a sharp spike in his back, for he knew it well. "Then you crawled to that gully, and that's where you shot the other two," the voice said. "Is that about right?"

"Are you gonna give it to me in the back, or can I turn around?" Bannack asked.

"You can turn around, as long as you do it real slow and keep your hands up where I can see 'em," Spencer said. "I've gone to a lot of trouble trying to catch up with you, Bannack. I think it would be downright impolite to just shoot you on sight. Besides, Judge Grant prefers to have you rot away in prison, so I have to give you the opportunity to surrender peacefully." He waited while Bannack turned around to face him.

"I figured it was you when Buster told me about a stranger who said his name was Frank Johnson," Bannack said. "I didn't expect to see you out here at Razor Creek, though."

Spencer smiled, pleased with himself, his Colt .44 held up comfortably before his chest. "I figured you might come by here to check it out, see if there was anything left, on your way back to town. So I thought it might be best to settle our little business out here. I might have been at a disadvantage in town. There're too many folks there who think you're a damn hero, instead of the common criminal you are. I gotta hand it to ya, you did a helluva job foolin' those people. It's better out here, just you and me."

"I'm surprised you didn't shoot me in the back," Bannack said.

"You know, I thought about that, but like I said, Judge Grant wants to put you back in prison. Yep, I thought about it, but you looked so damn feeble when you climbed down outta that saddle, I almost went over to offer you a hand. Five shots is what Buster said. Is that a fact?"

"Yep, that's the count," Bannack said. "It kinda slows me down a little."

"Well, it's been nice visitin' with you, Bannack, but I expect it's time to get down to business. Are you ready to surrender and go peacefully back to The Unit at Huntsville?"

"I'd rather not," Bannack answered.

Spencer smiled again. "I was hopin' you'd say that, although it would have been nice to have somebody to talk to on the long ride back. I reckon I'll still talk to you, even though you won't be able to answer. You know, since we've got a little history between us, with both of us workin' as special assistants to circuit judges, I'm willing to offer you a sportin' chance to save your life." He released the hammer on his .44 and dropped it back in his holster. "We'll settle our differences man to man. Whaddaya say?"

"I say that ain't all that sportin' of you, since you're the one with the reputation as a fast gun. I've got a better idea. Why don't you just go on back and tell Judge Grant I'm dead? Because as far as I'm concerned, John Bannack is dead."

Spencer chuckled, delighted. "I ain't ready to deprive myself of the pleasure of killin' you, Bannack. You're wearin' a gun. I'm giving you a chance to go down like a man, instead of an egg-suckin' dog. Now, I'm countin' to three and when I say three, I'm gonna shoot you down right where you're standin'. One! Two! . . ."

Both men anticipated the number, Three, and drew before Spencer actually said it. To the surprise of both, Bannack was a split-second faster and pumped a bullet into Spencer's gut, the shock of which caused him to discharge his firearm harmlessly into the ground. He doubled over in pain and dropped to his knees. Bannack charged toward him to take the weapon out of his hand and give him a shove that caused him to fall over on his side. Holding his belly, in excruciating pain, Spencer stared up at Bannack, who was as amazed as he was. He could only attribute his speed on the draw to the hours he spent with Daryl teaching him how to draw and shoot quickly. "You cheated," Spencer gasped painfully.

"So did you," Bannack responded. "I won't leave you to lie here like I was, hoping someone comes along to find you before you die." With that, he put his .44 to the back of Spencer's head and pulled the trigger.

Knowing Spencer was probably carrying a lot of money, his expenses paid for by Judge Raymond Grant, Bannack searched his pockets and his saddlebags and found a goodly sum. The toughest decision was to leave Spencer's fine gray gelding and saddle, but he decided it best not to be associated in any way with Frank Johnson's death. So he left the horse to drink in the creek when he rode away. Someone else could discover the fifth killing at Razor Creek and claim the spoils. "For a day that dawned with such poor promise, it's turning out to be much better than expected," he told the dun gelding recently ridden by Junior Dawson. "And thanks to Judge Raymond Grant, I can afford to replace you with a fine horse of my choosing."

It was just about dinnertime when Bannack rode into the stable at the north end of town. He was given a big welcome from Clem Shaw, who ran out from the back of the barn when he saw him pull up in the front. "Howdy, John, I'm sure glad to see you back in town. Buster told us what happened. Everybody's gonna be happy as hell to see you. I see you're ridin' a new horse."

"Yeah, this one's just borrowed," Bannack said. "It belongs to Ron Cord up at Tyson's Creek. I lost the buckskin when I got ambushed. I'm gonna have to buy a new one. I'll leave this one with you till I have a chance to take him back to Ron." He took the saddlebags and his rifle and walked out to the street. Clem walked out to the street with him.

"I'll take good care of him," Clem said.

"I know you will, Clem. Thanks."

He walked down the street exchanging greetings with several people along the way to the marshal's office, each one ending with a, "Welcome back, Marshal." Hearing people calling out greetings along the street, Daryl Boyd wondered what the cause. When he looked out the window and saw Bannack, he rushed to open the door and stood waiting on the steps. Buster, alert to the unusual sounds on the street, looked out his door and, upon seeing Bannack, ran out the door to inform the mayor, leaving a customer with half a haircut sitting in the chair. Within minutes, the mayor rushed through the door of the marshal's office to see what kind of shape his town marshal was in.

"I declare, you really had us worried there for a while," the mayor said. "I hope you're going to let Dr. Taylor take a look at that wound," he said, pointing at his bandaged shoulder.

"Yes, sir," Bannack replied. "I'm gonna let Doc take a look at a couple others you can't see under my clothes, too, although I'm satisfied the lady who bandaged me up did a pretty good job. She got all the bullets out but one in the back of my leg. I'll let Doc take a look at that to see if it needs to come outta there."

The mayor was amazed. The man seemed indestructible. According to what Buster Bridges had reported, their marshal had been shot five times, and here he was, already walking without even a limp for the bullet in his leg. "Welcome home, John," Mayor Glory said. "You take it easy and let those wounds heal." *And don't you ever think about leaving your job as marshal of this town,* he thought. As he went out the door, he almost bumped into Buster again, who had rushed back to his shop to apologize to a confused customer with half a haircut and quickly finish the job at no charge.

"Russell Sawyer told me to invite you to his café for dinner," Buster said. "Said it was a welcome back dinner free of charge."

"Well, that's mighty nice of those folks," Bannack replied. He was amazed by the reception he was getting from seemingly the whole town. He was not sure if his plan to hide in plain sight was still a good idea or not. But somehow it didn't seem right to abandon these folks in Glory who obviously wanted him to stay.

"If you don't mind, I'd like to go to Sawyer's with you," Buster said.

"Why, sure, Buster," Bannack responded. "I'd be glad to have you. We'll lock the office door and Daryl can go with us." That brought a smile of surprise to Daryl's face.

On the way across the street to the café, Buster started chuckling and had to comment. "I know one feller that'll be sorry he rode off somewhere today." When Bannack asked who he was referring to, Buster said, "That Frank Johnson feller. He was just hangin' around here, waitin' for you to come back."

"Maybe he'll show up again," Bannack said. "Did he check out of the hotel?"

"I ain't got no idea," Buster answered. "You wouldn't have no interest in whatever he's sellin', anyway."

You're right about that, Bannack thought.

"For what it's worth," Buster went on, "I wouldn't be surprised if Frank Johnson's not his real name. I think he didn't wanna use his real name 'cause he thought you might know it. I think he mighta been thinkin' about callin' you out, so he could add your name to his list of fast-draw killin's."

"You think so?"

"Yeah, I think so, and I'm afraid you wouldn'ta had

much chance against him in the condition you're in right now."

"You're probably right," Bannack said. "I am pretty puny right now. It wouldn't be much of a contest."

"You don't have to worry about it," Buster declared. "If he's still around, I'll keep my eye on him, and I'll cut him down if he shows the first sign of causin' trouble."

TURN THE PAGE
FOR A GUT-BUSTIN' PREVIEW!

**JOHNSTONE COUNTRY.
HOMESTYLE JUSTICE
WITH A SIDE OF SLAUGHTER.**

**In this explosive new series, Western legend Luke
Jensen teams up with chuckwagon cook Dewey
"Mac" McKenzie to dish out a steaming plate
of hot-blooded justice. But in a corrupt town like
Hangman's Hill, revenge is a dish best served cold . . .**

**BEANS, BOURBON, AND BLOOD:
A RECIPE FOR DISASTER**

The sight of a rotting corpse hanging from a noose is
enough to stop any man in his tracks—and Luke
Jensen is no exception. Sure, he could just keep riding
through. He's got a prisoner to deliver, after all. But
when a group of men show up with another prisoner
for another hanging, Luke can't turn his back—
especially when the condemned man keeps
swearing he's innocent. Right up to the moment
he's hung by the neck till he's dead . . .

Welcome to Hannigan's Hill, Wyoming.
Better known as Hangman's Hill.

Luke's pretty shaken up by what he's seen and decides to stay the night, get some rest, and grab some grub. The town marshal agrees to lock up Luke's prisoner while Luke heads to a local saloon and restaurant called Mac's Place. The pub's owner— a former chuckwagon cook named Dewey "Mac" McKenzie—serves up a bellyful of chow and an earful of gossip. According to Mac, the whole stinking town is run by corrupt cattle baron Ezra Hannigan. Ezra owns practically everything. Including the town marshal. And anyone who gets in his way ends up swinging from a rope . . .

Mac might be just an excellent cook. But he's got a ferocious appetite for justice—and a fearsome new friend in Luke Jensen. Together, they could end Hannigan's reign of terror. But when Hannigan calls in his hired guns, it'll be their necks on the line . . . or dancing from the end of a rope.

National Bestselling Authors
William W. Johnstone
and J.A. Johnstone

BEANS, BOURBON, AND BLOOD

A Luke Jensen–Dewey McKenzie Western

On sale now, wherever Pinnacle Books are sold.

LIVE FREE. READ HARD.
www.williamjohnstone.net
Visit us at www.kensingtonbooks.com

CHAPTER 1

Luke Jensen reined his horse to a halt and looked up at the hanged man. The corpse swung back and forth in the cold wind sweeping across the Wyoming plains.

From behind Luke, Ethan Stallings said, "I don't like the looks of that. No, sir, I don't like it one bit."

"Shut up, Stallings," Luke said without taking his gaze off the dead man dangling from a hangrope attached to the crossbar of a sturdy-looking gallows. "In case you haven't figured it out already, I don't care what you like."

Luke rested both hands on his saddle horn and leaned forward to ease muscles made weary by the long ride to the town of Hannigan's Hill. He had never been here before, but he'd heard that the place was sometimes called Hangman's Hill. He could see why. Not every settlement had a gallows on a hill overlooking it just outside of town.

And not every gallows had a corpse hanging from it that looked to have been there for at least a week, based on the amount of damage buzzards had done to it. This poor varmint's eyes were gone, and not much remained of his nose and lips and ears, either. Buzzards went for the easiest bits first.

Luke was a middle-aged man who still had an air of vitality about him despite his years and the rough life he had led. His face was too craggy to be called handsome, but the features held a rugged appeal. The thick, dark hair under his black hat was threaded with gray, as was the mustache under his prominent nose. His boots, trousers, and shirt were black to match his hat. He wore a sheepskin jacket to ward off the chill of the gray autumn day.

He rode a rangy buckskin horse, as unlovely but as strong as its rider. A rope stretched back from the saddle to the bridle of the other horse, a chestnut gelding, so that it had to follow. The hands of the man riding that horse were tied to the saddle horn.

He sat with his narrow shoulders hunched against the cold. The brown tweed suit he wore wasn't heavy enough to keep him warm. His face under the brim of a bowler hat was thin, fox-like. Thick, reddish-brown side whiskers crept down to the angular line of his jaw.

"I'm not sure we should stay here," he said. "Doesn't appear to be a very welcoming place."

"It has a jail and a telegraph office," Luke said. "That'll serve our purposes."

"Your purposes," Ethan Stallings said. "Not mine."

"Yours don't matter anymore. Haven't since you became my prisoner."

Stallings sighed. A great deal of dejection was packed into the sound.

Luke frowned as he studied the hanged man more closely. The man wore town clothes: wool trousers, a white shirt, a simple vest. His hands were tied behind his back. As bad a shape as he was in, it was hard to make an accurate guess about his age, other than the fact that he hadn't been old. His hair was a little thin but still sandy brown with no sign of gray or white.

Luke had witnessed quite a few hangings. Most fellows who wound up dancing on air were sent to eternity with black hoods over their heads. Usually, the hoods were left in place until after the corpse had been cut down and carted off to the undertaker. Most people enjoyed the spectacle of a hanging, but they didn't necessarily want to see the end result.

The fact that this man no longer wore a hood—if, in fact, he ever had—and was still here on the gallows a week later could mean only one thing.

Whoever had strung him up wanted folks to be able to see him. Wanted to send a message with that grisly sight.

Stallings couldn't keep from talking for very long. He had been that way ever since Luke had captured him. He said, "This is sure making me nervous."

"No reason for it to. You're just a con artist, Stallings. You're not a killer or a rustler or a horse thief. The chances of you winding up on a gallows are pretty slim. You'll just spend the next few years behind bars, that's all."

Stallings muttered something Luke couldn't make out, then said in a louder, more excited voice, "Look! Somebody's coming."

The town of Hannigan's Hill was about half a mile away, a decent-sized settlement with a main street three blocks long lined by businesses and close to a hundred houses total on the side streets. The railroad hadn't come through here, but as Luke had mentioned, there was a telegraph line. East, south, and north—the direction he and Stallings had come from—lay rangeland. Some low but rugged mountains bulked to the west. The town owed its existence mostly to the ranches that surrounded it on three sides, but Luke knew there was some mining in the mountains, too.

A group of riders had just left the settlement and were heading toward the hill. Bunched up the way they were, Luke couldn't tell exactly how many. Six or eight, he estimated. They moved at a brisk pace as if they didn't want to waste any time.

On a raw, bleak day like today, nobody could blame them for feeling that way.

Something about one of them struck Luke as odd, and as they came closer, he figured out what it was. Two men rode slightly ahead of the others, and one of them had his arms pulled behind him. His hands had to be tied together behind his back. His head hung forward as he rode as if he lacked the strength or the spirit to lift it.

Stallings had seen the same thing. "Oh, hell," the

confidence man said. His voice held a hollow note. "They're bringing somebody else up here to hang him."

That certainly appeared to be the case. Luke spotted a badge pinned to the shirt of the other man in the lead, under his open coat. More than likely, that was the local sheriff or marshal.

"Whatever they're doing, it's none of our business," Luke said.

"They shouldn't have left that other fella dangling there like that. It . . . it's inhumane!"

Luke couldn't argue with that sentiment, but again, it was none of his affair how they handled their law-breakers here in Hannigan's Hill. Or Hangman's Hill, as some people called it, he reminded himself.

"You don't have to worry about that," he told Stallings again. "All I'm going to do is lock you up and send a wire to Senator Creed to find out what he wants me to do with you. I expect he'll tell me to take you on to Laramie or Cheyenne and turn you over to the law there. Eventually, you'll wind up on a train back to Ohio to stand trial for swindling the senator, and you'll go to jail. It's not the end of the world."

"For you it's not."

The riders were a couple of hundred yards away now. The lawman in the lead made a curt motion with his hand. Two of the other men spurred their horses ahead, swung around the lawman and the prisoner, and headed toward Luke and Stallings at a faster pace.

"They've seen us," Stallings said.

"Take it easy. We haven't done anything wrong.

Well, I haven't, anyway. You're the one who decided it would be a good idea to swindle a United States Senator out of ten thousand dollars."

The two riders pounded up the slope and reined in about twenty feet away. They looked hard at Luke and Stallings, and one of them asked in a harsh voice, "What's your business here?"

Luke had been a bounty hunter for a lot of years. He recognized hard cases when he saw them. But these two men wore deputy badges. That wasn't all that unusual. This was the frontier. Plenty of lawmen had ridden the owlhoot trail at one time or another in their lives. The reverse was true, too.

Luke turned his head and gestured toward Stallings with his chin. "Got a prisoner back there, and I'm looking for a place to lock him up, probably for no more than a day or two. That's my only business here, friend."

"I don't see no badge. You a bounty hunter?"

"That's right. Name's Jensen."

The name didn't appear to mean anything to the men. If Luke had said that his brother was Smoke Jensen, the famous gunfighter who was now a successful rancher down in Colorado, that would have drawn more notice. Most folks west of the Mississippi had heard of Smoke. Plenty east of the big river had, too. But Luke never traded on family connections. In fact, for a lot of years, for a variety of reasons, he had called himself Luke Smith instead of using the Jensen name.

The two deputies still seemed suspicious. "You don't know that hombre Marshal Bowen is bringin' up here?"

"I don't even know Marshal Bowen," Luke answered honestly. "I never set eyes on any of you boys until today."

"The marshal told us to make sure you wasn't plannin' on interferin'. This here is a legal hangin' we're fixin' to carry out."

Luke gave a little wave of his left hand. "Go right ahead. I always cooperate with the law."

That wasn't strictly true—he'd been known to bend the law from time to time when he thought it was the right thing to do—but these deputies didn't need to know that.

The other deputy spoke up for the first time. "Who's your prisoner?"

"Name's Ethan Stallings. Strictly small-time. Nobody who'd interest you fellas."

"That's right," Stallings muttered. "I'm nobody."

The rest of the group was close now. The marshal raised his left hand in a signal for them to stop. As they reined in, Luke looked the men over and judged them to be cut from the same cloth as the first two deputies. They wore law badges, but they were no better than they had to be.

The prisoner was young, maybe twenty-five, a stocky redhead who wore range clothes. He didn't look like a forty-a-month-and-found puncher. Maybe a little better than that. He might own a small spread of his own, a greasy sack outfit he worked with little or no help.

When he finally raised his head, he looked absolutely terrified, too. He looked straight at Luke and said, "For God's sake, mister, you've got to help me. They're gonna hang me, and I didn't do anything wrong. I swear it!"

CHAPTER 2

The marshal turned in his saddle, leaned over, and swung a backhanded blow that cracked viciously across the prisoner's face. The man might have toppled off his horse if one of the other deputies hadn't ridden up beside him and grasped his arm to steady him.

"Shut up, Crawford," the lawman said. "Nobody wants to listen to your lies. Take what you've got coming and leave these strangers out of it."

The prisoner's face flamed red where the marshal had struck it. He started to cry, letting out wrenching sobs full of terror and desperation.

Even without knowing the facts of the case, Luke felt a pang of sympathy for the young man. He didn't particularly want to, but he felt it anyway.

"I'm Verne Bowen. Marshal of Hannigan's Hill. We're about to carry out a legally rendered sentence on this man. You have any objection?"

Luke shook his head. "Like I told your deputies, Marshal, this is none of my business, and I don't have the faintest idea what's going on here. So I'm not going to interfere."

Bowen jerked his head in a nod and said, "Good."

He was about the same age as Luke, a thick-bodied man with graying fair hair under a pushed-back brown hat. He had a drooping mustache and a close-cropped beard. He wore a brown suit over a fancy vest and a butternut shirt with no cravat. A pair of walnut-butted revolvers rode in holsters on his hips. He looked plenty tough and probably was.

Bowen waved a hand at the deputies and ordered, "Get on with it."

Two of them dismounted and moved in on either side of the prisoner, Crawford. He continued to sob as they pulled him off his horse and marched him toward the gallows steps, one on either side of him.

"Just out of curiosity," Luke asked, "what did this hombre do?"

Bowen glared at him. "You said that was none of your business."

"And it's not. Just curious, that's all."

"It doesn't pay to be too curious around here, mister . . . ?"

"Jensen. Luke Jensen."

Bowen nodded toward Stallings. "I see you have a prisoner, too. You a bounty hunter?"

"That's right. I was hoping you'd allow me to stash him in your jail for a day or two."

"Badman, is he?"

"A foolish man," Luke said, "who made some bad

choices. But he didn't do anything around here."
Luke allowed his voice to harden slightly. "Not in
your jurisdiction."

Bowen looked levelly at him for a couple of seconds,
then nodded. "Fair enough."

By now the deputies were forcing Crawford up the
steps. He twisted and jerked and writhed, but their grips
were too strong for him to pull free. It wouldn't have
done him any good if he had. He would have just fallen
down the steps and they would have picked him up
again.

Bowen said, "I don't suppose it'll hurt anything to
satisfy your curiosity, Jensen. Just don't get in the habit
of poking your nose in where it's not wanted. Crawford
there is a murderer. He got drunk and killed a soiled
dove."

"That's not true!" Crawford cried. "I never hurt that
girl. Somebody slipped me something that knocked
me out. I never even laid eyes on the girl until I came to
in her room and she was . . . was layin' there with her
eyes bugged out and her tongue sticking out and those
terrible bruises on her throat—"

"Choked her to death, the little weasel did," Bowen
interrupted. "Claims he doesn't remember it, but he's a
lying, no-account killer."

The deputies and the prisoner had reached the top of
the steps. The deputies wrestled Crawford out onto the
platform. Another star packer trotted up the steps after
them, moving with a jaunty bounce, and pulled a knife
from a sheath at his waist. He reached out, grasped the

man's belt, and pulled him close enough that he could reach up and cut the rope. When he let go, the body fell through the open trap and landed with a soggy thud on the ground below. Even from where Luke was, he could smell the stench that rose from it. He didn't envy whoever got the job of burying the man.

"How about him? What did he do?"

"A thief," Bowen said. "Embezzled some money from the man he worked for, one of our leading citizens."

Luke frowned. "You hang a man for embezzlement around here?"

"When he was caught, he went loco and tried to shoot his way out of it," Bowen replied with a shrug. "He could have killed somebody. That's attempted murder. The judge decided to make an example of him. I don't hand down the sentences, Jensen. I just carry 'em out."

"I suppose leaving him up here to rot was part of making an example."

Bowen leaned forward, glared, and said, "For somebody who keeps claiming this is none of his business, you are taking an almighty keen interest in all of this, mister. You might want to take your prisoner and ride on down to town. Ask anybody, they can tell you where my office and the jail are. I'll be down directly, and we can lock that fella up." The marshal paused, then added, "Got a good bounty on him, does he?"

"Good enough," Luke said. He was beginning to get the impression that instead of waiting, he ought to ride on with Stallings and not stop over in Hannigan's Hill at all. Bowen and those hardcase deputies might have their eyes on the reward Senator Jonas Creed had offered for Stallings' capture.

But their horses were just about played out and really needed a night's rest. They were low on provisions, too. It would be difficult to push on to Laramie without replenishing their supplies here.

As soon as he had Stallings locked up, he would send a wire to Senator Creed. Once he'd established that he was the one who had captured the fugitive, Bowen wouldn't be able to claim the reward for himself. Luke figured he could stay alive long enough to do that.

He sure as blazes wasn't going to let his guard down while he was in these parts, though.

He reached back to tug on the lead rope attached to Stallings' horse. "Come on."

The deputies had closed the trapdoor on the gallows and positioned Crawford on it. One of them tossed a new hangrope over the crossbar. Another deputy caught it and closed in to fit the noose over the prisoner's head.

"Reckon we ought to tie his feet together?" one of the men asked.

"Naw," another answered with a grin. "If it so happens that his neck don't break right off, it'll be a heap more entertainin' if he can kick good while he's chokin' to death."

"Please, mister, please!" Crawford cried. "Don't just ride off and let them do this to me! I never killed that whore. They did it and framed me for it! They're only doing this because Ezra Hannigan wants my ranch!"

That claim made Luke pause. Bowen must have noticed Luke's reaction because he snapped at the deputies, "Shut him up. I'm not gonna stand by and let him spew those filthy lies about Mr. Hannigan."

"Please—" Crawford started to shriek, but then one of the deputies stepped behind him and slammed a gun butt against the back of his head. Crawford sagged forward, only half-conscious as the other deputies held him up by the arms.

Luke glanced at the four deputies who were still mounted nearby. Each rested a hand on the butt of a holstered revolver. Luke knew gun-wolves like that wouldn't hesitate to yank their hoglegs out and start blasting. He had faced long odds plenty of times in his life and wasn't afraid, but he didn't feel like getting shot to doll rags today, either, and likely that was what would happen if he tried to interfere.

With a sour taste in his mouth, he lifted his reins, nudged the buckskin into motion, and turned the horse to ride around the group of lawmen toward the settlement. He heard the prisoner groan from the gallows, but Crawford had been knocked too senseless to protest coherently anymore.

A moment later, with an unmistakable sound, the trapdoor dropped and so did the prisoner. In the thin, cold air, Luke distinctly heard the crack of Crawford's neck breaking.

He wasn't looking back, but Stallings must have been. The confidence man cursed and then said, "They didn't even put a hood over his head before they hung him! That's just indecent, Jensen."

"I'm not arguing with you."

"And you know good and well he was innocent. He was telling the truth about them framing him for that dove's murder."

"You don't have any way of knowing that," Luke pointed out. "We don't know anything about these people."

"Who's Ezra Hannigan?"

Luke took a deep breath. "Well, considering that the town's called Hannigan's Hill, I expect he's an important man around here. Probably owns some of the businesses. Maybe most of them. Maybe a big ranch outside of town. I think I've heard the name before, but I can't recall for sure."

"The fella who was hanging there when we rode up, the one they cut down, that marshal said he stole money from one of the leading citizens. You want to bet it was Ezra Hannigan he stole from?"

"I don't want to bet with you about anything, Stallings. I just want to get you where you're going and collect my money. Whatever's going on in this town, I don't want any part of it."

Stallings was silent for a moment, then said, "I suppose there wouldn't be anything you could do, anyway. Not against a marshal and that many deputies, and all of them looking like they know how to handle a gun. Funny that a town this size would need that many deputies, though . . . unless their actual job isn't keeping the peace but doing whatever Ezra Hannigan wants done. Like hanging the owner of a spread Hannigan's got his eye on."

"You've flapped that jaw enough," Luke told him. "I don't want to hear any more out of you."

"Whether you hear it or not won't change the truth of the matter."

Stallings couldn't see it, but Luke grimaced. He knew that Stallings was likely right about what was happening around here. Luke had seen it more than once: some rich man ruling a town and the surrounding area with an iron fist, bringing in hired guns, running roughshod over anybody who dared to stand up to him. It was a common story on the frontier.

But it wasn't his job to set things right in Hannigan's Hill, even assuming that Stallings was right about Ezra Hannigan. Smoke might not stand for such things, but Smoke had a reckless streak in him sometimes. Luke's hard life had made him more practical. He would have wound up dead if he had tried to interfere with that hanging. Bowen would have been more than happy to seize the excuse to kill him and claim his prisoner and the reward.

Luke knew all that, knew it good and well, but as he and Stallings reached the edge of town, something made him turn his head and look back anyway. Some unwanted force drew his gaze like a magnet to the top of the nearby hill. Bowen and the deputies had started riding back toward the settlement, leaving the young man called Crawford dangling limp and lifeless from that hangrope. Leaving him there to rot . . .

"Well," a female voice broke sharply into Luke's thoughts, "I hope you're proud of yourself."

Visit our website at
KensingtonBooks.com
to sign up for our newsletters, read
more from your favorite authors, see
books by series, view reading group
guides, and more!

Become a Part of Our
Between the Chapters Book Club
Community and Join the Conversation

Betweenthechapters.net